ice deke

Milwaukee Steel Riders
Book Three

ellie k. drake

Copyright © 2026 by Ellie K. Drake Books

All rights reserved.

No part of this book may be reproduced in any form or by any electronic or mechanical means, including information storage and retrieval systems, without written permission from the author, except for the use of brief quotations in a book review. It is illegal to copy this book, post it to a website, or distribute it by any other means without permission.

All characters in this publication are fictitious and any resemblance to real persons, living or dead, is coincidental.

Designations used by companies to distinguish their products are often claimed as trademarks. All brand names and product names used in this book and on its cover are trade names, service marks, trademarks and registered trademarks of their respective owners. The publishers and the book are not associated with any product or vendor mentioned in this book. None of the companies referenced within the book have endorsed the book.

Editing by Casey Jones at Inked Edits Developmental

Cover design by Maldo Designs

Proofreading by Dr Mekhala Spencer at All The Proof Editing

To anyone who's had to climb an impossible ladder. To anyone who's had to hide who you truly are. And especially to anyone who's had to do both.

Do the hard things. Be vulnerable. Fight for your happy ending.

And to Kellsie—I miss you every single day.

authors note

Thank you for reading Ice Deke! This is a funny, spicy, hockey romance. If you're new to the Milwaukee Steel Riders—Welcome! This is book three, but can be read as a stand-alone. I recommend reading them in order, but if you want to read this one first, go for it! As with any book, you should know what you're getting into. Below are some themes I want to make sure you're aware of.

- explicit language
- multiple open door sex scenes between two consensual partners
- on-page alcohol consumption
- Stalking of MCs (not by one another)
- Discussion of childhood cancer and hospital visit (no deaths)
- Accidental pregnancy
- Kidnapping (Not done by MCs)
- Drugging someone's drink for the purpose of kidnapping (not done by MCs)

bougie's note

Hey, readers. It's me, your favorite Milwaukee Steel Rider, and hockey heartthrob, Jordan "Bougie" Boucher. First, I want to thank you for picking up this book. You know this is gonna be your favorite one in the series right?

But, before we get into that I wanted to give you a quick recap on what's been happening here in Milwaukee. Ellie says I'm one-hundo percent not supposed to talk to you. But, she doesn't need to know everything does she? This can be our little secret.

"I heard that."

"Shit, Ellie, you scared the puck outta me! Aren't you busy like…writing a book or something."

"You know I can hear your inner voice, right?"

"Girl. I'm just trying to give the people what they want."

"Mmmmm kay. You really think you know more about the Riders than me? Prove it. Why don't you fill the readers in on what's happened in the last two books if you're so smart?"

"Child's play Ellie. Let me just prepare myself…"

"Jordan, you can't go look this up on the internet."

Bougie's Note

"I know, I know. I'm just...*preparing*."

"Right. And I'm not sitting here rolling my eyes waiting for this show to begin."

"Patience, Ellie K. A good showman always takes his time. Now...where to begin......ahh I know...

So in the first book Ice Contact, Hayes Larson is the newest star (*debatable*) for the Milwaukee Steel Riders. He fell in love with our national anthem singer, Olivia Brooks. But the most important piece of information you need is that *my name* is mentioned in that book 30 times, and I am prominently featured in chapters 11, 35, and 49. I mean...the rest of the book is fantastic, but...I know what you're really looking for.

The second book, Ice Block, features my close, personal, and very best friend Vladi Volkov. He's the team goalie. He's grumpy, broody, and cranky as hell. He and Maggie James had a one night stand that went *very well*, but Vladi ghosted her afterward. *I. Would. Never.* Vladster and I weren't as close then or I would have told him to get his goalie stick out of his ass. Anyway...months later they end up get stuck in a hotel room together at a destination wedding for a week. *Yikes bikes.* I am featured heavily in Ice Block, including chapters 2, 16, 20, 26, 28, 47, 50, 51, and the epilogue. But most notably in Chapter 35—the section that happens to be one of the most highlighted scenes in the book. Would you expect anything less?

"Okaaaay Jordan. I think that's enough."

"Ellie. Please. I'm doing you a favor. They are going to devour all of these books knowing I'm in all of them!"

"Sigh. Fine."

"Thank you. Now, my dear readers and new BFFs, please enjoy this book all about me and my quest to find love in Ice Deke."

Yours Truly,

Jordan 'Bougie' Boucher

team roster

players

#9 Vladimir Volkov - Goalie 🇷🇺

#22 Hayes Larson - Center - *Assistant Captain* 🇺🇸

#68 Jordan 'Bougie' Boucher - Defenseman 🇨🇦

#91 Zack 'Z' Reeves - Right Wing - *Captain* 🇨🇦

#55 Colton 'Tay' Taylor - Defenseman 🇨🇦

#38 Erik 'EJ' Johanson - Left Wing 🇨🇦

#75 Connor McKenzie - Backup Goalie 🇺🇸

part one
march

1
jordan

"That wraps up another episode of Blabbing with Bougie, your home for all things hockey, being cocky, and living in Milwaukee. Join me next week when I break down what *really* goes on in the locker room between periods," I tease into the mic recording the end of my weekly podcast. "Today's episode is sponsored by Luca Bellezza Cosmetics and JJ Enterprises. Until next time, stay bougie, bitches!"

Dropping the headphones on the desk I lean back in my chair, a long breath escaping. Another episode done. I love my podcast. I love being an insider voice for the people. But being *on* all the time? It feels like the damn sky is sitting on my shoulders.

"Great job today, Bougie," my producer says from the booth. "I'll get working on this as soon as I get home. As usual, I'll have it edited and posted by Wednesday."

"Thanks, Jonesy! You're too good to me." I quickly shake off the weight of the world and tip him a salute, my signature grin sliding back into place.

"No, *you* are the one who's too good to me! I'm so grateful for this opportunity. You have no idea what this job means to me and my family."

Jonesy and his wife have three little kids, leaving chaos and love everywhere they go. He was working at MKE Arena as a security guard when we met. We'd chat about how he used to work at a radio station during college, and how much he loved it before life got in the way. I liked him so much that when my producer turned in his notice, I brought Jonesy on full-time to learn the ropes.

He was a natural. He's a hard worker, and it's evident he has a passion for this.

He steps out of the booth, making his way over as I stand to shake his hand. "Glad to have you on Team Boucher. You're coming to the game tomorrow night, right? The Riders should have sent you tickets for the fam."

"You know I'll be there! No way we would miss Bougie Bobblehead night. You still good to sign one for my kids' school auction?"

I clap his shoulder. "I'll sign that and anything else you want. Know what? I'll get you a team-signed jersey, too."

He shakes his head, a slight smile cracking his face. "Like I said, man, you're too good to me."

"Get home to that family of yours. I'll see you tomorrow night," I say as he heads out, the door clicking shut behind him.

I close my laptop with a smile and send my stack of notes flying toward the desktop tray. Jonesy is a great example of what I'm looking for in everyone I hire. You can teach someone a skill or help them refine it, but you can't teach them to be a hard worker or a decent human being. I've spent enough of my life around people who got a job because they had connections to someone, then acted like total dicks to everyone and *still* couldn't do the damn job. My dad instilled in me from the day I could talk to treat everyone, regardless of where they are in life, with respect and humanity.

Except on the ice—that's where all rules go out the window.

I turn off the lights in the studio and head upstairs to get changed. Walking through the hallway, I smile at the photos of my family on the wall. Most twenty-three-year-old guys probably don't have pictures of their family hanging around, but what can I say? They're awesome. But being a part of the Boucher family, one of the top real-estate developers in Canada, hasn't always been sunshine and roses.

Rubbing the back of my neck, I shuffle past the empty rooms of my house. Yeah, we have money. I'm never going to act like I should be pitied or believe anyone should feel bad for the things my life has afforded me, but wealth comes with its own problems. People think they know me from my celebrity persona and the names I've been called. Billionaire Bougie. The Trust Fund Troublemaker. And then, of course, the world came up with the term 'nepo-baby' which was hurled my way instantly in the form of the Nepo Nuisance. Honestly, I can own some of that. But my chronic insomnia isn't because I'm a billionaire or a troublemaker—it's because no one bothers to see beneath all that.

My parents had no involvement in me being good at hockey or my career on the ice, other than paying for my equipment and league fees. I worked my damn ass off my entire life to prove I was more than just a kid with money. I had no choice but to be the best. If I was on a team just barely cutting it, all anyone would say is how I only got the spot because of my parents' money. *I play because I fucking love it.*

When I was little, I put on a pair of skates, grabbed a stick, and fell in love with the sport. It's been my only constant. It's what drives me to do everything.

But all the chirping about me, my family, and how people think I got to where I am? That's where the gloves come off in treating people with respect.

In all honesty, I could not have picked a better sport than

hockey. A wicked grin spreads across my face. Someone calls you a name? Slam them into the boards. Someone tells you how hard it must have been for Daddy to pay your way into the league? Drop the gloves and give them a nice right hook to the face. And when the chirp hits harder than I'd ever admit, I throw my signature move their way—The Ice Deke.

As we square up, they don't notice me casually dragging my skate for a little snow. I toss a dramatic fake punch—big swing, total miss—then drop low into a textbook bend-and-snap, courtesy of my personal hero, Elle Woods. Then boom! I pop-up and give them a frosty face wash, gift wrapped by #68. I'm the first guy in the league to ever do that. I catch a glimpse of the awards and memorabilia from my career. *Where's my damn trophy for that?!*

Aside from being a first-round draft pick and the accolades that come with it, I have an OHL record for the most number of suspensions in a season. I fully own that shit. They were all my fault, and I would do them again in a heartbeat—no take backsies. Off the ice, I'm Mister Cool. Nothing phases me. Nothing gets to me. But when my skates hit that cold glistening sheet of glass? All my anger and aggression from the rest of my life comes out in full force. It's my outlet, my escape, and the spark behind my game.

Stepping into my bedroom, I seriously debate nosediving onto my bed, skipping the plans I have tonight in favor of some extra sleep. My shoulders slump as I realize I'll have to wait a few more hours. Some of the guys are going out to celebrate Colton Taylor's birthday. While the thought of having to be on again for the evening has me already regretting not plopping down for a nap, Tay's a good guy, and we need to celebrate. We aren't supposed to get too crazy since we are in season, but I make *no* promises as to my behavior tonight.

Not to mention, the game tomorrow night is all about me. The Milwaukee Steel Riders have chosen to honor me, star defenseman

Jordan Boucher, with a bobblehead night. It's exciting as hell to have my own little mini-me and, to be honest, a damn dream come true. But it's also slightly terrifying. My stomach twists, feeling like someone is taping up their goddamn stick deep in my guts. Because as much as the fans will pour out, so will the haters. I've learned to ignore them, but it doesn't mean it still doesn't get to me every once in a while.

Also terrifying—the fact that we fly out directly after the game. *I get to see* her *again*. The woman I've been pining after. The woman who haunts my dreams. Who acts like I don't exist. *Kennedy Kramer.* One of our team's pilots and everything I've dreamed of. Not only is she the most beautiful woman I've ever laid eyes on, but she's smart, successful, and she doesn't seem to give a shit about my family's money, as evidenced by the fact that she doesn't give me the time of day.

I'll never forget the first time I saw her. I thought my heart was going to crack through my ribs and fly down the aisle of the plane to get to her. The way her long, wavy blonde hair flowed down her shoulders. Her uniform hugged the curves of her body in the most perfect way. And that sexy as hell blue scarf around her neck.

My dick presses against the zipper of my jeans.

I see her every time we travel. I smile, say hi, and she just dismisses me like I'm beneath her.

Goddammit, I would like to be beneath her.

Sadly, she still acts like she doesn't know who I am when I speak to her. She seems to be literally the only person on the face of this planet that doesn't want to get to know me. It's fucking *torture*. The number of people who want to be my friend just because of my status, whether for hockey or my family name, is disheartening.

But not *her*.

I see how she acts around her friends. Once in a while, when I'm at a get-together, one of the WAGs will invite her. *Everyone loves*

Kennedy. I see the way she laughs. The way she makes everyone feel at ease. The way she seems to do everything in life with a sense of purpose.

And the way she does everything in her power to stay as far away from me as possible.

I've been sending her gifts. Anonymously. Not in like a stalker way, more like an I want to impress her way. I like to think of myself as a year-round Secret Santa—secret because I'm too much of a chicken-shit to sign my name. As if I didn't have enough on my plate, I keep a running list of gift ideas waiting for one to wow her so I can fess up.

Truth is, I would give everything up to focus on this full-time if it were actually working. I even bring her a latte every flight. Granted, she doesn't know it's from me since I have one of the flight attendants drop it off to her, but it's the thought that counts. *Right?* I groan, burying my face in my hands. I am so fucking confident in every other area of my life.

I run my fingers through my hair, ready to pull every strand out in frustration. *What's my problem being confident around Kennedy?* If Elle Woods were here, she'd help me figure out how to impress her.

I guess the fact that I got majorly burned by one woman and caused a massive PR crisis, endless shame and embarrassment, a complete change of my lifestyle, and, oh, I don't know, a million other things could be part of the problem. I swallow hard, trying to suppress the anger that still bubbles up, thinking back to that fucking disaster.

And let's not forget the other fun fact—the fucking bizarre messages I've been getting lately. Threatening texts from an unknown number. Texts that *specifically* say to stay away from Kennedy. I haven't told a soul outside of my dad and my cousin Hannah that I like her. *So how the hell does a random texter know?* I keep getting that creepy as hell feeling like I'm being watched every day. Yikes bikes. I've got my security detail on it, but that doesn't mean it doesn't freak me out a little. *Okay, a lot.*

I shake away the thoughts that have been eating at me for days as I grab a white T-shirt and throw on some jeans and sneakers, splash on a few drops of cologne, and head out to celebrate my friend.

Having rehashed the disaster my public life turned into a few years ago, I'll also be having some drinks to drown those feelings. Because even on my worst day, I know someone else is probably having a worser day than me. *Is worser even a word?* I shrug my shoulders and head downstairs to my car. Being my chipper self is why I'm known as Mr. Sunshine. Making other people feel special is the one thing outside of hockey that fuels the fire inside me. I do a final fit check in the mudroom mirror, flashing myself a smirk and a wink to get into character.

Tonight I'll be Jordan 'Bougie' Boucher, life of the party. And oh, do I bring my fucking A-game to a party.

2
kennedy

"I can't believe you're leaving us, Benny Boy! It's not going to be the same without you," I shout drunkenly across the table at the club. We've known each other for years, first through the Air National Guard, and now as one of the few rotating pilots I fly with for the Milwaukee Steel Riders. Well, he *was* anyway. He's worked his ass off studying to get more degrees and certifications, on top of all our flights, and he finally got his dream job with NASA. I can't say I blame him for leaving—NASA is cool as shit.

"I know, I know," he says with a sad smile, tears welling in his eyes. "I'm gonna miss the hell out of all of you! But NASA is calling, and I can't pass that up. But don't worry, I'll text when I get to Mars." He lifts his shot glass in salute to everyone at the table before knocking it back in one go.

"Just watch out for aliens trying to probe your anus, bro," one of our friends pipes up, getting a laugh and an eyeroll from half the table. "Let's all raise our glasses to a fun night out celebrating the one, the only, Benjamin Logan!" We all whoop and cheer for our friend, the tequila disappearing in an instant.

"You all want another round?" the server shouts over the loud baseline pumping from the speakers, the strobe lights creating colorful shadows across the table.

"Yes!" I shout. "Tabs on me. Even though *Benny* should be the one paying, since he's deserting me and leaving me with God knows who for a co-pilot the rest of the season. I swear to all things gin, I will drag your ass back here if I'm stuck with some pompous asshole who starts off with 'Oh boy, a female pilot. Sure you can handle a jet like this?'" I grumble in my ridiculous imitation of an idiotic man's voice.

Benny shakes his head with a scoff. "You'll be fine, Kenni! I mean, you'll never have anyone as perfect as me, but hopefully someone who is at least cool. Besides, you know Theresa and the rest of the flight crew won't put up with that either."

He's right. Theresa is a no-nonsense bitch. She doesn't take shit from anyone—including me—which is why I make sure to stay out of her way and on my good side. A shiver runs up my spine thinking about the few times I've mildly irritated her. That is one flight attendant you do *not* want to cross.

Still, having her in my corner doesn't take away the sting of someone questioning my ability to fly an aircraft.

Benny's one of the good ones who treats me like any other pilot. Sadly, some aren't. I have the same number of flight hours, go through the same rigorous training, and set all emotion aside to fly. I can't tell you the number of times a male co-pilot came to work in a bad mood, all pissed off about a baseball game, and had a horrible attitude the entire flight. But if *I* make any mention of emotion, I'm accused of being too sensitive or having PMS. I dig my fingernails into my palm at the double standard, the black cat inside me wanting to claw it in the face and then ask it to apologize. I hope that waitress gets back soon, 'cause I need to make another gin and tonic my bitch before spiraling further at the thought of who Benny's replacement will be.

But instead of a drink being set before me, my annoyance is furthered by a loud group of drunk guys waltzing in. I roll my eyes, then quickly realize it's not just any bunch of rowdy drunks. *It's the Riders hockey team.*

As one of the pilots, I see them on their flights, and I am actually friends with several of their wives and girlfriends, the WAGs as they refer to themselves. Maggie James, who lives in the apartment down the hall, is engaged to the team goalie, Vladi Volkov. *If you want to talk about two more people who don't put up with anyone's shit, add them to the list.*

My brow furrows. But I don't see Vladi in the group. This club doesn't really seem like it would be his vibe. Honestly, I don't see any of my friends' spouses here. They have a home game tomorrow night, then we fly out for several away games, so I'm guessing they are spending some time with their families before the road trip.

I can't say I'm not jealous. A heavy sigh escapes as the alcohol haze thins, allowing the thoughts I've been pushing down to creep back. While I'm a self-proclaimed badass bitch, and have achieved what I wanted in my career, my stomach churns as something inside me tries to claw its way out. Something I've been meaning to get around to but never really did. I've always been one to do things in my own way and in my own time.

Sleepless nights, wondering if I've waited too long. Wondering if my body is even capable of what I want it to do. *Why does there have to be a fucking time clock on starting a family?*

I shuffle in my seat, my eyes darting around the bar, knowing I've got to be the only person in here thinking about this while out at a club.

As I watch the last few players file in the door, an irritating heat rises in my throat as I recognize the one person I try to avoid like the plague—*Jordan Boucher*.

He struts in wearing jeans and a white T-shirt—probably the most expensive plain white T-shirt known to man, made by some designer I've never heard of.

He's young. He's cocky. He's unfairly and ridiculously handsome and, *dammit*, he knows it. He flaunts his wealth wearing designer everything. I've been around enough pompous assholes like him, their noses in the air and steeped in an attitude of being better than everyone, to recognize one instantly.

Every time we land, he waltzes down the aisle of the jet, *my jet*, and says hi to me with a smirk on his face like he owns the damn aircraft. To my knowledge, the team owns it, not that rich playboy. I see him in the tabloids, his arm draped around another girl in every picture. Pardon me for being the only female in America who doesn't want to be associated with him.

Growing up, my mom worked her ass off for everything we had. Tapping my fingers on the table, I can't help the corners of my lips crawling up my face, thinking about what a freaking rock star she is. She worked two jobs, made sure I went to the best schools, and did it all with a smile on her face. I knew how hard she worked, some days just so we could have food on the table. She always pushed me to be the best. To have more than she did. To never take anything we have for granted, and that hard work is the way to get what you want in life. And I fucking did that, and I'm damn proud of myself. And the fact that a guy like him just waltzed through life without a care in the world? My teeth grind, the bitter taste of his entitlement lingering on my mouth.

He's probably never had to work a day in his life.

And now he's made his way over to the bar, chatting up the bartender like he's her best friend. *Probably offering her a bunch of money to clear out the club so they can have it all to themselves.* My friends and I typically go to Walt's on Water, the best bar in all of Milwaukee, but decided to change it up for Benny's last night in town.

I'm quickly regretting that decision.

"Kenni? Earth to Kennedy!" I'm jolted from my thoughts as Benny waves his hand in front of my face, trying to get my attention. I look down at the table in front of me and see the fresh drink slowly melting. *Shit.* Fuck that jerk-face, pretty-boy, as usual, distracting everyone. I didn't even notice the waitress drop it off.

My arms tense as I practically strangle the two limes into the glass before picking it up and swirling it around, taking a bigger swig than I probably should. *Why do I let this asshole get me so riled up?* Maybe it's because on top of his effortless life, he actually *is* good-looking. Maybe it's because it's been a while since I've been with someone. Maybe it's the giant gulp of alcohol I just took, but with another few drinks, I would consider letting caution go to the wind with someone that hot. *Whoa, girl…abort mission.* For fucks sake I have bottles of gin older than him. I'm not going there. I am *never* going there. Despite his hotness, I could never put up with a conceited, egotistical, privileged rich boy like Jordan Boucher.

3
jordan

She's. Here. Oh my God, *she's here*. My eyes found her through the sea of people faster than a Where's Waldo world champion as my pulse raced in my chest harder than the EDM song playing at the club. *Does she see me? Does she know I'm here?* My stomach drops as I see the annoyed look on her face. *She* definitely *knows I'm here.*

"Bougie! You're spacing out again!" Connor McKenzie, our backup goalie, yells over the loud music. *Shit.* I'm for sure spacing right now—I always am when she's around. "Where you at tonight, man? Wait...are you daydreaming about your bobblehead night tomorrow? I'm so fucking jealous, asshole!"

I shake the cobwebs from my brain, trying to remember I'm here to be the life of the party. *Snap out of it, Jordan!*

"Yeah, man, I'm pumped as shit! My own little mini-me. Dreams can come true," I gush, placing my hand over my heart.

"Dude, if your head gets any bigger, you and your bobblehead aren't going to fit through the arena exit tomorrow," EJ says, his arm slung around his girlfriend Natalie. I roll my eyes, giving him a weak punch on his shoulder. They started seeing each other a couple of months back, and this is their first public reveal as a couple.

She seems nice, but I just get a weird feeling from her that she's not into him for the right reasons. *Especially since EJ asked me where to get her diamond earrings for their debut.* He has never been known for having impeccable taste in women. Everyone gets on me for having a different girl on my arm every time they see me on the news, but EJ tends to chase the ones who throw themselves at him. *Then again, maybe I'm just jealous because the one who I want to be throwing herself at me looks like she'd rather throw me off the top of a building.*

"Listen, I know we all get specialty placement on tickets and stuff," EJ continues, "but why did they have to give you and your giant ego a bobblehead?"

"You know what, EJ, that hurts," I say mockingly. "It's not my fault Jordan Joseph Boucher was born with a jawline perfectly ready for merchandising."

EJ scoffs as Natalie nuzzles into his chest. "More like a jaw perfect for punching."

"Oh, dear God…I'm going to puke," Tay groans, looking a little green.

"Are you sick from the shots or from Bougie's ego?" Mac asks him.

"Why not both?" Tay replies with a Joker-like smile and a more chipper tone than normal. He usually doesn't drink much, and I'm starting to see why.

"Come on, guys! We're not here to talk about me. We're here to celebrate Tay!" I shout, hoping to hide my level of distraction from my teammates. "And, of course, I'm here to provide Tay with everything he's ever wanted."

Tay's eyes widen with horror. "And what, exactly, is it that I've always wanted?"

"Entertainment!!!!" I scream at the top of my lungs as I run toward the bar. "Hit it, Ashley!" The DJ, who has been waiting for my cue, throws her thumb up over the crowd, a smile barely restrained across her face. I hear EJ mumble something like 'lord help us' as I hop onto the bar while Devil Went Down to Georgia pounds through the speakers.

4
kennedy

Everyone starts to hoot and holler as the pounding bass morphs into a country song—*oh dear God*. It's not just any country song; it's the most famous of famous country bar songs. I pick at the cuticles of my nails to the beat pumping through the speakers. Do I like this song? Yes. Is this song now ruined for me forever because of what's happening at this club? Also yes. My brows raise as I shift uncomfortably in my chair, as an annoyingly attractive man-child hops on the bar and begins performing the entire dance from Coyote Ugly.

"Yes!" Benny screams, my drink nearly spilling in shock. "I knew coming here was going to pay off!"

My mouth gapes open, my gaze bouncing around to see the rest of our table, hell, *the entire bar*, is clapping along, singing, and loving every minute of it. *Am I the only one who thinks this is ridiculously immature?*

"Don't you find this annoying?" I shout over the song. "Aren't we a little old for this?"

"Lighten up, Kenni!" he yells from the corner of his mouth.

"This is entertaining as hell! One of the top players in the NHL is doing full, iconic choreography to a kickass song…and he's actually really good at it! Holy shit, he's taking his shirt off." He cups his mouth and yells across the club, "Go Bougie!"

I swallow hard as my eyes nearly pop out of my head. I've heard rumors of him stripping the moment he boards the plane—most of the players do since they're required to wear a suit and they all change into comfy clothes before takeoff—but I'm too busy doing my pre-flight checks and preparing for takeoff to ever see it happen. Too busy doing my *actual job*, getting his ass safely from one city to the next, while he sits back there doing God knows what. He's probably back there every flight playing strip poker, texting supermodels, or some other dumb shit.

But there's no avoiding watching him strip now. It's happening. Right in front of me. And an entire club full of people. It's like a train wreck I can't look away from—a train wreck with a six pack that could crack open a walnut. His tan skin does nothing to hide the muscles beneath. I sit up straight in my chair, trying to push down the tension creeping up. Goddammit, why does he have to be so hot? And his arms…dear *God*, his arms. Every precise move of the dance highlights a different muscle.

The noise in the club fades; my attention and hearing solely focused on this spectacle as he is handed a pitcher of water and proceeds to pour it over his dark, wavy hair. My thighs squeeze together, betraying every signal my brain's firing to ignore the display of ripped muscles and pure sex. I swallow heavily at the sight of the water dripping down him like hot wax from a candle. Apparently, my body doesn't care that he's an arrogant, entitled asshole. *Traitor.* If he weren't so annoyingly cocky, I might even enjoy this. Goddammit! These athletes and their chiseled bodies. *Shit, I need to get laid.*

The song comes to an end, my lungs finally filling with air, and the entire club gives him a standing ovation as he takes a bow.

That's my cue to call it a night.

Just as I'm about to head out, I hear my name.

"Kennedy! Benny! What's up!" Erik Johanson, one of the players, yells from across the room. *Dammit.* He's a nice guy, but I was really hoping to sneak out before I was discovered by the team. I paste a smile on my face as he heads our way with a cute blonde on his arm.

"Hey, Erik, good to see you!" I say as I give him a hug from my seat.

"Good to see you too! Have you met my girlfriend, Natalie?"

I extend my hand to her. "I don't think so. Hi, I'm Kennedy."

"Nice to meet you. Erik said you're the team pilot, that's so cool! Do you make a lot of money doing that?"

Do I make a lot of money? Is this girl interviewing me for a loan application? I pull my hand back and shrug. "Umm…I do okay. Flying is a pretty fun gig. Except when I have to fly their tired asses back to Milwaukee after they lose," I spit out, jabbing Erik as he rolls his eyes. "Speaking of, don't you guys have a game tomorrow? Surprised to see you out tonight."

"It's Tay's birthday, so we're making an exception. Plus, we're playing Chicago. We *always* beat Chicago, so none of us are too worried."

My brows touch my hairline. "Wow, confident, huh?"

He shakes it off with a laugh. "I'm actually controlling myself tonight; just a couple and that's it. Tay doesn't drink much either, but everyone is buying him shots, so he'll probably have more than he should. I'll be dragging his ass to morning skate tomorrow." He looks around, chuckling as Tay downs another gulp with a twisted face. "What are you doing here tonight? Club 414 doesn't seem like your cup of tea."

"It's not," I say with a laugh. "I'd much rather be at Walt's, but Benny here is leaving us, so this was his choice."

Erik's eyes go wide, his jaw slack. "What?! Benny, you can't leave! What if it upsets Vladi's winning streak?! Shit…how did I not know this? Tay! Get over here!"

Colton Taylor walks our way, just a little off kilter, a scowl on his face after being-summoned. "Tay, did you know Benny was leaving?"

He rolls his eyes, shaking his head. "How did you *not* know about this?"

"Well, *someone*, apparently my roommate, forgot to tell me. You literally live across the hall! You can't tell me these things?"

My head jerks back and my eyes dart between them feeling like I've opened up some sort of can of worms. *Really wishing I had made my way to the door earlier.*

"I can't be responsible for all of your knowledge, EJ. You could educate yourself on things other than…ohh, I don't know…*yourself*," Colton snarks, crossing his arms and leaning in.

"Excuse *me* that I don't watch Jeopardy every night like a giant nerd and record it to catch the episodes on game nights. We need to ask Bougie if he knows about Ben leaving."

And that's my second cue to leave. My muscles tense at the thought of him making his way over here.

Why is that damn door so far away?!

"Nice seeing you guys, but I'm going to grab my tab from the bar and head out. I'll see you all after the game tomorrow." I stand and give Benny a hug. "Stay in touch, have so much fun, and keep your phone on so we can keep up on all things Taylor Swift!"

"You know it, girl!" Benny says, squeezing me tight. As I step back, I see our waitress walking by and flag her down.

"Excuse me, miss? Could I close out my tab? These guys can pay for the rest on their own."

She narrows her brows at me like I'm certifiably insane.

What am I missing here?

"Is something wrong?"

"No, ma'am, nothing's wrong, but your bill has been taken care of. The owner said your tab was on the house."

My jaw drops, my brain struggling to figure out what the hell is happening. "I'm sorry, did you say *the owner*? I don't know the owner here. Why would they cover my tab?"

"Apparently, they know you."

What in the Eras Tour is happening?

"Can I ask who the owner is?"

"Kennedy, how do you not know the own—" EJ starts to speak as Colton quickly slaps a hand over his mouth.

"Good seeing you tonight, Kennedy! We better get back to the guys. Catch you tomorrow!" Colton says, drunkenly dragging a protesting EJ as Natalie tries to keep up with them.

Well, that was weird as shit. I grab my purse and head out to grab a ride. How the hell would I know the owner? I shake my head, having no clue what that was, chalking it all up to the alcohol, and finally make my way out the fucking door.

The sting of the night air on my skin is a welcome discomfort compared to the battle that just ensued between my brain and my reproductive organs. When my rideshare arrives I collapse against the seat, the weight of the evening pressing down every inch of my body. My stomach twists that I let one annoying idiot doing a stupid dance ruin a fun night out celebrating my friend. An arrogant asshole flaunting his hot body should not have me racing toward the door ready to pull out every goddamn toy in my nightstand to relieve the ache between my legs. I can't believe I let the one guy from the damn team that annoys the shit out of me show up and get me so turned the fuck on I couldn't get out of the damn club fast enough. Grilled Cheesus, I need help.

5
jordan

A tiny piece of my heart and self-confidence fractures like a chunk of an iceberg drifting away as I watch Kennedy walk out the door. I couldn't even muster up enough fucking courage to talk to her when she's just here having a good time and not in an official 'in charge of an entire airplane' capacity. Why can't I just grow a damn pair and say any word to her other than hi?! I run my hands through my hair, fighting not pull out every strand. Maybe because I'm freaking scared shitless she won't say anything back. Or maybe I'm scared she *will* finally speak to me. Shoving my hands in my pockets, I rock back on my heels. I wonder if I'm ready for that…if I'll ever be able to trust a woman again.

Of course, I covered her tab. There is no way I'm letting the woman of my dreams leave my club paying a dime for anything. I bought this club a while back and had it intentionally renovated. I love investing in different businesses, especially in town, and this one had so much history in the community, I couldn't let it fail. I wanted to make sure it continued to be a staple for a long time. *But she doesn't know I own it.* I don't think she knows much about me at all, actually, other than what she's seen in the news. If that was all I saw, I probably wouldn't want to talk to me either.

It would have been so easy to just go over, say hi, and meet her friends. Be the life of the party like everyone expects me to be. I like Benny, and I wanted to say bye when I heard he was leaving. I cringe, taking a sip of my soda water and lime. Actually, I may have had a little to do with that. I have a friend at NASA who helped speed up his application, so I knew this was coming. I feel bad for Kennedy. I know they're close, but Benny deserves this. He grew up poorer than poor, working his way up from nothing. I'm super happy for him, and of course, I wanted to pay the tab for his sake as well. But mainly, I wanted to do it for *her*.

"Jordan, can I ask you somefing…somefi…some. Thing," Tay slurs, his eyes out of focus.

How many shots has he had? I flag down one of the waitresses and ask for a glass of water. He's *clearly* hit his limit.

"What's up, Tay?"

He darts his head back and forth, stumbling a bit.

"Tay, what the hell are you doing?"

"Shhhh…I'm making shhhure no one is around."

I narrow my brows. "Bruh…we're in a club full of people. There are people around us in every direction." His face falls, and my heart sinks. "But it's super loud in here, so I think you're good. What's going on?"

"I want to know why you can't just ask her out already?" he asks, sounding as sober as any other day.

My eyes snap wide, my heart in my throat as a strangled laugh bursts from my chest. *Does he know?* "I have no idea what you're talking about, Tay. I think that may be the tequila talking."

He sways, staring at the door we both just watched Kennedy walk through. "Jordan Joseph Boucher. I know."

My shoulders sink as sweat slides down my forehead. *Oh shit. He knows. How does he know?!*

"You have a thing for Kennedy."

"You don't know what you're talki—"

"Yes, I do!" he snaps, staring me dead in the eye. "I *know*."

"But…how?"

"Jordan, I know *everything*. I know you think *you* know everything, but I *actually* do. I have my sources. I have *all* the sources you could ever dream of."

Holy. Shit. Every muscle in my body tenses. I didn't want anyone to know. "Tay, please…please don't say anything."

He puts a hand on my shoulder. "Your secret is safe with me. I'm not trying to spill your business. I'm just…*confused*. You're the most confin…cofinan…*con-fi-dent* human being I know. Just ask her out already!"

"If only it were that easy," I groan, shaking my head as I sip my drink. "Have you seen how she reacts to me? I try to say hi when I get on and off the plane, but she just rolls her eyes. I don't know what I'm doing. I can't…" I trail off, my gaze dropping to my feet, not knowing how to tell him about how fucking hurt I've been before. "I just can't find the right way to get her to notice me."

"Just go up and talk to her like you do everyone else. Despite your slightly annoying personality, you never know…she might like you. Someone always wants the runt of the litter."

I glare at him down my nose, standing straight to remind him of the three inches I hold over his head.

He holds his hands up, tipping into my chest. "I'm kidding, I'm kidding. You know I love ya."

My stomach flutters as his words finally sink in. *What if she could like me, if she actually got to know me?* Then another thought hits. A terrifying one. My heartbeat is lodged in my fucking throat. If Tay knows…do other people know? *Shit.* Oh my God, is this somehow connected to the random texts I've been getting?

"Tay…wait…do you know anything about who's been texting me?"

He looks at me with wide eyes. "What texts?"

"Bro, someone's been texting me. Telling me to stay away from Kennedy."

"WHAT? Bougie, that's *not* cool. Have you told anyone? What if she's in *danger*?" he whisper yells as if anyone in this club could hear him over the music. "Maybe she needs to know?"

The blood drains from my face. "No. I haven't told a soul other than my dad and our head of security. Shit. I didn't even think about someone hurting her. *Fuck!* I figured it was just someone who had…I don't know…dibs on her?"

"Dibs?" Tay snorts. "Jordan, that is a completely misogynistic, antiquated, and ultimately ridiculous thing to say. You can't have 'dibs' on a woman. They aren't like the passenger seat of a car where you can just call shotgun."

I chuckle as I take another sip of my drink. "I know, I just meant…maybe she already has someone in her life. I don't know! I'm not like Hayes or Vladi or any of you. My social life…isn't what it seems."

He looks at me again, his eyes not blinking as if the tequila he's drinking is a truth serum. "I know."

I tilt my head. "What do you mean? What else do you know, Tay?! How deep does your espionage go?"

"You think I don't know you're *not* sleeping with all the women you're photographed with?"

Fuck. This guy needs to join the CIA when he retires from hockey.

"Why do you act like you're going out with all those women

anyway? Especially when you and I both know there's only one woman you're interested in."

"It's…" —I let out a loud sigh, running my fingers through my hair— "…it's fucking complicated. So complicated, I can't get into this tonight."

"Listen, all I'm saying is I know there's more to you than the playboy image you project. You should let people see it more often."

I swallow hard, his words hitting me like a hard check against the boards. "Seriously, who else knows about this?"

He tries to nudge me, tripping into the bar instead. "Don't worry, Bougie. Your secret's ssssafe with me."

"That is one-hundo percent *not* what I asked you. Come on, Tay. Who else knows?"

"I cannot rev…refal…re*veal* my sources."

I step closer, once again using the few inches I have to my advantage as he stumbles back a step.

"Fine. Maybe…maybe Johnny knows."

Motherfucker. Johnny, the bartender at Walt's, is the most caring and nosy son of a bitch around. He's everyone's fairy godfather, meddling in their lives in order to get them together with their fated mate like he's some magical spirit from the fictional world of Elfayne or something. *I should have known he would be in on this.* But, if he knows about me, I bet he also knows about Tay.

"Tell me, does Johnny know about *your* secret crush?"

Tay's shoulders slump forward, his eyes dropping to the paracord bracelet he fiddles with. "I didn't think you knew about that."

"Seems like we've both been keeping some secrets," I say, placing a hand on his shoulder. "Listen, you know you can talk to me, right? I'm here if you need me. And let's just keep all this between us for now. Well…us and that nosy-as-fuck bartender." I snort as we clink glasses.

"Agreed. And Jordan? You know you can talk to me, too, right?"

"You're a good guy, Tay. I hope we both get our happy endings at some point. Now, go celebrate your birthday with the rest of the group. Tonight is all about you!"

He smiles as he stumbles back to the rest of the group.

A loud sigh of relief escapes me. *Maybe he's right.* I just need to go for it. Paparazzi are all over me, women are always hitting on me, why should I be scared to go for it with the woman of my dreams? I down the rest of my drink, dropping my glass on the bar with a *clack*.

What could possibly go wrong?

6
kennedy

"I cannot believe I let you talk me into this," I sigh, sitting next to my friend Maggie James, waiting for the game to start.

"Kenni, it's the Riders! How can you *not* want to be here? Besides, it's Bougie Bobblehead night! Look at this cute little guy," she gushes, tapping the top of the figurine to make it wobble. "Vladi has one of himself at home, but of course, it's his typical grumpy expression chiseled on a mini statue. I swear that man knows how to be happy, not that anyone ever knows. At least Bougie is smiling!" The head rattles as she shakes the trinket. "I've never met anyone with a more positive outlook on life than him."

I roll my eyes as I pick up my box from under my seat, examining it to see if there's some magical feature I'm unaware of because I'm still not sure what the hype is.

"If I had everything in life handed to me on a silver platter I'd be chipper as a squirrel running loose in a nut factory too. Here," — I hand her the box— "you want mine?"

"Kennedy Judith Kramer! Don't you dare criticize my sweet, little Bougie. I know you're not his biggest fan, but he helped me get to where I am with my business. He gave me a chance when I wasn't sure I could do it on my own." My lips thin, the box dropping in my hand. "You should come hang out with us sometime. He loves all our Millennial pop culture references and, over time, he kinda grows on ya."

I shake my head, my nose curling. "So does a fungus."

She snaps her head toward me, a stern look on her face. "I swear, some days you and Vladi must've been separated at birth with your damn stubbornness." She pushes the box back into my lap. "Keep it. If nothing else, you can sell it and get some extra cash. The game was sold out, so who the fuck knows how much these things will be selling for."

I shrug, tossing it down beneath me. "*Fine*. At least I can make some money off his cocky ass."

"Great attitude, Kenni," she snarks, giving me a good side-eye. "Cheer up. At least you get to see our dear friend Olivia sing the national anthem, hopefully see some good fights, *and* we're in the seats with free booze!" Maggie shrieks as she cheers her drink with mine.

"In case you've forgotten…again…I'm not allowed to drink twelve hours before a flight. And since I have to transport the team, *including your fiancé,* directly after the game, I'll stick with my Diet Coke."

"Dammit! I always forget you're a pilot. Why don't you just come work for me? I'll find something cool for you to do at Little Fox Branding. Oh my God, you could model for my campaigns! We could do a whole shoot on female pilots using the new skincare line for Luca Bellezza! Holy shit, why did I not think of this before?!" She whips out her phone and starts furiously typing in her notes app. "This could be amazing. Think you can get all your friends on board with this?" Her entire body freezes. "Oh damn…'on board'? I just made an airline pun! Holy tits, this could go viral."

I shake my head with a laugh. "I'm not sure I'm model material, Maggie."

"Kenni," she waves her hand at me. "You don't even know your own hotness. That means you are for sure model material. You are gorgeous. I would kill to have your skin, your hair, your profession…"

"Well, this just took a weird stalker turn."

She laughs, her head falling back. "True. Too bad I simply don't have the time to stalk you. But seriously, I'd love to use you on the campaign, and you know Shelly would be all about it too."

Our friend Shelly owns Luca Bellezza Cosmetics, and Maggie's branding firm does all her advertising. They are the ultimate girl bosses. *And* Maggie's best friend, Olivia, still works for her. She certainly doesn't need the money being married to one of the Riders' star players, but Maggie makes the job fun and treats all her employees with respect. *Something I wish flying would involve.* I stifle a groan. *Why did fucking NASA need to steal Benny away?* Maggie and Shelly don't put up with *any* of the patronizing 'old boys club' bullshit. My teeth grind on their own, wishing that wasn't still a thing with a lot of the older male pilot population.

Don't get me wrong, some of the male pilots are amazing, truly great to work with, and have respect for me and all the other females in our profession. When I see I'm on a flight with them, I rejoice. Sadly, there are still a lot that aren't.

I've worked my way up through the ranks in both the Guard and the airline, but *still* have to deal with this shit. I stare at the half-eaten pretzel in my lap, my appetite gone with the looming uncertainty of who my new co-worker will be tonight.

"Oh, pre-game's about to start! I see Olivia down there," Maggie says, tapping my leg.

The usual hype video plays on the Jumbotron as the refs and opposing team skate out onto the ice, and the coaches head to the bench. My heart is pounding, the bass from the music beating against my chest. The energy in this arena is electric, sparks igniting the fans as a motorcycle revs through the speakers.

Maybe watching these grown men fight one another with blades on their feet will get me out of my funk?

"Ladies and gentlemen! Tonight, in honor of Bougie Bobblehead night, we have a special performance for you prior to the starting lineups from our very own bobblehead honoree," the announcer's voice booms through the speakers and the crowd starts to cheer, "please welcome to the ice, nummmbeerrr sixty-eight, defenseman, Jordan Booooouuu-cher!"

Nope. Not getting me out of my funk. Funk is now at one hundred percent as strobe lights flitter across the ice and a familiar song kicks in. *Don't tell me he's skating out to—*

"Oh my God!" Maggie cheers next to me. "It's Ice Ice Baby."

The muscles in my jaw clench. *Please God, no. Just...no.* Let this not be happening.

But it is. It's happening.

The entire arena erupts as the spotlight finds him skating around like he's doing a goddamn figure skating routine all while holding a miniature version of himself like it's the fucking Stanley Cup.

Did he just do a sit spin? Holy hell on toast. I shift in my seat and shake my head as the crowd conveniently changes the words to replace baby with Bougie every time the chorus hits.

My eyes narrow as my stomach twists. He is ridiculous. He is juvenile. He is...godammit he is fucking good and that sit spin could rival Michelle Kwan's.

Stupid fucking athletes and their stupid fucking talents.

"This is incredible! He's doing ice dancing moves in hockey skates!" Maggie shouts. I look over at Coach Calhoun, his arms tightly crossed as if he's about to murder his own defenseman. I laugh louder than I should. *Guessing Richy Rich didn't get pre-approval for this.*

I nudge Maggie, jutting my chin toward the bench. "I don't think the coaching staff is very happy."

She stops clapping along momentarily to elbow me. "They'll get over it."

"I'm not sure I will."

"Lighten up, Kenni, or I'm going to send you and Vladi to Grump Camp this summer!"

Sinking into my seat, I suck my teeth. "I am not a grump!"

"Says the blonde who's had a permanent scowl on her face the entire pre-game!"

I force myself to relax. Almost. Maybe she has a point. *Maybe I should chill.* I know he's a professional athlete, and I'm sure he works hard, and all that, but something just burns me that he gets to literally skate around like an idiot and make millions of dollars without really trying.

Especially since he doesn't even need the money.

The crowd erupts again as he ends his short program with his hands over his head while a burst of flames shoots out from his fingers. I roll my eyes and take a deep breath. I suppose he *did* put in a lot of effort here. I will never admit this out loud, but between this and the bar dancing the other night, he is one hell of a showman.

"That was amazing!" Maggie shouts, "But now I feel bad for Liv having to go after Bougie on Ice."

"Yeah…I don't know how the hell she's going to follow that."

I head out after the second period to change into my uniform and get to the airport before the team arrives. A long sigh escapes as I drive away from the twenty thousand people fawning over a damn bobblehead. I will never admit this to Maggie, but the game and the antics leading up to it were a welcome distraction from the knot in my stomach about who my new co-worker will be. I inhale, then slowly exhale. I'm sure it will be fine. Maybe it'll be Benny 2.0?

I reviewed my flight plans earlier today, but after arriving at the FBO where the private flights takeoff, I focus my energy on peeking through them again.

"Hey, Kennedy," Theresa's voice echoes through the crew lounge. "Heard you actually went to the game tonight. You get a bobblehead?"

I roll my eyes. *Am I the only one in this town that doesn't give a shit about this little statue?*

"Yeah, Maggie dragged me with her," I say, reaching down into my bag and pulling out the giveaway. "You want this?"

She laughs. "Nah, I already have one coming. Funny enough, I spent all day today chasing my grandson around the indoor play café, and all he could talk about was wanting a Bougie Bobblehead. He has no idea we're taking him to the game in a few weeks with all his friends, and Mr. Boucher offered to bring signed ones for them all. You keep that one."

I scoff and shake my head at the thought of the publicity he's probably getting for making a cameo at a kid's birthday party as I shove the box back in my bag.

Why will no one take this damn thing from me?

"Look at this." She holds her phone out to me, a photo of her and her grandson on display, both of them wearing Riders jerseys with #68 on them. "Isn't he the cutest?"

I can't help the grin that creeps up my face. Despite the number on their jerseys, the photo is adorable. "Definitely the cutest. How old?"

"He turns seven in a couple of weeks. We'll be on the road again for his actual birthday, so that's why I arranged the surprise for him. You know how it is, missing things, so my husband and I have always tried to make my crazy schedule work." Pride fills her smile, a rarity for her since she's usually dealing with keeping the flight crew, and occasionally rowdy players, in line. "You ready to head to *tropical* Columbus, Ohio?"

"Yeah," I snort. "Nothing like going from one cold Midwestern town to another. We need more games in Miami."

She lets out a laugh. "No argument here. I'm gonna go grab the manifest and check on the catering," she says over her shoulder as she heads off.

I pull my iPad back up to focus on my flight plans. *I try anyway.* I slouch forward, and my thoughts drift off as if they've already taken off down the runway. I love my life, love my job.

There's nothing better than being a pilot and flying all over the world, meeting cool people, and doing something I love. But seeing a glimpse into Theresa's personal life has me wondering. A heaviness sits on my chest as I pick at my cuticles—could I actually have what she has? Is there someone out there for me? Someone to laugh with, travel with, have adventures with. Someone who knows what it's like to climb their way up what seems like an impossible ladder in life. Someone who is ready to settle down and start a family.

As much as I'm on the go, I've always wanted that. I love kids, and the desire to have my own has always been strong. My lips thin. It's challenging with my job, but there are ways to make it work. But even if I could figure that out, there's still the nagging issue of finding someone to have a baby *with*. I've considered donors and adoption and all the things one does. I've started the adoption paperwork more times than I can count, but despite my outward demeanor at times, there's still a part of me that wants to do it with a man by my side. My stomach twists at the thought of a man who probably doesn't exist outside my thoughts. And yet, I long for him.

"Who are you?"

I peer over my shoulder, spotting a middle-aged man in a pilot uniform staring me down as if I've somehow stumbled my way in here after getting lost at the mall. A bitter taste forms on my tongue like I just bit into the pith of the lime in my gin. I can only assume he's asking who I am because no one else is in a pilot uniform, and I happen to have tits.

This is off to a great start. Thanks for leaving me, Benny.

But, of course, I am a professional, so I put on my fake as hell smile as I stand to greet him. "Hi, I'm Kennedy, first officer on this flight."

He sneers. "No. The paperwork says K. Kramer. I was told I'd be flying with Kenny today."

"Yep! I'm Kenni. Short for Kennedy. Nice to meet—"

"Didn't think you'd be a woman," he interrupts, ignoring the hand I'm extending to him.

I grit my teeth, pushing my shoulders back. *Dear God, please give me the strength not to strangle this idiot and get fired.*

"Ainsworth. Captain Chaddwick Ainsworth, but you can call me Chadd. With two d's," he says, finally shaking my hand as his eyes drag up and down my frame and I do my best to not vomit through my smile.

I officially hate this guy.

I return to my seat and wipe my hand on my pants to wash the douche's sweat off my palm.

Stay calm. Stay focused on the pre-flight brief. Don't let this one pompous ass defeat you.

I remain cordial as we review the fuel plans, takeoff data, and the weather one last time before heading out to the jet. My feet are heavier than usual, doing my walk around the aircraft, looking for

Ice Deke

anything that may be off, my steps slow and measured. *All good.* I nod, a small smile on my face. I like checklists. I like order. That's another reason this profession is so great. Consistency. Excellence. Achievement. Of course, there is always something new that gets thrown in the mix during a flight, but the repetitiveness is like a heartbeat—one that hits at different rhythms but always keeps beating. Flying is a lifeline when I need it. It's consistency and chaos mixed together, and, for some reason, that combination gets me fired up for every flight.

I barely step onto the jet when his voice cuts through the flight deck like it owns the very air in the plane.

"I loaded your flight plan into the box since you took the scenic tour on the walkaround. Started the pre-flight without you as well—I'd rather not waste time double-checking your work."

This fucking guy. The air is thick, my hand shaking as I take my seat, tugging at my uniform a little too hard.

"Okay, sweetheart, let's start the checklists." He doesn't turn to face me; he just starts looking things over on his own. *This is my worst nightmare.* "Do you need me to explain those to you?"

Does he need me to bitch slap him off this jet?

I take a deep inhale, trying to compose myself, and refuse to respond. Just begin the checklist, and it'll be over before I know it.

"Oxygen?"

"Tests at one hundred percent."

"Flight instruments?" I say, giving him the next item on the list.

"Heading, zero-one-one. Standby heading, zero-one-two. Altimeter, two-niner-niner-two." He lists off the readings as we mark them complete and verify everything is in working order. I notice him peering over to my side of the panel to ensure I'm giving him the correct values.

A pit forms in my stomach knowing that if a man were in my place, he wouldn't do that. He doesn't fucking trust me simply because I'm female. They *never* trust me to fly. *Great.* I roll my shoulders back, remind myself I earned my spot here despite whatever fucking Chadd believes, and finish the damn checklist.

As we wait for fueling to wrap-up, this already feels like the longest sixty-minute flight I've ever flown, and we haven't even taken off yet. My eyes flutter closed as I force a breath deep into my lungs. Not to mention what the rest of this long-ass season will be like if this asshole is on the jet.

Can this day get any worse?

First, I had to witness the spectacle that is Bougie on Ice while listening to all his adoring fangirls, and now I'm forced to sit next to another cocky, pompous, better-than-everyone man-child.

I'm officially changing this flight plan to take me directly to the nearest spa.

7
jordan

Late in the third, we're only up 6–5. We *were* up by four, but the Chicago Saints must have done some sort of sorcery between periods and went on a goddamn run. The way Vladi just slammed his water bottle down in his net lets the entire arena know he's fucking pissed. *Great.* And in the most unsurprising news of the night, Tay is not on his game. He puked on the bench after his last shift and is now back in the locker room getting fluids.

Guess him getting shitfaced drunk the night before a game wasn't the brightest of ideas after all.

So here we are, up by one goal with only minutes left on the clock, and I have one objective – keep the puck the fuck out of here.

Chicago pulled their goalie, risking the empty net for an extra man to cover in the defensive zone. My heart races, every one of my senses on high alert—this is my time to shine. The puck heads my way, my eyes laser-focused on the black disk, and I clear it away from the crease, sending it toward Chicago's empty net. Thank fucking God it's out of our zone.

Chicago's defenseman Miles King races to the puck, taking it behind his own goal, setting up a play with thirty seconds left on the clock. I shift my weight back and forth, trying to anticipate what their move is.

"Bougie, watch Fox—he's been sneaking in the crease all night shoving Vladi and the refs aren't calling shit."

"Got it, Larsy!" I scream at Hayes Larson, our center and badass motherfucker. He's a great leader on the ice—I can only hope to be like him one day. He's earned his alternate captain title ten times over. And he's a fucking good guy. *And* the love he has for his wife, Olivia, is straight out of a fairy tale. *One I wish I had.* But now King is skating toward us to try and tie it up and force overtime. He crosses the blue line, firing off a shot on goal. Vladi blocks it, but there's a scrum in front of the net over the rebound. His stick gets caught in one of the other team's skates as he fights to free it, but it's no use.

I watch in horror as it skids across the ice just as Chicago's center passes to Fox. Right in front of me. Right in front of the net. The blood drains from my face as Fox unleashes a shot, the puck moving in slow motion toward the goal. My stick can't reach it, Vladi's stick is gone, which means he's scrambling to do something, *anything,* to stop this shot.

I've got to do something. I lunge toward the other side of the goal, diving on the ice between Fox and Vladi, releasing a sigh of relief as a sting of pain hits my chest.

Shot. Blocked.

The horn signaling the end of the game goes off, and I, Jordan Joseph Boucher, have made a defensive play to win the game. My teammates rush the goal to tap Vladi's helmets with their own, afterward treating me with a round of pats on the back and echoes of 'nice dive' and I let out a yell, my lungs still burning from the game. This is one of those moments that make me love hockey. We have a lot of shitty games, losses, injuries, workouts, practices…but when we all come together as a team, when we do whatever it takes to win and succeed? That makes it all worth it.

"Great job in the o-zone tonight, boys! We kept them on their toes the entire sixty minutes, had good shots on net, and continued firing them in until they hit. Defense, we need to do a better job of keeping pucks out of the crease. Tonight's game puck goes to EJ with his goal and two assists," Coach Cal says after the game in the locker room. We all shout and cheer him on. EJ's had a rough few games, but he's finally found his groove again tonight.

"Thanks, Coach," EJ says, taking the puck, eyeing it for a moment, lips pressed together before making the usual post-game celebratory speech. "I felt great tonight, and that's all thanks to everyone in this locker room. Onto the next one!"

"Boucher!" Coach barks as I jolt in my seat. "My office. *Now*."

Shit. I can't say I wasn't expecting this, but to get called out in front of the entire team? *I might have gone too far this time...*

I follow him down the tunnel to his office space here at the arena. I swallow hard, waiting in the doorframe as he walks behind his desk.

"Sit," he growls, staring me down like a grizzly bear about to attack—and I'm his next victim.

"First of all, you're lucky I didn't bench your ass after that goddamn pre-game stunt. Just because you have a fucking give-away on a game night doesn't entitle you to do whatever the hell you want. That was disrespectful to me, to your teammates, and to the league." He sighs, pinching the bridge of his nose. "You know you'll be fined for this."

"Yes, sir," I solemnly whisper. I'm not naive enough to know there won't be a fine, but I am enough of a prick to not care. I can pay for it, I can *always* pay for it, but if I hint at all that I am not worried about the money, that's going to make this worse.

"Second, you are a damn good player. You have the potential to be one of the top defensemen in the whole goddamn league." My heart lifts, the idea of finally being seen for *me* rushing to the surface. "But your attitude and your lack of maturity are becoming a problem. A big one. I try not to say anything when I see you in the press with your flavor of the week, but when this type of immature bullshit spills onto my ice, it becomes my issue, and we can't have that. Not on my team."

"Sorry, Coach." My stomach knots tighter than the laces on my skates. I wish I could spit out the words that I don't want to have to fake having a girl every night. I regret the mistakes I made. I regret the outcome. I regret all of it. I wish I could tell him the truth. *Except* for the bobblehead skating routine—that was one-hundo percent worth it. I run my hands through my hair, wanting to pull the strands out at the direction my life has taken.

"Don't 'sorry Coach' me. Fucking fix it."

"Yes, sir."

"Get dressed and get ready for the flight. This is your last warning, Boucher. I will place you as a healthy scratch if you ever do something like that again."

I nod and walk out of his office, feeling like a kid who got sent to the principal's office. I deserve it. I was an idiot for doing that, but I'll own up to my shenanigans. But the fact that my coach, and everyone else, thinks I am actually sleeping with all those girls? I exhale every last bit of air from my lungs, hoping it takes the weight of the last few years with it. I want something real. I want something meaningful. Blonde hair and a silk scarf flash through my mind. I want *her*.

"Bougie got in trouble! Bougie got in trouuu-ble," Mac sings as I shuffle down the aisle to my seat on the plane.

"Shut the fuck up, Mac." I tighten the grip on my bag, stopping at his row. "At least *I* made a save tonight."

"Enough," Vladi grunts behind me. "Both of you."

"Fine," Mac spits. "But if I got called into Coach's office like that, he'd sure as shit be making fun of me."

"I didn't say he wouldn't," Vladi growls. "I simply said *shut up*. And that means shut the *fuck* up."

Mac raises his hands in surrender, his eyes wide as we walk past him to our seats. I plop down against the window, my muscles tense as I try not to throw my bag beneath the seat.

Vladi sits next to me, calmly stowing his luggage as if we didn't nearly fight one of our own. He is my seatmate on every flight. I'm basically his good luck charm, and despite his pretend hatred of me, he never lets me sit anywhere else. I hold back the smile threatening to crack across my face. He kind of just totally defended me. I'm not sure if I should be scared or...I look at the mountain of a man out of the corner of my eye. Actually, I don't know what the hell to think right now.

"Jordan," he says, taking his earbuds out of their case.

I snuggle up to his arm. "God, I love it when you call me that."

"You love it when I call you your name?"

"It makes me feel special."

He rolls his eyes and shakes me off before speaking in his slight Russian accent that makes everyone swoon.

"That pre-game shit was absolutely ridiculous. Yet, sadly, not out of the ordinary. However, you've been pleasantly distant from me lately. It's not normal. So, are you going to tell me what's bothering you?"

Goddammit, this goalie really does see everything. But...this is very friend-ish of him, something I genuinely never expected, so I'll allow it. My shoulders slump as the weight of everything that's been going on the past few months settles over my body.

"It's nothing. I've just...I've got some stuff going on. But I swear, Vladi, I'm not letting it affect my game. Those goals were not my fault."

"No. They were Tay's fault. You saved him from my wrath with your dive to block the final shot. Thank you for that. But it's not your game I'm concerned about. It's your demeanor. Dare I admit it has been slightly less peppy than usual? Not un-peppy by any means, but not fully obnoxious."

My brows raise to my forehead. *Wow, he's good.* I haven't been my normal exuberant self since I started getting the threatening texts, their presence constantly gnawing at the back of my mind. And now that Tay brought up the fact that Kennedy could be in danger, I'm even more worried about it.

"You know you can talk to someone about it, yes? Perhaps Larsy? Or Zack?"

I snort. I know this is his broody goalie way of telling me I can talk to him without ever admitting it. That's his personality, and I fully accept it. He's one of my best friends, whether he will ever admit it or not. He couldn't give two shits about my money or my family's status. And that's why I love that damn goalie so much.

I buckle my seatbelt, settling in for takeoff, and see Vladi about to pop in his earbuds.

"Wait! Before you zone out, can I ask you about it?"

He lowers his hands with a loud sigh. "If you must."

"You know what, nevermind." I sink down low into my seat.

"Jordan. Tell me."

I dart my eyes around the plane, making sure no one is listening. My teammates are still filing onto the aircraft, too absorbed in their own worlds, as well as the coaches, equipment managers, the social media and broadcast personnel, team physicians, and everyone else who travels to away games with us. To be honest, some of these folks are new this season, shoot, even the last few games, and I haven't seen them before. Still, I don't want anyone to hear my business.

Clearing my throat, I fiddle with my headphones. "Let's say I like this girl. But she wants nothing to do with me. And every time I try to talk to her, she kind of, totally, entirely ignores me. I didn't know what to do, so I started sending her presents anonymously, and now—"

"Jordan," he interrupts, "Are we talking about Kennedy?"

My eyes nearly pop out of my head as I swallow hard. *Fuck... how does he know too?!*

"What? No. I mean...maybe? I mean...shit! How do you know?!"

"Do you truly think Maggie wouldn't drag me down the hall to see Kennedy's diamond-encrusted leopard? No one else would send a gift like that but you."

Goddammit. "Okay, so let's *pretend* it is her." He raises his brow. "What...what do I do? I stopped sending gifts because that wasn't working, and I realized I don't even know how I'm going to tell her they were all from me. But that doesn't matter because I still don't know how I can get her to talk to me."

He rubs his hand along his jaw, staring at the back of the seat in front of him. "I can tell you she doesn't seem to be into grand gestures. She travels a lot, and she's seen parts of the world we've probably never been to. A giant animal statue is not the way to her heart. She seems like the type to be more about small gestures—ones that don't cost anything but have meaning. You actually do many of those things despite hoping people never know that about you. Try to find a way to show her that side of Jordan Boucher. Obnoxious gifts will not work."

Apparently, Russian Yoda is back now that he has his own love life figured out.

"Let's say you're right. I wouldn't even know how to do that."

Vladi nods with a smile as he slides his earbuds into his ears. "You'll figure it out."

Well, that was zero help. I groan, banging my head against the seat. *Russian Goalies.*

"Thanks anyway, Vladster."

"Don't call me that."

"But you love my nicknames, Vladinator!"

"I do not. Now, leave me to my music, or I will rat you out to Olivia, who we all know can't keep a secret."

I swear my eyes pop out of my head. "Point taken."

When we finally land, I jump up to grab my things and walk single file toward the front of the plane. I swallow hard, my pulse racing even more than usual. Standing in the front galley is Kennedy, smiling and nodding at everyone as they exit. And there, in her hand, is my bobblehead. She's holding me. In. Her. Hands. Oh. My. God. Breathe Jordan. Breathe. *Holy shit. What do I do?* Do I say something? Do I see if she wants me to autograph it? Is this one of those moments where I can do something that doesn't cost any money? As I step closer and closer, she's still smiling. *Does she see me?* Oh God. I'm going to vomit. *Pull it together. You can do this.*

As I finally make it to the front of the line, I stand right in front of her. *This is it. This is my moment.*

"Hi. Did you, um…want me to sign that for you?" I ask with a shaky voice, pointing to the box in her hand.

She tilts her head, her eyes squinting at me like a book she's trying to decide if I'm worth keeping or donating to the library. *Be brave. Stay calm.* Maybe she'll read the first chapter and want to get to know me more.

"I have a Sharpie in my bag; I don't mind…if you want—"

"I'm good." She dismisses me with a snarky smile, turning around to grab her roller bag, acting like she's busy with anything else so she doesn't have to talk to me.

Donation bin, it is.

Shit. I nod quietly, hoping none of my teammates paid much attention as I step off the plane. My heart sinks into the pit of my stomach as if it were the Heart of the Ocean necklace from Titanic. And it's probably going to stay at the bottom of the ocean for eighty-four years with how bad this hurts.

8
kennedy

Sitting at the hotel bar, my best friend Ginny in my hand, I squeeze my lime in and swirl her around as I replay today's events like a re-run of The Office. Except Michael Scott isn't funny. He's super annoying, and his name is Chaddwick. I swear, some days I want to strangle people like Chadd. Okay, maybe I just want to strangle *actual* Chadd. Who the hell talks to a co-worker like that? We are supposed to be a team getting the Riders to and from their destinations as safely as possible. This isn't some pissing contest about who has more power. There's an element of trust between the flight crew to do our jobs, and I didn't have that today. I love flying, but people like him, days like today, make me despise it.

The hair on the back of my neck stands on end. Speak of the devil, he's headed my way. *Fuck my life.*

"Hey, sweetheart," he says to the bartender, and I smirk at the eyeroll she's hiding behind her smile. "Johnny Walker Blue, two-fingers, neat."

Classic dick move—ordering an expensive scotch. *As if I give a shit.* And unlike the bartender, I'm not serving him, so I let my eyes roll back so far I get an instant migraine as he takes a seat at the barstool next to me. *Great.*

"Well, hello again," he says, his voice lower than before. "Guess we'll be seeing each other a lot this season."

I stare deep into the abyss of my drink as I reluctantly nod my head. "I guess so." My stomach churns—he's right. I have to see him a lot. Every. Damn. Flight. *Great.*

"I upgraded my room to a suite. I've stayed at this hotel before, and the standard rooms are so small it's almost unlivable."

I peek over from the corner of my eye. "You having a dance party in there or something? I go to my room and go to sleep."

"These trips get so lonely. I like a little extra space in case I want some company."

My ice clinks against the side of my glass. "Good for you."

The waitress brings him his whisky, and he hands her his card to start a tab, leaning forward in his seat as he watches her walk away. *This guy never stops, does he?*

He takes a sip, then shifts his body toward me. "How about you? You ever get *lonely* on these trips? I'd be happy to give you some company."

Is he trying to hit on me? After he just ogled the waitress? After he insulted my ability to carry out my duties today? My brows narrow, and my jaw clenches. He's out of his mind if he thinks he's going to win me over by ordering an expensive drink and telling me he's lonely. *Of course,* this is my new co-worker. Congratulations, Kennedy Kramer! You've won a free roundtrip ticket to your own personal hell.

I swivel to face him, scooting farther away without caring if he sees. "I enjoy my alone time."

"You could enjoy some alone time with me."

"I'm pretty sure alone time implies being by yourself, Chadd."

"Come on; don't you want to have some fun? These trips get so boring."

"No. I enjoy the solitude. I get caught up on books, binge-watch trashy TV, and get a good night's sleep so I'm prepared to do my job."

He leans in closer, placing his hand on top of my arm resting on the bar. My entire body cringes at his touch as the bile rises in my throat.

"You can just relax on the flight tomorrow night. I'll let you know when I need help, but I can handle the jet on my own. That's basically what I had to do today anyway."

A furious fire rips through me like a stick of dynamite exploded in my chest. *How. Fucking. Dare. He.* One damn day into having a new pilot and I'm already being harassed and demeaned.

"I can *relax?*" I spit out through gritted teeth. "On a flight where I am scheduled to be flying? That's not how it works, and you fucking know it. We split the duties, like a team, for the safety of everyone on board. I did my job *to perfection* today. And, unlike you, I take it seriously."

"Don't be so uptight, sweetheart. A pretty thing like you doesn't want to end up with early wrinkles from that scowl."

"Don't call me sweetheart," I say through gritted teeth. But this joker doesn't get the hint. He doesn't see I'm two seconds away from destroying my entire career by punching him in the face. My fist shakes in my lap as I contemplate doing it, desperate to throw caution to the wind and use my training so I don't actually break my knuckles, when someone steps up next to me, the presence all encompassing.

"Sorry that took so long, babe. I could *not* get my agent off the phone—what a yapper!"

The room spins around me, my body frozen in place like a raccoon caught mid-dumpster dive. Shock is not even an accurate word to describe what's happening as I watch the one person, who may be cockier than my captain, extend his hand to Chadd. My pulse races, my stomach drops, trying to figure out what hell is happening here. And whatever it is, it just keeps getting worse.

"I don't think we've been properly introduced yet. I'm Jordan Boucher, Kennedy's boyfriend."

9
jordan

A few minutes earlier

Rolling onto my side with a huff, I punch the hotel pillow, willing it to fill with more feathers. Goddamit, why can't things be magic like in the movies so I can get some fucking sleep? She dismissed me. *Again*. Why do I let this get to me? Why do I let her cold response hit my heart like a tranquilizer dart, making my entire body completely numb? *If only the metaphorical tranquilizer would help me sleep.* I don't even know how long I've been tossing and turning. I've flipped over my pillow at least ten times. I've tried counting in English. In French. Imagining bobbleheads jumping over my bed. Anything to get me to relax.

Nothing's working.

There is one thing that helps me sleep sometimes. A glass of red wine. Doesn't matter if it's a cabernet, merlot, or pinot noir. All of those make me drowsy super-fast and don't affect me the next day if I just have one. I roll out of bed and step over to the mini-bar in the room. *No dice.* Only some imported beers, whiskey, and vodka. Dammit. I need to get some sleep. We have a game tomorrow, and

I'm already on my last warning with Coach. I need to be playing at my best.

The last thing I need is to be tired as hell *and* play like shit. My head flops toward my side table. I could order room service, but that'll take an hour. I slam the fridge closed. *Fuck it.* I throw on sweats and my 'I am Kenough' hoodie, grab my wallet, and head downstairs.

As I step into the lobby, my gaze locks on the bar like my phone connecting to the Wi-Fi—instantly wanting to log in and explore. *She's here.* My heart drops into my stomach seeing the one person I can't have. Just like a random Wi-Fi signal, I don't have the fucking password. I rub my tired eyes, hoping the action will press the 'forget network' setting. *It doesn't.* I can't be around her again right now. I can't see her beautiful face and take another rejection. Not tonight. I shuffle my feet, wanting to retreat to my room like a damn turtle back into its shell. But wine is the only thing that's going to help me sleep. *Fuck.* I was a ninja turtle for Halloween one year. I'll just channel that energy and hide inside my shell in plain sight.

I take a seat in a corner booth away from the bar. I'll just order a drink and head on my way. Easy peasy. But goddammit, I still see her. *I'll always see her.* The server comes by, and I order a glass of Bonanza, my favorite cabernet. It seems fitting for the state of my life, and it knocks me out for a solid eight hours. The name sounds as ridiculous as my persona, and the word means a windfall of good fortune, which I could fucking use right now.

Especially with Kennedy.

I can't help but stare at her, wondering what it would be like to just go up and say hi. To have her *actually* respond. But as soon as that thought enters my mind, some guy approaches and takes the seat right next to her. *Who the fuck is that?* My breath catches. Does she have a boyfriend? He looks like a douche. *Oh shit.* That's our new pilot. I saw him standing behind Kennedy earlier on the plane.

Goddammit. He's sitting a little too close to her for my taste. My stomach drops…she looks…*uncomfortable*. My teeth clench as he leans close, as if whispering in her ear, but I see her flinch. I see her shift away in her chair. I see her hand clenched into a fist in her lap. *She is not into this motherfucker*. I am also not into this. Rage pulses through my veins as he reaches over to place his hand on her arm. I watch her cringe as she pulls her arm back enough to break contact without being overly rude.

What the fuck is happening to me right now? I don't know why my feet are suddenly the most confident motherfuckers in the world or why my heart is beating out of my chest. I don't know how I'm standing next to her or why the next words come out of my mouth.

But they do.

Words I've wanted to say for a long time fall out like teeth after a puck to the face.

"Sorry that took so long, babe. I could *not* get my agent off the phone—what a yapper!" I say, looking at her with pleading eyes, hoping she won't balk. Hoping she can see what I'm trying to do. She blinks, her face amazingly blank. *So far, so good.*

I turn my attention to face dipshit. "I don't think we've been properly introduced yet. I'm Jordan Boucher, Kennedy's boyfriend."

His eyes narrow. "Chadd. With two d's," he says, deadpanned as he reluctantly extends his hand. "I wasn't aware you two were dating."

"It's new. But it was love at first sight, right, babe?" I turn my gaze to see her staring back, her lips tight like she wants to thank me and murder me all in one swift move. I swallow hard—the combination of those two things is weirdly hot.

But in the best moment of my entire twenty-three years of life, she opens her mouth and says the unthinkable:

"Yeah, Chadd. This is my boyfriend. Jordan. Everything okay with your agent...*babe*?"

10
jordan

Ohmygod. Ohmygod. Ohmygod. Ohmygod.
    She spoke. She spoke to me. To *me*.
My breath catches. What is breathing anyway? Do I need air? Fuck I *do* need air. I have no idea what I'm doing, but she spoke *actual* words to me. She hasn't asked me to leave. *She called me* babe. I'm gonna throw up.

11
kennedy

Oh my *God*—this cocky son of a bitch is talking to me. I would like to request a refund from the universe. Chadd sneers. *Make that a demand.* I glance at the idiot standing beside me, flashing me the same damn smirk that's on his fucking bobblehead. On the other hand, I'll take this cocky ass over Chadd degrading me for another thirty minutes. At least he has an ass worth checking out. One that could probably bounce a quarter up to a cruising altitude of thirty thousand feet. I clench my jaw at the series of events that have led me here. *Can this day get any fucking worse?*

12
jordan

Chadd darts his eyes between the two of us, looking more confused than a boomer trying to figure out tap-to-pay. I have no doubt he's questioning this—the legitimacy of our confession—but if there's one thing I know how to do, it's sell a performance. I inch closer to my scene partner, hoping she can keep up. And hoping I don't pass out from the fact that Hotty McPilot is staring next to me in this show.

"How long have you two been together?" Chadd spits.

Kennedy looks to me. "Do you want to tell him, *babe*?"

Fuck, why is her calling me babe so hot?

"It's been a couple of months. Our mutual friend, Maggie, lives in the same building as Kennedy and introduced us. She thought we might hit it off." I place my arm around the back of her chair, careful not to actually touch her. Something tells me she could probably go toe-to-toe with me in a fight. *I'd like to keep my face for the moment.* "Sure enough, she was right."

"Are you sure you're allowed to date one of the players?" he asks with a smug look on his face. Just as I open my mouth to speak, she lays a hand on my chest and shoots me a look that says 'I've got this.'

"Actually, *Chadd*...I'm allowed to date whoever the hell I want," she fires back, her voice firm and confident. *Holy fucking fuckballs, Kennedy Kramer is* officially *the woman of my dreams.* "I'm not directly employed by the Riders, which means we're not technically co-workers. Not to mention, I fly my friends and family all the time, as I'm sure you do as well." She stands and grabs her purse, my chest burning from the imprint of her hand as if she left a brand on my skin. And now she's staring Chadd down like a lioness about to devour its prey. My pulse races, all of it flooding south.

I have never been more turned on in my life.

"But you, *Chadd*, you *are* my co-worker. And you've been hitting on me, not to mention questioning my ability to do my job, since the minute you stepped into the flight deck," she snaps before turning her attention to me. "What do you think? Should we report him?"

My pulse races, my muscles tense at the thought of him doubting the talent of the best pilot in the entire fucking world. This fucker would be worth every second of a ten-minute misconduct. But I stay focused because...*dear God, this is all my dreams come true.* The way she's playing along. The way she seems like she's all in. The way I want to have moments like this forever. "I one-hundo percent think we should report him. But we've been trying to keep this relationship under wraps and away from the paparazzi, so how about you just leave my girlfriend the hell alone and we call it a day. Do we have a deal?"

Chadd's face turns a deep shade of red, anger and embarrassment shooting from his eyes as he shakes his head, refusing to admit defeat. *Good.* Just as he opens his mouth to, no doubt, insult Kennedy again, I step forward to tower over him. I can't take this fucker anymore. A warm hand grips my arm, goosebumps pebbling all the way to my fingers. *She's got to stop touching me so I can concentrate.*

"Listen to me, Chadd, with two d's," I whisper through the menacing smile I give all my opponents. "You don't know me, and you sure as hell don't know her. Mind your own damn business. And if you ever talk to her like that again, I will destroy you. Myself, and the entire team of players at my disposal, will make your life a living hell. You will never fly for an NHL team again. You got me?"

He grits his teeth staring at us as if fire is about to shoot out his mouth like a dragon, but he doesn't make a move. Doesn't say a word. Yet another person speechless at the stellar showmanship of Jordan Joseph Boucher.

Fucking crushed it.

"Come on. Let's get out of here," Kennedy whispers as she glides her hand down my arm to grip my hand and drag me away. Like a puppy following its new owner, I fucking follow her. But not before getting in a couple more digs at the douche-nozzle that's been harassing her.

I blow a kiss over my shoulder. "Bye, Chadd! Hope you're not mad. If you get sad, go cry to your dad!" I yell as she continues to lead me toward the elevator.

Holy. Fucking. Shit. That was fan-freaking-tastic. And, by some miracle, she's *still* holding my hand. I swallow hard, my heart beating in my throat. God, she smells good like vanilla and sugar, and like I want her to be mine forever.

I glance at her through my peripheral vision. *She's right here.* Next to me. Acknowledging me. Her hand perfectly molded in mine. I flash her a warm smile, hoping she's feeling what I am. Feeling this instant, overwhelming need to be together always. My stomach flips, the world tilting just enough to feel like I'm getting the rom-com moment I've always dreamed of when her fiery green eyes meet mine.

DING!

As soon as the elevator doors open, she pulls me inside and hits the button for the twentieth floor. That's *my* floor. *Oh my God. Does she want to come to my room?* My downstairs elevator shaft rises rapidly at the thought. But shit—I'm not ready for...

THUD!

My entire body jolts as the elevator comes to a dramatic stop between floors, and Kennedy Kramer shoves me up against the wall. *Yep. It's official.* The elevator in my pants has achieved liftoff, and the woman pressing into me is going to make it burst right through the ceiling like the end of Willy Wonka. The way she's looking at me like she wants to devour me...

"What *the fuck* did you do back there, Cashanova?!"

I swallow hard, my eyes wide. *I'm beginning to think I may have misjudged this.* "What are you talking about? I was helping you! Wait...did you just call me *Cash*anova?"

"Yes, you jerk. I didn't fucking need you and your rich boy ass helping me. Now you've made things a million times worse!" she yells as she steps back and flicks me with her finger.

I clutch my bicep. "Ow! What the hell was that for? How did I make it worse? That guy was mauling you with his dumb pilot hands!"

Her face turns a shade of red brighter than the stop button she just pressed. *Shit.*

"Dumb pilot hands? What the hell does that even mean? I'm a pilot...do you think I have dumb pilot hands?"

"No...I don't think...I mean, you have hands, and you're a pilot, but they aren't dumb, they're...they're..." *Shit. How do I tell her they are the most perfect, softest hands I've ever held without sounding like a total creep?*

"What's the matter, Mr. Ego? At a loss for words?"

I mean...kinda yeah. "No. I just...I mean...you went along with it. You were smiling. You were holding my hand."

"Because there were *people* watching. Specifically fucking *Chadd*," she says as she takes a step back and runs her hand over her face, the sigh she lets out crushing my soul. "What the fuck do we do now?"

My gaze falls, my stomach twisting like a knotted ball of skate laces fresh out of the dryer. "I just thought, maybe, if you had a boyfriend, he would leave you alone."

"I have to see him every flight."

Yeah...I'm starting to rethink this whole thing now. My vision blurs as my breaths get shorter. We're in an elevator. Trapped. *Is there any oxygen in here?* Oh man. I don't do well in tight spaces where I can't quickly get out.

Fuck.

"Quick question..." I squeak. She looks at me like I just told her I thought the world was flat. "Could we maybe...um...start up the elevator again?"

Her nose wrinkles, and if I weren't searching for air, I might think it was cute. "Why?"

"I may be a little..." I clear my throat, "...claustrophobic."

"Fuck my life," she grumbles as she hits the start button.

Thank God.

"Thank you. I'm...I'm sorry. I was honestly just trying to help. I didn't mean to make things worse."

"Well, you did," she spits out as we reach the twentieth floor. "This is my floor. I'm going to bed. We'll figure this out in the morning." As she steps out of the elevator, I follow, and she gives me a painful look over her shoulder. "Do. Not. Follow. Me."

I flinch. "I'm not following you."

"Then why are you walking behind me?!"

"I, um...my-my room." I point over her head. "It's on this floor."

Her shoulders slump as she lets out a loud sigh. "Of course it is. Why *wouldn't* I be on the same floor as my new *boyfriend*?"

I mean, if we were dating, this would be kind of perfect.

As we walk down the hall, I stop at my door and notice she pauses one door past mine. *She's in the room next to me.* I'm gonna need a very, *very* cold shower.

My hand shakes as I reach for my key, realizing I may have actually made this worse for her.

"Kennedy. I'm...I'm really sorry. I really was just trying to get him to leave you alone."

Her gaze shifts toward the gray-patterned carpet. "I know. But this," —she looks up, gesturing between us— "complicates things for me."

For once, I really am at a loss for words. I've already said I'm sorry. I know she won't let me comfort her. I want more than anything to tell her I think she's the most amazing woman I've ever met, but even my dumbass knows that would not go over well. So I just nod and stare at the carpet as well, clearing my throat. "Goodnight then."

"Night," she says as she taps the card on her door and disappears behind it.

I unlock my own door and step inside. This was the first real encounter I've had with her. And while I thought it was going well —she didn't. *Shit, I really screwed this up.*

I kick my shoes off and flop down on the bed, the weight of my actions making me sink further into the mattress. It feels like I swallowed a rock, and it found a new resting place in my stomach. *She's embarrassed to be seen with me.* The way people will view her...I'm sure her life as a female pilot is hard enough. My three older sisters have struggled to be taken seriously in their professions, even with my family connections, and I'm guessing Chadd the Gonad has a fucking loudmouth and will blab our lie everywhere.

I throw an arm over my eyes with a groan. She'll have co-workers who view her as dating a guy who, for all intents and purposes, acts like a complete himbo. They'll assume she's with me for my money. They'll assume, like everyone else, that my money *somehow* helped her get to where she is. *I would give anything not to be me right now.* Just to be a regular guy pining after a girl so far outside of his league is hilarious. A guy worthy of dating someone like Kennedy. No…not someone like her. *Actually her.*

My phone pings. I want to ignore it and lie here like the Michael Jordan crying meme trying to fall asleep. But my heart races as I jolt up in bed. *Holy shit, maybe it's her.* I don't think she even has my number, but maybe she got it from someone? As I look at the screen, my heart races for an entirely different reason. I was wrong. Very, very wrong.

> **BLOCKED NUMBER**
>
> I told you to stay the fuck away from her. Doesn't look like you're very good at following directions.

Another *ping;* a photo of Kennedy and me by the elevators appears under the text. We're holding hands. Smiling at one another. A warmth spreads through my chest seeing us like that. I *wonder if it could ever be this way between us.* But my breath catches in my throat. I feel like I'm being chased in a dream where I can't run fast enough to get away.

Who the fuck took this photo?

13
kennedy

"Why the *hell* is Bougie blowing up my phone at this hour like a firework display, asking me for your number?" Maggie interrogates me over the phone as if I've just admitted to living a double life. Shit, is that what I've just done? My stomach churns.

Why the hell is he asking for my number?

A defeated sigh escapes me as I put her on speaker and continue getting settled in my room. *This day has gone on forever.* "It's a long story."

"Good thing Vladi's in Columbus with you and the rest of the Riders because I've got all the free time." Sheets rustle as she settles against her pillows. "What's going on? He said he needed your number because, and I quote, 'the fate of the universe rested on him talking to you.' Spill it."

I can't help the giant eyeroll that escapes before shoving my uniform shirt in the laundry bag. "That's a bit dramatic."

"Bougie is known for his flair."

I tug my pajama top over my head and briefly explain that

Chadd was hitting on me, and Jordan came over to us and announced he was my boyfriend.

"What?! Jordan Boucher. The Most Eligible Rider Bachelor Bougie? You guys are dating?!" she screams.

"No! We are definitely *not* dating. He just said that in a lame attempt to rescue me." I scoff. "As if I'm some damsel in distress that can't take care of myself. And now I have to somehow tell Chadd with two d's we are not dating. Then he'll start hitting on me again, *and then* I'll have to either suck it up and deal with it or report him and get labeled as the 'difficult female pilot' and…shit." I groan as I twist my hair up into a messy bun. "I can't with this. Just put me on one of those burning Viking rafts and float me out to sea."

"Oh, stop, Kenni. It's not that bad." Maggie teases like this is the most normal thing in the world.

"Not that bad?" I laugh in disbelief as I drop down on the bed, leaning against the headboard. "This kid is a twenty-something acting like he's God's gift to women, hooking up with people left and right without a care in the world, and now fucking Chadd thinks I'm associated with him. I don't know how to make this go away."

Maggie sits quietly for a moment, which is very unlike her. *It's actually the most un-Maggie thing ever.* My brows pull together, the silence hanging like the scene in a thriller right before the jump scare.

"Maggie? Did I lose you?" I worriedly ask.

"No, I'm here. I'm just…thinking."

I'm for sure scared now. "This can't be good."

"Hear me out…" she hesitates, "but what if you didn't have to break up with him?"

I shoot upright. "I'm sorry, *what?* Are you delusional?! We aren't even dating to begin with!"

"No, no. I know *that*. I mean...I get it. But what if you *were* dating?"

My fingers twitch as I shake my head. "In what universe would I *ever* date someone like Jordan Boucher?"

She huffs out an irritated laugh. "Kenni, think about it. If you kept up the ruse, it would give you an excuse to hopefully keep Captain Can't-Take-a-Hint away without having to report him. He knows there will be hell to pay from Bougie. He can't be *that* stupid and desperate. It's actually kind of perfect."

"Maggieee," I groan, "You know I love you. But...no. Hell fucking no."

"Why not? Listen, Linda, I know you think he's this crazy rich playboy douche-nozzle. But...Bougie's more than what he seems. He has a heart of gold. I know he can be a little immature, but underneath that, he really is special."

"A *little* immature? The player who did a figure skating routine before the NHL game he played in? That's frat boy level immature. I'm in my thirties. There's no way in hell I can date, or pretend to date, someone like him," I scoff. *Despite his hotness and the fact that he stood up for me, it's a hard pass.* I will admit—he honestly did give me the out I needed tonight. The worst part is I shouldn't have needed saving. I should be able to sit at a bar with any member of the flight crew without feeling like a piece of meat. And despite the progress the world has made, we're not there yet. At least Jordan allowed me to walk away without causing a bigger issue with Chadd.

My phone buzzes in my ear, pulling me from my thoughts.

"Hang on; I'm getting a text—oh my God. You gave him my number?!"

"He made it seem like it was life or death! I know you don't like him, but just think about it. At least hear him out about whatever crisis this is."

I shake my head, not wanting to give this another thought, but I suppose I can play along for the moment. At least for my friend's sake.

"*Fine.* But we're having mimosas when I get back, and you're paying."

"Deal. Just text him back."

"Also, why does he need my number? He's literally in the adjoining room next door."

"Ohhhh!!! Well, *that* is quite the development! Maybe you could go next door and…you know…*talk it out.*"

"I don't like the tone you just used with me," I say as she cackles.

"Love ya, girl—keep me posted!"

"Love you too, xa

> UNKNOWN NUMBER
>
> Hey. It's Jordan.
>
> Jordan Boucher…from the Riders and the bar and the elevator earlier.
>
> Can you call me?
>
> Or meet me?
>
> I don't want to be too forward to ask to come over, but…we have a problem.

"Shit."

14
jordan

If the carpet in this room were ice, it would need resurfacing from the pacing I've done since I messaged her. *Did I text the wrong thing? Did I upset her more?* Of course, I fucking upset her... this is *all* going to upset her. Maybe she's already asleep? God, I need to talk to her before I'm sucked into tomorrow's game day schedule. My throat tightens, the clock on the nightstand impossibly bright with a time that's far too late to be okay. *Fuck, I really need to get to sleep.*

Out of the corner of my eye, my phone glows like the neon light in front of my favorite arcade bar. My heart pounds in my chest as I dart over to grab it. *Holy. Shit.* It's her.

> **KENNEDY**
> Fine. I see we have adjoining rooms. Open your side and knock on my door.

My knees buckle as my jaw drops. She's not just on the other side of the wall—*our rooms connect.* If this isn't the gods of love and hockey looking down on me, I don't know what is.

My hand shakes as I gently knock. Stepping back, I rock on my heels, waiting for her to answer. My pulse races faster than a mouse on the run from a cat, trying to escape the possible wrath in store from bothering her this late at night with what I have to tell her.

Fuck.

But there's no more time to panic because there she is, standing before me wearing sleep shorts, a T-shirt, and that same fire I saw in her eyes earlier, but now it's burning even more, and I realize, it wasn't a fire of passion, it was a fire ready to burn me alive. My throat tightens—*I'm not saying I wouldn't let her.*

"Hi…" I swallow hard, trying to get the words out, "um… thanks for opening your door."

Eyes narrowed, she crosses her arms. *Yeah. She definitely looks like she wants to murder me.* "What is so urgent that we have to talk right now?"

"Can I, um…" I point to the table and chairs in her room, "Can we sit down?"

She sighs, and I swear I see her eyes fighting not to roll. "Sure. Why the hell not?" she spits, her voice thick with sarcasm. "Why would I turn down the one and only Prince Charming, who just announced to my coworker we're *dating*, from conniving his way into our adjoining rooms?"

My body curls in on itself like plexiglass warping after a hard check. *Well, this is off to a fabulous start.*

"Okay…out with it," she snaps, collapsing into the chair opposite me. "What's going on?"

I swallow hard. I'm not ready to tell her any of this, but I also know I have no choice. "Do you have, like, a boyfriend or a husband or a partner or something?"

The muscles in her perfect face tighten, her lips pursing together. *God, she's gorgeous when she's angry—even if she looks like she's going to kill me.*

"*That* was what you needed to talk about?"

"No!" I throw my hands up, "No, no, no. I...I got a weird text. It was a photo—"

"A photo of *what*?"

I furiously tap my foot on the floor. Would she take this better if it were in Morse code? Fuck. I have to spit it out. "A picture of us."

Her eyes widen, a look of horror flashing across her face. "What do you mean of *us*?"

I let out a loud sigh. "Here." I slowly slide my phone across the table. "It came through a while ago. This isn't hotel security footage. I think someone..." I scrub my hand down my face, "I think someone was watching us."

"Us?" She shakes her head, waiving her hand between us. "There is no *us*. There is you, and there is me. The end."

My chest tightens. *Shit.* "Sooo about that..."

Her eyes nearly bulge out of their sockets. "Fucking hell. Am I going to need another drink for this?"

I wince. "It might not be a bad idea."

"Fuck," she mumbles, walking to the mini-bar and perusing the lackluster selection I saw earlier. "Goddammit, there's no gin." She snatches a vodka seltzer and slams the fridge door shut, cracking the can open and shotgunning the entire thing. My jaw drops quicker than an opponent I knocked out on the ice. *Stay calm, Jordan. Do not come in your pants over the hot woman shotgunning a drink.*

I take a deep breath and continue as she takes her seat, "I don't think there's any way this could be Chadd McLimpdick." She twists her lips in an adorable attempt to hide her smirk. To be honest, I'm hiding a smile as well. *Maybe there's hope for us yet?* I bite my cheek. *Focus, Boucher,* she *will* murder me if I don't act like this is serious. "There's no way he could have run out of the bar to snap a photo that fast. That guy is a total Unc."

She blinks. "Unc? What the hell is that?"

"It's like..." my brain falters as if my blade caught a bad groove in the ice, "I don't know, it means an old guy. He's old. Like an uncle."

"Got it," she says, her brows narrowed with a look that says she totally has *not* got it. "And you're right. From that angle, there's no way he would have been able to run out of the bar and take our photo without us noticing," she says, her voice softening just a tad as she slides the phone back to me. "Who *did* take this?"

I shake my head, my pulse finally settling enough to think more clearly. "No clue. That's what I'm trying to figure out."

"Did the message say anything? Or was it just the photo?"

Cue my pulse shooting back to one billion beats per minute. If I show her the message, she'll know someone is telling me to stay away from her, then I'll have to explain that I have a massive crush on her, and everything will change. My stomach twists. *I'm not ready for that.* I don't want to lie, but...that wouldn't *really* be a lie. This is just not revealing that I like her. Yeah. This is fine. *Totally* fine.

"The photo came from a blocked number," I say, pulling my phone back across the table. *Not a total lie.* "That's why I asked if you had a boyfriend or something."

She shakes her head. "Nope. No one. Why would it have to be a boyfriend?"

"No reason." *Except that I want to date you.* "Just making sure."

"Obviously, this is nothing new for you, though, right? You're used to being photographed with women every day."

I drop my gaze. I didn't know it was possible for words to slice through my chest like a freshly sharpened skate blade, but lucky me, I just found out. I suck in a deep breath, reminding myself she's only seen the side of me I let everyone see. My acting skills and my ability to improvise in any situation are two of my biggest strengths. I take in a deep breath, exhaling a defeated sigh. At times like this, I kinda wish I sucked at it more.

Maybe then she'd see the real me.

"Listen. I know what you probably think about me. The media likes to paint a picture of me, but it's not all what it seems."

She pulls her head back, her eyes narrowing. "So you *don't* have a different girl on your arm every few days?"

"I mean, I do. But—"

"Look." She leans forward, crossing her arms on the table. "I don't need an explanation, I just need to know why this is a problem."

I nod. "Right. I contacted my publicist after I got the text. She did some digging and confirmed it's already been leaked to several paparazzi websites. So, as of tomorrow morning—"

The blood drains from her face.

"Everyone will see this."

"Yeah." I scratch the back of my neck, my stomach sinking between my toes.

She nods in quiet acknowledgment as my shoulders slump forward. *God, I hate seeing her disappointed.*

"Kennedy, I know I've said this a million times, but I truly am sorry," I say, watching her sit in silence, staring at the table with glossy eyes, her lips curved in a frown I would give anything to erase. The realization of being the one who did this twists in my chest.

Fuck, Jordan. You really screwed this up.

I did what I came to do—I told her the news. It's time to admit defeat, once again not knowing how to talk to this woman, and go back to my room to fail some more at sleeping.

"I'm gonna go." I push my chair back. "I'll give you some time to process—"

"Wait." She places her hand on mine. My eyes fixate on where our skin is touching, a warmth I've wanted for so long settling in. Forcing my gaze from her hand to her face, she continues, "I may have an idea."

15
kennedy

Damn Maggie and her ridiculous ideas! If this were the Eras Tour, this is where I would sing, 'Look What You Made Me Do.'

I can't believe I'm about to suggest this, but she may be right. Especially now that there is a damn photo of me holding hands with Richy Rich.

I push my shoulders back, taking control of the situation. This is what I'm trained to do—find the alternate path in crisis.

"What if we...*pretend* we're dating?"

His eyes go wide, blinking faster than a red fire warning light in the flight deck.

"What did you say?" he whispers with a very surprised tone to his deep voice.

"We can decide in the morning if you want to think about it. But, what if we did keep dating—"

"Yes!" he shouts louder than necessary with only two people in the room.

I cock my head. "You're sure?"

"Yep. I'll do it. I'll help you out." He scoots his chair back up to the table.

"Well, um…" I mindlessly pick at my cuticles. "Like I said, you can think about it first."

"Okay, I'll think about it." He places his chin on his hand like he's the goddamn Thinker statue.

And now I'm thinking of him naked and wondering if he's as chiseled as a statue. *Fuck.*

"Let's see…I got you into this mess. Seems only fair I help you get out of it. Okay! Done thinking." He puts both of his hands down on the table in front of him. "My answer is still yes."

My heart pulses in my throat. *He's agreeing to this.* What have I gotten myself into?

"If we do this, it's just to help keep Chadd off my back and not make me seem like your latest one-night stand."

His eyes soften. "Kennedy, I would never—"

I scoff, holding my hand up. "Stop. Everyone says you're a nice guy, and I'm going to try to give my friends the benefit of the doubt, but I also know you like women. I'm not going to be the joke of the tabloids. I have a profession. One I've worked damn hard to achieve at this level. If we're going to pretend we're dating, you can't be out with anyone else."

He leans back. "Deal. Not a problem."

I narrow my brows, my cuticles threatening to bleed from their torture this evening.

"You can just cut off other women just like that?"

"Yep," he says with a smile I've not seen from him before, his gaze never leaving mine. "Consider me gone for any other woman but you."

Shit, that was kind of sweet. *Nope. Abort. Do* not *go there. This is all for show, Kennedy.*

"Okay then. It's settled. But…what about you? I mean, this is really helping me out, but doesn't this hurt your precious playboy image?"

He runs his hands through his hair, the strands falling back across his forehead. He twists his lips as if he's debating some sort of admission.

"Honestly, I could use the positive monogamous relationship PR as well. Coach got on my case about the pre-game performance last night; he's worried my lifestyle is bleeding onto his ice."

"I'm shocked," I say, my tone dry and not at all shocked.

He smirks. "Yeah, yeah. I know. What can I say? I like to have fun. I try to make hockey games enjoyable for the fans who spend their hard-earned money to come see the Riders. The antics, the fights…Nothing I do is just for me. It's for them. I want them to leave feeling like it was the best night of their lives."

"And that's what the girls are for, too? To make them feel like it was the best night of their lives?"

"No. It's," —his gaze drops— "it's complicated. But Coach told me he wants to see more leadership, on and off the ice, and this could really be good for me too. Although I really don't care about that. This is about helping you. Coach can go suck a lemon. I want to make sure everything is okay for you and try to undo any damage I did tonight."

The slight creeping upward from the corners of my mouth doesn't surprise me as much as it should. My pulse flutters at how genuine he sounds. He's got to be doing this to save face. But, this being all about me? *I do like the sound of that.*

"You're right about one thing. This *is* about me. But I suppose if this helps us both, that makes it a little more mutually beneficial. So we're agreed? We pretend we're dating and, hopefully, this gets us both a better image?"

"Agreed. Should we make this official somehow? I can have my family attorney draw up a contract if you want, or…"

I lean back in my chair, my arms falling to the side. *Is this day ever going to end?*

"I don't really want a paper trail. Unless you're planning to screw me over?"

He shifts in his seat, a flicker in his eyes disappearing as quickly as it came. Smoothed back into his handsome, unreadable face. But the softness of it lingers, humming in the air.

"I know what you think about me—that I'm some rich playboy who only thinks about myself—but I swear to all things hockey." He places his hand over his heart, "I would *never* do anything to hurt you."

His sincerity hits me, tightening my chest, my throat forcing a swallow to keep my voice steady. My eyes slowly rake up and down his face, his arms, his chest, like I'm doing a walk around of a jet, looking for anything that might be off. I know his exterior perfection doesn't mean he's not hiding something underneath. And yet, for some strange reason, I feel like he's being truthful.

"Thank you. And I'm sorry for how I reacted earlier in the elevator."

He huffs out a laugh. "All good. We'll just call it our first argument."

I let out a slight chuckle. He is maybe, sort of, a *little* funny. *If you're into that sort of thing, which I definitely am not.*

"I guess that's true. Maybe before we make this official, we should set some guidelines?"

"Bet."

My eyes dart back and forth. "What are we betting on?"

He laughs again, the sound warm and calming after the stress of the night.

"Nothing. Bet means like…yes. Okay. I agree."

"Christ on a cracker, we're from different worlds," I huff as I pinch the bridge of my nose. "Okay, so we need a backstory, obviously. I like what you said earlier about how Maggie introduced us. Let's stick with that."

"Works for me."

"And maybe we should talk about when we end this."

16
jordan

"End this?" My voice cracks. "For sure. Let's figure that out." The words taste more sour than eating a mustard packet to help my leg cramps during a game. How am I this close to the woman of my dreams, in a hotel room, talking about ending our relationship?

My chest caves in like I took a penalty shot to win the game, and I hit the fucking post. *What if...what if I don't* want *to put an expiration date on this?* I don't want this to start like a container of yogurt—more like yogurt-covered raisins where the expiration date is more of a suggestion than a warning.

Well, now I just want to eat my feelings.

I take in a deep breath and let it *out* again. I can't tell her I don't want to end this. She'll think I'm a stage five clinger. But I can't walk away from this either. This is my chance to finally show her how different I am. To show her I'm more than just a spoiled rich asshole. To show her I'm *actual* boyfriend material. My mind races with how much time I would need to prove this to her while balancing my crazy ass hockey schedule.

"How about…" *Fuck, Jordan, use your brain. Think!* "after the playoffs?" I spit out. "That would help me a lot with Coach and not stress about a breakup, *a PR breakup,* until afterward. Would that be okay?"

She twists her lips. "When do the playoffs end?"

"June, if we make it to The Cup finals. One more win and we'll clinch the division, so we're in a great position to make a long run. I have to plan like we're going to go all the way this year."

Her gaze lifts to the ceiling as my pulse quickens, silence filling the space. Her eyes drop back to mine, a slight crinkle in her brows. My heart furiously pumps blood throughout my body, straight to where I don't need it to go right now. This woman is sexy when she's angry, happy, sad, and deep in thought. *Dammit, why did I wear sweatpants?*

"A few months works for me. That'll give me time to figure out what to do about Chaddwick Ainsworth, the most arrogant man in the world."

I smirk. "I thought I was the most arrogant man in the world."

"You fell one place in the rankings. Don't get too excited."

I can't help but let out a laugh. I'll take one spot down. I will actually take *any* spot she gives me. But hopefully I'm off the list by June, the Cup in my hands and her on my arm.

Kennedy groans, dropping her head into her hands. "I guess there's just one last thing we need to discuss."

I tilt my head, narrowing my brows. "And what's that?"

"PDA."

I freeze harder than Paulette in Legally Blonde when the UPS guy walks in. My breath leaves my lungs and doesn't come back. *How do you find air when you're drowning in a sea of Kennedy Kramer?* I swallow hard.

"PDA. Right." I clear my throat, fighting to keep my voice even. "How do you want to handle that?"

"Obviously, they'll want us to hold hands. They already saw that in the photo, so we're stuck with that." The hint of irritation in her voice doesn't slip past me. What does she think I am? A lizard? My hands may be a little rough, but dammit, I moisturize.

Still...she's agreed to hold mine.

I bite the inside of my cheek, holding back my excitement and desperate to keep a straight face. Honestly, she could maul me like a bear at this point, and I'd be fine with it.

"Right. Holding hands is fine with me, too."

She peeks through her fingers, still hiding her face. "Then there's PDA beyond that."

"I'm fine with whatever you're comfortable with. You just tell me what's allowed and I'll respect it."

Kennedy slumps, picking at her nails once more. "I figured you'd want to have your tongue down my throat the second you entered my room."

Fucking hell, this woman. I mean, she's not wrong, but she has got to stop talking about tongues because my dick is swollen more than a can of soda someone put in the freezer too long. Unless I decide to set up a permanent residence here, I will eventually need to leave this table. It would be weird to sleep sitting like this.

"Let's stick to hand holding and hugs," she suggests, bossy as hell, and I am fucking here for it.

As if I'd *ever* say no to anything with her.

"Yes, ma'am."

She winces. *Shit.* "Oh God, please don't call me *ma'am*. That makes me feel old."

"How old are you?" My eyes go wide. "Wait...shit...you're not supposed to ask a woman that. Dammit. I'm sorry."

She leans forward, propping her elbow on the table, resting her chin in her palm.

"It's fine. We need to know these details if this is going to work. I'm thirty-four. You?"

Fuck. I don't even want to tell her. I don't want her to think I'm as immature as my image and my age make me seem. But I have to...

"I just turned twenty-three earlier this month—March 1st. When's your birthday?"

"September 5th," she says with a defeated sigh. She's trying to keep it together, but I know she's freaking out. Growing up with sisters, I learned that composed on the outside usually means turmoil inside. I catch the subtle way she bites down on her nail. The slight waiver flips my nerves on their head. My muscles go tight, barely stopping me from reaching across the table to pull her into my arms until she feels safe. But...we aren't even past holding hands. *I can do this.* I'll just do what I always do and break the tension with my wit and personality.

"I was thinking, since you don't want any sort of contract, we could shake on it. If you want, we can even have our own *secret* handshake that only we know what it means," I say with a wink as she lets out a laugh and rolls her eyes. My lips curl up at the sound, my chest filling with pride. *Even with the eyeroll, I still made her laugh.*

"I think a normal one is fine. So...we have a deal?" she says, extending her hand.

I delicately grab her hand in mine, giving it a firm shake, my eyes never leaving hers. "Fake dating it is."

For now.

17
kennedy

Waking up to the sound of my phone buzzing incessantly like it's personally offended I'm still asleep is not the way I wanted to start my morning. I flop my arm over my eyes with a groan. I had aspirations to do so much today. I was going to sleep in, lie in bed for a good hour doom-scrolling social media, order an almond milk vanilla latte to my room, then doom scroll until I passed out. I have no obligations to be anywhere until nine tonight.

"Is it too much to ask that my phone not pop off like a popcorn maker at seven in the goddamn morning?" I gripe to myself. Apparently so because as I lay here trying to ignore the rattling on the nightstand next to me, I realize it's not going away.

I roll over, squinting at the blinding light on my phone. My eyes widen as much as they can this early in the morning, my body fumbling out of the nest of pillows as I jolt straight up in bed. My entire screen is filled with notifications. Every social media app. News alerts. Missed calls. Unopened texts.

"What in the actual fuck?"

MAGGIE

Girl...call me ASAP.

OLIVIA

Kennedy...Oh my God...Bougie?! 😮

KARA

Kenni, we JUST had brunch and you didn't tell me about you and Jordan? What the hell?! What is going on??

SHELLY

Dammnnnn girl! A hot younger guy? Yaaasss! 🔥

MAGGIE

911! Did you do what I think you did?! Holy tits this is amazing. I need details!! Call me ASAP.

JORDAN

👋. Hi. Me again. Jordan.

From last night and next door.

Your new boyfriend.

I have to take off soon, but if you don't mind knocking on my door when you're up, I think we need to chat about a few more things if that's okay with you? K. Let me know 😊👍❌✔️😊

Well, this is a fucking fantastic disaster.

I curse under my breath as I clumsily make my way to the bathroom to take care of business and brush my teeth. *Wouldn't want my new boyfriend to know I have morning breath.*

I shuffle over to the adjoining door and open my side. My knuckles barely graze the wood before it's flung open wide. Heat burns low in my gut, my knees suddenly unsteady. My eyes are still sleepy, but, unfortunately, my hormones are wide awake and staring at the male figure before me. His Riders' T-shirt does nothing to hide his muscular arms, nor do his tight as hell gray joggers hide the thick thighs beneath. He's wearing a backward baseball cap for God's sake.

My breath catches in my throat—*it is too goddamn early to have this kind of hotness thrown in my face.* Thank God women aren't subjected to something visible like morning wood. *Did he have morning wood today? FUCK.* I shake my head, not prepared for the onslaught of thoughts running through my mind. Especially since they don't seem quite as annoying as they once did.

God, I really need to get laid and not be thirsting after this way too young for me, egotistical, sculpted as hell man-child standing at my door. My jaw ticks. *Shit. I can't get laid.* I have a fucking boyfriend now—one who is standing in front of me and getting my sleep shorts much wetter than I'd like. I certainly can't fucking sleep with *him*! *Deep breaths, Kennedy. Let's just hear what he has to say.*

"Good morning. Hope I didn't wake you," he says, his voice gruff with sleep and a soft curve to his smile.

Dammit. His smile is kind of sweet. I mean…if that was the kind of thing that got me going. Not me, though. Nope. I don't go for cute smiles and broad shoulders.

I sway back and forth, arms crossed tight across my chest. "Shockingly, you didn't wake me—it was the other eighty thousand notifications that did. Yours came after I was already up."

His lips twist, his nose crinkling as his cheeks heat. "If it makes you feel any better, I had just as many. I'm guessing you figured out the photo is everywhere?"

"I think everywhere is an understatement," I snort. "I get *you* having all these notifications, but…how do these people know who *I* am?"

He leans against the doorframe as he shakes his head. "Internet detectives are no joke."

"For real. So, what did you need at this God-awful hour?"

"Right. So listen. I'm not sure if I'll have to do press after the game tonight. Hopefully not, but it all depends on how the game goes. If I do end up in the hot seat, they'll for sure ask about us, and that will be my formal announcement about our," —he motions his hands back and forth between us— "relationship."

"*Fake* relationship," I quickly correct him. A low pull tightens in my core, my body betraying me. "This is all just an arrangement."

He exaggeratedly nods. "Right. Yep. Our very fake relationship. Got it," he says, biting his lip. The tension in my muscles let loose. "I, um…I also wanted to tell you that my cousin, Hannah, is my PR agent. I gave her your number so she can give you a call later. I figured your phone was blowing up like mine, and I thought I'd pass her number along so you would answer and not think it was spam. She just wants to talk to you and let you know she's here if you need anything."

I narrow my eyes. "You think I can't handle myself in front of the media? I'm quite capable of taking care of mysel—"

"Oh God no!" he interrupts. "It's nothing like that. She's just… Hannah and I have always been really close. The Bouchers learned a long time ago to not trust many people outside our family. She owns her own PR company; I trust her with my life. And I trust her with yours. I don't think you need help. Not at *all*. I just…I wanted to offer it in case you didn't want to deal with the insanity that's coming. The media's brutal. They suck balls, actually, *and* we play Columbus today. We've had some bad blood with them recently, so this is only going to fuel the fire." He rubs at his shoulder, the tension in his body practically vibrating. "Game days are really crazy. I have a routine, and I get really anxious if I don't stick to it, so I…I just wanted you to have someone to chat with about all this if I'm not around."

A quiet sigh escapes. It is still too fucking early to deal with all this, but…his offer is a nice gesture. *At least he's being somewhat helpful. And not annoying me…for now.*

"I appreciate it. I guess it couldn't hurt."

"Here's her number," he says as he hands me a torn piece of paper from a hotel notepad.

My lips twist in a wry smile. "You know, you could have just texted me her info and went on your way."

"Yeah, I know. I just…" He pauses, his eyes looking to the floor before popping back up to mine. "I still feel bad about last night, and I wanted to make sure you were okay."

My heart skips a tiny beat at his thoughtfulness. I swallow it down quickly, putting my fortress back in place. "I'm fine. Thanks for the info."

"Sure. No problem. Also…there's one more thing."

It's fucking too early for one more thing. My knuckles go white against the edge of the door. "What is it?"

"Hannah thinks we should go on a date."

Grilled Cheesus take me now.

18
jordan

"She thinks we should make a public appearance to make this seem legit." I shuffle my feet, trying not to count each individual strand in the carpet before I spiral completely out of control. "I wanted to do this right and ask you if you'd like to go on a date. With me. We have an off day in Dallas this week." Her brows furrow. "You'll be there, too, since it's between away games, so I thought maybe that would work…"

My stomach dips after I finally word vomit everything out in what seemed like one long thought. *Deep breaths, Jordan. It's only the woman of your dreams. We're fake dating, so she* can't *say no. Right?* I didn't know my pulse was even capable of reaching this speed. I glance at my watch, waiting for some sort of alarm to go off as she thinks. *She has to say yes, right?*

"Yeah." She leans against her doorframe. "I mean…I guess we're fake dating, so we should go on a fake date."

My heart feels like it's going to shoot like a rocket out of my chest.

I put a death grip on the seam of my shirt to keep from smiling like a psychopath and try to focus on forming some sort of coherent response.

"There's a place in Dallas where all the big athletes dine when they are in town. Hannah suggested it, saying it would be good to go there just to make this seem legitimate. There will be media out front, like always, and she'll tip them off to make sure they're looking for us. Is that..." I swallow, "would that be okay with you?"

She slowly nods. "I guess if we are *dating*,"—she air quotes—"we'd better act like it. Let me know the details, and I'll be there."

She'll. Be. There. *Ohmygod, ohmygod!* Flipping my thumb against all my fingers, I try to stay calm, but my excitement is fighting to get out like a rabid dog who hasn't eaten in days. *Breathe, Jordan.*

"Okay. This is...it's gonna be great. We'll go to dinner, be boyfriend and girlfriend...all fake, of course." *Not fake to me, though. This will never be fake to me.* "Oh! Did you pack anything other than pilot clothes? You know what...it's okay. Hannah can get you hooked up with something to wear if you need it. I'm sure you look just fine in jeans and a T-shirt, that's just not the vibe of the restaurant, but if you need anything else, just—"

"Call Hannah," she interrupts, her lips pursing together as her eyes narrow. "Got it. I'll figure it out."

"Right. Yeah. Okay. Well, I'd better get going. Hope things calm down with your notifications. Okay...well...bye."

"Have a good practice or morning skate or whatever..." she trails off as she closes the door.

"Morning skate!" I shout at the wooden wall between us.

My shoulders slump. *Great.* I'll just go to the arena and make it seem like my every hope and dream isn't right here and obligated to go on a date with me. This is the best thing that's ever happened to me. I drop my head against the door.

No big deal.

"Yo! You and Kennedy?" EJ yells from across the locker room as he laces up his skates. "Why didn't I know about this?"

"Once again, EJ, if you'd pay attention to things outside of yourself every once in a while, maybe you'd pick up on things like this," Tay snaps as he tapes his stick, quickly looking to me with a very bizarre side-eye.

My stomach clenches. *Oh fuck. Tay knows.* Goddammit—I'll deal with that later.

"Bruh, you're dating Kennedy?" Mac chimes in with one brow raised. "The hot-as-hell team pilot? I saw the picture online of you two holding hands. What the fuck does she see in you?" He smirks as he tightens the strap on his pads.

I grit my teeth. "Funny, Mac. The only thing *your* hand is holding is your lonely dick. And yeah, she's my girlfriend. If you refer to her as being hot again, you'll be the first one going into the boards tonight; screw the players from Columbus."

"You can't slam a goalie into the boards."

I narrow my eyes. "Watch me."

"Enough!" Zack silences the room as he's lacing up his skates. "This is not the time or place for this. We are here to practice. We win this game tonight? We win the division. Save the Bougie harassment for when we're celebrating. Got it?"

Murmurs and mumbles fill the locker room, everyone disappointed that their chance to tease me evaporated with a single word. I drag my hand down my face at the way everyone found out about this. I'm not sure how I thought it *would* go, but it wasn't some photo being leaked to the media. My gut twists. *Fuck. I need to sell this.* If I sit here angry and pouting, my entire team will know something's up.

"It's fine, Z." I stand at my shoebox of a cubby in the visitors' locker room. I swear these things suck so bad. *If I ran a league, every team would have locker room equality.* "It's true. We've been trying to keep it under wraps, especially from the media, but now that it's out…" I don't even try to contain my grin, "Yes, we're dating. It's new, but she's the best freaking thing that's ever happened to me. We are, in fact, the new celebrity 'it' couple. So chirp all you want! I scored the hottest girl in the world, and you can all suck it. In fact, to honor my new relationship being public, I'd like to recite an original poem—"

I barely get the words out before the entire room erupts with groans, and balls of wadded-up tape slam into my chest. *Works every time.* Though, if I do say so myself, my poetry game is top-notch.

As I sit back down to finish getting dressed, I see Vladi staring me down from his locker. *Shit.* He knows this couldn't have happened this fast. *It's gonna be a fun plane ride home after the game tonight with him grilling me.* Fuck we need to let Maggie know about this, too, since she's the *reason we met*.

I pull the laces on my skates tighter than usual. This fake dating thing just adds more things to keep track of in the Jordan Boucher Public Persona Facade.

Everyone grabs their gear and heads out to the ice. Pushing my shoulders back, I put my gloves on and reach for my stick, ready to slip into a mask that feels more comfortable. As I turn to walk out the door, someone grabs my arms and pulls me to a stop. When I look up, Vladi stands before me. My eyes widen. My pulse races. He doesn't say a word, just stares into the abyss of my soul, and it's scary as hell. I swallow hard, afraid he's going to use his wolf claws to rip me to shreds.

"What?"

"Keep your focus on your game."

I force a smile. "Of course. Vladinator, you know I got your back on the ice! No pucks in your crease on my watch."

He doesn't respond, just nods and walks out the door.

Fuck.

19

kennedy

"That was the longest two hours of my life, Kenni—I need details!" Maggie screams on the other end of our FaceTime call.

"Geezus, Maggie, I haven't even had coffee yet." I run my hand across my face. *So much for a relaxing day.* "You *do* know the point of the phone is so you don't have to yell, right?" Her eyes narrow. "Don't side eye me, miss 'what if you did date him.' You and your ridiculous idea got me into this mess and…" I pinch the bridge of my nose. "I suppose I did agree to it. Sorry, it's…shit, it's been a morning."

Another notification pops up on my phone. *Fuck.*

"Who is it? Is it Jordan?!" she screeches, still too loud for my morning ears.

"It's Kara. I'll call her back later."

"Don't you dare!" she warns. "Get her on the phone now! We'll have a virtual catch-up session. I'll add Olivia and Shelly."

My head shakes, my thumb itching to just hang up, but the mere thought of having to recount this story multiple times is a fate worse than death. *There's no avoiding the inevitable.* "Fine. Hang on—let me add Kara."

After we get everyone on the call, I see them all foaming at the mouth for details. They look like a bunch of crazed owls—every damn one of them wide-eyed and ready to swoop down and snatch up the latest bit of gossip.

"Today's emergency meeting of the Brunch Babes has now commenced," Kara proclaims in a very regal tone. Her husband being the captain makes her the official First Lady of the WAGs. "Kennedy Kramer, you are hereby subpoenaed for interrogation as to the details of your new relationship with Jordan 'Bougie' Boucher. Please place your hand on the Gideon's Bible in the hotel room so we can swear you in."

Everyone laughs, easing some of the nerves and tension in my body. I lean against the headboard, pulling a pillow in my lap. *God, I love these gals so much.* I love my family, but found family are like a warm hug on a shitty day. I can't even be mad right now because, if the situation was reversed, I'd be doing the same thing.

Here goes nothing.

"Yes. We're dating. *Fake* dating. Emphasis on fake. However, the fake thing is a secret. And I'm specifically calling that out for you, Olivia."

"What?! I've been so much better lately! I haven't told anyone that Maggie and Vladi bought that new sex bed thing."

Maggie's face reddens darker than a beet with a glare of pure irritation aimed directly at Olivia. "It's called a *swing*, Liv, and *I* haven't told anyone else either, thank you very much!" Maggie snarks, admonishing Olivia for spilling yet another secret.

An awkward smile stretches her cheeks. "Shoot! Sorry about that. Well…at least it's just us on the phone."

"I want to hear more about the sex bed thing." Shelly smirks.

"Thanks, Liv," Maggie snaps. "Whatever. It's fine. I'm not

embarrassed. Vladi will be pissed when the guys find out, but he'll get over it. I'm less concerned about that leaking than this secret about Kenni and Jordan."

"Your secret is safe with me. Promise"

I roll my eyes, only half believing her. I do think she'll keep this within the group. But, a lump forms in my throat and I swallow it down—it's only a matter of time before the boys learn the truth.

"Enough stalling. Kenni…spill. How the hell did this happen?" Kara asks.

I fill them in on all the details from the bar last night, the photo, the idea—*stupid fucking idea, damn Maggie*—and how it all came to fruition. All their mouths gape the entire time as they hang on my every word. Damn, does our group love to hear the tea. *I mean… same, but not when it's about me.*

"So now we have to go on a date when the team is in Dallas. He *literally* asked me if I brought anything to wear other than *pilot clothes.*" I wince, slumping down in the bed. *What the hell have I gotten myself into?* "Guys, I can't do this."

"Yes, you can," Kara pipes up. "This could be good for you! It seems like a good solution to your problem, *and* there are a lot worse things I can think of than having a hot, young guy at your side."

"Young guys are trending right now, Kenni," Shelly says with more enthusiasm than I'd like. "Men have been dating younger women for decades—it's about damn time we got ourselves some good-looking younger men."

"Can we please stop using the word young? It implies that I'm old, and I already feel like I'm in my nineties. You know me. When I'm not working, I sit my ass on my couch and do nothing. He seems to want to go out every night and go to all these fancy things. Not my cup of tea."

"Oh, come on. It's fun to get all dolled up and go out once in a while!" Olivia says. "Maybe he's just going out all the time because he'd be sitting at home alone, too. Some people don't like being by themselves. I know I'm one of them. When Hayes is away, I'm constantly trying to fill my schedule just to not have to sit at home by myself. Maybe Jordan is like that. You never really know what's going on behind closed doors."

My nails tap a nervous rhythm against the back of my phone case. *I love my friends, but why do they keep defending him?* "I can't imagine that playboy being scared of being alone."

"Regardless of his reasons, I think you should give this a shot," Kara says seriously. "Then give us *all* the details. Are you going to have to kiss?" Her brows raise to the top of her hairline as she squeaks. "Oh my God, you *are*! Have you practiced it? Talked about it? Did you guys write up a PDA contract or something? What are the rules here?! Ahhh! I'm so excited for this!"

Kara is indeed way *too excited about this.*

"No," I scoff, "We have not practiced shit. No contracts. We'll hold hands and stuff, but we will *not* be kissing. Maybe a peck on the cheek. Nothing more. *Ever*."

"Kenni." Maggie looks like she's a teacher about to scold me. "No one will believe you're dating if you only give each other a peck on the cheek. If you were in a real relationship with that hot piece of ass, and he's with *your* hot piece of ass, you would not be able to keep your hands, or your tongues, away from each other."

"Mags, oh my God," Olivia yelps, her cheeks blushing.

"I'm just saying! Bougie wasn't named Hottest Rookie in the NHL last year for nothing."

"You know Vladi would murder you if he heard you say that." Shelly giggles.

"I'm just saying he's hot in a brother-like way. I mean...shit, there's hardly a bad-looking man on the entire team! Am I right?" Maggie exclaims as everyone else nods in agreement.

Great.

"Listen…I'm not saying he's ugly, but…uggghh…what have I gotten myself into?!" I cover my face with my hand. I mean, he *is* attractive—I won't deny that—but I'm also not going to admit it out loud, especially not to my nosy as shit friends. My sexual frustration of not having had any in a while is too much to even consider making out with him. "Even if he is, just because someone's good-looking doesn't mean we're compatible for dating, or fake dating. His rich boy attitude isn't going to cut it for me. Besides, he's the one who got me into this whole mess to begin with!" The muscles in my jaw tense. *I'm* the one who's going to have to make changes to my life to accommodate this. *I hate this already.*

"Okay…I think we've had enough of the Kennedy show for today. I need to figure out what to do with my life, and I think his PR rep is supposed to call me or something. I'd better go get in the shower and prepare for this *super fun* day."

"Keep us posted! We want to know about any tongue action ASAP!" Kara yells as I roll my eyes.

"Bye, girls! Nice chatting with you, as always. Not weird at all that you're pressuring me to make out with my fake boyfriend!" I singsong before hanging up.

I could *never* have a long-term relationship with someone so much younger than me. He's from a completely different world. A different generation, for fucks sake. He had to *explain* slang terms to me. I thought I was hip, but nope! Old as fuck apparently. I groan, finally pulling myself out of bed. I'm a Millennial. We *used* to be the young ones. Now we're just in the ancient civilization category with the Gen Xers and the Boomers. *How did this happen?* I swore when I was younger that I would never be old like my parents, convinced I would always stay hip to the pop culture and trends. I roll my eyes as I turn on the shower. *When did adulting become boring?*

My shoulders slump as I toss my clothes in a messy pile on the floor. When I finally step in, the warm droplets soothe the tension in my muscles from all this stress. I breathe in the steam, leaning back to wet my hair. *This is relaxing.* But my stomach turns, wishing I were able to shut off my mind like I could the faucet. I smile, knowing my friends were helping me not freak the fuck out at what I've gotten myself into. Telling me that he's sweet. That he doesn't want to be alone. I lather up the shampoo, biting the inside of my lip. *I mean...I don't want to be alone either.* I push my shoulders back. Him not wanting to sit at home by himself does *not* mean he's ready to settle down and start a family. The hollow ache in my chest cries out as a reminder—I *am* ready for that.

But, at the end of the day, they were right about one thing—he is attractive. Something nice to look at for a few months at least. *I suppose it could be a hell of a lot worse.*

Finally clean, I stare into the abyss, my anxiety still racing through me like a jet hitting the runway at full speed. *I need to relax.* I bite my lip. If there's one thing that helps me do that, it's getting myself off while thinking about a nice, age-appropriate man. My hands wander across my skin, down past my stomach, thinking about running them down someone's chiseled abdomen. My fingers squeeze my nipple, imagining how it would feel if it were someone else. Their mouth teasing the sensitive bud—worshipping every inch of my body.

I push my fingers inside my aching entrance, lubing myself up enough to rub gentle circles around my clit. Not directly on it. Just to the side. Just the right amount of pressure. *Just the way I like it.* God, what would it feel like for this to be someone else's fingers? Rough, callused, and firmly caressing me the way I want. Rubbing myself faster, harder, thinking about being in control over him. To sit on his face, suffocating him with my cunt, feeling his tongue fluttering across my clit, getting me as close to the edge as I am now. How hard would his dick be lying there while I ride his face and find my release with his mouth? What would it feel like if he were here, picking me up and using his thick as fuck thighs to hold me steady while he thrusts inside and presses me against the wall? Our tongues colliding as my hands dig into his sculpted shoulders so hard they leave a mark.

Oh God.

The pressure builds, warmth flooding my core, and I can't hold it in anymore. I fully let go, and my orgasm hits me hard. My body shakes uncontrollably as I moan, a name escaping my lips that shocks the hell out of me.

"Jordan."

My entire body quivers as I float down from my peak. *I fucking needed that.* I collapse against the shower wall, the chill welcome against my flushed flesh. The water prickles my overly sensitive skin as it calms the fever running through me. My pulse is barely steady as my eyes pop open and my hands fly to the wall to steady myself. The relaxation I clawed free is ripped away, my throat closing as the realization hits—there is only one thing that would make this situation a million times worse.

Goddammit. I want to fuck my fake boyfriend.

20

kennedy

Sitting at what I am forever referring to as the Table of Disappointment, I mindlessly study my flight plans for tonight. Work has always been an escape, and *fuck* do I need an escape right now. My stomach groans, reminding me of the other thing I need. Food. A knock on the door has me grinning ear to ear.

"Finally," I whisper, as I push back my chair from the table.

My head tilts as a petite woman in a pink blazer, with the most perfect Barbie ponytail I've ever seen, stands before me. I shift my eyes down the hall, trying to figure out if my food is on the way or if this is some sort of bizarre joke. My pulse quickens. Please, God, tell me this is *not* a singing telegram. That seems like a stunt my immature *boyfriend* would pull.

"You must be Kennedy. I'm Hannah Lavoise, PR rep for the Boucher family," she introduces herself.

My head pulls back. "Oh. Hi! Yes, I'm Kennedy." I extend my hand to shake hers. "Please, come in. I'm…sorry, I'm confused. Jordan said you were going to call me…"

She smiles widely, her blue eyes bearing a resemblance to

Jordan's. "He did. But once he left for morning skate, he called and asked if I wanted to come and meet you in person. He didn't want you to have to deal with this alone. I don't get very many chances to see him play in person, so it was a good excuse to hop on the family plane for the day."

My jaw clenches at the unpleasant reminder of rich assholes on jets. But I let it go, realizing Hannah doesn't fit that mold. And now something tugs in my chest, a spark that's too sharp—*he's making sure I'm okay.*

"It's nice to meet you, Hannah. You really didn't need to come all this way."

She waves me off. "It's really nothing. Someone has to check up on my cousin once in a while. Can we sit down?" She gestures to the table. *The goddamn Table of Disappointment.*

I purse my lips, preparing for another *fun* conversation. "Sure, after you."

At first glance, Hannah looks sugary sweet, like a poof of cotton candy, but the confidence in her speech demands respect—*this woman is on top of her shit.* She's in full-on crisis management mode, giving me a play-by-play of what to say to the media. Where to go. What to avoid. I try, and fail, to stifle the yawn that escapes. I do appreciate her professionalism, but I'm also exhausted and would rather ditch the niceties and cut to the chase.

"Hannah, I appreciate everything you're saying, and I know your job is to treat this as a business transaction between your cousin and me. But…can I ask you a favor?"

"Of course," she says in her extremely professional tone, but the slight tilt of her head gives her curiosity away.

"Would you shoot straight with me? I know you're trained to talk corporate and say the right things, but I'm not big on bullshit. Jordan says we can trust you, and he seems to have a lot to lose if this gets out, so tell it to me like it is. What am I going to be dealing with here?"

She huffs a laugh, her eyes narrowing as she leans forward in her chair. "JJ said you were no nonsense, and he wasn't kidding. I'm the same actually. How about we start over?"

"I'd like that." I smile, my cheeks appreciating the slight reprieve from the perma-scowl I've had on my face most of the day.

"Perfect. So, the Boucher famil—crap. Sorry. *My* family. We're very…guarded. Every story about us in the news is because we allow it to be there. It's not that we're hiding anything; we just prefer to keep our lives as private as possible."

I can't hold back the snort that escapes. "Jordan Boucher likes to keep his life private? He's got a new story about him on a gossip site every day."

She smiles through her teeth, something hidden behind her eyes. I blink. She seems intelligent, but there's *no way* she's a fan of her cousin's rich playboy image and having to cover up what can only be a multitude of indiscretions, right? She must be good at her job, though, because outside of what I've seen about his latest flings, there isn't much else about him out there except for his hockey stardom.

Clearly, she's a PR genius.

She takes in a deep breath, fiddling with the hot pink pen resting on top of her pink notepad. "Believe it or not, JJ prefers to keep a lot of his life private. His public persona is…well, that's a little complicated."

My jaw clenches. *Why does everyone keep telling me it's complicated without elaborating? And JJ?*

"I'm sorry, JJ?"

Her eyes go wide. "Oh my gosh, sorry about that. Bougie? Jordan? He goes by a thousand names. I'm not sure what you call him."

Is this what they mean by complicated? His fifty-thousand names?

"Jordan is all I've ever called him. You call him JJ?"

"All the family does. His middle name is Joseph, and it just kind of stuck when he was a kid." A small smile softens her face. "JJ and I have always been super close. He has three older sisters, and I have two older brothers, so we were always left to our own devices while they were all out doing older-kid stuff. Plus, our parents were the closest of all the Boucher siblings. We actually lived on neighboring lots in Montreal. If we weren't all at one house for dinner, we were at the other for game night and movies. I honestly can't imagine growing up any other way than having that big house full of people, a million kids running around, and all the memories we made. Because of that, we have always been tighter with each other than the rest of our family. He's actually more like a brother than a cousin."

I rub my fingers across the seam of my sleeve as warmth spreads through my chest. I open my mouth to ask a question, but my brain can't seem to send the words fast enough before she continues singing the praises of the immature fake boyfriend I've accidentally acquired. The one that, apparently, has a warm, loving, super close family.

"Oh! You should see him with his nieces and nephews. Talk about uncle of the year—it's like no one else exists when he comes home to visit. Everyone loves Uncle JJ." Her eyes go out of focus, a memory I won't get to see taking hold. "Family is everything to the Bouchers. He keeps trying to get me to move to Milwaukee now that I own my own PR firm, but that involves things like work visas, moving literally everything I own, and leaving all the delicious Canadian snacks behind. Who knows, though, maybe someday down the road I'll find myself in the States again."

My body stills as my brain officially has a computer blue screen of death, trying to comprehend her words. *This is not what I was picturing when he said his PR agent would call me.* Especially now that she's here. The way she's talking about him is in no way, shape, or form the Jordan I've seen. Or the Bougie. Or JJ. Or whatever the hell we're calling him today. I glance toward the door between our rooms. *Are we talking about the same person?* She's talking about him as if he's being nominated for a top gentleman of the year award despite living the playboy life every night.

Grilled Cheesus, make this make sense.

"So, how about you, Kennedy? Are you close with your family?" she asks.

The corners of my lips turn up, thinking about them. "Yeah. They live in South Carolina. We're not as close as your family. With my crazy travel schedule, I don't get to see them as much as I'd like, but we still text and call as much as we can. Our family group text gets a little unhinged at times."

Hannah's laugh is boisterous and full of understanding. "Oh God. Our family group text would probably have you running for the hills! We love each other, but I swear our love language is giving each other shit every moment of every day. And you'll never guess who the biggest shit-giver is."

I grin, feeling relieved to finally hear a believable characteristic about him. "I would expect nothing less."

"Family is everything to us, so I love to hear you get along well with yours. And while you're in this relationship, you're my family too. JJ is my client and my family, but he's also one of my best friends. Anything I'd do for him, I'd do for you as well."

My heart warms, the kindness easing the twisting in my gut. *Is this some sort of weird fever dream?* I figured Jordan's PR cousin would be a total hard-ass bitch who shamed me for even suggesting we fake date. I swallow back the thought as I realize I'm doing to her *exactly* what people do to me as a female pilot. Making me feel like I have to fit into a certain mold or act a certain way when in reality we're just two women with cool-ass jobs.

"Thanks, Hannah. I appreciate that." I'm shocked to realize I truly mean that. "So, tell me what to expect with all the attention that comes with being Jordan Boucher's latest fling."

A wince crosses her face, her nose crinkling as if she's upset by the description of him. She said he's her best friend. She knows how he acts. *What the hell am I missing here?*

She leans forward, placing her elbows on the table, resting her chin on her hands. "I've done this with celebrity couples before. Now that it's out in the open, if they see you out a few times, they'll usually back off. In my experience, seeing you leave a restaurant together after a nice dinner will squash any rumors of you two doing this for publicity."

I snort. "That is exactly what we're doing."

"Precisely," she laughs, "and they'll get their precious photos, then move onto the next 'it' couple, assigning them their precious ship name."

My jaw drops. A 'ship' name? *Fuck.* "Do we...do we have a ship name?"

She nods. "They're calling you Jennedy."

My head shakes like I'm watching the world's slowest tennis match. *How the* hell *am I part of a celebrity couple called Jennedy?* I sit at home. I read my books. I work, go on a vacation or two. I'm *not* a celebrity couple with a ship name.

"I guess it could be worse," I mumble.

She purses her lips, her brows narrowing slightly. "Kennedy... are you sure you're okay with this? If not, I can talk to JJ, and we can come up with something—"

"It's fine," I spit, not wanting her pity. "Fake dating was my idea. I'm all in. It's just...it's hard to wrap my mind around all this."

"I can imagine this is quite the upheaval in your life."

"Just a bit," I say, my voice dripping with sarcasm as *another* news alert pops up. "My poor phone hasn't had a break all day."

She smiles and sighs in understanding. "I promise it will calm down. Turn it on do not disturb and make sure all your favorites are set to ring through. That will help until the media dies down."

"Will do." I pick at the edge of my nail with my thumb. "What exactly do I need to wear for this date?"

"Oh!" She bounces in her chair as her eyes light up like a Christmas tree. "I almost forgot!" She reaches into her houndstooth bag and passes across an envelope. "This is for you. It's a black card, no limit, so get whatever you need!"

I straighten in my chair and raise a hand to stop her. "Hannah. I do well for myself. I don't need a credit card. I am quite capable of buying my own clothes."

"I know, I know. I appreciate that, really, but listen. JJ wants to make sure you have everything you need; that's all. You don't have to use it. But…" She grins mischievously. "If it were me? I would be running to the hotel spa and getting a massage and a stiff drink."

The warmth and humor in her words loosen something tight inside me. I suppose I could capitalize on this. *Just this once.*

"You know what? That's not a bad idea. I think we'll get along just fine. And…hey. Thanks for just chatting with me like a real person and not just a client."

"Anytime. Like I said, I'm here if you need me at all. If you need someone to talk to about all of this, or need a fit check, I'm happy to help."

"Thanks." I flash her a warm smile.

She checks her watch, a small frown marring her features. "I should get going. I'm going to meet with another client while I'm in town," she says as she goes back into full business mode, packing up her bag. "Also, Kennedy? One more thing."

"Sure, what's that?" I ask, my voice wavering like a jet hitting a pocket of turbulence.

She twists her lips. "I know this is just an arrangement, but JJ's been through the wringer. Even though this is fake, just keep in mind you both have real hearts."

Her words sink in, curling low in my gut. This isn't real. This is fake. *How the hell would real hearts ever be involved in this?* He may be attractive, but there's a lot more that I'm looking for in a relationship. We are *not* compatible, and there's no way in hell he's in the same place I am.

I shrug, lifting my hands in surrender. "I'm just trying to come out of this with a positive public image. I'm not trying to hurt him. Promise."

"Good," she says with an uneasy smile as I walk her to the door. "It was really nice meeting you, Kennedy!"

"You too, Hannah." I close the door after she flits down the hall like Glinda floating off in a pink bubble.

Grilled Cheesus, I am fucking confused.

I feel like I'm trying to put together a puzzle, but none of the pieces fit together. *Jordan has a completely different personality around me.* He seems nervous, scared almost. All anyone can talk about is the way he does nice things for people. Add to that the way Hannah gushed about him and his family and how close they are, how she asked me to, in not so many words, not hurt him. I stare out the window as my thoughts spin like an out-of-control ceiling fan about to crash onto a bed some poor sap is sleeping on beneath it.

Why the hell am I starting to think there may be something more to Jordan Boucher? And where the hell is my damn room service?!

21
jordan

After our on-ice celebration, my teammates and I strut down the tunnel with shouts of 'let's fucking go' on the way to the locker room. I hand my gloves to the equipment manager and start to peel off my layers of clothing at my locker stall. As I toss my jersey into a giant blue bin, I glance at the white board in the front of the room, smothering my disappointment.

"Media: 9, 38, 68, 91"

Fuck.

Seeing my number on the media list is no surprise. We won. We clinched the division. I had great hits and played a fantastic game. And they won't give a damn about any of that. They never do. My heart sinks—as usual, this has *nothing* to do with my game.

They swarm Zack first, like wasps buzzing in his ear. He skillfully answers questions about the win and how we clinched the playoffs.

I continue to disrobe, removing my pads and my T-shirt, trying to cool off after the fury of the third period. As I hang everything on the hook, I hear their questions shift to grilling him about what he knows about my new girlfriend. A sour feeling settles in my stomach like a glass of spoiled milk. As much as I don't mind being the center of attention, I don't want anyone else to bear the burden of my latest drama. My teammates are used to it, but for fucks sake, we *just* clinched a playoff spot—literally minutes ago. I flop in my stall and take my skates off, my fingers tangling in the laces. *Can we not fucking talk about the win?*

"I'm not here to comment on anything other than the game. We're excited to clinch this early, and we're going to keep working toward improving our record to get the best seed possible," Zack responds like the class act he is. I hear the annoyance in their voices as they thank him for his time, dismissing him as professionally as possible. They are no longer interested in him, not really, eagerly beelining in my direction. Anyone else might be unprepared. But me? I'm *always* ready.

I grind my teeth. Welcome to the show, motherfuckers.

"Jordan! Great game. Can you verify the rumors that you're dating Kennedy Kramer? She's the team pilot; isn't that against the rules?"

I smirk. *Fuckin' Gene.* This guy is the worst. He thinks he's the goddamn Willy Wonka of media with his questions.

"Wow, Gene. Thanks for mentioning the game at all in that line of questioning. Yes, I did have a fantastic game, thank you very much. Did you see my diving save in the second? Classic Jordan Boucher move! I'm surprised I don't have my own special trophy for diving saves at this point, to be honest."

Gene looks at me with a scowl. *You're welcome, fucker.*

"Anyway, how are you doing, Gene? Tell me about your love life," I ask, flashing him a maniacal smile.

"I'm not here to talk about me; we're here to talk about you. Are you in a relationship with Kennedy Kramer?" he asks, his voice barely audible over the clicking of cameras.

"I'm *so* glad you asked about how excited I am to be headed to the playoffs! We've fought really hard, battled some incredibly tough teams, and it's exciting as hell to see all our work pay off."

A collective groan fans through the sea of reporters. "Enough with the deflection, Boucher. Are you going to answer or not?"

God, this is fun.

"Well, Gene, now that we've gotten the hockey out of the way, I can confirm I am in a committed relationship with the most beautiful woman on the planet, Kennedy Kramer."

An audible gasp echoes from every media member in the room. Then the questions pour in ten at a time.

"How long have you been dating? Is she the one?"

"Are you allowed to date the team pilot? Are you officially off the market?"

"Can we get a quote about how serious this is?"

I force my winning Bougie smirk. As always, I'm ready to keep the show going. Only this time, my heart pounds in my throat, in my ears, in my dick, through every part of my body. This time... there's no acting necessary.

"You want a quote about how serious this is? She's the woman of my dreams, and I've never been more serious about anything, or anyone, in my life outside of hockey. She's accomplished in her career. She's smarter than I am, that's for damn sure. She's amazing at everything she does, and that doesn't even account for how gorgeous she is. She's the best thing that's ever happened to me. She's my whole world, and I've never been happier. So yeah, you could say this is serious."

My hands shake, a truth that's been buried so deep, finally finding the light of day. *Focus Jordan.* I take a deep breath through my nose, my chin in the air to keep the show going for the audience.

"Now, do you have more questions about my game? If not, I

think we're done here. Why don't you go talk to the man who only let in one goal from forty-one shots tonight? Vladi...you're up!" I yell across the locker room, hoping to divert their attention elsewhere.

I let out a sigh of relief as they make their way over to our goalie, swallowing down the giant lump in my throat. *I gave them a fucking statement, alright.* That was the first press statement about my love life that was actually true.

Hopefully, that statement, the *actual* truth about how I feel about Kennedy, will keep them off my back for a bit. Plus...I need to shower and make a call.

"Hey, JJ! Great game tonight, bud; we're so proud of you!" my dad says over the phone after the game. The team is packing up and making their way to the bus, but I snuck out for a quick minute to make sure my dad knew what was going on.

"Thanks, Dad. Can't believe I'm going to the playoffs this year. Two years in the league and I, somehow, am going again. Some guys don't make it here for years."

"You really lucked out getting drafted by Milwaukee. You guys have a hell of a team. You could take it all the way this year!"

The corners of my lips tip up. My parents are always my biggest cheerleaders, even if they never fully understood my draw to hockey. "Yeah, well...this is the first step. One game at a time, just like we've always said."

"Exactly. I'm proud of you, son," he says, his slight pause sitting heavy between us, "but you never call this soon after a game. Everything alright? Is this about what Hannah told me earlier? She filled me in on the situation."

I bite my lip. I hate having to do this over the phone, but my dad is more than just my dad. He's my best friend who knows everything about me. And I can't help but love him for it every day.

"Yeah, it is. With game day prep, I didn't have a chance to call you, and I figured you had questions, and—"

"JJ, it's okay. I know your game day routines. It's been a bit of a crazy day here as well, dealing with all of this. I know you're probably still processing everything. Listen, bud…it's going to be okay."

I run my hands through my freshly washed hair, tugging at the smooth strands. "Is it though?" I glance around the small janitor's closet I found, triple-checking no one is around. "What if I screwed everything up? We can fix a PR crisis. I know that. Hannah is the best, and we've been changing the narrative on things for as long as I can remember. I just…I just never expected this to happen with…"

"With Kennedy," my dad finishes the thought for me.

I nod. "Yeah."

When your dad's one of the only people you can trust to not leak things to the media, you have no choice but to confess that you like someone to him. It's honestly been that way most of my life. When there are only two men in the house, you learn to stick together and have each other's backs.

"How has her reaction to this been?" he asks, the worry in his voice not relieving the ache in my chest.

"Have you ever seen those videos where a cat gets pissed, then hisses and lunges at someone with their claws?"

My dad cackles. "So, it's going well then?"

"She shoved me against a wall in an elevator, and I genuinely feared for my life," I recount the incident to him, leaving out the part where I was more turned on than a fully pre-heated oven. "But, after her initial shock, I think she's better. Maybe? Hell, I don't know. Being anything but friends with women is not my strong suit. Funny enough, the fake dating was *her* idea."

I close my eyes, my heart twisting in my chest.

"I think she's embarrassed to be seen with someone who has a reputation like mine, and this makes it seem less grotesque. She's got her own career, and now she's tangled up in this mess and… God, I really fucked this up."

"I will not tell your mother you used that language," he chides in a jokingly stern tone, "but I see where you're coming from. She seems like she's got a great career and a level head. When Hannah and I were talking today, we thought this may finally be a way out for you. A way to get rid of the image we all played into. A way to finally show the world who you really are and all the great things you've accomplished." My eyes burn, the weight that's been so heavy on my shoulders for so long loosening just enough I can breathe. "Let me ask you something. Why did you go up to her at that bar? What gave you all this confidence after being afraid to talk to her for so long?"

I shrug. "I saw that guy hitting on her, and I could tell she wasn't into it. She looked like she was in trouble, and I wanted to help her. No one should ever be put in that situation."

My dad hums in agreement. "Then you keep showing her that, JJ. You have such a good heart—don't ever forget that. If I were a betting man, I'd think if she starts to see who you really are, she'll see that heart of yours too."

"I hope so. I just…I don't know how to get over this fear of talking to her. Or opening up to any woman again. I can't even speak to her without getting all tongue-tied and sweaty. Got any great words of wisdom for that?"

"Think about your pre-game nerves. A little nervousness gets your adrenaline going, so just take a deep breath and be confident. Play your game and don't be anything but yourself. That's all you can do. If she's the right person, she'll appreciate it."

My jaw falls. "Wow, Dad. That's deep. You sound like Vladi," I say, wondering where all these people get this advice and why my dumb ass can't just follow it. "Okay, I gotta hop on the bus to the airport. Thanks for the help."

"Anytime, son. You know I'm always here if you need me. And like I said…look at this as a way to get out of where you've been. Love you, bud."

"Love you too, Dad."

Ending the call, I tap my phone against my lips. God, I lucked out with the most amazing parents. My mom and dad have been supportive of me my entire life. Never pressured me to do anything I didn't want to. Never held unrealistic expectations of me. Even when everything came out about my past relationship and we all decided to lean into me being a playboy, they always said it was my decision.

I walk out of the closet, seeing a group of Rider's interns and staff walking by, a few of them looking this way as the door clicks behind me. I suck in a sharp breath. *Did any of them hear me?* Shaking it off, I make my way through the arena to the bus, thinking about how they've had one of those perfect marriages people dream of. Always so happy together, even with four kids, including a little shit like me, wreaking havoc in the house. I asked my dad, once, how they dealt with all of us, and he said it was both the greatest irritant and the most fulfilling joy they ever had. After we'd all gone to bed, they would laugh, give each other shit about how they could have handled things better, and simply vent about all the trouble we'd gotten up to with one another.

Fuck, if I don't want that for myself too.

The hollow pull tightens again, right in my fucking ribcage, like it does every goddamn day. I should be a typical twenty-something out partying and living it up, and I certainly go out and hang with my teammates as much as I can and have a great time, but I would give that up in an instant to have something special like my parents. *Something real.* The kids. The chaos. A woman by my side, giving me shit and living a crazy, perfect life with me.

More specifically, the one I'm currently fake dating.

I shake my head as I climb up the stairs onto the bus and find my seat. Right now, she sees me as a reckless twenty-three-year-old partying my life away and sleeping my way around town. My stomach twists tighter than my freshly taped stick. *I have to find a way to help her see past that.* I wish I could change things. I wish I could take away the self-doubt, the fear, that I'll get hurt again. But just like being down at intermission, the only way to win is to view this as a clean start. To focus on the future. And focus on how to make Kennedy see what's underneath this mask I've been wearing.

Time to start showing her the real Jordan Boucher.

22

kennedy

Arriving at the hotel in Dallas after the game, I stumble into my room, kick my shoes off, and flop down face-first on the bed. I open my mouth to scream my frustrations into the mattress. But I can't. I am so damn tired; the thought of expanding my lungs more than necessary is exhausting. I thought I would be relaxing all day, but between the endless notifications going off, calls from my friends and family, and going over flight plans, I barely got a chance to relax.

Thankfully, I got a quick nap in after chatting with Hannah, otherwise I'm not sure I would've made it through the post-game flight. Chadd was tolerable on the flight—not sure how long that will last, but at least I survived. *I'm ready to hibernate in a cave for a year.*

The minute we got in the shuttle to the hotel, I started getting tagged in a million notifications on social media. Specifically, the one of Jordan announcing our relationship after the game. I watched it—the shirtless man with an incredibly sculpted chest declaring I was the woman of his dreams. I watched again, to make sure I heard everything correctly, since I was too distracted watching his muscles ripple across my screen. And then a third time, needing to be certain I caught it all, noticing the way his throat bobbed as he spoke. My breaths became quick, my thighs clenching together as I watched it a few more times for good measure—until I remembered I was on a bus filled with other people.

If I weren't so damn tired, I'd watch it again here in bed...for science.

It's a great speech. I swallow hard, realizing he ticked off every item on the checklist of things I've been waiting my entire life for someone to say. *But it's not real. This is all for show.* One thing I'll never doubt about him is his ability to perform on demand. If I didn't know any better, it would have been a nice declaration if I were even into that sort of thing from a guy, especially one like him, which I'm clearly not. It was just another of the many performances from hockey's greatest showman.

Flipping onto my back, I stare at the ceiling, wondering what the hell I've done. *Was this the right decision?* I could just admit to Chadd this was all a ruse and deal with the fallout. I flop my arm over my face. Shit, I cannot lower myself to admit to him this was all fake.

I'm pulled from my thoughts by the sound of paper rustling. I quickly sit up, finding a piece of paper shoved under the door from the adjoining room next to me. *Is he in there? How is this happening again?*

I walk over to pick up the paper and unfold it to read.

Kennedy,
I hope you're doing okay after everything today. This has all been a lot, way more than I ever would have

thought.

Sorry I didn't get to check in on you until now, game days are always crazy somehow. Sleep tight, and I'll see you tomorrow night.

Your boyfriend, Jordan.

P.S. Open the mini-bar

A tired smile creeps up my face as I huff out the smallest laugh. *Is it my exhaustion or does some of that rhyme?* I did hear rumors about a filthy poem he wrote for Hayes Larson's bachelor party.

I can't remember the last time a guy wrote me a note, let alone one with pen and paper. The slightest of flutters runs through my stomach, warmth filling me before I quickly squash it. Just because he's not thinking only about himself for one minute doesn't mean anything. *Everyone has their moments.*

I read the last line again, my eyes peeking up from the paper toward the mini-bar. Walking over I slowly pull the door open, half afraid I'll find some immature joke. I suck in a sharp breath as I stare at what's before me, blinking a few times to make sure it's not a mirage. I reach out and touch a bottle. *Nope. It's real. Really, truly real.* The entire fridge is filled with nothing but Aviation gin, bottles of tonic water, and a container of freshly cut lime wedges.

I tilt my head to the side, that damn flutter in my gut back again and stronger than before. *How did he know?* I guess I ordered a gin and tonic at the bar last night, but he wasn't there that long. And this is my favorite brand. All of it is my favorite.

I grab the ingredients to make myself a nightcap, knowing it's *exactly* what I need after this horrific day and snatch the ice bucket to fill in the hallway. But…it's already full. I'm not going to deny that being able to make myself a drink without having to schlep down the hall to get ice is a welcome luxury after this day. *How the hell did he arrange all of this?*

I make my drink, finding a piece of paper and pen and the nightstand, and sit at the small table by the window. *You know what? A drink by my side and a gorgeous view of downtown Dallas lit up across the night sky. This isn't half bad.* Writing down a few things, I fold the piece of paper and push it under the door between our rooms.

I walk back to bed and, for some ridiculous reason, I'm...I'm smiling? *What the hell?* I do *not* smile by myself in a hotel room. *It must be the alcohol hitting my stomach.* My gaze shifts between my bed, the door to his room, and my phone.

Apparently, Jordan Boucher is taking this fake dating thing pretty damn seriously. I think I just got my second wind to watch that video again.

23
jordan

"The car service will be outside the hotel at seven, and I won't tip off the press until you're already at the restaurant, so you can hopefully at least enjoy dinner without being harassed. Oh! And the reservation is under your name, not one of your aliases," Hannah says over the phone.

"Dammit, Hannah. I was really hoping to show up as Glen Coco tonight."

She chuckles. "I'll keep that in mind for the next date."

I catch myself in the mirror grinning like a fucking idiot at the thought of another date. But it fades as quickly as it came, my stomach clenching at the thought of me royally screwing this up. "Hannah Banana...do you think she'll even go on another date with me?"

"I think she will," she answers, her voice warm and confident. Something loosens in my chest at the way Hannah and all my family believe in me. It makes me think maybe...*Maybe* I can actually do this. "When I flew to meet her in Columbus, she wasn't nearly as overwhelmed as you thought. She just needs to see the other side of you. The *real* you. Show her that."

"The real me is *so* amazing, right?" I joke, trying to calm myself down.

"I wouldn't go *that* far," she quips. "But in all seriousness, just be yourself. You're amazing, JJ. Let her see that. Just don't let my compliment go to your head."

"Too late," I tease, the fluttering feeling in my gut overwhelming. "Thanks for setting all this up and for flying to see her the other day. Let's just hope this works. For the media."

"Right. Just for the media. Nothing else other than a date," she snarks with a wink.

"Fake date."

"It's not fake to you." *Well, if that isn't the fucking truth.* "Hang in there, JJ. You'll do great. Text if you need me."

I set my phone down and pick up the tiny note I've held onto all night long.

> J -
> Thanks for the gin. The fresh limes were a nice touch.
> - K

I've read the note a thousand times. Memorized it. Eleven words, two letters, and two dashes—the dashes seem important for some reason. She could have used a comma, but I feel like this was an intentional choice. *Seems more...personal.* I've traced every inch, feeling the ridges where the pen indented the paper and marveling at the way she wrote a cursive letter 'J' like my grandma used to in all my birthday cards. I set it down, afraid it will disintegrate if I touch it anymore. But as simple as it is—just like her—I want to hold onto it forever.

I sit on the edge of my bed, my hands shaking and sweating like I just finished a game that went into double OT. *Get it together, Jordan. It's just a date. A fake one.*

I take a deep breath in through my nose, then slowly exhale out my mouth, just like they taught in the yoga class I take to improve my flexibility. It also helps keep me calm off the ice, especially in situations like tonight. Plus, I'm a sucker for anything that includes built-in nap time.

I wipe my palms on my pants one last time before putting on a spray of my cologne. *One* spray. Some of my teammates, specifically EJ, drench themselves in this shit, and we all have to suffer when we get on the bus. You can fucking taste it. My mouth, on the other hand, is so fucking dry I can barely swallow. *Goddammit, Jordan, calm down! You are one of the most popular players in the NHL. You can do this.*

If only I had a pre-game routine for a date. *Should I do my pre-game routine?* Dammit, I don't have time. If only I'd been on a date with anyone outside of the one person who ruined my life. The one selfish motherfucker who got me into this life of secrets. The one person I would pay to poke skewers through her eyes. I ball one hand into a fist, pounding it into the other at the slightest thought of that time in my life. *Fuck.* I take another deep breath, slowly letting the air back out to calm my heart rate.

Don't go there tonight, Jordan.

I can only look ahead and focus on the task at hand. The simple task I'm scared to death of. It's just a door in front of you, one you've literally knocked on before. This time is no different. *Except for the fact that the woman you've been pining over for months is on the other side.* The piece of wood seems so thin, but it represents the giant roadblock between us. But the door she once slammed shut in my face has cracked open the tiniest bit. She talks to me now. And every tap of my knuckles carries the weight of what I stand to lose.

Last time, we weren't officially fake dating.

Last time, she wasn't obligated to hold my hand.

Last time, I wasn't about to take her on a date.

I open my side of the adjoining doors and knock. Oh shit. Should I have walked out into the hallway to knock on the real door? Do I leave and go there? What if I do, and then she opens this door? *Oh, God. I'm spiraling already. Deep breaths, Jordan.*

The door opens, and I feel like a gust of wind blows through, nearly knocking me off my feet. My lungs gasp for air. I thought nothing could eclipse how stunning Kennedy looked the first time I saw her on the plane.

I. Was. Mistaken.

Tonight, she's flawless—and she's dressed like this to be with *me*. Her long blonde hair cascades in soft waves past her shoulders, and her green dress hugs the curves of her hips so fucking perfectly my knees feel weak. And if that wasn't hot enough, she's wearing a leather bomber jacket over her dress in a perfect mix of femininity and badassery, and I want to obey her every command. I swallow down the lump in my throat, my body instinctively swaying toward hers.

She gazes at me, the flecks in her emerald green eyes mimicking the color of her dress. Her lips are pursed together as her brows slightly raise. *Oh shit. I'm staring.* I haven't even said a word to her yet. *Geezus, Boucher, pull it together!*

"Hi."

"Hi."

I run my fingers through my hair. "Are you ready to go? I have a car waiting for us downstairs."

Her nose scrunches. "It's not some fancy car or a limo, is it? I don't need to be treated like some celebrity. I don't need to be wined and dined."

Shit. Hannah didn't get into specifics about this. "It's a car service." I rub the back of my neck. "I'm not sure the specific make and model, but it's not a limo. At least...I don't think it is. But it would really throw off the image we're trying to portray if we show up in a beat-up Toyota Camry." She huffs out a laugh, the grip on her purse strap loosening. "You really don't like all the fancy stuff, huh?"

"Not really. I fly so many rich assholes, they've turned me off the *high life*, no offense."

I smile as I shrug. "None taken."

"They show up to the airport in ridiculous sports cars with their designer luggage, and they treat my crew and me like we are the lowest of humanity despite literally being in charge of their lives."

My teeth clench at the thought of anyone treating my girlfriend, fake or not, that way. "That would irritate the shit out of me, too. You know, maybe you've just been around the wrong rich assholes. We're not *all* bad."

She scoffs, "Yeah, right. And black licorice is delicious."

I laugh at the thought of how gross that stuff is. "While I do feel the hit from that dig, I do agree that anyone who likes black licorice is a psychopath."

"Right? That stuff is nasty!" We both let out quiet laughs, sparking something deeper inside me. She's never talked to me like this before—like we're not just pretending. Like I actually belong in her world. And in this moment, I can't stop wondering if the road we're on could stretch to something more. Like we could actually go from fake dating, to friends, to forever.

24

kennedy

When I'm traveling, I always try to find unique places to eat. Some place with great online ratings, good food, and an amazing atmosphere, but nothing too fancy, because usually I'm eating alone. I know some people thrive on dining solo, and I do it all the time, but something about sitting in a fancy white napkin restaurant by yourself just feels odd.

And now here I am, in one of Dallas's top restaurants, which has at least one Michelin star, where you have to spend an entire paycheck just to purchase an appetizer. But I'm not alone. *I'm on a date. A fake one.* And so completely out of my element. Perusing the menu is enough to make me lose my appetite. There's a seafood tower listed at 'market price.' *What does that even mean?* Do they take you behind the building and remove a kidney as payment? And you certainly can't ask what the price is, otherwise they'll think you're cheap. I like things to be spelled out clearly—here are the goods I will give you in exchange for this amount of money. I shift in my seat as I continue down the menu. *Goddammit, half the* menu is listed as 'market price.' I know this is nothing more than a publicity stunt, and I know he's paying, but...*fuck*.

"Good evening; my name is Gary, and I'll be the head server this evening," a waiter says, approaching our table as another gentleman fills up my water glass and yet another one drops off a basket of bread. "This is Nick and Brady; they will be assisting your table tonight." I tap my nails against the back of the fancy as hell menu. *Three waiters feels excessive.* "If you'd prefer sparkling water, just let us know, and we can arrange that. Can I start you with any drinks before starting your courses?"

I dart my eyes between Gary and my date sitting across from me. I feel like Jack at dinner on the Titanic, not knowing which piece of silverware to pick up first. Except Kathy Bates is not here to instruct me. Only a twenty-three-year-old kid who was born eating at these kinds of places.

What the fuck have I gotten myself into?

"Give us a minute with the drink menu, Gary," Jordan says with a surprising air of confidence.

"Very well." Gary bows his head, walking off to somewhere in the back of the restaurant.

Probably taking the kidneys of the folks from the table next to us, who did in fact order the seafood tower.

Jordan sets his menu down gently, propping his elbows on the table and lacing his hands beneath his chin. "I'm guessing this place is too fancy for you?"

"I just…do we need an entire team of waiters to serve us?"

He laughs, his eyes sparkling with something I haven't noticed before. A small smile creeps up on my cheeks seeing him like this. *He's in his element.*

"I know, right? It's a little ridiculous. Watch this," he says with a smirk as he leans back in his chair and proceeds to take a large drink of his water. When he sets it down half-full, Nick waltzes over seconds later and refills the glass. "Thanks, man."

I glance between the retreating man and Jordan's now pristine drink.

"They never let your glass get less than half-full. It's a game that Hannah and I used to play when we were little. We would set it up so each of us would drink half our glass consecutively, so the poor guy had to keep coming back. It was fun until our parents caught on and we got in major trouble. I feel bad now, looking back on it, but I also saw my dad give the poor water refill guy a huge tip when we left, so it all worked out in the end."

"That was nice of him. Most people wouldn't. Working in an industry catering to the wealthy, most people just expect that kind of service."

He shakes his head. "Not Joseph Boucher. My dad taught all of us to respect and be kind to everyone. He didn't put up with any goofing off either." His cheeks heat. "I may have been in trouble quite a bit."

I set my menu down, crossing my arms on the table. "Shocking someone like you wouldn't be on your best behavior at all times."

"Got me pegged on that one for sure," he says with a smile, quickly looking down at the menu. "Do you know what you want to order yet?"

My shoulders slump, my cuticles shot and fully picked into a crackly state. "Is there a steak on the menu I don't have to order by the ounce?"

His face falls. "Sadly, not here. I'm sorry...I know this isn't your vibe. Hannah suggested it because she knew the press would show up when they got a whiff of us being here. Next time, we'll go somewhere more casual."

I narrow my brows. "Next time, huh?"

He stares at his menu as if he's studying to take an exam. "Yeah.

For sure. I mean, this is just for show. We can keep things low-key going forward. Just a couple of appearances here and there should do the trick."

He was so confident a moment ago, and now it's almost as if he's...nervous. *That can't be right.* How can a guy this cocky and egotistical be nervous? Maybe he gulped his water too fast? Of all the times I've seen him around our friends or with the team, he's never been like this. I shake the thought from my mind as I see Gary coming back. Maybe I should test just how confident he is here.

"You know what? I'm really not a picky eater. Why don't you order for both of us?"

His brows furrow as he looks at me like I'm half crazy, but the waiter is at our side now. *What're you going to do, Boucher?*

Without missing a beat, Jordan turns to him and starts speaking. "We'll each have 4 oz of the snow beef wagyu, cooked to the chef's preference, with a side of truffle frites, and a deep-fried lobster to share." He looks at me with curious eyes to see if that order is acceptable. I nod as a heat pulls low in my core. *Damn.*

"Oh! And she'll have a gin and tonic with a lime, Aviation if you have it, and I'll have a glass of Cab." He hands the menus back to the waiter, who walks off to place our order, then collapses back into his chair.

The entire time he was talking to the waiter, he seemed as though he was on top of the world. But now? He's back to getting ready to have his blood drawn while being deathly afraid of needles. *Am I really that scary?* Am I blood-draw needles? I let out a loud sigh that disappears into the quiet hum of the restaurant. We sit in silence for a few minutes as he looks anywhere but at me. I lean back in my chair, my arms still crossed as I study every inch of his expression. Looking for what? I don't know. But this is *not* what I was expecting from the prince of social media.

Nick comes by to refill my water glass...*again*...and the waiter returns with our drinks.

"Cheers to a successful...*relationship*," I say, tilting my gin toward him, hoping to break the awkwardness with a toast. "So...I suppose since we're here, we should probably share something about ourselves. Just in case nosy people start asking."

His eyes brighten. "Yes! Like in the movie The Proposal."

I lean forward, surprised he even knows one of my favorite movies. "You know that movie? The one with Sandra Bullock?"

He snorts. "Who *doesn't* know that movie?"

"I just thought, maybe, that was a little..." How do I say, *'you're too young to know that movie,'* without making this age gap thing weird? "...before your time."

He laughs, picking up his drink for another sip. "Kennedy, I am the youngest of four siblings and the only boy. I was what you call a *surprise addition* to the Boucher family." He smiles into his drink. "My sisters are quite a bit older, and I love them dearly, but the amount of chick flicks I was forced to watch as a child should have been illegal. I can quote every episode of Gilmore Girls, I can sing every song from every High School Musical, and sometimes I sit around and watch Mean Girls for fun."

"Seriously?" The word slips out as a half-laugh, half-snort.

"It's true! Just don't let word get out...I have an enforcer image to keep up."

"I'm not sure how well you're keeping that secret; I heard what went down at Hayes and Olivia's wedding. Did you really recreate the courtroom scene from Legally Blonde?"

A wicked smile bursts across his face. "What, like it's hard?"

I can't help but let out a full-on laugh. "I'm impressed. I was bummed I couldn't attend, and even sadder when I heard I missed that. It's one of my favorite movies."

His eyes light up a bit more. "Really? Wow. I had you down for a How to Lose a Guy in Ten Days fan."

"Also a classic. But there's something about a powerful blonde working hard to achieve what she wants, and realizing it's more than just chasing after a man."

He nods, the muscles in his jaw relaxing. The tension he had moments ago seemingly gone now that we've had some actual conversations other than 'hi, we have to date now.'

"So, Jordan Boucher, what do you want to know about me?"

25
jordan

What do I want to know about her? The limit does not exist. Each beat of my heart aches to uncover every. Single. Detail. Her innermost thoughts. Her goals in life. Does she sing in the shower? Does she replace the toilet paper over or under? Even mundane details like what brand of toothpaste she uses. Apparently, all I want to know are things located in the bathroom...*God, why does she make me so nervous!* I take a deep breath to calm myself. Don't scare the gorgeous woman away with weird questions. *Just keep it simple, Jordan.*

"How about we start with something basic—what's your coffee order? In The Proposal, he got her coffee every day. I mean, that was his job, but still. This is very important boyfriend information."

Also, I will get you a coffee every day for the rest of your life if you let me.

The corners of her lips tip up enough to form the slightest of smiles. My heart soars. *I'll take it.* "I'm a serious coffee addict. I get a vanilla, almond milk latte every morning. And I always get it hot, even if it's one-hundred degrees outside. I know everyone is into iced coffee right now, but if I want a cold drink, I don't want it to be coffee, if that makes sense."

I nod, affirming her answer while trying to calm the panic in my chest. I've made a grave error getting her a cinnamon dolce latte every flight. I just figured if I got her the drink that sounded the sweetest, maybe she would feel some sort of sweetness toward me. *That was stupid.* Not to mention, she doesn't even know they were from me. *Shit...what was I thinking with all this secret admirer stuff?* Also...double shit. My stomach twists as I realize I've been getting her 2%, not almond milk. Oh my God! Have I been poisoning her? *Stay calm, Jordan. Ask a follow-up.*

"Almond milk, huh?"

"Oh yeah, I can't drink real milk."

Triple shit. "You're lactose intolerant?"

"Sort of. It's really weird. I can eat any other dairy. Cheese, ice cream, yogurt, I'm fine. But if I drink a glass of milk? Nope. My stomach won't digest it."

Quadruple shit on a hockey stick. "What do you mean it won't *digest* it?"

She winces, and I think I've overstepped. *Quintp- oh, who am I kidding? I fucked up.* I open my mouth to apologize, but she continues, "I probably shouldn't elaborate on that sitting in a fancy restaurant."

I snort. "Do you know the kinds of things hockey players talk about in the locker room? On the bench? At dinner? I promise you can't gross me out."

"I guess I didn't think about that; I figured it would be maybe un-ladylike to talk about throwing up an entire glass of milk in a fancy place like this." Her lips twist into a half-smile.

"Oh shit." I bite the side of my tongue. "That sucks."

"It's something to do with the pasteurization process, I guess. At least I can still have ice cream! I need *something* to drown my sorrows in outside of gin once in a while. So, what about you? What's your coffee order? Can you drink milk?"

"Yes to milk, and my coffee order is easy—a double double."

She leans further across the table as if getting closer to me will make this make sense. "I consider myself pretty fluent in coffee, yet somehow, I don't know what that is."

"It's a coffee with two creams, two sugars. It's a Canadian thing."

"Oh damn. I just remembered you're Canadian." She glances around the room, her voice a whisper. "Are we committing international fraud?"

"You know, this is more like The Proposal than I thought. Except I'm not being deported…that I know of." *Would she marry me if I were?* Blood starts rushing through my veins at the world of possibilities opening up at the very thought.

"Thank God we only have to date and not get married."

I suck in a sharp breath as if she picked up the steak knife on the table and stabbed me in the heart. Taking that as a quick no to the 'would she marry me' question. I slowly nod, not even knowing how to respond. I remind myself of what Hannah said, what my dad said. Just keep showing her the real me. This is only a first date. I run my hands through my hair. Plenty of time to work on the fake…or real marriage proposal if needed.

When our food finally arrives, it's a nice break to focus on eating instead of how my heart keeps flipping between full-blown racing and the ache of feeling like it's been crushed. Thank God for frites. Carbs always make everything better.

Once we've finished nearly everything, both of us nosh on the crisp little potatoes covered in the world's most delicious truffle oil. Despite the mix of emotions I'm facing, I can't help but smile. Seeing her enjoying all the food I ordered—especially the frites—steadies my shaking hands.

At least I got one thing right.

"Aren't these to-die for?" I say as I pop one in my mouth, and she does the same.

"I have never eaten fries these good. Honestly, I've never eaten *any* form of carbohydrate this good. And this little aioli dipping sauce?" She groans, her eyes rolling into the back of her head, "I would like to dive into a barrel of this and eat my way out."

I huff out a surprised laugh, something warm punching my ribs at the glimpse of humor I didn't expect from her—and dammit if it doesn't match mine. "I'm demolishing these like they owe me money."

"Same," she chuckles, the sound soothing something that's been wounded inside for so long. "I'm a total foodie. Traveling as much as I do, I love finding new restaurants and sampling dishes I've never tried before. My favorites are the hidden dives only the locals know about. They always have the best food."

"Bet. I follow a strict diet routine when we're in season to help with rest and recovery—it's a whole boring thing—but when it's a cheat day," I glance around the dining room, "I'd never pick a place like this. Don't get me wrong, the food here is great, but...I'm more of a casual guy. There are some awesome diners in Milwaukee I love to sneak into. That's one of the things I miss the most from Montreal...the diners. Tim Hortons. The poutines. Why those aren't popular in Wisconsin with the clear abundance of cheese curds, I'll never know."

Her smile looks nearly impressed. "Right? Why aren't they a thing there?"

"Over the summers, I used to eat at this one diner in Montreal every day. Same order, same poutine. *Fuck,* it was good. They have over forty different types, but I just like the OG version best. Just potatoes, curds, and gravy," I say as I pop a few more fries in my mouth. "Then I started dating someone who only liked fancy places like these, even for just a quick lunch. She was kind of controlling and said it wasn't a good look to eat there, so I never made it back. They probably thought I died. I should have…" I suck in a deep breath, looking down as I try to steady my shaking hand, pressing it into the table. I may have just made a big mistake letting my guard down.

I have no idea why I'm even telling her any of this.

My stomach churns. I don't like reliving that part of my life. I must have let my feelings slip through onto my sleeve somehow because a warm hand now rests on top of mine.

"Hey. I know we don't know each other well, but whoever that girl was, she didn't deserve you." Her gaze locks with mine for just a moment. One fleeting, glorious moment. "You have to give me the name of that place for the next time I'm in Montreal. But I have to be honest, I'm not sure they can beat these fries or frites or whatever the hell you want to call them. Someone would need to pry these out of my cold, dead hands to make me stop eating them. I'm making these frites my bitch," she says, pulling her hand away from mine, the chill of its absence sinking in immediately. But I see she's only moving away to attack the plate of food once more as she takes several fries, dips them in the sauce, and devours them in a perfect mirror of my actions just a few minutes ago. I grin at the accuracy of her frites monologue, dangerously on point and endearing. And then my eyes lock in on the cutest little drop of aioli on her lip. She must notice me staring, because she immediately asks me, "What?"

"You have, um…you have aioli on your face." I gesture toward my own lip, showing her where it is.

"Oh my God," she gasps, eyes wide as she grabs her napkin and wipes her mouth. "Did I get it?"

I try my best not to smile, but I can't hold it back. "Not quite. May I?"

She nods, and I lean across the table. Cupping her chin, I delicately run my thumb across the bottom of her lip, my touch lingering a little longer than it should. Her gaze locks with mine. For just a moment, time seems frozen. My skin grazes the lips I've wanted to kiss for so long. My pulse races, wondering what it would feel like to be touching her like this cradled together in my sheets.

My heart can't reconcile that this isn't real. I blink, the spell broken. Time hasn't stopped. We are in a restaurant full of people on a very fake date. But for a fleeting moment, it looked like she might have seen beyond the mask I wear day in and day out. Past the one screaming rich, playboy, troublemaker, and getting a tiny view of the hopeless romantic buried deep inside me. If only this moment could last forever. But just like every second on a clock, it ticks by, time marching mercilessly on, and I pull back to my side of the table.

"Got it."

"Thanks," she says with a shy smile, shifting to quickly take a sip of her drink.

I can't help but notice the blush in her cheeks. The way her eyes dart to avoid my gaze.

That moment didn't last forever. But something shifted. That door between us cracked open just a bit more. And I'm going to do whatever I can to never let it fully shut again.

26
kennedy

We stand side by side at the glass doors of the restaurant, watching the storm unfold before us. It's not only the literal storm outside, but a blinding swell of people with cameras and cellphones and those weird mini mics. *Holy shit.* I was expecting one, maybe two people, but there are *dozens* of media personnel. All of them standing around in raincoats with umbrellas covering their hungry cameras, some already snapping pictures of us through the water-covered windows. *Is this normal for him?* I edge closer to my date before I realize what I'm doing. *How does he deal with this every day?*

This night has already proved to be nothing like I expected. I can still feel the flush on my cheeks from his thumb dragging along my lip, which was ungodly hot. No. *No.* Maybe they poured my gin and tonic too strong. *Yeah. That has to be it.* I sneak a glance at him. It can't be because a very handsome, a very well-dressed, way-too-young-for-me man with thighs that could crack open a safe dabbed a bit of aioli from my face. And it most certainly could *not* be the urge I had to lick it off his thumb. It was clearly because the aioli was so delicious, I hated it going to waste. *Yep. That's all that was.*

"Hey," he whispers, a breath away from my ear, pulling me from my thoughts. The thoughts I should *not* be having. "You ready for this?"

I swallow the lump in my throat. *What the hell am I doing?* "How does one even prepare for this? These people are standing in a torrential downpour just for a *chance* to get a photo of us walking to the car."

"If you've changed your mind, I can make a call, and we can slip out the back door. They've seen us through the windows. It's okay if you're not comforta—"

"No," I say, forcing down the anxiety clawing at my chest. "I agreed to this. I'm good."

"You sure? I'm serious; if you don't want to do this—"

"I'm good. We made this deal for both of our sakes, and I'm here to hold up my end of the bargain. So, grab my hand and let's make a run for it in the rain to the car and pray I don't slip and fall in these heels."

He flashes me a warm smile, his gaze locking on mine. As if he's memorized exactly where my hand rests at my side, he reaches for it—and the way his fingers curl around mine feels like he wants nothing more than to keep me safe. My eyes burn. *I don't need saving.* I'm the one in command in every area of my life. I'm the one who decides what I do when. So, can someone in the universe please explain why this feeling of someone looking out for me is strangely comforting?

The way he's been around me has been...unexpected. I replay all the times I've been around him. He hasn't been cocky or arrogant. He's been...kind. Thoughtful. Helpful even. And seemingly worried about me. *Does he worry about me?* I trace his profile out of the corner of my eye. *Oh God…nope, nope, nope.* I shake the idea of him having an inkling of a feeling toward me out of my head. This is fake. He can't. *I* can't. We could never work. We're totally wrong for each other. But the rush of adrenaline, my pulse racing like it's found something it's been seeking for a very long time, transports me back to that night at the hotel, standing in front of the elevator. *Was that only a few nights ago?* I was so irritated with him for butting in, for causing all of this, but now? With our hands joined again, my perspective is redirected. *He did that to keep me safe.* I snap myself back to the present and the blinding flashes through the glass.

"Okay," he whispers as his thumb rubs along mine for just an instant, sending a chill down my spine. "I've got you."

He pushes the door open as a staff member from the restaurant hands him an umbrella. As he takes it, I replay the conversation with my friends earlier this week, biting the inside of my cheek. *We're never going to convince anyone this is real if this is just a run to the car and hop inside.* I've kissed lots of guys. I can do this. And this will just prove that we have no physical connection. We couldn't possibly. This is just me and my hormones, and being around a hot guy who just inhaled a plate of fries with me. Surely, that's what I'm all worked up about. And the gin…of course! The *gin*! It has to be. I can do this.

I grab his arm. "Leave the umbrella. What do you say we give them a show? That is…if you don't mind getting a little wet."

He narrows his brows, his eyes bouncing between mine, then shrugs. "It's, um…totally up to you."

"Any limits I need to know about, rich boy?"

"Limits?" His voice cracks as his Adam's apple bobs in his throat. "What limits are you talking about?"

"Do you trust me?"

He looks at me with a little glimmer in his eye, almost like I've just asked him the most absurd question in the world. "Yes."

"Good." I pull him with me into the pouring rain and head straight down the long sidewalk to the car, the Chauffer waiting with an umbrella at the open door. But when we get there, I turn to face him, not an ounce of hesitation in me as I place my hands on his cheeks and press my lips against his.

I did this for the media.

I did this to put on a show to imply this is very real.

I did this to prove to myself that while he's extremely good-looking, there couldn't possibly be any physical chemistry between us.

But as he gently wraps his arms around my waist, I can't help but open my mouth to him. And as his tongue glides along mine, a warmth spreads through my chest that slowly crawls lower, pooling at the apex of my thighs. The rain trickling down my skin does nothing but amplify the feeling of want and need. A shiver pulls in my core as my body leans into him.

This was all to prove a point to myself. *I'm quickly realizing I fucked up.* Feeling his hands on me, pulling me into him like he wants this—like he wants me—has created this sudden, intimate connection that's doing nothing to prove anything except that I want him more.

But as fast as it started, it ends. A clap of thunder startles us both, probably nature's way of reminding me this is not real. We take a step back from one another, our chests heaving. He stands stunned, his mouth still agape as he gasps. He finally blinks and motions for me to get in the car before following behind me.

The car door shuts, the hot air thawing our chilled skin. Silence fills the air, the pitter-patter of raindrops on the window the only noise marking the awkwardness. Both of us are soaking wet. Seeing him run his fingers through his dark hair is making me want to pull him in again and do more than kiss in the back of this car. He crosses his legs, turning his body toward the door. *I can't tell what he's thinking.* What am *I* even thinking? *Shit, Kennedy, what did you do?* I think I made this situation *way* worse. He probably didn't want to kiss me. This guy is the entertainer of the century. He knows how to play to the cameras, especially with a woman on his arm. This is par for the course for him. I pick at the hem of my dress. I thought he would be gloating. Bragging. Talking about how I should be impressed by his kissing skills. *Not* that I think he has skills. Not at all. The damp feeling between my legs is from the rain. Yes, that's exactly what's happening. He does not have skills. He was just...just...just...*goddammit, that was a really good kiss.*

Fuck.

I can't take sitting here in silence the whole way back to the hotel. I need to say something, *anything*, since I was the one who did this.

"You, okay? Was that...okay?"

He snaps his head to mine, looking like he's struggling to breathe. "Yeah. It was..." —he clears his throat and shifts in his seat — "it was fine."

A tightness pulls in my chest. *Did he not feel what I felt?* "Fine?" I huff. "Great. I was hoping it would be *fine*."

"I didn't mean—"

"Jordan. I'm teasing. It was just for show, right? Hopefully, that was enough proof for them to think this is real."

His gaze falls to the floorboard as he lets out a loud sigh. "Yep. That should do it."

My heart sinks. *Why do I feel like there's more he's not saying?* I still don't understand why this guy, who is normally so confident, seems like a scared kitten, stuck in a storm drain, waiting to be rescued whenever he's around me. Does he think I'm a flood that's going to come in and drown him? He's like those Sudoku puzzles I do on my phone when a flight is delayed. Every time I think I know which spot to put the number in, he does something, and I have to redo the entire row. I'm going to figure out how to crack this guy's code. Come hell or high water.

27
blocked number

I am a sensible, rational person. And I have been very patient. My instructions have been crystal clear. *Are the words 'stay away from her' so difficult to understand?* It seems simple to me. And yet, somehow, I'm being ignored just like I've been overlooked my entire life.

I'm fucking sick of it.

I pick up my phone, tapping my foot as my fingers fly across the screen. My pulse is thrumming through my veins like a raging river, ready to finally take back what's mine.

If Jordan Boucher thinks he can ignore me, he's got another thing coming. It was one thing when his relationship seemed one-sided. I thought releasing that photo would drive them apart, but that clearly backfired. I don't know what the hell they think they are doing, but they won't survive everything I have planned.

Ice Deke

> Look who made the news again. I'm disappointed. Why won't you listen to me? Since you seem to need the reminder, know this is my last message before things take a turn you won't like. I'll say it to you one last time.

> Stay the fuck away from Kennedy Kramer.

part two
april

28
jordan

Gliding backward on the ice, my opponent comes straight for me, all my senses on high alert. Watching for the slightest shift in movement. Listening for his teammates calling out to him. Keeping my eyes directly on his chest to make sure I have him, while using my peripheral vision to focus on his eye movements to see if anyone else is in the way. I know Vladi is behind me, but my goal is for this puck to not get anywhere near his crease.

My senses may be locked on this game, but it's nothing compared to when Kennedy kissed me. It's been weeks since our date. Weeks since I held her hand. Weeks since she grabbed my face in the rain and pressed her lips to mine. That lightning strike that seemingly pulled us apart? That was nothing more than an electric shock jump-starting my heart to beat for her even more.

I've struggled to fall asleep every night, thinking about our kiss and wondering if she's awake doing the same. *Does she feel it too?* Does her heart pound as fast as mine every time my phone buzzes, hoping it's her? Does her breathing get so fucking fast when she sees me walking down the aisle of the plane, the same way mine does when I catch a glimpse of her at the other end? At least that's one bright spot—she *does* say hi to me now. We've made small talk and texted here and there, making sure we had a plan and a story if anyone asked what we were doing or where we'd been. And we figured people would want us both to remain professionals on the plane, so no need to flaunt things there. But fuck me. If she were really mine? I would be flaunting her everywhere. Kennedy is everything. And that kiss did nothing but provide even more proof. *She's the one.* But she still seems...*annoyed* that we're dating. That this is an inconvenience. How do I get her past this? How do I get her to see me in a different light?

And, of course, this is all happening during the playoffs. Which I'm happy to be in the midst of—hell, we even agreed we'd keep dating through these games—but there's not a lot of time for socializing or figuring out how to woo the girl of my dreams into falling in love with me. *How the fuck do I even do that?* Shit. I'm so out of my element here.

Niko Koskinen from Green Bay passes to his teammate and whirls by me toward the net. *Fuck.* It's game five in the first round of the playoffs. We're up three games to one on the Bobcats. Win this, and we move on. What's even more at stake, though? Win this, and my fake girlfriend isn't going anywhere. My legs burn as I tear after him, my pulse thrumming in my ears louder than the fans. We're up by one goal late in the third. It's not do-or-die tonight, but we are itching to clinch. Having a few extra days of rest during these brutal rounds is a nice perk. You don't want too much rest, but almost all of us are playing with some sort of injury, bad bruise, sprain, or are in a lot of pain, especially this late in the season, so a little rest is welcome. I myself am nursing a bruised ankle after I took a slapshot to the skate. It's painful, but it's the playoffs. We push through.

Right now, the only pain I'm focused on is the pain-in-the-ass

Koskinen, from Green Bay, who is trying his best to get me off my game. I'm crowding the douchebag enough that he can't get a shot off, so he skates behind the net, and I get in a good hit right into the boards.

Then I hear it. The fucking whistle. *Fuck.*

"In the box sixty-eight," the ref says as he skates up to me.

"What? That was a clean hit. What are you even calling here?"

"Boarding," he says, skating me over to the box.

"He leaned into the boards!" My arms fly up in disbelief at this stupid-ass call. "This is horseshit, and you know it! That was a fucking clean hit."

"Keep it up, Boucher, and I'll toss you."

Fucking fuck. The last thing we need right now is to be on the PK. I slam myself down in the penalty box and beat my stick against the glass. "Fucking piece of shit ref!" I continue to grumble well after the official has skated away to announce the penalty over his damn little pussy of a microphone. That was not boarding, and that damn ref knows it. I see Coach Cal trying to argue the call as the entire arena erupts in a chant of 'ref you suck.'

But it's no use. This isn't a call they can review, so a face-off right in front of Vladi's net is set to go down. Two minutes and thirty seconds. If they can just hold them off for the power play, we can return to full strength. I can barely keep myself seated on this damn bench, desperate to be back on the ice, but I need to rest my legs so I can go full throttle the last thirty seconds once I'm out of here.

Luckily, my teammates have cleared the puck out of our zone a couple times, but Green Bay is bringing the puck down the ice again.

Goddammit! I hate not being out there.

Fifteen seconds left in my penalty. Green Bay has gotten off a couple more shots, but, as expected, Vladi is playing out of his mind tonight. He wants nothing more than to bring a cup to the city that's done so much for him. I want to do everything possible to help him with that. I watch the official in the box step over to the door, watching the seconds count down, jumping out of the box when the clock hits zero, and skating toward Vladi as fast as my legs can take me.

Number eighty-seven for Green Bay passes to his teammate just as I enter the zone. I intercept it, a smirk on my face, and pivot, heading toward Green Bay's goal. I see Larsy racing toward their net as well, and we fly up the ice. It's two on one. We have the puck. I could take the shot, but Larsy's got the better angle, so I zoom toward the net and just as I approach the goalie, getting him to shift his weight to my side, I pass the puck back to Larsy, who pops it into the back of the net just as the horn sounds. Our home crowd screams, and our teammates clear the bench and form a giant dogpile on the ice.

We fucking did it! We're moving on. *God, this feels good.* I love this team so much. It's such a special group of guys. Even though they give me a lot of shit and call me dumbass rich boy names, I still love every single one of them.

And now it's time to do the classiest thing in all of sports—shake the other team's hands. It only happens at the end of a series, and it sucks to be on the other side of this receiving line, but the handshake in hockey shows how much respect we all have for one another. But waiting in the line this time, instead of thoughts of the next round, the next game, and what could be for our team, my thoughts aren't on hockey. *They're on her.*

I instantly spotted her in the crowd when I skated out during warm-ups, unable to stop the stupid grin from spreading across my cheeks.

She's here with all the WAGs, because thanks to our arrangement—she is one. She's not been to the away games. She's doing her pilot stuff. And that's her job, so I get it, but tonight is a home game—*and she's* here. *Is she thinking about me now?* I smile like an idiot as I go through the motions and shake hands. They have no idea my grin is not sportsmanship, but about the woman in the stands, I'm anxious to see.

After handshakes and celebrations, I grab a quick shower and change back into my suit. As I head out of the locker room, I see most of the WAGs waiting in the hallway for us. Maggie, Olivia, Kara, and—oh my God. My jaw drops, my stomach twisting into knots. *Breathe, Jordan...Breathe.* Standing next to Kara, wearing a blue embroidered jacket with the number sixty-eight on the sleeve, is Kennedy. She's wearing *my number*. Am I allowed to cry? Cause I kinda want to cry. Girls cry in movies all the time; why can't I, dammit?! But I suck in a sharp breath and flash her a smile as I get close.

"Hi."

"Hi."

Great start, Jordan. Maybe say more than one word next time. "So... what's this?" I say, pointing to her jacket. "You're wearing my number?"

"I'm technically your girlfriend, so...yeah." She bites her lip as she leans against the concrete wall. "Also, Maggie said I had to."

I look over to Maggie, who gives me a wink and mouths 'you're welcome.' *Does she know I have a thing for Kennedy?* How much does she know? Do her and Vladi sit and gossip about us at night? I can't really picture that. I feel like she asks him how his day was, and he just grunts.

"I'm flattered. It's kind of a big deal to have someone wear your number."

"So I've heard."

"Are you, um," —I swallow back the nerves that have my throat closing up— "are you coming out with everyone after the game? We're all going to Walt's to celebrate."

She forces a smile that sends my heart plummeting to the floor. "I don't know; I'm kind of tired. I think I'm just going to—"

"Oh no, you don't!" Kara shouts as she and Olivia quickly move to her side, looping their arms around hers. "Kennedy Kramer, you are coming out with us. My parents are taking the kids home, and we're going to spend this *one night* celebrating. We have no idea when they'll be at home for a series clinch again, so we are going to have a good time!"

"Yes, Kennedy, you have to come! There is no excuse. You don't work tomorrow. The team has an off day. You don't have Guard stuff," Olivia says, counting out the reasons on her fingers. "You're coming."

"Well," Maggie chimes in, "sounds like Kara and Liv have my speech covered. So, it's settled. You're coming."

I dig my fingernail into my palm, trying to hold back the smile as these feisty women gang up on her. And every word they say gives me a little more hope she'll say yes. She looks at her friends, who are all giving her a look like they know she's about to make up another excuse. Her brows narrow as a fake smile creeps across her face. "I guess I can come for a couple drinks."

"Great!" Maggie grins. "You're riding with Bougie. We'll see you guys there!"

"What?!" Kennedy and I both shout, looking at Maggie wide eyed.

"Yes! You're dating. You have to ride together. It's the law. WAG law. See you there!"

My heart jumps from the floor back into my chest, beating fast and hard. *Is she riding with me? In my car?* We haven't been together in a car since...since...the most powerful, explosive, mind-blowing, life-altering kiss in the history of the world.

Ice Deke

What the fuck do I do?

29

kennedy

I'm going to strangle Maggie. Hello, awkward—party of two—here for our reservation of a cringe-worthy car ride. Because we kissed and have not talked about it. We've sent a few texts here and there to coordinate things—each one from him having a ridiculous amount of emojis. During away games, we've still, somehow, had adjoining rooms. And every time I arrive at the hotel, my minibar is fully stocked with all of the ingredients for my gin and tonic—fresh ice and limes included. Every night, I make my drink, sit on my bed, and stare at the door between our rooms, wondering why the hell I'm lusting after my fake boyfriend.

And now here we are, walking through the tunnels of the arena to the player parking lot. Our footsteps echoing off the concrete are the only sound cutting the thick tension. And with each step, I remind myself this isn't real. *It could never be.* He's too young. Too cocky. Too…way too fucking handsome. Based on my very rational and very analytical analysis, we could never work. It's like flying. Follow the flight plan and arrive at the destination. My brain is well aware of how this works, but my body seems to only remember that goddamn kiss. And his biceps. And his thick as hell thighs. And—no. *Hell no.* I can't go there. He needs to focus on the playoffs. And I need to focus on literally anything else. I pick at my cuticles because if I don't, I'm not sure my mind will win this war; it's raging with my hormones.

Walking past the rows of player cars, I realize I don't even know what kind of car my *boyfriend* drives. I'm guessing it's some sort of tricked-out sports car I can't pronounce with every extra imaginable. He comes to a stop beside a black Range Rover. Is it expensive? Yes. But at least the doors don't open in an upward motion.

"Huh."

His face crumples. "What?"

"Nothing."

"It's *not* nothing. You just said 'huh.' What was the 'huh' for?"

"I just…I just figured you'd have some ridiculously expensive sports car with weird doors."

He winces, his jaw clenching as if the sting of my words hit deeper than he's willing to admit. My stomach churns. Maybe I went a step too far? *Ugh…why am I such a bitch?* His eyes narrow.

Shit.

"Jordan, I'm sorry. I didn't mean—"

"It's fine," he interrupts, his face surprisingly neutral. But I know he's not fine. I feel like I just got the stereotypical line women usually say to men. That's *my* line.

He steps closer, trapping me against the side of his vehicle. My pulse races as his gaze locks on mine. The hard lines in his eyes sharpen as if something inside him snapped.

"I know you think I only like lavish things, but just so you're aware," —he leans in, our faces a breath apart, the tension crackling — "I don't buy things because of the price tag. The things I have? It's because I *want* them."

My breath catches, his arm reaching behind me, caging me in.

CLICK.

He opens the car door, stepping back to open it for me. "Come on. Let's head out."

I nod, trying to catch up with what he just said. He technically has *me* at the moment…*is he implying?* No. He can't be. I settle into the car and buckle my seatbelt.

What. The. Fuck. Was. That?

30
jordan

*W*hat the fuck just happened?! *The things I have are because I want them.* Did some alpha male biker bro just invade my body? The confidence that took over that first night at the hotel bar re-appeared out of nowhere, pushing me forward again. *Maybe it was the win tonight?* Or the fact that she seems to be annoyed with me for something I have no control over. How do I show her I'm more than my family's money?

My palms are sweaty as I grip the steering wheel, my courage abandoning me. *Thanks for nothing, alpha male biker bro.* Now I have no idea what to say. I place my arm behind her seat as I back out of the parking space—also using it as an excuse to catch a glimpse of the beauty in my car. The fire in her eyes isn't one I've seen before. After that first incident with Chadd McDingleberry, she was full of angry fire. Tonight? She was...*intrigued*. Fuck, I'm so out of my element here. *Where is Vladi when I need him?*

The drive out of the parking garage is quiet, the turn signal ungodly loud as I turn onto Water Street. I need to break this tension. And show her I am more than the things I own.

"So, how's your week been? Is the media still outside your place?"

She lets out a breath as if the whistle finally blows to end conditioning. "It's been okay. They finally stopped camping outside my apartment. Only a few still hang around when they think I'll be leaving the building, and there's usually one waiting for me at the coffee shop across the street when I pick up my drink in the morning, but he seems harmless." She laughs, the sound tired. "I think Maggie is secretly bummed they aren't there anymore. She'd never admit it, but she was hoping for her fifteen minutes of fame. She's been wearing her Little Fox Branding hoodie, hoping they'll post her online instead of me."

I grin. Her description of Maggie is, well, accurate. But the hair prickles on the back of my neck at someone still lingering. *Especially* after getting more threatening texts.

"How far across the street is the coffee shop? Are you still against having a security detail? Does the guy at the coffee shop seem sus?"

She scoffs. "Oh, God no. Wes is an older guy who takes some photos on the side. We chatted the other day, and I let him snap a photo of me picking up my coffee. Like I said…harmless. And *please,* no security. I can take care of myself. The last thing I want is some creepy secret service guy following me around."

"You do know I'm not the president, right? I don't have secret service. But I can have someone patrol your building to make sure you're safe with all the extra attention coming at you. You know… maybe we should just do that anyway."

"Jordan, I'm a *Major* in the Air National Guard. I take charge of entire planes full of people and supplies, sometimes even rowdy, obnoxious hockey players." I see her crack a smile out of my peripheral vision, and I can't help but smirk back. "I'm fine. I appreciate the offer, but it's not necessary. Plus, it wouldn't be a good look for me."

I narrow my brows as I find a spot outside Walt's. "Just know the offer stands if you ever feel uncomfortable. Some of these press people can be really pushy."

Her soft smile is genuine. "I'll keep it in mind."

Putting the car in park, I take a deep breath as we get ready to face the next obstacle in our fake relationship. "Ready to go to our first official hangout with our friends?"

She stares at me with pleading eyes. "Do we have to? I feel like Maggie's out to get me tonight."

I let out a loud laugh. "I'm not gonna lie, you're totally in her crosshairs. Come on, let's get this over with."

31
kennedy

I'll give him credit. As much of a bitch as I was earlier, he's still a perfect gentleman, racing around to open the door for me. The boldness he found is still going strong, his fingers lacing through mine as we head into the bar. His thumb grazing mine, and his goddamn scent, has a warmth spreading through me before I can stop it. My brain is, once again, willing my body to not react, but it's not happening. I'm too aware of the sexy as hell man leading me inside, his thumb moving slightly along mine. *Goddammit, Kennedy. Focus. Don't let your guard down now; your nosy-ass friends can smell blood in the water.*

As we walk inside, everyone else is already pulling together tables like they own the place. At this point, they basically do. This place has become a Riders staple ever since Hayes joined the team. He met Olivia singing here one night, and the owners, Walt and Johnny, have become like family to us all. Even to me, who really doesn't have a connection to the team like everyone else. *Until now.* While I know I'll always be a part of the Walt's family, this connection with Jordan, being a WAG, is only temporary. Just through the playoffs. Why am I feeling so much excitement for them moving onto another round when their season being done means I could end this whole thing? I shake the thought from my mind, remembering these really are my friends and I truly do want them to succeed.

Yep. That has to be it.

"Bougie! Kenni!" Johnny shouts as soon as we walk in. "Good to see you two! Kenni, you want the usual?"

"You know it, Johnny!"

"And what are you drinking tonight, Bougie?"

"I'll just have a water."

Johnny's eyes dart between us for a couple of seconds, something unspoken about his order, but he nods and goes back to making drinks. "You got it. One water and one gin and tonic for the happy couple."

"Go grab a seat," Jordan says, leaning toward me. The unexpected feel of his breath along my neck sends goosebumps flying across my skin. "I'll grab our drinks."

I pull away and immediately head over to my friends and plop down in the old wooden bar chair, focusing my attention on one person in particular.

"Thanks *so* much, Maggie, for suggesting that wonderfully awkward car ride."

She snorts. "Kenni, you're *literally* dating him. Like it or not, you can't just avoid him in public. You also can't sit here and talk to us all night either—you have to hang out with him," she whispers as she rests her head against my shoulder. "There are other people here, so you have to actually do girlfriend stuff tonight."

"I wouldn't have to if my dear sweet *friends* hadn't forced me to come out," I shoot back with enough sickening sweet sarcasm to drown the entire bar.

"Kennedy." Kara jumps into the conversation, reaching across and grabbing my wrist. "It's one night. You haven't been seen together since you movie kissed him in the rain; people need to see celebrity couples out in public."

"What about you? You and Zack hardly ever go out!"

"First of all, we have been married for over ten years, so there's no need to convince everyone we're together. Second, we have four children at home, and that's not really conducive to going out on the regular. Third, you're 'dating'," —she holds up air quotes as she speaks— "a young, hot hockey player. You *should* do fun stuff together. A night like tonight? A good WAG would support her man after a big series-clinching game," she says, taking a sip of her martini with a matter-of-fact look on her face.

"Kennedy," Olivia turns in her chair to face me, "what's so bad about Jordan anyway? Would it be the worst thing in the world if you were dating him for real? He is so damn sweet. Did you ever think maybe he's awkward because he's smitten with you?"

I scoff. "Olivia, I know you live in la la land with your perfect relationship. I mean, that man worships the literal ground your highness walks upon, but there's no way in hell Jordan Boucher is *smitten* with me. He's a twenty-three-year-old who could literally walk into a modeling agency and pick a wife out of a line-up if he wanted to. He has no interest in some thirty-four-year-old who wears a short-sleeved dress shirt with epaulets."

"What the fuck is an epaulet?" Maggie asks, looking at me like I just told her I was from another planet.

I shake my head and roll my eyes. "The striped patches on my shoulders? I've told you this before."

She takes a sip of her drink, blowing bubbles with her straw. "I can't keep up with your pilot fashion. All I know is you wear a scarf because you said you don't like the tie. Which, I happen to agree with, but that's not the point. Olivia is right! Have you *seen* the way he looks at you? Didn't you catch him looking for you in the stands? What if Jordan just thinks you're hot and gets all tongue-tied because of it? Or maybe he's just a sucker for a woman in uniform? I mean…Even I would consider that."

I let out a loud sigh as the rest of my friends cackle. They are well-meaning, but they also suck right now. *Goddamit.* I do think he's hot and want to, maybe, do some fun stuff with him. No way they are right about him feeling the same way. I need Ginny here to give me some wisdom. *Where the hell is my drink?*

32
jordan

"You gonna tell me what's up with the water tonight?" Johnny asks while I wait for our drinks. I cringe, already knowing this is going to turn into an interrogation. "You *always* order a scotch and Splenda after a win."

My stomach twists. *Nailed it.* "Goddammit, Johnny; you don't miss anything."

He smirks, knowing he is well-versed on all things Riders, both on and off the ice. "Well, you haven't stopped by lately. I know ya'll are busy with the playoffs, but don't think I don't keep up with all my Jordan Boucher love life news on social media. And if you think I'm gonna chalk that up to a random coincidence, you got another thing coming. Now…you gonna fill me in on what's going on with you two or should I go grill Maggie?"

"We're dating now, okay?" I let out a defeated sigh. There's no use avoiding him. He always knows *everything*. "We're dating, and I'm…*beyond* happy to have the woman of my dreams by my side."

He glances up as he long pours the gin, and my stomach twists once more. "You know I don't put up with bullshit at my bar. I saw you two swapping spit on every news site a few weeks back, looking the happiest you've ever been, and now you're acting like you have to wait for your drinks, like I wouldn't just bring them over to ya, and sulking like you didn't just make it to the second round of the playoffs." He jerks his chin across the bar. "And she's sitting over there not looking any better."

I run my hand through my hair fighting to not pull out every strand. "Johnny...Fuck! You know I like her, okay? And now I'm scared shitless to say the wrong thing and get caught up in someone who isn't into me...I've been fooled before, and I really don't want to go down that road again." I drag my hand down my face, leaning heavily against the bar. "Every time I find the tiniest bit of confidence, thoughts of my former life pop back up, and... goddammit! I don't know what to do. I was so confident with her earlier tonight, and now? Now I am terrified to go over and talk to her in front of our friends."

"Let me tell you something, Jordan, if some part of her didn't like you to some extent, she wouldn't be doing this in the first place. Kennedy Kramer is not going to fool you. I know you're a great performer, but that kiss? That was all her. I saw the shock in your eyes." The corner of his mouth lifts, his eyes finding Walt in the dark. "There's something there."

He's wrong. "Where do you come up with all this shit, Johnny? There is no way she's into me. Even if she was, how the hell do I get her to stop thinking I'm just some spoiled rich kid who only cares about money and myself?"

He sets our drinks on the bar and throws a towel over his shoulder. "Keep showing her you're more than that. Give her a window into the side of you no one else gets to see."

I blink. That's what my dad said. That's what Hannah said. *Maybe that's what the body-invading alpha biker bro was trying to tell me, too.* My ribcage is assaulted from the pulsing behind it, anticipation spreading through my body like the last few seconds in the penalty box. "You know what, Johnny? I changed my mind. I'll take that scotch and Splenda after all."

He flashes me a wicked grin, grabs a glass already waiting with Splenda, adds in the ice and scotch, and slides it across the bar with a wink. I take a sip, knocking back a bit of liquid courage.

Time to stop being a little bitch and date the shit out of Kennedy Kramer.

As I weave through the crowd toward the big group table, I see Kennedy wedged between Olivia and Maggie. I stand across from her, setting the glass on the table and sliding it her way.

Olivia practically jumps out of her chair as I look for a place to sit. "Jordan…here! I'm gonna go sit with Hayes. You can have my seat."

Heat crawls across my cheeks as little smirks light up the faces of all her friends. There is *no one* in the entire universe who loves playing matchmaker more than the Milwaukee Steel Riders and their significant others. I walk around the table to sit next to Kennedy. Everyone else is deep in conversation, clinking glasses, and celebrating our win. But my mind is not on the next round of hockey. It's focused on one thing—figuring out how the hell to show Kennedy the real me. I wish I could just say 'hey, I'm not really the rich fuckboy you think I am.'

Shit…maybe that would be easier.

"You changed your drink," Kennedy says, surprising the hell out of me. "Johnny seemed pretty shocked by your water order. Is this what you normally get? You drank a cabernet in Dallas. Are you a big wine drinker?"

I smile; the thought of her remembering my drink order makes my heart pound in my chest. "I do like wine. Sometimes I have a glass to help me get to sleep. But after a win, my go-to order is a scotch and Splenda."

"Ha! Like Michael Scott on The Office?"

I laugh. "Yeah, you're a fan?"

"Who isn't? I don't even work in an office, but it's such a funny show." She tips her glass toward me. "I guess you don't work in a typical work environment either."

"You've been to my office. Just ice, sticks, and sweat. And a grumpy goalie who rivals Stanley Hudson with his short dialect and brooding nature."

Her eyes sparkle as she lets out a roaring laugh. "Dear lord! Vladi really is a real-life Stanley, isn't he? I can just picture him saying, 'Did I stutter?'" She leans in close, heat radiating from her body to mine as she whispers, "Do you think he likes pretzel day?"

We both burst into a fit of giggles as her hand rests on my arm. I glance at the delicate flesh touching mine, goosebumps quickly spreading across my skin, meeting her gaze as I look back up. The air thickens as her joy fades into a sweet smile, and I match it with my own. *Maybe Johnny was right. Does she have a thing for—*

"Hey, Bougie!" The moment is interrupted by EJ shouting down the table. "We're gonna go to 414 after this. Can you hook us up with bottle service?"

Kennedy tilts her head, her gaze darting between my loud-mouth teammate and me. "Jordan..." she whispers, looking me dead in the eye, my stomach twisting like I just got caught with my hand in the cookie jar. "Why is Erik asking you for free drinks at Club 414?"

Shit. *Fucking EJ.* I'm gonna swap out his laces for some hideous ones next practice.

I shrug. "EJ's just a big mooch. Never wants to pay for anything," I say, shooting laser beams at EJ. "Buy your own drinks tonight, asshole! That salary extension's burning a hole in your pocket."

There. Problem solved.

Until dickface opens his mouth again. "Oh, come on, Bougie! You own the damn club; you can't hook your teammates up? Lame!"

I slowly face Kennedy, her lips pursed, and her jaw clenched tighter than I thought physically possible.

"You own Club 414? As in...*own it*, own it?"

I flash a cringy smile, my heart plummeting to the floor. *Yet another example of me having a lot of money that I'm sure she'll hate.* "Would you believe me if I said no? That it was a gift I inherited from a long-lost relative?"

She shifts in her seat to face me, crossing her arms. *This can't be good.* "No. Spill it."

"Okay. Yes. I own Club 414. Along with a few other businesses around Milwaukee and Canada."

Her expression doesn't change, but my pulse fires on all cylinders, wondering how she's going to react. My tongue wets my lips, and I can see the wheels spinning as if she's trying to put the pieces together. I see when it finally clicks, spots dancing across my vision.

"Wait...when I was there celebrating Benny's last day, my bill was covered by the owner..."

"It was me," my confession spills out of me before I grab my glass and take a drink, my throat suddenly dry as hell. *This 'show her you're more than your money' thing is really going well.*

She blinks. "Why did you pay for my tab? I'm quite capable of—"

"It was for Benny," I say quickly, thanking all the hockey gods for helping me come up with that half-truth. "He was cool, and I wanted to make sure he had a nice send off."

"For Benny..." she drawls, nodding slowly. "Right. Well, that was very nice of you to do that. For *Benny*."

"Yep. That's me. Super nice doing things for only Benny."

She leans back, breaking our connection. The amount of money

I would pay to know what she's thinking right now is endless. *Does she know I did it for her?* I love Benny, but this was one-hundo percent for her and her alone. Running my hand through my hair, trying to calm my nerves down and figure out how to quiet her suspicions, I'm saved by the literal bell ringing above the door to Walt's.

"You've got to be fucking kidding me," Kennedy spits as we see a couple walk in, hanging all over each other.

I flinch as the woman trips over an occupied table, the man making no attempt to catch her. *Did I say walking? I meant stumbling.* They've both had *way* too much to drink.

And the man leading a very drunk woman to the bar is none other than Chadd fucking McDickwad, III.

33
jordan

"What the hell is he doing here?" Kennedy grumbles through gritted teeth.

Without a second thought, I put my arm around the back of her chair, the hand in my lap balling into a fist. The fucking audacity of this guy showing his face here. We deal with him as our pilot because we have to, but seeing him at Walt's, at a known Riders bar? The enforcer in me wants to pummel him into nothing more than a heap of dust on the floor. *God, if only I had this guy on the ice right now.*

"And who the hell is he with?" I say to everyone and no one all at once.

As if summoned by magic, Tay appears behind us, leaning forward to almost whisper in our ears.

"That's Mara. She's the new production assistant for the broadcast crew. Just started a couple months back. Apparently, the former assistant Bridget got accused of selling her employee tickets online, which is a big no-no."

I look over my shoulder as he smiles and walks away. "No

wonder she looks familiar," I mumble, a chill running down my spine at anyone who would be willing to be seen with Chadd with two d's. "Are they together?"

"Apparently, the poor thing." Kennedy clicks her tongue. "Why the hell is she wearing sunglasses inside? At night?"

I can't help but snort. "I mean, if I were with Chadd McLoser, I would want to dull my senses so I couldn't see him too."

Kennedy chokes on her drink, slamming it down as she tries to swallow while gasping for air. After a moment, panic sets in as her cheeks redden, patting her chest to help swallow down the gin. *Is she okay? Did I kill her with my joke?* But she regains her breath and laughs hysterically, laying her hand against my arm. My fingers itch to cover hers. This patting my arm when she laughs thing is quickly becoming my new favorite thing in the entire world. *Apparently, she likes my jokes.* I gotta tuck that little nugget into my arsenal of Things Kennedy Likes because I could listen to the sound of her laugh every day.

"Oh my God! I would gouge my eyes out if I had to look at Chadd McDouchenozzle more than I have to. Sitting with him on a flight for hours at a time is a *struggle*." She fakes a full-body shiver as Chadd tries to take his date's sunglasses off, and she swats his hand away, sending both of us laughing at the sight of the two of them.

That's when he clocks us, his eyes glassy but focused. I suck my teeth. I'm guessing drunk Chadd is not going to be happy seeing us here. Without saying anything to Mara, he glares and heads our way. Man...I hate being right.

"Is that our other pilot?" EJ asks down the table. My heart soars; everyone loves and knows Kennedy by name, while he's nothing more than the 'other pilot.' *Serves him right for being a giant dick.*

"Looks like it. What the hell is he doing here?" Larsy asks, the whole table quieting as he stumbles toward us.

"Kennedy," Chadd singsongs with a goddamn smirk on his face. "I see you are still trying to cradle rob your way to the top."

I grit my teeth wishing I could stick, gloves, shirt this guy and beat the shit out of him with only a five-minute penalty. I take a deep breath, calming the fighter in me, reminding myself that my off-ice personality is always supposed to be smiling and friendly, even if my smile is psychotic. I slowly stand to face him. *God, do I want to punch his smug little face.* But I keep my cool, like I always do, and chirp him like an opponent.

"Chadd McDoubleD! I see you've finally found someone to get your dick wet with. Was it hard to find one who doesn't mind it being the size of a baby carrot?" Several of my teammates snicker, their wives just as pleased knowing how badly he's treated my girlfriend. Fake or not, she's mine to defend.

"Wow. *Real* mature, Boucher." He takes a step toward me. "I guess when someone gold digs for money, they don't exactly get the cream of the crop, do they?" he taunts as he pokes me in the chest.

As if we planned it, my entire team stands up from the table, like we're reenacting a scene from a movie where someone pisses off the main character and the whole bar backs them up. I don't bother hiding the smirk twisting my cheeks. *God, I love these guys.*

"You need to stop talking," Vladi growls, and fuck if that isn't scary.

"This is a Riders bar," Larsy pipes up. "You don't get to come in here and insult Kennedy, Bougie, or anyone else. This is our home."

"This is a public place. You don't *own* this bar," Chadd squawks, puffing his chest while his date is still over at the bar ordering drinks.

"No. They don't," Walt booms, walking over to our table. "But I do. And from what I heard you say to Jordan and Kenni, I'm going to have to ask you to leave. We don't tolerate that kind of talk here."

Damn, Walt. You go, Glen Coco. I fight back the mist in my eyes between him and my teammates coming to our defense. *Hold it together, Jordan.* Don't cry in a bar or you'll be chirped the rest of your life.

"You're going to let a bunch of goons dictate what happens in your bar?"

He crosses his arms, Johnny leaning against the bar top over his shoulder.

"Damn straight I am. This bunch of goons are my family, and we treat family with respect."

"Thanks, Walt," Kennedy says, standing up and linking her arm around mine. "I can take it from here." I thread my fingers through hers, squeezing lightly and letting her do her thing. "Listen Chadd, we don't need to get along, but we also don't need to be around one another outside of work. I'm here celebrating my boyfriend and his team's big win tonight, and we were here first. We're not working, so there is no reason for you to be over here. I wish I could say it was good to see you, but I was raised to believe lying is wrong. Now, go back to Vanessa Von Ray-Ban over there and enjoy your drinks on the other side of the bar."

Chadd's jaw tightens as he seethes. "Her name is Mara."

Kennedy and I exchange a quick glance and begin hysterically laughing, no one having any idea about our joke from earlier.

"What are you laughing about?" Chadd asks, looking like smoke is going to pour out of his ears as his face turns a deep shade of red.

"Oh, nothing. Nothing at all," I manage in the midst of my giggles.

Kennedy doubles over, unable to breathe, she's laughing so

hard. But she regains her composure to get out another dig. "Oh! Hey Johnny, play I Wear My Sunglasses at Night on the jukebox!"

Chadd finally gets the joke, stomping his foot as he storms off, waving off the drinks and dragging Mara out the door, pulling it shut with an exaggerated slam.

"Such a shame they didn't want to stay after all—wonder why?" I say after composing myself.

"Probably going to go home and file a formal complaint against sunlight," Kennedy whispers, and we double over again. Seeing her smile, hearing her laugh uncontrollably, makes me want to be with her even more.

"Speaking of going home," she says, sliding her arm from mine, "I think I'm gonna head out. Maggie, are you ready to go?"

Maggie snorts and gives us a look like we're certifiably insane. "Kenni...I am *not* taking you home. I'm staying at Vladi's tonight. Your *boyfriend* is your ride. I'll see you Sunday for brunch."

I swallow hard at the thought of another awkward car ride. But also...I don't want her to leave.

She turns to me, her lips twisting. "This is your night to celebrate. I can order an Uber if you want to stay longer with your team—"

"No!" I interrupt quickly. *Awkward or not, I still want to be with her.* "I'll take you home. It's not a problem. I was just getting ready to leave anyway."

She scoffs. "I can't imagine you wanting to go home early."

I still don't think she gets it—I will go anywhere she does.

"It's been a long day, and I haven't been drinking like the rest of these fools. Plus, I see them constantly. They can roast me another time. Come on, let's go."

We say our goodbyes, several members of the team hoot and holler as we walk away hand-in-hand. *Mental note: give them shit about that later.*

The ride to her place is actually *comfortable*. If I didn't know any better, I'd assume this feels more like what a real relationship should be. Our nerves seemingly disappear as we continue making jokes at Chadd's expense, the conversation flowing like a clean breakaway on fresh ice. She laughed even harder when I told her I was seriously debating going full-on Crazy Rich Asians on his ass and buying the damn company they fly for so I could fire him. She made me swear not to do it. And I did.

She doesn't need to know I may have had my fingers crossed.

As we pull up to her building, her phone buzzes. She sighs, and my stomach twists. I can only imagine the texts she's getting from the WAGs, not to mention social media clips of her being at the game, but as I put the car in park, she screams, "Oh my God. Oh my fucking God!"

I whip my head toward her, my heart pounding. "What? What's wrong?"

She looks at me, her eyes filled with horror, and slowly holds her phone to my face. There's a photo of the two of us at the arena when I'm opening the door for her to get in my car. *It's actually kind of cute for a pap picture.* But the message beneath it makes my blood freeze:

> BLOCKED NUMBER:
>
> Your boyfriend doesn't like to listen, so I'm hoping you will. Stay the fuck away from Jordan Boucher.

"That text you got that started all this?" Her eyes bounce everywhere, her mind too frantic to focus on anything specific. "Now they're texting me."

Fuck. Fuck, fucking, fuck, fuck.

My heart drops to the pit of my stomach. *I can't avoid this any longer.*

Ellie K. Drake

"Kennedy, we need to talk."

34
kennedy

"What the fuck is going on, Jordan?" My hands shake as I stare at the back of my phone, my knuckles white. "Who is this? How do they have my number?"

He taps his head against his seat as he stares into the abyss of the steering wheel. "I honestly don't know who this is. But...*fuck*, I need to tell you something."

My heart sinks like a boat anchor in the nearby lake. "Is your... is your family some sort of Canadian Mafia or something? Does that even exist? Am I going to be wearing cement shoes at the bottom of a giant vat of maple syrup?" My eyes flutter closed, my swallow heavy and forced. "Did you know I hate the smell of that shit? When someone brings a McGriddle on the plane, I need my own barf bag! Oh God. I cannot die by drowning in maple syrup."

"Kennedy. Okay...just...take a deep breath and stay calm. My family is not in the Mafia. We don't own any maple syrup factories. And I'm probably going to have my citizenship revoked, saying this, but I also don't like maple syrup. I just eat my pancakes with—"

"Butter," we say at the same time. He flashes me a warm, timid smile and, for some reason, that actually calms me down, my hands a little steadier than before.

"Exactly," he adds. "If it's a good pancake, you only need butter."

"Right?" The tension eases a notch. It's oddly comforting how in sync we are about food. "Or a warm blueberry compote on top. Now *that* is my dream pancake."

"Hell yes! Blueberries are my favorite. I swear I can eat blueberry anything."

"Okay, I know I'm freaking the fuck out, but now I really want pancakes."

He laughs. "You know what…I'm actually starving after the game and all the excitement at the bar, and now your text." He hesitates for a moment, looking as if he wants encouragement. I drop my phone, relaxing enough to let him know I'm past the initial panic.

He bites his lip. "There's an all-night breakfast place not far from here. You um…you wanna go? We can talk, and I can explain more about my hatred of maple syrup and," —he runs his hands through his hair, his eyes darting back toward the steering wheel— "tell you about the other texts I've been getting."

Defeat washes over his face. I'm still unsure what the hell is going on, but for some bizarre reason, I trust him. He's done nothing other than look out for me.

Just as I'm about to say yes, my stomach lets out the loudest growl I've ever heard. "Well," I chuckle, "apparently my stomach is on board. Let's go."

After a short drive, we find a booth inside Millie's, an old 50s-style diner with red leather booths and a jukebox in the corner, vinyl records spinning inside. The sound of bacon sizzling on the flat-top behind the counter and the smell of plates on the pass-through window have my stomach itching to dive in.

"How have I lived in Milwaukee for years and never heard of this place?"

He flashes me a smile that's sexier than I'd like to admit, warmth I don't want to think about spreading through my chest. Especially after getting a text from a stalker and him telling me we need to *talk*.

"It's one of those 'if you know, you know' places. They don't advertise, and there's no social media. It's just good food, good people, and pancakes as good as those frites we had in Dallas."

My eyes nearly bulge out of my head. "You're lying. No food could be better than that."

"Wait till you try these pancakes—you'll regret that statement."

"I seriously doubt it."

"Jordy!" A sweet, older-looking woman with long gray hair pulled back in a bun comes over to our table and flips over the coffee mugs before filling each one. "Didn't think I'd be seeing you here for a while with the playoffs. Congrats on the win tonight!"

"Thanks, Beverly."

"And who is this lovely young lady with you?"

"This is Kennedy. My girlfriend"

A sweet grin crawls across Beverly's face as she winks at Jordan, then looks to me. "You snagged yourself a hell of a man there, Miss Kennedy. I wouldn't be here if it wasn't for Jordan Boucher."

I blink slowly at yet another person talking about how much he's helped them. One more piece to the puzzle of figuring him out. I got the corner piece at Walt's when he told me he owns Club 414. *Does Beverly have the piece that will help this whole thing fit together?* "What do you mean?" I ask, but before she can reply, Jordan abruptly shifts the conversation.

"I'm ready to order, Bev. I'll have the usual. Kennedy, do you know what you want?"

I glance between the two of them, wondering what the hell he doesn't want her to say. Also wondering if I can test my theory again about us being pretty in sync with food, and the fact that I kind of like him ordering for me. *Why is this a thing?* Never in my life have I wanted someone else to order for me. I close my menu, not having read a word. *Screw it.* I make enough damn decisions during the day—he can make this one.

"You know what? Bring me whatever he's having." My eyes catch his, my heart racing. "Let's see if you can go two for two."

His lips twitch. "You heard the lady, Beverly, bring it!"

"Alright, two Bougie specials coming right up!" Beverly whoops as she waltzes behind the counter to put in the order.

I clasp my hands around the warm cup of coffee in front of me, taking a delicate sip. I don't normally drink black coffee, but I feel like it's going to be the lifeline that gets me through whatever he's about to say. "So…we're here, and food is on the way…explain to me what the hell is going on before I freak the hell out again."

He slumps against his seat as he lets out a loud sigh, his gaze dropping to the table. "That text we got that first night with the photo of us at the hotel? That," —he pops his eyes back up to mine, his body curling in on itself— "that wasn't the first text."

I set my coffee down so hard it sloshes over the edge. "I'm sorry…what?"

"Yeah. I've been getting them for…a while. Long before that night at the hotel bar. Only, there was never a picture included until then. I didn't tell you because I didn't want to freak you out. I thought it was maybe a pissed-off fan or something. I realize now that was a mistake. I'm sorry," he trails off. "I told my security detail about it, and they've been extra vigilant about things, but the texts still come in fairly regularly. But that night…Hannah told me the photo had been leaked online and was going public, so I had to let you in on it. I didn't, *don't,* know what any of this is about. Please don't hate me."

I tap my nails along the side of the coffee mug in a rhythm I'm convincing myself will make this make sense. But it's not. My fingers still. The warm feeling in my chest from earlier shifts into a fire, and I'm scrambling to find the extinguisher.

"Let me get this straight. You were getting texts from this random psychopath before that night? And now they are texting *me*?!" I whisper-yell, painfully aware we are in public and desperate to not cause a scene. Granted, we are practically the only ones in here, but I don't want to upset poor sweet Beverly.

He nods, his eyes locked on the coffee in his cup, which he's doctored with cream and sugar. The cream dilutes the color, as it seems he's been diluting the truth of what's really going on here.

I take a deep breath, praying it will give me the will to hear him out. "Jordan. I'm trying *very* hard to stay calm. In fact, it's a good thing you suggested a public place because, while I'm ready to flip out and call the police, I'll start with a few questions."

He flinches. "Got it."

"First of all, what the hell does any of this have to do with *me*? Second, the text *I got* said 'my boyfriend doesn't like to listen.' All I've known about is *one* leaked picture of us. You said there was nothing else but a photo from a blocked number. Now you're telling me they sent you other messages. What have they said that you aren't listening to? What the fuck are they asking you to do?!" The words race out of my mouth in a rushed whisper.

He clears his throat as he runs his fingers through his hair. "The texts...they always tell me to stay away from you."

35
jordan

This is the part where I crawl under a rock and die. I want to run. I want to hide. The churning in my gut is not from the surprise biscuits and homemade jam Bev dropped off; she knows they are my favorite—it's the imminent dread of Kennedy's reaction. I shift in my seat. Things are escalating, and I need to let her in on what's going on. My knee bounces under the table. If this is the end of our fake relationship, and any hope for a real one, I guess it was good while it lasted.

She's still staring at me, her eyes filled with shock and disbelief. "To stay away from me? Like...Kennedy Kramer, me?"

I nod, watching the cream dancing in my cup. "Yeah."

"Why would someone want you to stay away from me? Wait... is this why you asked me if I had a boyfriend that night?"

"Yes." *Among other reasons.* "I thought." I scrub my hand down my face. "I thought someone was jealous seeing us together and was threatening me because of it."

"And you didn't think that would have been *helpful* information for me to have had?"

I'm starting to pick up the vibe that she's a smidge *angry.*

"I didn't..." I groan, my words getting caught in my throat. "I didn't mean to keep it from you. You had a stressful day, then we had the whole shenanigan with Chadd McScumbag. I thought it would freak you out even more."

"Well, I'm certainly freaked out now!" she shouts a little louder than either of us expects.

I wince, raising my hands in surrender to Beverly's concerned look from across the diner as I mouth *sorry*. She shakes her head and goes back to work, releasing me so I can turn my attention back to the most beautiful, angry woman I've ever seen, waiting for her to breathe fire from those gorgeous lips I can't stop thinking about and burn me alive. *That actually might be less painful at this point.*

"Maybe..." she speaks softly as she stares into her drink, her eyes not meeting mine. "Maybe we should just end this fake dating thing. Stage our breakup now, and this will all go away. Right?"

My heart stops, and it's a few moments before it finds its rhythm again. *She's right.*

"Yeah. If that's what you want, we could do that," I whisper. I've got to find a way to convince her this isn't the answer.

She nods, her gaze still locked on the steam rising from her mug. "It's probably for the best."

Call the coroner. My life is over.

Unless I can miraculously think of a way to keep her. *I can't lose this.* I tap my foot furiously on the floor like Elle Woods before the drinking fountain scene where the pool boy gets irritated for stomping her last season Prada shoes at him, and then she asks douchebag Warrner what brand her shoes are, and he doesn't know and...oh my God. That's it. The douchebag!

"But..." I singsong, "it still doesn't solve the other problem we have—Chadd McTwatWaffle. And despite him having a new girlfriend, who apparently has a fear of fluorescent lights, I think he'll continue to be an issue even if we break up."

I hold my breath as her eyes pop up to mine, an intrigued look in them I haven't seen before. "Yeah. Yeah, I guess you're right. That doesn't solve the Chadd issue."

"I say we just stick with the plan to at least keep that asshat away from you."

"Okay."

I exhale, the tension slightly melting now that she's not leaving. *Thank fucking God.*

"Okay." I nod. "And we're going to get you security until we find out who is doing this."

She glares at me. "Security? No. I don't think so. How about we just call the *police* like rational people?"

I scrunch my face. "I know this probably sounds like another rich people thing you won't like, but I know what is going to happen if we involve the police. We'll file a complaint that will sit on someone's desk for months, and nothing will happen. Then, if there's a snoopy person at the police station looking to score some extra cash, they'll leak the report to the media. I've been dealing with things like this my entire life, and my family realized it's better to control things ourselves as much as possible. And before you ask again, no, we are not Mafia, and we do not 'off' people."

She huffs a slight laugh, lifting some of the weight off my chest. "So…how many texts have you gotten from whoever this is?"

Dammit. I swallow the lump lodged in my throat. *Fuck.* I don't want to tell her this, but there's no more avoiding this. "Maybe once or twice a week."

"Every *week*?!" she whisper-yells, forcing a smile as she sees Beverly coming over with our order. Kennedy leans across the table. "Holy shit, Jordan. For how long? When did these start?"

"Here we go!" Beverly comes over with a tray full of plates, just in time to help me stall and think about how to tell Kennedy that I've been pining after her for months and that someone figured out I was sending her gifts and wanted me to stop. At least when Kennedy places me in her own personal death row, I'll go out with a great last meal.

"Thanks, Bev," I say, grateful for the welcome interruption.

"You two need anything else? Do I need to grab syrup for the lady?"

"Oh no. She's Team No Syrup."

She smiles with a wink. "Holler if you need anything and I'll be back with some coffee refills in a bit. Just gonna make a fresh pot."

I slowly turn toward Kennedy, who, shockingly, is not staring at me, but at the breakfast for dinner laid before us. "Good *God*, this looks and smells amazing. Are those hash browns with cheese and onions?"

I smile, knowing I picked correctly once more. "Yep. Do you like them that way?"

"Smothered and covered is the only way to eat them."

Be still, my heart. "Right?!"

She takes a bite of the delicious potatoes, and we, once again, bond over carbs. And dammit, I'm so here for it.

"Listen, I'm still mad...like, *really* mad, but...Grilled Cheesus, this is delicious. You weren't kidding about the food here."

"I take my cheat days seriously."

"These pancakes..." she groans, her eyes rolling into the back of her head, making my cock twitch, "I apologize. I stand corrected. These are the best things I've ever eaten."

I flash her a wicked smirk. "I'm glad you can finally admit I have a superior food palate."

She glares at me as she takes another bite of pancake—*yep, she's still pissed.* Her lips twist as she chews, and I can tell she's thinking hard as she devours the fluffy goodness. We sit quietly for a few moments, and I give her some time to process all of this. *God, I'm such an idiot.* My hands shake with every bite I take, wondering what she's thinking. She said she was mad. Is she like…*mad* mad? Or just…mildly irritated?

Fuck. If only I could see inside that beautiful head of hers. But I don't have to wait long to learn what she's mulling over, her voice breaking the rhythm of knives and forks as she asks another question.

"So, back to the texts." *Shit.* My mouth goes dry, and I take a sip of my coffee as she continues. "How long did you say you've been getting them?"

"I didn't," I say, quickly shoveling a giant bite of pancake in my mouth, savoring the glorious blueberry delicacy as I try to avoid her question at all costs.

Her glare tells me I'm not going to get away with this. *Dammit.*

"Jordan, if you don't want me to call the police right now, I'm going to need to know everything so we can figure this out."

"Every-hing?" I mumble, my mouth still full of delicious, golden-brown avoidance.

"Yes. Every detail. Every text. Everything that seems out of sorts. Every…" she trails off as her eyes widen with absolute panic. "Oh my God. Son of a bitch—I completely forgot."

"What?"

"When we were at the game, I got a message from the apartment complex that I had a package delivered. I've been getting random gifts lately. Apparently, there's another one there. They all come with a poem, too. That's creepy, right?" She wipes her lips with her napkin. "Do you think this could all be connected?"

I shoot up straight in the booth. *Ohhhh shit, double shit, triple shit* on a hockey stick. Pull yourself together, Boucher. "Oh no. For *sure*, no. I mean, probably, definitely not connected. I mean..." I clear my throat, "I wouldn't even say it's creepy *per se*. Maybe it's just... someone trying to do something nice?"

Her lips twist, my heartbeat thrumming in my ears. "Yeah. Maybe. I thought it was a secret admirer or something, but now that I know these people are threatening us, and apparently have my phone number..." She pushes her plate away, trapping her lip between her teeth. "Do they know where I live? Having another package delivered this same day has to be connected, right?"

My pulse skyrockets throughout my entire body. *I didn't send her anything.* I haven't since I talked to Vladi, and he said that was not the way to impress her. *Fuck.* "Beverly, can you grab our check?" I shout across the diner, and she nods, giving me a thumbs up and heading to the register. Then I look to Kennedy. I swallow hard, knowing *everything* is going to have to come out tonight. As much as I want to, I can't keep this in any longer. "We gotta go."

She freezes, coffee cup half raised. "Why? What's happening?"

"I'll explain on the way." She sets her mug down and grabs her purse.

"Beverly, never mind!" I shout, setting some cash on the table. "This should cover it. If not, I'll hit you next time I'm here."

"Jordan," Kennedy says, calming some of the anxiety humming through me, "you just put down two hundred dollars. I think that'll cover some pancakes."

"Oh. Yeah. Right. Okay." I reach for her hand before stopping myself. "Let's go."

"Good seeing you, Jordan! Kennedy, don't be a stranger!" Beverly waves as we race out the door. As we get into the car, I try to take in a deep breath to calm myself down for more reasons than I care to admit.

One, Kennedy could be in real trouble.

Two, I could be in real trouble with Kennedy.

Three, I'm going to have to tell her I was the one sending the gifts.

Four...all of the above, *and* we get murdered in the process.

God, please *let there be an option five.*

36
kennedy

I didn't know a Range Rover could go this fast, but apparently, all it needed was Jordan Boucher racing to my apartment like a maniac to make it go pretty damn quick. And my heart isn't far behind, feeling like it would register higher than the speedometer in the car. He hasn't really explained why we are flying through the streets of Milwaukee, outside of the fact he realized I was right and all of this could be connected. I still feel like I don't have the full picture, but I'm too consumed with thoughts of exactly what is at my place to think coherently.

He parks in a spot that *definitely* isn't mine, and we run into the lobby like we're on the Amazing Race, trying to get to the next clue. Heart in my throat, I beeline for Sean, our concierge, waiting patiently, and without judgment, at the desk. "Hey, Sean," I gasp, "I got a message that I had a package today?"

"Oh yes, Ms. Kramer, we placed it in your apartment per your request. Is everything okay?"

Shit. "Yeah, it's fine. That's exactly what I asked for with the delivery. Sorry for the panic. Thanks."

I look to Jordan, forcing a brittle smile, still not quite understanding why he's here, what else he's being tight-lipped about, *or what the hell is going on.*

"Let's go," he says, grabbing my hand and leading me toward the elevator.

"Jordan." I drag my heels. "You don't have to come with me. I'm sure it's nothing."

"No way. No fucking way. We're going together to see what this is," he says, squeezing my hand.

I twist my lips as I consider arguing with him, but from the way he's holding my hand, and the long-ass day we've had, I don't want to be alone tonight.

"Okay," I whisper, allowing myself to follow his lead. "Let's go."

Taking the elevator up to the 10th floor is the longest damn elevator ride of my entire life, but when it finally dings, we speed-walk down the hallway, and I tap the key fob against my door. Red light.

"Shit! I hate this damn door. This freakin' key has to hit just the right spot."

Jordan snorts. "You do live here, right?"

I give him a wicked side eye. "Yes, I live here. But this stupid door is impossible."

"Here," he says, holding out his hand. "Let me try. I have a knack for hitting things in just the right spot."

A shiver runs up my spine thinking about what other spots he may be able to hit. I still feel like he's keeping something from me, but my body responds anyway—that damn undeniable heat pooling low in my core. *Shit...I need to stop reading romance books with morally gray men.*

I hand it over and, sure enough, he unlocks it in one try.

"How...how did you do that?"

He shrugs as he hands back the key. "I watered Maggie's plants when she and Vladi were out of town and got the hang of it. I also may have, you know, accidentally killed one of her plants, and she absolutely threatened bodily harm if it happened again."

I snicker, breaking the tension as the door clicks open. But now...I pick at my nails, almost scared to enter. Jordan slowly pushes open the door, and we both inch inside as if a creepy clown is going to pop out of a closet.

"Anyone there?" he yells, glancing around the dark space, then whispers, "Stay here; let me walk around and make sure no one snuck in."

"Jordan, this building is secure; there's no way someone walked in here without security knowing."

"Will you just let me check? Please?"

I let out a defeated sigh, a part of me glad he's here with me and I'm not alone. "Fine. I'll stay here."

What happens next can only be described as Jordan Boucher acting like he's an undercover agent for the FBI. Shuffling down the hallway with his back against the wall, he darts around corners, holding his hands in the shape of a gun like he's one of Charlie's Angels. I stifle a laugh at the ridiculous manner in which he's ensuring the safety of my apartment.

"Are you seriously laughing?!" he whisper-yells down the hallway. "Someone could be trying to murder me right now!"

"How did this escalate to murder?" I retort as he tiptoes down the hall, shaking my head in disbelief. As I step into the kitchen, my eyes catch on a little plush teddy bear sitting on the counter with a balloon attached. The tension flickers away, and I suddenly feel ridiculous for racing to get here. "Jordan...oh my God, Jordan, stop. Come look at this. I think we may have overreacted."

He walks back into the kitchen and stands next to me, placing his hand around my waist. Standing this close, his scent floods my senses. He smells like juniper, and citrus, and—fuck, he's like a walking gin and tonic, and my mouth is salivating for him more than the drink. Not to mention my thighs clenching together at how he's being ridiculously protective. *Why is this so intoxicating?*

"The coast is clear," he pants as if he's just run a marathon.

"Thank *God* you were here," I tease as he rolls his eyes at me. He actually rolls his eyes at *me*. It's so immature, so ridiculous, and somehow, it's...charming.

"Look..." —I gesture to the stuffed animal on my counter— "...someone sent me this cute guy and a balloon. I think we let our imagination get the best of us. It's probably from my mom."

He leans over my shoulder, a smile relaxing his face. "Oh, look! It's one of those bears that talks. Push the paw and see what it says."

I'm expecting the bear to say something cute like, 'you're amazing' or 'world's best daughter' or 'I miss you beary much.'

Not. Even. Close.

Chills crawl down my spine as deranged circus music crackles through the speaker, every distorted note twisting through the air. I freeze, ridiculously waiting for a car full of clowns to drive through my apartment, forcing me to rock back on my heels. Then the bear blinks. It fucking *blinks*. I sneak a glance at Jordan, his eyes matching my horrified state. His fingers tighten around my waist as a deep voice curls around us.

"Roses are red, violets are blue, stay away from Boucher, or I'll come for you."

As if that wasn't already scary as hell, the arms start swinging up and down, and we both scream like little girls.

I grab the bear, balloon in tow, and slam it on the floor, violently stomping it to death and popping the balloon with my shoe as Jordan screams louder, covering his eyes. I grab a pan out of the cabinet and continue smashing the shit out of the stuffed animal from hell until the music crawls to a stop.

"Is it...is it dead?" he squeaks, his hand on my shoulder, peering around to see if the bear was silenced.

"Yeah." I let out a relieved sigh before whirling around and pointing the pan at the scaredy cat in question. "Jordan, what the fuck was that? Why is someone telling me to stay away from you?"

"First of all, can we *please* get rid of the deranged Build-A-Bear? It's looking at me."

I blink. "Are you seriously scared of a stuffed bear?"

"Well, *that one* for sure!" He tiptoes forward, leaning for a closer look before shivering and scurrying back to the safety that's, apparently, behind me. "My sisters had one of those talking bears with the cassette tape that read you stories, and they used to scare the shit out of me with it. I was convinced it was going to come to life and eat me in my sleep! You would have thought having older sisters would be a lot of hair and make-up experiments, and while it was some of that, my sisters loved torturing me with stories about dolls killing me in my sleep. So, *excuse me* if I don't want that damn bear staring at me while we talk."

I smirk. This man tried to protect me from a murderer, but he is also scared of a talking bear. It's surprisingly adorable. "If I put it in the trash, will that make you feel better?"

"Yes! Please. Thank you." He sighs, his facial expression relaxing.

I set the pan down in exchange for a pair of kitchen tongs, not wanting to touch this damn thing either, and throw it in the trash can. Just as I'm ready to grill him about what the hell is going on, my eye catches a glimmer across the room like a shooting star in the night sky. My breath catches in my chest as I remember that half the things in my apartment could be from this person. A pit forms in my stomach. "Oh my God. The other gifts…are they from this creep too?"

He pipes up quickly. "I think the word *creep* may be a bit harsh."

"Jordan!" I spit out, digging through the junk drawers in my kitchen. "You just hid in a corner from a stuffed animal. I think creep is a fitting description for the person sending me this stuff!" I move to the next drawer. "I know I have a hammer here somewhere," I mutter to myself.

"Did you say a hammer?"

I dart my gaze to him, his eyes wide with fear. *I guess I was louder than I thought.*

"Yes." I continue rummaging through the drawers of random crap, desperate to find it. One would think someone with a job requiring my level of precision and focus would be completely organized at home. Not me. I don't get paid to be organized here.

"Um…what do you need it for?" Jordan asks, his voice shaky.

"Ah ha! Here it is," I shout in triumph, walking over to the stupidly giant diamond-encrusted leopard.

"Kennedy? What are you…oh shit! What are you doing?"

"I need to crack open this leopard to see if there's something fucked up inside. I've been *dying* for an excuse to break this thing." I raise the hammer over my head, my tongue sticking out of the corner of my mouth, aiming right for the head of th—

"STOP! Don't hurt Neil!" he shouts.

I freeze mid-swing, my gaze snapping to him. "Who the fuck is Neil?"

"Neil. Neil Diamond." He gestures toward the monstrosity before me. "The leopard."

I shake my head as I blink. *What the fuck is happening here?* "His name is Neil?!"

Jordan rubs the back of his neck. "My parents are big Neil Diamond fans, okay? I know every song by heart."

"Okay...I'm not surprised by that. What I am surprised about is how the hell you know this leopard's name," I say, my brows narrowing, my mouth hanging open in shock.

"The leopard wasn't from them. It was um...from..."

"Who was it from, Jordan?"

His eyes lock with mine. He runs his hand through the long waves of brown hair before finally whispering, "Me."

37
jordan

It's finally here. The moment my life ends. My stomach twists. *Kennedy Kramer knows I've been sending her gifts.* She's staring at me with a hammer, still held over her head, ready to strike. Except now her eyes are dead on me.

"*You?* You sent this to me?" she says, slowly lowering the hammer to hold in front of her chest.

"Not the bear! Just Neil." He glances around the room. "And the espresso maker. And the guitar. And some roses. And a few other things here and there…"

She tilts her head, tapping the weapon into the palm of her hand. "All of this was you? Even the poems?"

I drop my eyes to the floor, unable to hold her gaze to say one simple word. "Yes."

"Jordan," she says, her voice eerily calm. I can't look up. I can't face her disappointment. *I just got her…I'm not ready to lose her.* Her heels tap the floor, then another. "Look at me."

I force my eyes up to see her still holding the hammer in her hands. Is she going to crack my skull open? Is this it? *Fuck.* At least I'll go at the hands of the most beautiful woman to ever exist.

"Every one of these gifts came with a poem. The *same* poem. 'I see you in my dreams, in every sunlit sky; I see you in the morning when you barely pass me by. Like waves drawn to the shores, you've pulled me in with force. I'll long for you until'..." her voice trails off as if she's afraid to say the last line.

"I'll long for you until the day when I am finally yours," I finish it for her.

She drops her arm holding the hammer down to her side, a slight wave of relief washing over me. Not completely, because she's still holding the damn thing, not that I think she would hurt me, but I *did* just admit to being her secret admirer. *And* we're both getting texts from a random stalker guy.

I really fucked up.

She takes a deep breath, holding it in as if it will make this whole situation disappear. *If only.*

"Jordan..." she says, her voice still steady and composed. "I'm going to need you to explain."

I let out the breath I have been holding. *She's going to let me explain.* She's not immediately kicking me out. My heart does a dance of relief, but quickly pauses. *Is this just the calm before the storm? Fuck.* My guts churn; we are already in the eye of the hurricane. The only way through this is to let the rest of the storm pass. "I promise I'll explain and I'll tell you anything and everything. But...could you just do me one quick favor?"

Her eyes narrow. "What in the world do you need me to do?"

"Maybe could you just like...put the hammer down? I'm still creeped out by demonic Paddington, and you holding a hammer while I'm confessing my sins isn't helping."

She shakes her head, huffing out a defeated laugh as she sets it down on the coffee table before flopping down on the couch. I sit down as well, but all the way on the other end. *That hammer is still a little too close for comfort.*

I swallow the lump in my throat, preparing to say what I have wanted, but also not wanted, to admit for so long. "When I started sending you gifts, I honestly had no plan of how I was going to tell you it was me. But never in a million years did I imagine it going like this."

Her nose curls as she catches a glimpse of Neil. "Why were you sending me all this stuff?"

"Because..." I run my hand through my hair, hoping there is something magical in the product I used that will give me the strength to spit this out. "Because I like you. The first time I saw you, you were the most beautiful woman I'd ever seen. The way your eyes sparkled all the way down the aisle. Your sexy as hell uniform." A groan slips out before I can stop it. "Goddammit, Kennedy, you wear the hell out of that scarf." Her scowl cracks as the corners of her lips tip up. *If a half-smile through her anger is all I'm getting...I'll take it.*

"Every trip, I watched you smile and say goodbye to everyone as they stepped off the plane. You seemed so kind, goodhearted, and like you really cared about getting us all from place to place and being a part of the team. But..." my voice trails off, wondering if I should even continue. But I owe her the truth. *It's the least I can do now.* "You treated everyone like that...except for me."

A flicker of surprise crosses her face, her gaze dropping to the floor. "Jordan...I—"

"Kennedy, it's...this is all on me. Let me get this all out before we get into anything else. Please?" She nods, her eyes focused on the couch cushion. "All I wanted was to talk to you. To get to know you. But every time I walked by, you seemed put off. I thought, maybe, if I sent you some gifts, you'd realize I liked you and, maybe, I'd get the courage to...I don't know...ask you out sometime." I rub the back of my neck. "I was so scared you'd say no. And, somewhere deep inside, I decided silence would hurt less than rejection. Call me crazy, but there's just something about you. I felt it the minute I saw you, like some sort of magnet was pulling me toward my other half. I don't have much experience with relationships, but I know my heart. It lost its will to find love a while back. It hasn't wanted to beat for anyone. Ever. Until you."

Her lips tighten, her cheeks flush. Is she embarrassed I'm telling her this? Is she going to turn me down? *Focus, Jordan. You have to get this off your chest.*

"I was…I was hurt before by someone I dated. Hurt is actually an understatement. I trusted someone who only wanted me for my money. But the fact that you wanted nothing to do with me? I felt like you didn't give a shit about my money."

"You picked up on that, huh?"

I nod. "All my life, I've been around women. My sisters, my cousins, all my friends. I'm comfortable around women I'm friends with. I know how to do that. But…" I pause, twisting my hands around the fringe on a nearby throw pillow, needing a moment to pull my thoughts together. "The real me, the one behind the public persona, is…not great around women I want to be *more* than friends with. As you can clearly tell by the predicament we're in."

She offers me a weak smile, giving me a moment to recenter.

"Then I started getting the texts telling me to stay away from you. I am so secretive about so much of my life, I don't know how anyone could have figured that out. I never thought it had anything to do with you, just some crazed fan or something. As the texts got more frequent, I started to worry maybe you were being watched too." Her face goes pale as she stiffens in her seat. "And then I was going to tell you, but after the whole incident with Chadd and you suggesting we fake date, I thought it was a great way to get to know you better and actually be around to keep you safe." I gasp for breath. "Wow, this sounds bad. I sound ridiculous."

She sits on the couch, staring at the TV despite the screen being black as night. Probably because my life is basically a train wreck of a reality show, and she's trying to figure out how the hell she ended up with a starring role.

God, I fucked this up so bad. Another knot forms in my stomach, this one twisting my insides like a towel being rung out in the sink. She's not saying anything. She's not looking at me. She's essentially in a catatonic state. And *I* put her in it. *Fuck.*

"I'm so sorry, Kennedy. I never meant for this to get so out of hand. I didn't mean to keep all this from you. I'll just…I'll go," I say as I stand up and walk toward the door. The doorknob is cold in my palm as the heaviness in the air presses down on me.

"What are you sorry for?"

I freeze, glancing over my shoulder. She's still staring straight ahead, not moving a muscle. If she'd spoken any quieter, I would've thought I imagined it. Her words hit me in the chest like a slapshot I didn't see coming, my heart pounding so loudly I hear it in my ears.

"What?" I turn around, my head refusing to believe what my heart is hoping for.

She stands and walks toward me. Every step is a choice. Every inch closer, making my heart explode in my chest. *What is she doing?*

"I said…what are you sorry for? Are you sorry for being attracted to me?"

I swallow hard. "I…umm…yes? Or…no? I…I don't know what you want me to say." I point behind me. "Do you want me to leave?"

She takes another step. "If I want you to leave, I'll ask you to leave. What I truly *want* is for you to give me some answers. I knew there was something more to you, but I couldn't put my finger on it. So, I'm going to ask you some very simple questions, and you're going to answer me," she says with a firmness that makes my knees weak as she takes yet another step. "Do you understand?"

"Yes," I whisper, my voice cracking in fear and excitement.

"Did you send me all these gifts to try and impress me?"

"Yes."

"Did you do something to help Beverly with that restaurant?"

"Yes. I..." *God, she's going to hate me for this.* "Her husband passed away and left her in a lot of debt with the diner, so...I paid it off." I wince, convinced she's going to kick me out. But she doesn't. She looks almost...grateful as she continues her line of interrogation.

"Were you the one bringing me a coffee that suddenly switched to almond milk recently?"

"Shit," I say, realizing she has me figured out. "Yes."

Her eyes ice over. "Did you have anything to do with that first photo to try to trick me into fake dating you?"

"No! Kennedy, I swear to all things hockey, I would never do that."

"Good." She smirks, taking another step and stopping inches from my face, her intoxicating vanilla smell surrounding me. I suck in a sharp breath. Her scent fills this entire apartment, but now that she's standing so close, my chest tightens, and everything fades away.

"Are you attracted to me?"

I look at the floor, but she grabs my chin, tipping it toward her gaze. "Eyes on me, pretty-boy. Answer my question." She leans in closer as I stare deep into her gaze. "Are. You. Attracted. To. Me?"

"Yes." The word barely escapes as a whisper.

"Did you enjoy our kiss?"

"Yes."

"Do you want me to kiss you again?"

I don't know if my answer will be right or wrong, but there's no hesitation in my response. "Yes."

And just like that night we got ourselves into this mess, she shoves me against the wall, pinning me in place with nothing more than her palm. Only this time, the fire in her eyes has morphed from one that wants to destroy me to one that wants to consume me. My pants feel tight as hell as she utters one final word, 'Good,' before she slams her lips to mine.

My hands instinctively wrap around her waist, pulling her tight. Feeling her body against mine is everything I've ever wanted. She opens her mouth, and our tongues collide, feverish and passionate and so much more explosive than Dallas. I have never been more turned on in my life. *If she leans into me any more, she'll feel just how into her I am.* She runs her hands through my hair, her nails scraping my scalp. *It's hypnotic.* Kennedy Kramer has me in a trance I don't ever want to end. She's kissing me. Here. Alone. No cameras, no media. Just us. She runs her hands down my back, dragging her nails around to my abdomen, my hips jerking at the fire she leaves behind. She reaches for my belt, pulling my tight-ass pants toward her. *Goddammit, I want this.* Want her. But fear of the past rears its ugly head. I gently grab her wrist, stopping her from going any further.

"Kennedy. I...it's...it's been a while."

She steps back. "Does it look like I care?"

I huff out a laugh. "No. But...my life is really...complicated."

"I think we've already passed complicated. Is there more you're keeping from me, pretty-boy?"

I flinch. "Kinda, yeah."

She breaks the connection, her curious eyes not leaving mine. "Then stay here tonight and let's get it all out in the open."

"What? You wa...want me to stay? Here?"

She turns to walk into the kitchen as a soft laugh escapes. "To be honest, part of me really wants to be pissed at you for not letting me in on all this sooner. My brain is telling me to kick you out and find a way to call off this whole fake dating thing right now. But another part is telling me to hear you out. Besides, after a creepy stuffed bear, the photos, and everything else, I really don't want to be here by myself." She grabs a glass and some ice from the freezer. "And...I'm honestly interested in getting to know the real Jordan Boucher. Not the one in the press. Not the hockey player. I want to get to know the guy who helped my best friend start her own business. The one who has Beverly at the diner wrapped around his finger. The one who made me laugh uncontrollably tonight. Because, despite my better judgment, I'm attracted to him too."

38
kennedy

Sitting in my T-shirt and sleep shorts on the couch, Jordan walks back in after grabbing his phone charger and his toiletry bag out of his car to stay the night. I am still unclear what is happening to my body here. Part of me feels like I should be... pissed? More upset? Angry? But the part of me that starts to see behind the cracks of the facade he wears every day is strangely drawn to him. He mentioned magnets, and dammit if that didn't send goosebumps running across my skin. God, I sound like a teenager having a goddamn boy over when my parents are gone for the weekend. *Goddammit, Kennedy, control your ovaries.*

This could never work. I'm in my freaking thirties, and he's in his twenties. *Early* twenties. *What the hell am I thinking?!* I need to stop this before things get more complicated. But as he shuts the door behind him, his eyes run up and down my body, leaving behind the fucking goosebumps again. He sets his bag down by the front door and slips his shoes off, never taking his gaze off mine. My thighs clench together, once again at war with every rational thought. Christ on a cracker, this man is hot. *Well, there goes the stopping this right now part.*

He sits on the couch ridiculously far away from me. *Again.* How is this guy, who is a total playboy in the news, a truly respectful gentleman in my apartment? This is not what I was expecting. He was the one who stopped our kiss. He was the one who pulled back. I pick at my cuticles—this entire situation is making me need a manicure. I'm not used to this. Most guys are more pushy. Is he…is he scared of me? Does he not like to take the lead? I guess I *have* initiated both of our kisses. Not that I'm mad about it. I'm used to being in control and, to be honest, it turns me on, especially with him.

"Are you scared to sit close to me? You know I don't bite."

"You have attacked me with your mouth twice now."

I smirk. "Are you complaining?"

"No," he says with a wicked smile. "Just…stating a fact. I thought you wanted to talk and get everything out in the open; if I sit closer to you, I'm afraid I'll be too much for you to resist."

I let out a loud laugh. "There's the extremely humble Jordan Boucher I see around everyone else. Glad he showed up tonight."

His cheeks flush as he shifts on the couch. "Happy to oblige."

"Do you want something to drink?" I ask as I swirl my heavy pour of gin.

He sucks his teeth. "I could probably use a drink for this."

"You got it. I have…gin, gin, oh, and some gin," I say as I get up to make him a drink.

"No…you stay there. Relax," he motions to me to sit back down. "I know how to make a drink. Especially with your many options."

I don't stifle the smile creeping up my face as I hold my hand up in surrender. He quickly sees the bottle of gin I have on the counter and finds the tonic water in the fridge.

"Glasses?"

"Cabinet to your right," I say, gesturing with my head toward the correct door.

He makes his drink and returns to the couch, sitting a little closer to me than before. I'm not mad about it, but there's something in his eyes as he knocks back half the drink that dampens the thrill running through me. His hand shakes just a hint as he sets his glass down and leans back in his seat.

"So…tell me what I need to know about you," I say once he finally gets settled.

"I need you to promise me, swear on your life, that this does not leave the room," he mumbles, a shakiness to his voice.

"I would hope you've realized I'm not that kind of person. We have enough dirt on each other that we could get the other one canceled in a heartbeat. Even if I wanted to, I couldn't. This is just between you and me. I swear."

"Okay. Yeah. It's just…this is…God, it's fucking embarrassing."

I scoot next to him, my legs curled at my side as I tuck my feet under the throw pillows, settling in. A dull ache weighs heavily in my chest, my actions twisting tightly inside me. I bite my lip, realizing I owe him an olive branch before he spills the rest of his story.

"Listen, I know I can be kind of a bitch sometimes. Okay, most of the time."

"Kennedy, you're not a—"

"Yes. I am. Before you share whatever it is you need to get out, I want to apologize. I had a lot of preconceived notions about you. I thought you were selfish and conceited, and…I don't say this often, but I was wrong." I grab his hand, pulling it into my lap, the roughness surprisingly soothing as I choke out my words. "I was a bitch for ignoring you before. And I'm sorry about earlier. I insulted you about your money and your car, and that was wrong."

His brows narrow; it's as if someone's never apologized to him before. Yet another surprising reaction from this man.

"Thank you. I know my family has money, but it really is such a small part of my life." A warm smile spreads across his face. "You'd probably be surprised if you met them in person. We're not like some of the rich families you see on TV. Everyone has a job. Everyone works hard. My dad, especially, made sure we all had a path to independence. He always said, 'We have money now, but you never know what can happen'." He chuckles. "When I would complain about people on the ice chirping about my family's money, he would always tell me the best way to prove them wrong was to work your ass off and show up every day."

My smile matches his. "Your dad sounds cool."

"He is. Joseph and Maria Boucher are pretty badass parents, if I do say so myself. But seriously, thank you for the apology."

"Can I still call you Richy Rich?"

He smirks. "Yeah. I'll let that one slide."

"Good. Now that we've cleared the air, I'm ready for story time. Tell me why you pulled away from our kiss."

39
jordan

Holy. Shit. She apologized. She wants to get to know me. *Me.* My heart does a cautiously optimistic flip in my chest. She wants to kiss *me—more* than kiss me, actually. *Wait…is this some sort of weird dream?* Did that bear have some sort of hallucinogen in it? Or is this because I chugged her gin? I would have to be flat out drunk for her to be asking to get to know me more. Right? I rub my hand across the stubble on my chin. I can still feel my face, so I'm not drunk. *This is real.* I take a deep breath, trying and failing to calm my pounding heart before I lay all my cards on the table.

It's now or never.

"When I was eighteen, I met this girl, Angelica, at a party after a game. She was pretty and showered me with a lot of attention. I'd never had a girlfriend before—I honestly never had time—but we hit it off and started dating. After a month or so, our fooling around was really heating up, and she started pressuring me to sleep with her. I know, I know. What guy wouldn't want a girl throwing herself at him, right? Fuck." I rub my forehead with my hand. "God, this is so cheesy—I can't believe I'm even talking about this."

"Jordan," she says, giving my hand, still resting in her lap, a squeeze. The small gesture steadies me, my chest lifting enough to keep me going. "Listen, we all had a first time, and almost all of them are awkward in some way. Mine was in the back of a pickup truck after a football game. Let me tell you, leather seats in August are not sexy. Seriously…it's nothing to be embarrassed about. Go on."

Okay, now I'm trying not picture her with another guy in a pickup truck. *Focus, Jordan.*

"I just always dreamed of it being special, you know? I wanted to have a deep, meaningful relationship with a girl I was madly in love with, woo her, then have a super romantic night where we did it for the first time with candles and rose petals. You know…" —I shrug— "the works. Blame all the chick flicks my sisters made me watch, but that's just how I'd always imagined things. But Angelica just kept pushing. One night, she begged me, told me she loved me. I convinced myself that it was romantic enough. I told her I loved her, too, and I decided to just give in and go for it. She knew…" —I rub my hands across my pants— "she knew I was still a virgin. It wasn't because I was saving myself or anything, I just am very…I don't know…picky, maybe? But she said she was a virgin too, so I figured at least we'd have this. To be each other's firsts. So…we had sex."

I run my fingers through my hair, feeling the strands sticking up at odd angles, my ears ringing as I find myself back in that damn room at eight-fucking-teen.

"What I didn't know was that she'd been lying to me the entire time. She just wanted me for my money. Nothing more. She…she videotaped us. We were at her apartment, and I didn't know she had a hidden camera in the room. There was no audio, but it was damning. Then she leaked it to the press. After it was out, I confronted her, embarrassed and ashamed, my first time was plastered all over the internet. She didn't care. Added insult? Turns out she wasn't a virgin either."

Her jaw tightens as she places her other hand on top of mine. The anger brewing in her gaze at everything I'm telling her reminds me of Vladi. *Is she a touch him and die type of woman?* Holy shit. *She is.*

"My whole world came crashing down in a matter of hours. She said she had interviews lined up and that she was going to tell them it was my first time, that she faked everything, and that I was a horrible lay that didn't know what I was doing, and...*fuck*..." My eyes burn, but I *refuse* to shed any more tears over this. "It was so bad. I felt so betrayed. Looking back, I should have picked up on so many little things about how everything was always about her. How dismissive she was to me at times, like not letting me eat at my favorite poutine place. Even her brown eyes always seemed cold. I was a complete fucking idiot. I immediately called my dad to tell him I fucked up, which meant we had to react quickly."

She squeezes my hand again, an empathetic smile on her face as tears shine in her eyes. "Jordan. I...I can't even imagine what that must have been like. The fact that someone did this to you? *God*, I wish I could punch her in the throat!"

"I like to imagine I'm poking her eyes out with little kabob skewers."

We both snort, a welcome relief from the heaviness in the air. "I...I wish I had words to say other than I'm so sorry that happened to you. That is not what anyone's first time should be like."

My knuckles go white, holding onto her hand like a lifeline I've never had before. One I didn't realize I desperately needed.

"We hired the PR company Hannah had just joined and came up with a plan. The video was already out—there was nothing we could do about that—but we could pay Angelica a ridiculous amount of money for her silence. A sex video online created a playboy image, so we made it seem like I did this all the time and that someone just happened to film me and leak it to the media." My laugh is jaded, years of masks and press forcing me deeper into the cushions. "It's not that I'm embarrassed to express my emotions. But…being an enforcer, I had a reputation I felt like I needed to keep up. Be the big tough guy everyone was afraid of. The draft was a couple months away, and a long, drawn-out trial would been a terrible look for me, my family, and exposed us to way more than a celebrity sex tape. Shit, we've all seen those. Luckily, the playboy persona played right into the image I was trying to project. And the PR team thought this was the best thing for my career, so we just…leaned into it."

"You keep saying they thought this was the best thing. Did you think it was the right decision?"

My heart flutters. No one has ever asked me if I thought this was the right thing to do. No one has ever asked me how I felt. *How can someone who has just seen through the cracks in my mask see what I've been hiding for so long more clearly than anyone else?*

"No. I wanted to tell everyone she was lying. To make a statement. But I was barely out of high school; I didn't know what the fuck was the right thing to do. And, right or wrong, I made the decision to go with it. I *did* have a choice. Was it the right one?" I shrug. "I'm not sure. I'm not sure I'll ever really know."

Talking about all this has the anger that's been slowly burning deep inside reigniting like a fire with a fresh log thrown on top. I grit my teeth. The flames that were almost out are now at full height and eager to burn the world down. But a soothing motion running across my hand sends a calming chill through me as Kennedy rubs her thumb along mine.

"Did you love her?"

"No." I shake my head with a huff, shifting my gaze to our hands. "I only said it because I felt like I had to say it back. I honestly didn't even know what I was doing, but I knew somewhere deep down I didn't love her." I lift my eyes to meet hers. "She wasn't the one."

It's almost ironic that the person I am falling in love with is the one comforting me while I relive this horrible, life-altering event. One I never wanted to share with her. Yet somehow, she's making it not as bad as I thought it would be. Something about the way she's looking at me, not with pity or disgust, but with compassion and understanding, lets me take my first deep breath since sitting on the couch. I want to be in her arms. I want to feel every bit of her body pressed against mine right now. Even the gentle touch of her hand on mine gives me the strength to get the rest of this sham that's been my life out.

"All of those girls I've been photographed with, the ones you see on my arm in the press? I've never slept with them. They were all staged photos. Some were friends of my family, acquaintances we knew we could trust to keep quiet. Every single one fully vetted with a signed NDA. Hell, even Hannah would pose with me sometimes. She has quite the extensive wig collection, believe it or not."

Kennedy's brows narrow, her head tilting to the side. "You've never been with any of those women? Not even one?"

"Nope." I shake my head. "Unfortunately, the only person I *have* slept with is mother-fucking Angelica. I didn't even want to do it. I just felt so pressured. And I was a complete fool for not seeing that she was only into my money. And then, for the grand finale cherry on top of it all, I find out I'm horrible in bed."

"Jordan." The quiet reassurance in her voice dulls the rage bubbling under my skin. I wish I were in the middle of a game and could punch someone. But sitting here with her? She feels like the cool air that hits the minute you skate onto the rink—burning my lungs in the best way possible. "You couldn't have—"

"Kennedy, don't. I know what you're going to say. I've heard it from my family a million times."

Her eyes widen as a snarky expression crosses her face. "You're a mind reader now? You know exactly what I'm going to say?"

"I've heard it all before," I say in an irritated singsong voice. "I wasn't a fool. I couldn't have known. It'll all be okay…same shit, different day."

"Hmm," she says, her eyes piercing directly into mine. "That's not at all what I was going to say."

I look at her, confused. *Maybe I mistook her compassion for hatred?* She does seem like she hates me most of the time.

"It wasn't?"

"No," she says softly. "Jordan, how do you know?"

I crinkle my face once more. "How do I know what?"

"How do you know you're horrible in bed?"

My pulse thrums in my ears. Her hand, still resting on my thigh, grounds me as the room feels suddenly void of every bit of air I'm trying to breathe in. "Well…I'm…" I clear my throat, "I'm an athlete. We perform. We're told if we're good or bad or what to improve on. We don't question it. We work hard and train harder to get better, stronger, faster. I guess I figured if she said I was bad, she was right. Add to the fact that it was my first time…what else am I supposed to think?" I shrug, pursing my lips together.

"What if she was wrong?" Her gaze shifts, as if she's speaking to something inside of me and not the external persona she's seen. "I can't imagine someone like you, who puts their all into every aspect of their life, being bad at anything."

My heart skips a beat—a beat that makes me question everything I've ever thought about myself. "I…I don't know. I guess I never thought about it."

"Did *you* think it was bad? Did it feel good to you at all?"

Is this woman a pilot or a therapist? My stomach is twisted into a thousand knots, but...goddammit, she's asking me every question I've been too afraid to ask myself. "I mean, obviously it felt *good*, but it...it didn't feel right. I don't know; that probably doesn't make any sense."

"It does." Her reassurance, once again, was a welcome surprise during this weird-ass conversation. "Sex is a release; it's meant to feel good. But I think when there's an emotional connection, it can be so much more."

Heat creeps up my neck. My dick is having a really hard time controlling himself right now, between talking about sex and her fucking hand rubbing circles on my thigh. I don't want her to stop. I want her—*badly*. But I'm scared to let myself go there. Not until I know she's one hundred percent in this for me. Not for fake dating. Not for a release. Not for one night. *I want this to be real.* Tonight gives me hope—but not certainty.

She yawns and, like clockwork, one slips from me, the chaos of the day finally wearing us down. I look at my phone and see it's two in the morning. *Fuck.* And seeing the date, I realize I have a commitment tomorrow...er...today actually. *Double fuck.* This is one thing I can't half-ass either. *Maybe this is a way to keep showing her the real me.*

"It's been a long day. I think we both could use some rest. I'm actually meeting up with a friend later and can't cancel, so I should probably sleep."

"Oh. Okay." Her lips purse as she reluctantly nods, her eyes dropping to the floor.

Is she disappointed I have plans, or that we have to stop talking? My fingers twist in my lap, guilt setting in either way. *Hopefully, my idea will make it up to her.*

"I was actually wondering if...if you'd like to join me? I'd love for you to meet them, and it might be a nice way to get our minds off all this."

She flashes a tired smile, a flicker of something I'm too scared to believe in her gaze. "I'd like that. You sure I'm not imposing?"

"Promise. I'll need to run home in the morning to change clothes, but I'll be back here around ten to pick you up, if that works."

"Just one question," she asks, playfully drawing out the words. "What do I wear for this mystery date?"

My eyes widen. "I never said it was a date."

"What if I want it to be?"

My lips curl, my dick fighting not to follow at the thought of taking her out sometime. "I'll take you on a real date. And not some stuffy restaurant where they fill the water after you take one sip. It'll be the most perfect date you've ever been on."

"That's quite the declaration there, Richy Rich." She snorts.

I wink as I stand, offering her my hand to pull her up beside me. "Go get some rest. I'll see you in the morning."

Kennedy tilts her head. "Jordan, I have a giant king-sized bed. Why don't you just sleep in there with me?"

"Just need a pillow, and I see a blanket right there. I'm all set," I say, still holding her hand in mine. "But, how about a goodnight kiss?"

She smiles and steps closer, but doesn't fully close the distance between us. And for the first time since I've met Kennedy Kramer, I feel brave enough to step forward, cupping her cheek and leaning down to kiss the most gorgeous woman I've ever met. She loops her arms around my neck, pulling me in closer, deepening not only the kiss, but this connection. She presses flush against me, and I feel her body rubbing against my erection through my pants. We both moan at the thought of where this could go. But my mind gets the better of me again, and I take a step back. Her lips are flushed and swollen. My hands flinch around her waist using every inch of my willpower to not pull her in for more. But when I'm with someone again, I want it to be forever.

I'm just not sure we're there yet.

"Are you sure you won't join me in bed?" she says with a wry smile.

"I would, but I don't think you could resist me. Goodnight, Kennedy."

40

kennedy

Thank God I don't have work today because I got zero point zero hours of sleep last night. Lying in bed, I roll over to avoid the beam of sunlight sneaking in through my shades. My exhaustion does nothing to calm the heat still swirling through my body as I remember his mouth on mine, his hands curled around me, the feeling of him pulling me in and holding me like he never wanted to let go.

Trying to sleep last night was like all those nights in the hotels, knowing he was just on the other side of my door. *Except he was in my freaking apartment—my home.* Which, for some reason, is even hotter. I flail on the bed like a starfish, my emotions all over the place with everything going on. My body is feral for this man.

Gin and sex are my go-to stress relievers, but since my liquor cabinet and the person I want to have sex with were both in the main living area of my apartment, I *may* have silently relieved some of that last night when I couldn't fall asleep. I *hope* it was silent anyway. Had he walked in on me touching myself, I would have proved him right—I wouldn't have been able to control myself.

He was right to sleep on the couch.

As I crawl out of bed to get ready to meet his mystery friend, I marvel at the amount of self-control he has. The number of times I thought about walking to the couch and at least snuggling up with him should probably be illegal. Hell, this whole thing should be off limits. He's twenty-three, for God's sake! But...every time I convince myself this could never work, something about him draws me back.

Kissing that man is a drug, and I am officially addicted. I swear that man's thighs, the ones that stretch the seam of his pants when he sits down, are my weakness. What is it about a man with nice thighs that gets me so worked up? *I wonder how much he squats?* Fuck, now I'm picturing his thighs and that ass of his in a squat position. *Snap out of it, Kennedy!*

Obviously, admitting I'm attracted to him physically is an understatement. But last night, something shifted. I bite my lip. *I finally got to see the real Jordan.* He let down his guard—*for me.* These past few weeks, I've seen little pieces of the real him. He's funny and sweet and thoughtful, and he can unlock my goddamn front door like he's done it a million times. But last night, he laid his soul bare. Every last drop. I saw the pain in his eyes, the hurt he hides day in and day out. My pulse quickens thinking about the girl who did this to him. I'm not a crazy possessive person, but if I ever find fucking Angelica, I *will* use my jiu-jitsu training to take her down.

I'm still ninety-nine percent sure he's intimidated by me—or, at least, he was. *He's been doing all of this because he had a crush on me.* And he had the chance last night to have me...but instead he acted like a complete gentleman, asking if he could kiss me goodnight. Then he left it at that—nothing more.

I'm used to random one-night stands, meeting a guy at a hotel bar, and hooking up just for some fun. My stomach clenches, bile clogging my throat as the realization hits me. Here I was being judgmental about him hooking up with all those people, when in reality, he wasn't.

I was.

God, I feel like a piece of shit. I have done nothing but ignore him, acting like I was better than him, when he's done nothing but keep trying. Fuck if that doesn't make me want him even more.

As I brush my teeth and try to do something with my bird's nest of tangled hair, I admit to myself there's something incredibly sexy about him wanting to take things slow. *He's in control here.* And it's kind of…sweet? Grilled Cheesus, I have never done *sweet* with any guy. I've only dated complete assholes who would find out I was a pilot and immediately ask if I had joined the Mile High Club. I roll my eyes. *So* original.

But not Jordan.

This is nothing like any other relationship I've been in before. *Maybe that's the point?* Shit…Kennedy, you aren't *in* a relationship with him. I slam my hairbrush on the counter, reminding myself that the relationship part is fake. He wouldn't even want this to be real…*would he?* I'm jolted from my thoughts as a text comes through.

> JORDAN:
> On my way back to your place! Be there in 15. Please check for talking bears. 🐻

Shit. I hurry to finish my make-up and find something to wear. I still don't know where we're going. He said casual is fine, but dear God, what do I wear? What says, 'I like you, and I respect your boundaries, but also I want to rip your clothes off, tie you to my bed, and sit on your face?' *Jeans?*

I decided on some leggings and an oversized crewneck, fancying it up with a necklace and earrings and cute tennis shoes. I throw my hair in a quick pony and decide the elevated Sporty Spice look is fine for this non-date.

I finish getting ready and race downstairs, a strange feeling hitting my gut as I wait in the lobby. My stomach flips, and I can feel my heart beating in my throat. *Am I...excited? What the hell is happening to me?*

When we arrive at our destination, we walk into the building hand-in-hand. My pulse races and my eyes blink like they are trying to talk in Morse code. Jordan must sense my anxiety, squeezing my fingers gently.

"Are you okay? If you don't want to come in, I get it. I know this is a lot."

I can say with all honesty, this is the last place on earth I would have thought we would end up. The giant giraffe painted on the wall, the colorfully decorated elevator banks, and the cheerful music playing are a disheartening contrast to the mood of everyone walking by. All the bright and cheerful artwork is a distraction that will forever fall short. Walking through the lobby, there's no laughter, only quiet whispers between parents and children. Some are here for a quick visit. Others are simply fighting to survive.

I swallow down my emotions. "No. I'm okay. I'm just... surprised. It's really cool that you do this."

He shrugs as we walk toward the visitors' desk to check in. "Remember when I told you how I like to entertain the fans at the games? This is why. You never know what someone's going through, and if there's anything I can do to help them have a better day...I'll do it."

Now it's my turn to squeeze his hand, choking back the tears threatening to fall at this caring and compassionate side of him. I loop my other hand around his arm as a wave of guilt makes my feet heavy for ever misjudging this man.

"Hi, Janet," Jordan says as we approach the desk. "I brought a friend today…" He pauses as he flashes me his impossibly charming smile. "My girlfriend, actually. This is Kennedy."

A wide smile spreads across Janet's face, her eyes darting between the two of us.

"Well, I'll be damned. You've never brought anyone with you, Bougie. Nice to meet you, Miss Kennedy. Here are your badges," she says, handing us each a little sticker with our names, Floor Seven, and a word I never thought I'd have to read on it.

Oncology.

"Miss Kennedy, you snagged yourself a keeper. He'll show you where to go. Oh, and welcome to Milwaukee Memorial Children's Hospital."

41

kennedy

We knock on the doorframe of room 706 and see a sweet, teenage girl wearing a Steel Riders pom-pom hat lying in a bed, hooked up to an IV pole, watching a show on an iPad.

"Hey, Kellsie, got time for a visitor?" Jordan says as we stand in the doorway.

Her sunken, tired eyes light up. "Jordan! I wasn't sure you'd make it with the playoffs going on. Come in!"

He smiles as we enter the room. "Where's your mom?"

"She went down to the cafeteria to get something to eat. She'll be back soon," she says as Jordan walks over to give her a hug. "Wait...oh my gosh!" Her excited squeal pierces the air. "Is this who I think it is? For real?"

He laughs and turns to me, waiving for me to come closer. "Kellsie, I'd like to introduce you to Kennedy, my girlfriend."

I nervously walk to her bedside to shake her hand. "Nice to meet you, Kellsie. How do you know who I am?"

She scoffs. "I saw you two making out on the internet with the rest of the world."

My cheeks heat as I shake my head, and Jordan runs his hand through his thick, dark waves. I've seen him do that a million times, but today it catches me off guard, settling deep within me. Not out of cockiness, but almost as if he's as embarrassed as I am to be called out by a teenager for our kiss. He subtly smirks at me, and I can't help but embarrassingly smile back.

"If you two are done making out with your eyes, I have some questions," Kellsie teases as she crosses her arms, interrupting our ridiculous glares at one another. I blink in shock, wondering if I'm in a hospital or a courtroom.

This girl is serious.

"Questions?" Jordan and I answer simultaneously.

"Yep! Jordan, you need to go find something else to do so I can interrogate her alone."

My eyes go wide as I see this sweet, innocent girl, dealing with far more than any teen should ever have to, looking at me like she's got a scalpel hidden under her pillow, more than ready to slice me up if I don't meet her standards.

Jordan laughs. "It's okay, Kells. She's been vetted."

"So? I love you, but you can't vet someone you made out with. That's against the rules," she grumbles, glaring at him like a parent who is going to ground him for a week. "I'm serious, Jordan…get out of here!" She shoos him out of the room. "Just give us five minutes. I'll be able to tell by then."

He looks to me, his eyes almost comically big, as if asking permission to leave me alone with his youngest bodyguard.

"I can handle myself," I say to him. *Surely, I can handle a harmless teenager. At least…I think she's harmless.*

He nods as he walks toward the door. "I'll go grab us some coffees." He gives me a quick peck on the cheek, and the small, quiet gesture has me ready to melt into a puddle. I jolt at the smile lifting my lips, straightening my spine. *What is wrong with me?* I am a badass woman who does not whimper over stuff like this. *Pull yourself together!*

"Behave yourself, Kellsie!" he throws over his shoulder as he closes the door behind him.

I turn to face Kellsie, a slight twitch in my jaw as I search for something to talk to her about. "So, tell me about—"

"What are your intentions with Jordan Boucher?" she interrupts, her sunshine smile nowhere to be found. *Wow.* This got intense quickly. *And how the hell do I answer this question?* Cue the nervous stomach. I never thought about my intentions, other than things that are *not* appropriate to discuss with a teenage girl.

"Well, we've been dating for a few months. I guess, right now, my intentions are to just keep dating him."

"Interesting." She taps her fingers on the tray across her lap. "You don't want to marry him for his money?"

I can't help but snort out a laugh as I take a seat in the uncomfortable guest chair next to the bed. "To be honest, his money is the least attractive thing about him. I don't care about any of that."

"So you *are* attracted to him then?"

I blink. *Who the hell is this kid?* Does she have some sort of magical truth serum running through her IV?

I look down at the tiles, hiding the stupid smile that hijacks my face. "Yeah. I am."

"Good answer. If you said no, I would have *known* you were lying. I saw it in the online kiss." My brows kiss my hairline as Kellsie rolls her eyes. "I have a lot of free time to analyze videos, plus I saw the way you blushed when I brought it up a few minutes ago. I can tell he *really* likes you. I'm just making sure you're not going to break his heart."

My stomach drops, the guilt of how I've treated and misjudged Jordan creeping in. And after everything he confessed to me last night? Damn, do I appreciate her looking out for him.

"Wow, you guys are close?" I hum.

The genuine smile lifting her lips steals my breath. "Jordan's the best. He comes here when he's not on the road, and we just sit and gossip. He gives me all the tea on the Riders, and I give him all the tea from the hospital and catch him up on our fav reality dating show, *You're the One*. Have you seen that show?" I shake my head, fighting my smirk, realizing Jordan binges reality dating shows. "Oh my God! It's the best. There are rumors next season may feature a hockey player, and I am going to riot if that's not the case."

"Jordan watches *You're the One*?"

"Oh...he does. He knows all the contestants and sends me messages to talk about who got eliminated if he's on the road. We also watch all kinds of movies and learn TikTok dances. He's the coolest."

My heart is beating out of my chest as I lean closer, listening to this young woman talking about how cool my boyfriend is. *Well, fake boyfriend.* The more I get to know him, and see the pieces of his heart I've never seen before, the more I want to take the word fake and throw it off a cliff.

"Yeah, I'm starting to realize there's a lot more to Jordan than I thought," I mumble.

"I like that you call him Jordan. Everyone here calls him Bougie. Not me. I hate getting called nicknames at school when I'm feeling well enough to go, so I always call him Jordan. Plus, I feel kind of special getting to call him by his real name."

"I only call him Jordan, too," I say with a bit of a laugh, not really liking his nickname either.

"You know, you didn't answer my earlier question," Kellsie says with all seriousness. *Shit.* "Are you going to hurt him?"

My breath stutters, all the air having left my lungs. As much as he used to annoy me, as much as I thought he was just some crazy immature playboy, the thought of me doing anything to hurt him hits like a punch to the gut. He's done so much to keep me safe, to protect me. Not to mention the thought of anyone else hurting him makes me want to roundhouse kick someone in the face. *This is normal, right?*

"Kellsie, I would never hurt him. Sometimes..." My voice sticks in my throat. "Sometimes relationships don't work out, but I swear I will never do anything to hurt him."

She tilts her head, her eyes closed deep in thought, then finally nods once. "Good answer. And if you do hurt him, I have a scalpel hidden in here, and I *will* find you."

"I guess I'd better keep my promise then." I laugh, the two of us seeming to have the same sense of humor. "So, how long has Jordan been coming to visit you?"

"The Riders did an event here last season, and we just kinda clicked. He said he had sisters he misses like crazy, and I have a brother I don't get to see very often since he's away at college. The day he came, I was watching the Barbie movie on my iPad, and we talked about Ryan Gosling's performance and how he was robbed of the Oscar. He's the shit."

My eyes widen as I clutch my chest. "Are you allowed to swear?"

"When you have cancer, your parents really don't care if you cuss. There's a lot of downsides, but that's definitely one of the perks. Also, getting to cut in line places 'cause you're sick."

I offer her a smile, stunned at her optimism. "I'm really glad you can find the bright side of things."

She shrugs. "No one knows when their last day is going to be. I hope mine is a long time from now, but you never really know. It's just a lot more likely for me to go sooner, so I try to live every day doing whatever I want."

"I'm sure that's hard some days," I whisper.

"Yeah, it can be, but if I dwell on what's going on with me, it's too depressing. That's why I like following crazy shows on TV and chatting with people like Jordan. And you! He told me you're a pilot. That's badass!"

"I have to admit, it's a pretty cool gig."

"I think it would be *so* cool to get to fly a plane. Being stuck here in this damn room makes me wish I could see new places that don't have snails painted on the walls."

I snort as I look around the childish decor. "I guess they really don't have teen rooms here, do they?"

"No. But at least it's better than the adult floors and their stupid beige walls. Why is everything beige?" She shivers, sticking her tongue out. "No one likes that color."

"Oh my God, Kellsie...*same*. I hate beige. It is not in my color wheel," I say as we high-five.

We're still chatting and laughing as a knock at the door interrupts us.

"Can I come back in?"

"Yep!" Kellsie yells toward the door.

Jordan peeks his head in, looks at her, then looks back to me, his smile disarming. "Kennedy, blink twice if she's holding you hostage."

I stand with my arms raised as he comes back in to join us. "I'm fine. Kellsie's pretty damn cool."

He smiles wider than the entire hospital floor as I bite my lip, trying to keep my ovaries from melting into a complete puddle.

"Well, Kellsie, what's the verdict?" he asks with a shaky voice. I pick at my nails as we wait for her response, as if he really does take her opinion seriously.

Honestly, I think he does.

She looks back and forth between the two of us, pursing her lips and taking her sweet time deciding exactly the right words to say.

She smirks, finally letting us off the hook. "She's cool. I approve. You can keep dating."

Jordan clutches his hand over his heart, very dramatically acting like she's revived from an actual heart attack. *"Thank God. I was really hoping I didn't have to break up with her."*

"What?!" I say, my voice just as shocked as his. "You would really have broken up with me if she didn't approve?"

"She's the boss! You're lucky she said yes," he says, leaning in to kiss me on the cheek as a full army of butterflies fills my stomach. A nod of approval from his teenage friend, a kiss on the cheek, and my knees are threatening to betray me. He stays close to my cheek as if telling a secret only to me, but saying it loudly enough for Kellsie to hear. "Be glad she said yes because I talked to her mom in the cafeteria about seeing if we can get her to a playoff game this season."

"Seriously?!" Kellsie screams as her face lights up with excitement. "I'm supposed to be going home in a few days. Oh my God, pleeassseee let my doctors clear me to go!!!"

"I hope so, Kells! We'll get you tickets in the suite with all the WAGs, and you know I'll hook you up with whatever you want."

"Could I get my own nacho bar?"

"I think we can arrange that. I can bring a nacho bar here if you want one. How about we set up a nacho bar for the entire floor and all the staff tomorrow? We can celebrate the Riders making it to the next round *and* you, hopefully, getting out of hospital jail soon. That work?"

"That would be sweet! Hospital food is the *worst*."

"You got it, Kells." He laughs again, pulling a Sharpie out of his pocket. "So…what do you have for me to sign today?"

I take a step back as Jordan follows Kellsie's very detailed directions to grab a stack of things across the room to sign. It's not even hockey or Riders' merch. It's a lot of random items; some stuffed animals, a book, a weird-looking bottle of shampoo, and one of those hospital water bottles with the ounces listed on the outside and a giant bendy straw. He gracefully signs everything she asks him to, chatting with her the entire time, asking how things are going with school, what she thinks the Riders need to do to bring the Cup home this year, and, of course, talking about how they can't wait for the next season of their favorite reality dating show to start back up. A look passes between them before they burst into the theme song simultaneously with a bunch of 'ooo ooo's as they both wave their arms in matching hand motions.

Watching these two interact is cuter than a litter of newborn puppies. Something tightens in my stomach as my mind flips back to when I saw him dancing at the club a couple of months back. *I was so irritated at him for showboating on that bar.* I was bitter that he was flaunting his hot body and his dance moves to get attention. I was so put off by everything.

I was wrong.

This side of him? His compassion. His ability to make everyone around him feel magical. His *heart*. He did all this with no cameras, no media, no photos, no recognition.

I was so caught up in preconceived notions about a rich hockey player with more money than God, I failed to see the real Jordan. And now all I see is this incredibly tenderhearted, loving human. One who also happened to mention that he was attracted to me. A warmth spreads through my body. But this isn't lust. It's not attraction. It's not infatuation. And it's fucking scary as hell.

This fake relationship is starting to feel more real than I ever imagined.

42
jordan

"Thanks for taking me with you today," Kennedy says as I look for a parking space outside her apartment. "I really didn't know what to expect when we got there, but everyone was amazing. Especially Kellsie."

"Yeah, she's a pretty cool kid," I say, shifting the car into park. "I'm glad you got to meet her."

"Same. *And* we got her approval of our relationship, so it's a good day all around."

"Oh, for sure. If only this weren't fake."

Her smile fades as she looks down at her hands clasped in her lap, nervously picking at her nails.

"Right. That's what I meant. At least our *fake relationship* is cool with her."

My leg shakes against the floorboard. There's something she's not saying. The way her eyes don't meet mine. The way she's fidgeting. *She's hiding something.*

"Is it okay to park here?"

"Oh, Jordan. It's okay. It's been a long day; you can just drop me off and head home…" Her voice trails off, her shoulders flinching as she catches a sensitive part of her nail.

"Kennedy." I turn to face her, grabbing her hand as her gaze drops to where our palms meet. I don't know where the hell this boldness blossoming inside me is coming from—it all started that damn night in that hotel bar when my feet took off like a racecar toward her—but it's here. And I'm leaning into it.

"I'm staying here tonight. After all the weird texts, especially now that you're getting them too, and the damn bear I'm going to have nightmares about for the rest of my life, you're not staying here by yourself. In fact," —my leg is now shaking at ludicrous speed, but I have to do this. For me. For her. For us— "I'm moving in."

She jerks her head toward me, her eyes nearly popping out of their sockets. "You're *what?*"

"I'm moving in and staying here with you until we can figure out what the hell is going on with all this stalker shit. Unless you'd rather let me hire a security detail for you. You said you didn't want that, and I want to respect it, so I figured this was the better option."

"You're moving? Into my apartment? When?"

"Now. I packed up some stuff this morning, and I'm going to stay here tonight."

I can see her breathing pick up, her gorgeous chest rising and falling with every word I speak. I rub my thumb across hers, easing the tension or whatever the hell this is, and trying to calm myself down as the silence stretches between us. My heart drops. *She may say no.*

"You think you can keep me safe, pretty-boy?" Her eyes dance. "You do remember that *you* hid behind *me* when that damn bear started talking?"

I snort. "That's fair. But I also thought maybe your badass self could keep me safe, too."

"From evil stuffed animals?"

"It's an epidemic," I say as we both chuckle, my thumb still brushing hers. "Listen, obviously I can't force you to let me move in, but with everyone thinking we're dating, no one will question me being here all the time. It keeps you from having security, keeps us both safer, and around each other most of the time, and we'll be together when we need to travel with the team." I bite the inside of my cheek. "Now that I'm saying this out loud, that is a lot of togetherness."

She smirks, her eyes reflecting a glimmer of something mischievous behind them. "You say that like it's a bad thing. Do you want to spend more time with me?"

I swallow the lump in my throat, instantly reverting back to my shy, awkward, 'I don't know how to talk to women' self.

"I uh...Yeah. Yes. I do."

"Good." She points to a garage door ahead. "You can park in the guest area in the underground parking."

I pull out from the curb and quickly find an open spot in the garage. I grab my bags out of the trunk, my heart pounding as we hop in the elevator up to her floor. As we get to her apartment, she hesitates.

"Do you need help with the key again?" I ask, giving her my signature smartass smile.

She looks back over her shoulder as she struggles, but finally pops open the lock.

"No," she gloats, motioning for me to walk in behind her. "However, I do have one condition for you staying here."

"One condition? What's that?"

"You're not sleeping on the couch." She closes the door and locks the deadbolt behind her. "You're sleeping with me."

43
jordan

"Say what now?" I drop my bags to the floor in shock while she calmly walks through her apartment like she didn't just tell me we are going to be sleeping in the same bed. *Yikes bikes.*

"I said, you're sleeping in my bed. None of this couch shit. You're in the playoffs. You need good sleep. I'm not sure of my mattress quality compared to yours, but it's at least better than my sofa cushions. So," —she turns to face me— "you're sleeping with me."

For the love of all things Elle Woods did she just say I'm *sleeping with her*? My heart pounds in my chest like a drum line directing the signals to my dick at full speed. *I need to find a way to calm this down, or sleeping in a bed with her is going to be torture.*

"Kennedy...I thought we talked about how," —I gesture my hands between us— "you can't control yourself around me."

She takes a step toward the door, and the déjà vu hits me full force. Except this time her eyes rake up and down my entire body, my pants are ungodly tight with no hiding the full-on erection I have, and *fuck* if she doesn't stare right at it as she continues to stalk closer *Why is this woman always walking toward me like I'm her goddamn last meal?!*

"Well, I'm *not* having a security detail and, apparently, you're not leaving," she murmurs, moving forward another step. "If you want to stay here with me and, as you say, keep each other safe, this is my rule." Her voice is a whisper against my lips, before she leans to the side and picks up one of my duffels. *Goddamn this woman and her witchcraft.* "Grab the rest of your stuff and bring it into my bedroom, pretty-boy, before I drag you and your bags in here with me."

Holy fucking fuckballs. If my dick wasn't trying to escape my pants before, it sure as hell is now. I nearly trip as I pick up my bag as fast as possible and follow her vanilla scent, tracking her like a K-9 unit meticulously trained for search and rescue.

My pulse throbs in my throat, the mix of her beauty and her take-charge attitude intoxicating. My tongue wets my lips. I'm fully drunk on Kennedy Kramer. *And I never want to be sober again.*

She tosses my bag in the corner near the closet as I timidly set my other next to it, the thud echoing off the hardwood floor. I made sure to pack enough to stay for several days without having to run home. I am dying to take her to my house someday. To show her more of myself and my personality, but I wanted her to be comfortable. I thought this would be better. My eyes blur, spots dancing along the edge of my vision. And now she's ordering me to sleep with her. And while Downstairs Jordan is ready and firing all cylinders, a heavyweight pulls me back down, making it hard to take in air.

She's not her. She's not trying to trick you.

Kennedy is everything that's good in the world. Angelica was everything that's bad. I take in a deep breath, forcing the shaking in my hands to still.

"You, okay? You look a little pale?"

"Yeah…I'm…I'm fine. I just…"

"Hey." She turns me gently to face her, her fingers warm against my skin. "I don't want to make you uncomfortable. I can behave."

I laugh louder than I should. "It's not that. I just…I haven't slept in a bed with a woman since Cruella."

She snorts at the nickname for the woman who nearly ruined my life, my muscles relaxing at the sound. "If it bothers you that much, I can sleep on the couch."

"One-hundo percent no. This is your place, Kenni. You're sleeping in your own bed."

Her lips tip up at the corners, her smile shyly crawling across her face as her gaze softly drifts into mine. "You called me Kenni."

I swallow hard, squeezing my eyes shut. "Oh, shit. I'm sorry. I didn't mean to call—"

"It's okay," she reassures me. "I like it. That's what my friends call me."

I take a deep breath, realizing I'm not in trouble. But the pang of disappointment hits my chest. "Friends. Right. We're *friends*. Fake dating friends."

She cocks her head as she dissolves the distance, her chest touching mine. "Exactly. We're just…*friends*. But…" she says in a long, drawn-out, singsong voice. "I've been thinking."

I suck in a sharp breath. Her lips are *right there,* so close to mine I can nearly taste them. "You have?"

"Mm hmm. Since we're friends, and friends help each other out, what if I can help prove you wrong?"

"Wha…what? Wrong about what?"

"That you're bad in bed."

Shit on a fucking hockey stick. Is she implying what I think she is? That we? *Ohmygod, ohmygod, ohmygod.* My lungs burn like I just inhaled pepper spray. I need air. *I can't breathe.* Find the air in the room, Jordan, and breathe. It. In. I take a breath, barely enough to calm my nerves, let alone speak. "And how..." I clear my throat and continue, "how would we do that?"

"We practice," she responds like she's telling me tomorrow's weather forecast, meanwhile, my eyes expand wider than this big ass apartment.

"Come again?" I squeak. *Does she know what she's implying? We're not practicing pickleball dinks and volleys. This is like...sex stuff.*

She smirks. "You're a fantastic kisser. What if you're fantastic at other *things* too? You are ridiculously talented at hockey. You perform as if you were born to stand out. I'm just saying there's a pattern here. But I want you to know that I'm not doing this to trick or hurt you. We wouldn't do anything you're uncomfortable with. I just thought since we're fake dating and living in the same apartment, per *your* request," she says, poking a finger at my chest, "why not have some fun and help you along the way."

My chest rises and falls rapidly at her words, her touch. "Kennedy, I don't want you to do this out of pity."

"This is not pity," she says sharply. "Look. You're worried about not being good, so who better to test that with than your fake girlfriend? The one who happens to be attracted to you." My eyes bounce between hers, her words almost making sense. "Do you trust me?"

"Yes."

"I don't want to freak you out, but I need you to pick a safe word. Not because we're doing anything crazy, not yet, but I want you to feel comfortable. Okay?"

"Okay."

"Good. Now, what's your safe word?"

My eyes go wide. *Fuck.* I never in my life thought I would need a safe word. *Isn't that some 50 Shades shit?* But the way she's making sure I'm comfortable makes my heart melt and my dick leak. "Frites."

She lets out a wicked laugh. "Frites, huh?"

I shrug. "It's just what came to mind."

"It's perfect," she says softly, placing a hand on my cheek. "If you need to stop, you say frites, and we stop. Got it?"

"Yes."

"Good." She steps back and removes her T-shirt, casually holding it out to the side, before letting it slowly drop to the floor. My mouth dries as she removes her leggings. Kennedy Kramer is standing in front of me in nothing but a bra and panties. Seeing her like this—the smooth curve of her hips, the glow of her skin, the soft curls falling across her bare shoulders as she shakes them free—has me seeing stars.

I. *Am. Unwell.*

"Give me your hand."

I respond immediately, my hand unsteady. She places my palm on her shoulder, gently guiding it down between her cleavage. I feel her eyes on my face, but I can't tear my stare away from our intertwined fingers. She drags our joined hands further down her abdomen, placing them directly between her legs. *Her panties are fucking soaked.* I suck in a shuddering breath as she rubs our hands across the wet fabric, pressing my fingers against her.

"Does this feel like I pity you? Does this feel like I'm doing this as a favor?" she asks as I shake my head. "Or does this feel like I want you? Like I want you as badly as you want me?"

"*Fuck.*"

She takes her free hand and tips my chin up, forcing me to look directly in her eyes as my heart threatens to beat out of my goddamn chest.

"You didn't answer my question. Does this feel like I want you?"

"Y-yes, you're…" I swallow. "You're so wet."

She presses my hand into her even harder. "*This* is what you do to me, pretty-boy."

"Jesus fucking Christ, Kennedy. I'm going to come in my pants if you don't stop."

She flashes me a sultry smirk. "Do you *know* how hot it would be if you came in your pants? You not being able to control yourself around me? That's hot as fuck."

"If you keep doing this, your wish will come true."

"Good," she says with a wink. *A goddamn wink!* "Now fucking kiss me, pick me up, and take me to bed."

She barely finishes her sentence before my lips crash against hers. *Fucking hell, this woman.* I'm more nervous than being in an opening face-off, but I feel it down to my core that I can trust her.

I lift her up, not breaking our kiss, and grab her ass, groaning against her mouth as her legs wrap around my waist. My knees bump into her bed, and I gently set her down, hovering over her and kissing her like my life depends on it. My skin buzzes, my vision blurs. I'm completely consumed by the woman underneath me. I'm not fucking sure how I stop myself.

My chest tightens as my brain catches up to all this. It's still so new and—I want to, *need* to, take this slow. I roll over to the side, needing to take a breath.

"Kenni…I just…I need a little break. This is…*God*, it feels so good, but it's so overwhelming."

"Jordan. Look at me," she says, sitting up to face me. "We'll go as slow as you want. There's no pressure here. But…" Her tongue traces her bottom lip. "I have an idea."

44
kennedy

I have never wanted to fuck someone so badly in my life, and here I am with the only man who has ever been hesitant in return. My body aches for this man like I need him to survive, and *goddammit*, I need some relief. But even more, the ground shifted like an earthquake, shaking me open. Seeing him so broken, witnessing a side of him that helps everyone but himself, carved out a space inside me I didn't know existed. My breath catches as it hits me—*this is starting to feel like more than just attraction.*

I place a reassuring hand on his shoulder. I want to help him. He deserves a do-over. He deserves to know that one mistake doesn't define the rest of your life. I'm going to give him a boost of confidence to get him where he should be. I want more than anything to have him buried deep inside me. *But he's not ready for that.*

And I'm still trying to untangle a world of emotions I don't recognize.

"So...what's this idea?" he asks, his deep voice shaky, but curious.

"I'd like to be your coach."

"My what now?" he sputters, his eyes wide and his jaw unhinged.

I huff a quiet laugh. "Your coach. Let me teach you how to do things. Let me show you *exactly* how to make me come."

His brows narrow. "Kenni…I'm…I don't know…you want to coach me?"

I pat his chest. "I'm a flight instructor. I know how to walk someone through pushing the right buttons, staying calm under pressure, and reaching the final peak. You've had coaches your whole life, right? They tell you how to do a drill, and you do it." He nods slowly, still confused. "Just pretend I'm your…your…clit coach," I say as a smirk flitters up my face at the fucking fantastic alliteration I just came up with.

"Clit Coach? Fuck, we need to trademark that," he quips as we both laugh.

"Can you follow instructions? Do you know right from left? Up from down?"

"Wait, your right or my right?" I lift a brow, not breaking eye contact. "Yes, Kenni, I can follow directions."

"Good. Then we won't have any problems."

His brow creases, his lips tight before the words rush out of his mouth in a tangled mess. "And you swear to God you won't fake it? Promise you'll tell me if I'm doing something wrong."

My heart softens just a little more. "Look at me, pretty-boy." I cup his cheek. "I promise. And, since we've been sharing secrets, I'll let you in on one of mine. I have…I have a tell."

"A what?"

This sweet, innocent man. "A tell. If I've had a real orgasm, my clit pulses like it has its own heartbeat. You can feel it, so you'll know."

His head pulls back. "Seriously? That's a thing?"

I nod. "Every woman reacts differently, but that's what happens for me. Are you interested in seeing how it works? You want to make my clit beat for you?"

His Adam's apple bobs as he swallows hard. "Yes."

I gently grab his hand, placing soft kisses on it before running it down my body again. Placing it right between my legs, once again letting him feel what he does to me.

"We're going to go slow, so just use your hands to tease me through my panties. Just gentle, slow circles."

He does exactly as I ask, and *fucking hell*. Warmth pools low in my stomach, my toes curling into the sheets. The heel of his hand presses into my clit as his fingers slowly explore what's beneath the damp fabric barrier.

"Is this okay?" he asks, his voice unsteady.

My heart swells more than the area he's rubbing between my legs. *He's nervous.* It's the sweetest and hottest thing I've ever experienced in my life. *And I am more than okay taking the lead here to make him feel comfortable.* "You touching me like this is why I've been touching myself every night. Imagining this very moment."

His groan echoes low in my room. "Kenni. You've...you've been getting yourself off thinking about me?"

I smirk. "I told you, pretty-boy..." My chest heaves, tremors flooding my senses, "You're not the only one fighting attraction here."

His eyes shut closed as his head tips back. "Fuuuck."

"We'll get to that," I tease, finally getting him to let out a real laugh. "Jordan. *Relax*. You're doing fantastic. There is only one thing you could be doing better."

His eyes fly to mine. "Tell me. I'll do it."

I lean up, whispering in his ear, "Kiss me while you slide your hand under my panties and rub my clit."

He flashes me a wide grin with a confidence that nearly undoes me. "Yes, Coach," he whispers as he places his lips on mine.

I drag my teeth along his lower lip as he shudders. He gently slides his hand as I instructed, his touch warm against my skin. My back bows off the bed in response, his finger slowly sliding between my lips, finally reaching my most sensitive place.

Fucking hell, there is no way this man could be bad at anything.

"Oh God. That's…that's perfect. Just like that." I can barely get the words out, the heat in my core the size of a forest fire.

"You're sure…this feels good?"

I grip his chin, ensuring he can't look away. "Listen, pretty-boy. You said you trusted me. *I* will fucking tell you to change something if it's not working. Got it? Now put your fingers in my pussy and stretch it the fuck out. Do you understand?"

"Fuck," he mutters under his breath. "*Yes.* Fuck yes."

He slides his fingers farther down, easing one into my dripping cunt.

"Goddammit, that feels good," I reassure him as his finger moves in and out of me, reveling at the burn as a second, then third finger fills me completely. Every movement, every thrust of his hand, feels like something he's done a million times.

Like this is something I don't ever want him to stop doing.

"I'm getting," I gasp, my nerves on fire, "I'm getting close. Finish me off on my clit." He pulls his fingers out, the instant emptiness of their absence only relieved by his gliding up to my clit.

My breaths are short as my chest heaves, the fiery urge building inside like a pressure cooker. But I want him to feel exactly where my favorite spot is. The one that makes me lose control in an instant.

"Move your finger…" I say between pants… "just off to the side." The pressure builds in my core, all the blood rushing between my legs. "Fuck…just like that. Just a little more—Ah!" He does exactly as I ask with the precision of a sniper. "Just a bit more to the side...ohhhh, holy fuck. Right there."

I'm writhing against his hand. It's been so long—there's no prolonging this. "JJ...*shit*...I-I'm coming."

A breathless moan escapes me, my body shaking. His hips thrust against my leg. His hand is still working me until he's sure I'm done, as he groans, panting, unable to control what he's experiencing as well.

"Fuck, Kenni!" he screams with several more slow, deep thrusts. I still, a satisfied smile softening my face as I realize he's reached his own orgasm.

Holy. Fucking. Hotness.

The bliss of this much-needed orgasm, and the fact that he just came in his goddamn pants, nearly sends me over the edge again. He collapses on his back next to me with a full-body sigh. He's spent. I'm spent. Both of us are trying to recover from the euphoria flooding through us.

"Come here." I motion for him to roll back my way.

"Kenni, no." His voice is shaky, the man desperately trying to regain his composure. "I'm a mess, I—"

"Do I look like I care? I said, come here." His body tenses, my voice softening as I try to calm his fear. "I need you to feel what you did to me on the first fucking try."

He does as I ask, and I take his finger, placing it next to my clit, letting him feel the still pulsing heartbeat that's thrumming only because of him, only *for* him. I'm not sure if I'm still shaking from the orgasm, or if it's because my heart is starting to beat for him as well.

I'm not sure it will ever be the same after being with this man.

His gaze, gleaming with astonishment and curiosity, locks on mine. "Holy shit. I...I did that to you?"

"You did." I offer a tired smile with the only energy I have left in my body after that. "Jordan, you're not bad in bed. Not even a little bit. You listened, you hit the perfect spot, and it was fucking fantastic. The fact that you did all that, *and then* came without me so much as touching you? I've never been more turned on in my life."

A shy smile creeps up his face. "I told you you'd get your wish. Want to know what finally pushed me over the edge?"

"Please tell me so I have this information for future coaching sessions."

His gaze softens. "You called me JJ."

Now it's my turn to be astonished. "I did?"

"Yeah. Turned me the fuck on. Only people I'm super close with call me that. Not even my teammates know that name. How did you hear it?"

I rack my brain trying to remember, my shoulders relaxing as it dawns on me.

"Hannah. She kept calling you JJ, and I guess I must have tucked that away somewhere. Sorry, it just sort of slipped out."

"I liked it. And after that?" He sheepishly grins. "We've definitely reached a new level of…*closeness*."

I nod with a laugh. "We did. And you…holy shit, you're a quick learner. You did amazing. Better than amazing, it was an elite athletic performance. Which is why I want to just lie here and die from the most amazing orgasm I've ever had."

"There is no way that was the most amazing org—"

I place a finger on his lips. "Don't you dare finish that sentence. No more of this self-deprecating shit. We're done with that. Jordan…" I pause, remembering what he said. "*JJ*, I will never lie to you. You are the most confident motherfucker in the world outside of this one little area. We're going to make you the best fucking fucker there ever was. No one will ever be able to question your skills. Are we clear?" He nods as the reality of a looming end date for this agreement creeps back in.

I feel it too.

"I assume you have practice tomorrow?"

"I need to leave around eight."

"Well then, we need you to get some rest."

"I don't know if I'll be able to sleep much after that."

I laugh at this soft, sweet man sprawled in bed with me. He's so different from his public persona. This side of him, the sweet, scared guy coming out of his hidden mask, is something I feel lucky to witness.

"If you think you won't be able to control yourself, I'm happy to put up a wall of pillows in the bed—"

"Hell fucking no. I've dreamt my whole life about cuddling after sex. Well…sex-ish? Sex adjacent, I guess? You're not gonna steal that away from me."

I laugh before placing another kiss on his lips. "I would never deprive you of that. I know my resting bitch face doesn't project this, but I am a secret snuggle addict. Just don't tell anyone; I have a badass bitch persona to uphold."

"I wouldn't dream of it. A badass bitch and a hockey enforcer cuddling in bed? No one has to know," he says in a comical whisper.

"Perfect. Let's get cleaned up, put on comfy clothes, order food, and snuggle."

"The night of my dreams," he murmurs as he drops a kiss on my lips and heads toward the bathroom.

The giddy smile I've been fighting all night finally breaks free. I'm not going to lie—this does feel pretty perfect. My pulse is still racing from this entire day. These feelings, these emotions, are foreign and a little scary. It's like I'm taking control of a jet for the first time. Once I pushed past the fear, I reached heights I never dreamed of.

But this is one of the weirdest damn flights I've ever been on.

45
jordan

I, Jordan Joseph Boucher, made a woman come so hard she had a pulsing clit. My own pulse races as if my heart has never had blood pumping through it until now. I'm lying in bed trying, and failing, to get some shut-eye. How do you sleep with the woman of your dreams curled against you? How do you close your eyes when the most beautiful creation is here for you to admire? How do you find rest when the moment you've been dreaming of is finally here?

You don't.

I could stay up all night staring at her. The warmth of her body wrapped in my arms is all-consuming—everything else pushed aside until nothing exists but her. A tear wells, spilling down my cheek. The fact that a woman like her would be the one to see past all the walls I've had in place for so long...*It doesn't feel real.* She didn't judge me. She didn't get angry, even though she had a right to. She didn't try to use this for her own gain. Well...she *did* use me for the orgasm, but I'm not complaining. And since I finished too, we'll just call this one a draw. And the fact that she told me her tell?

That she gave up the one thing most women hold close to their chests? I brush my fingers across her cheek, pushing aside a stray piece of hair that's fallen across her face, still in awe that I'm this close to her. There can never be any faking it with me, and that seems monumental. The amount of trust I have in her went through the roof after that.

It's two in the morning, and I am wide awake watching the rise and fall of her chest, making sure she's still breathing and that this isn't some sort of fever dream.

Wait…how would I know if this *was* a dream? What if *all* of this is a dream? Or, even worse, what if I fall asleep and I wake up and it's all gone? I normally count sheep, but I can't stop counting her freckles to settle myself.

If I'm ever going to get over my past, I'm going to have to try to trust again—to let her see parts of me I'm scared to show anyone. We made it pretty far down that road tonight. Being here curled up with her, something pulls tight in my chest, a sense that I was right to open up to her. As if she can hear my thoughts, Kennedy stirs in her sleep, cuddling closer and pulling my arm tight to her chest. Warmth spreads across my skin like a blanket fresh out of the dryer. I've never felt anything like this—as if everything I've ever wanted in the world is wrapped up in my arms. I know what I want to call this, but the cautious part of my brain is struggling to catch up. Struggling to let go of the pain of my past. But there is one thing I know one billion percent: I never want to let this go.

part three
may

46

kennedy

Sitting on my couch with my friend Ginny in my hand, a bag of sour cream and onion chips on my lap, and watching The Notebook with a box of Kleenex at the ready was not the way I thought this day was going to go. But getting called into work to discuss a *personnel matter*, that ended up being an anonymous report about a bad landing, means I'm upset and desperate to drown my feelings in gin and Ryan Gosling. Just as I'm about to get a refill on snacks, the door pops open.

"Hey! I'm back," Jordan says, surveying the situation of me lying out across the couch in baggy lounge clothes. My hair is in a messy bun. Chip crumbs on my shirt. I literally look like a trash panda that infiltrated the apartment. Meanwhile, he looks like he stepped off the cover of a goddamn fitness magazine wearing a tight-fitting Riders shirt, his damn gray joggers that hug every inch of him, and a piece of his still-damp hair falling in front of his face. My eyes trail over him, my body heating more and more at every inch I see. *Grilled Cheesus, take me before I die of embarrassment.*

"Kennedy Kramer!" he shouts in disbelief. "The Notebook and gin at 2pm? *This is clearly a cry for help.* Are you okay?"

I quickly try to clean myself up, wiping the crumbs off my chest and sitting up straight. "Just…" I clear my throat, "I've just had a bad day."

"Give me your glass," he says, holding out his hand.

"Jordan, I'm not drunk—"

"I know—I'm getting you a refill. You're a quart low."

I can't help but smile, a warm feeling spreading across my chest. The last couple of weeks have been insanely busy for us both. Between him being in the middle of the playoffs, me having two weeks of mandatory guard duty, being in different cities and on different sleep schedules, we've only been able to fool around once. We were both exhausted but too amped up to be around each other without exploring, and he said he wanted to 'get in more practice' on his finger drills. *I wasn't about to complain.* Honestly, he doesn't need any more practice. He's better with his hands than anyone I've ever been with. He pays attention, remembers every little detail…the man has skills. *Fuck that girl for ever making him feel like he wasn't good enough.* I grip the edge of a throw pillow, wishing I could strangle that bitch. But I can't change his past. All I can do is help him gain back his confidence.

But right now? I'm the one who needs the pep talk.

"You wanna talk about it?" he throws over his shoulder as he empties the melted ice into the sink.

I lean my arm across the couch and word vomit, as the pop of the gin bottle echoes across the room. "I got called into work today because someone reported me for a bad landing. But the flight in question? I wasn't the one flying at the time. I was on the radio, so it couldn't have been me. I don't get who would do this."

"First of all, yikes bikes. Second, you would *never* have a bad landing because you're perfect and can do no wrong. Third," he pauses, looking back at me, "explain this to me like I'm five. What do you mean you were on the radio, so it couldn't be you?"

I snort, realizing he doesn't know the first thing about my job. It's sort of cute. *Okay, maybe a lot cute.* He walks back to the couch, handing me my drink and curling up next to me. He even made a little slice in the lime to put it on the rim of the glass. *Goddammit, he's thoughtful.* My stomach flutters at this confident, caretaking side of him. I run my fingers through his hair, his body relaxing against mine, and the stress of the day finally begins to melt away. *So different from that first time he was here, thinking I was going to crack his skull open with a hammer.*

"So, on a crew aircraft, one pilot is flying, and the other is monitoring instrumentation and manning the radio. And we switch each leg. If you pull the recordings from air traffic control, you'll hear *me* on the radio—not Chadd. We got clearance to land, you can hear me talk to ATC and confirm. *That's* why I'm so confused. Why would someone report me when all we have to do is pull the tapes and listen? It's like someone wanted to make me go through all this extra shit to prove it wasn't me. It will be fine, but it's…" I let out a defeated sigh. "This is humiliating. Why would someone do this? Even during our debrief, Chadd fucking acknowledged the landing was a little rough."

"Can you appeal this and get it off your record or whatever?" he asks as he finds a stray curl and tucks it behind my ear.

"I did. It's just a hassle." I scrub my hand down my face. "I just really didn't need this right now, you know?"

"Do you think it was Chadd McDumpsterFire?"

I snort, loving that he has a new nickname for my co-worker every time he comes up in conversation. "I have no fucking clue. I didn't think he was *that* pissed about us dating, but who else would even know to do this?" I let out a defeated sigh, my shoulders slumping forward. "I'm just so pissed. And then I turned on the TV and this movie was on and everything came crashing down in a big, depressing, full-on crying session."

"I'm sorry, that sucks ass. I would be pissed too. Fuck I'm pissed for you! My offer to Crazy Rich Asians buy the airline still stands."

I lean into him as I laugh. "Thank you, but buying the airline isn't necessary. I'll figure this out. I just can't work out who in the hell reported me. And why? Anyway, sorry to bombard you with this just as you came in the door. How was practice?"

He narrows his brow. "Kennedy, you didn't bombard me with anything. We're," —he gestures between the two of us— "we're friends, right? I'm here to talk about anything you want. Chadd McDipshit, work stuff, lady time troubles. Whatever it is, I'm here for it all."

My heart flips at his sickeningly sweet nature. The fact that he's also, apparently, not embarrassed to talk about shark week is damn cute. *They must make them different in Canada.*

"Buuut," he singsongs, "we are done with the pity-party starter pack here." He snags the remote, finding something else to watch on TV. "Now this! *This* is a much more uplifting movie to watch. Ooo! And it's almost at the dance scene! Come on up! Off the couch." He grabs my hand, pulling me up to join him, as I watch Jennifer Garner doing the same to Mark Ruffalo.

"Jordan. No. *Hell* no. I am not doing the Thriller dance from 13 Going on 30. I look like trash, and I do not dance except to sway awkwardly during songs at a Taylor Swift concert."

"Don't care. Come ooonnn," he whines, "it'll be fun! We're doing it."

He doesn't seem to be phased by the laser beams of death shooting from my eyes. My stomach twists, realizing he's not letting me out of this.

He stands beside me and counts off 'two, three, four' as he starts to tilt his head to the side, while stomping, making the iconic zombie-dinosaur motion back and forth across his chest, clapping his hands above his head, then sliding across the floor with an impressive shimmy. He glances over his shoulder with a smile. His infectious grin falls when he notices I'm still frozen in place. "Kennedy Kramer, come on! Dance with me!!"

I shake my head, but, for some stupid reason, my body betrays me, and I join in, surprised I remember the moves. *I'm at least dressed like a zombie.* As we shuffle our feet, stepping forward and tilting our heads to the side, I begrudgingly admit this is kind of fun. We dance. We laugh at how bad a dancer I am, and he promises to give me lessons, claiming to be a better instructor than I am. *Doubtful.* Glancing over at him, seeing his eyes light up, has the corners of my lips tipping up, effortlessly getting me out of the funk I was in earlier.

As the song ends, and the movie goes to a commercial, Jordan wraps his hands around my waist and dips me as if we've just ended a slow dance. He pulls me up, my face a breath away from his, with a smile that makes my lungs struggle to breathe. "Feel better?"

"I do," I say, just the slightest bit out of breath. "Thank you. I *really* hate to admit this, but…I needed that."

"I know," he says, leaning down, his eyes fixed on my lips. God, I want this man so bad. The way he makes me feel. The way he comforts me. I never thought I wanted any of this. But here I am, in the arms of someone who makes me feel as if I asked for the world, he'd give it to me in a heartbeat without question. I bite my lip, my pulse stuttering. Wanting him physically is one thing. But this? Wanting more—wanting something that matters, something real? Wanting him like this is a problem for a thousand reasons.

But right now, with the space between us shrinking, his fingers flexing against my waist, I can't remember one of them.

We're pulled from our thoughts as his phone vibrates in his pocket, and I hear mine chime at the same time. *Weird.*

"Just ignore it," he says, pulling me in a little tighter. "It's probably someone from the group chat."

Maybe he's right. But thoughts of work are still there, and my muscles tighten. "Let me make sure it's not work after everything today."

We both grab our phones and simultaneously read the message as we cover our mouths with our hands. My heart thrums in my ears, my entire body shaking.

What. The. Fuck.

> **BLOCKED NUMBER**
>
> Peek-a-boo…I see you! Thought I'd start a group chat since you both seem to be ignoring me. I want to make sure you get this one. Stay the fuck away from each other. This is your last warning…or we'll have a real Thriller on our hands.

And included with the message is a photo of us.

In my apartment.

Dancing to Thriller.

"Holy fucking shit!" Jordan screams as he drops to the floor, urging me to fall to the ground with him. I duck behind the couch as he army crawls to the window and reaches up to pull all the curtains shut. "They can see us!"

"What the fuck is with this person! Why are they doing this? Listen…I know you don't want to go to the police, but we are in over our heads here. We need to involve the authorities."

He stands up wearily, as if he's unsure the curtains are truly blocking the view.

"Yeah. Yeah…you're right. Let me call my dad and have him get a discrete security detail here. Kenni…" He extends his hand to help me up. "I know you don't want security, but we're beyond that point right now."

I throw my arms wide. "Jordan, we need to call the police!! This has gotten out of hand."

"What do you think this person is going to do if we call 911? They are around here, somehow watching us, which means they'll *know*. All we're going to do is piss them off even more than they already are when they see a bunch of cop cars pull up outside the building." He places his hands on my shoulders, his eyes bouncing between mine. "I know you're going to call me Richy Rich when I say this, but Ray, our head of security, is legit the best at this kind of shit. He is a former CCIS."

"What the hell is CCIS?"

He huffs a light laugh, easing the tension a bit, as he drags his fingers down my arms to hold my hands. "Canadian Central Intelligence Service. It's like the CIA here in the States. That's basically the police, right?" I drop my chin in a stilted nod. "Let's run this by him and get a security detail here. I'll make sure it's discreet, and no one knows that's what they are doing but us."

I run my hand down my face, all of this adding to the shit day I've already had. "Okay. *Fine.* I'll allow it. I just can't imagine who would be doing this. Should we stay somewhere else? It's one thing for them to send a creepy bear via delivery, but it's another to send a picture of us doing something that happened less than five minutes ago."

He pulls me in tight, his grip like a weighted blanket, calming me down amidst all the chaos. "I think we stay here. You have a doorman downstairs, and we can get some security here ASAP. I think if we move locations, they'll be watching and follow us out. We fly out to Denver in the morning, so let's just get through tonight, and we'll figure out a plan from there."

I nod my head against his chest, "Okay," the only word I can muster out.

I don't know who is trying to scare us, but it's fucking working. *I'd still rather call the police*, but as much as I hate to admit it...he's right.

"Come on," he says, dragging me back to the couch. "Now that we've got the windows covered, let's find another movie to watch, and we'll order in some food while I send a message to Ray."

"So you're going with the 'feed me and tell me I'm pretty' method?"

"I didn't say you were pretty—*I'm* the pretty one, remember?" he says with a smirk.

I double down on my glare, teasing him with a little smack on the arm.

"Plus," he says, tucking a piece of hair behind my ear. "I would never call you pretty. That word doesn't come close to how beautiful you are. You're gorgeous, Kenni," he says as he presses his lips to mine. "Now, come on...let's watch How to Lose a Guy in 10 Days."

47
jordan

I hate travel days. We get our meals, take them on the plane, eat them on the way to land in another city, then practice, work out, and have dinner. It's honestly more exhausting than the games. Add in the fact that I've been worried sick about Kenni all fucking day, and I feel worse than a dying phone battery with no charger in sight. I know she's here in the hotel. I gave her strict instructions not to leave. I feared for my life at the glare she gave me, but was also rocking a semi at the fire in her eyes. However, she reluctantly agreed it was safer for her to stay put. Ray has a guy stationed in the lobby. I saw him earlier, draining some of the tension from my shoulders, but still. *I need to see her.* I need to see she's okay.

Walking into my room, I kick off my shoes and beeline to the adjoining door. How in the hell this arrangement keeps happening, I have no clue, but I'm not questioning it.

The door swings open before I even have a chance to knock. "Wow, that was fast, did you hear me come in, or—"

Lips slam into mine as she pushes me back into my room, shoving me down onto the bed.

"Hi." She climbs on the bed, her legs straddling my hips as my dick throbs against her. "This okay, pretty-boy? You need to use your safe word?"

"Hi back," I respond with a smirk. "And yes. This is one-hundo percent okay. More than okay; this is *okay* to the nth degree."

She laughs as she leans down to slide her nose along mine. "I've been cooped up in this room *all day,* thanks to you and your security detail," she whispers between kisses along my neck. My hips press against hers as I wrap my arms tighter, pulling her close. "I'm stressed with all this stalker shit," —another kiss on my pulse point — "and there's *one* thing that *always* helps me relax." She draws out her words as she reaches for the waistband on my joggers, my dick twitching in response. This woman overwhelms me in a way I never could have imagined. *Fuck, I want her to overwhelm me in every way possible.*

"This..." I pant, "This is what you do for stress relief?"

My stomach grumbles, making her stifle a laugh. "Sounds like you're hungry." She moves her lips to my ear, "I don't have any frites, but I do have something else you could eat."

I suck in a sharp breath. *Is she?* "You're not...you're not talking about food, are you?"

"Nope," she says, popping the p.

Holy fucking fuck balls, this woman. "You mean eating, *with my mouth,* on your—"

She sits up as she grabs my hand, running it down her body down to where our hips meet. "Your mouth right. Fucking. Here," she says, pressing my fingers between her legs.

"Fuuuck, Kenni." I dart my eyes from our hands back to meet her gaze. "Are you sure?"

"Do I feel *unsure,* pretty-boy? When I want something, I ask for it. You've mastered fingering me. Graduated with honors, in fact. And now?" She leans back, pulling her shirt off and tossing it onto the floor. *She's not wearing a bra.* With no bra on, her tits are on full display. Right in my face. *I want to kiss every freckle across her chest. I want to feel her shake underneath me. I want—Shit.* I'm gonna come in my fucking pants again if I don't calm down. *Maple syrup. Demonic bears. Pucks to the face.*

"It's time to test your skills elsewhere. I want to feel your tongue on me. And once you've made me come, I'm gonna put my tongue on you and make you do the same. Unless..."

"Nope. Allllll good here. Give me the cap and gown, play the fucking pomp and circumstance, 'cause I'm ready to graduate," I choke out, convinced that if I don't get to say them, I'll lose my ticket to heaven.

"You know your safe word if you need it?"

I nod. "I don't need to eat frites tonight. Just you."

She jerks her head back, her mouth agape. "Jordan Boucher, look at you with the dirty talk."

A smirk crawls up my face. "I thought about that line the first night I picked my safe word; I've been waiting to drop that one on you."

She laughs, and dear God, the sound goes straight to my heart, healing just a bit more of what I thought was cracked beyond repair. *I want her. I want this. I want—oh fuck it.* The alpha male biker bro invades my body again as I flip her onto her back in one swift move. I kiss her, our tongues colliding as she runs her fingers through my hair.

Her hands tangle in the damp strands, her strength keeping me from the euphoria of her lips. "Slide my pants down, take off my panties, and get between my legs, pretty-boy."

Heat crawls through my stomach as I shift between her thighs. The way she tells me what to do tugs something sharp and low through my body. My dick has achieved full lift off, my pants so fucking tight I see stars, as she lifts her hips to help me remove her clothes. I slowly drag them down her legs, goosebumps spreading like wildfire across her skin. I gently set everything to the side, kissing back up her mouthwatering legs toward her goddamn gorgeous pussy.

"Does this feel good?" I flip my eyes to meet hers, hesitation tightening in my chest.

"Jordan, you are *annoyingly* good at everything you do. Be the confident motherfucker you are in every other area of your life and go down on me like you haven't eaten a meal in a goddamn week. I promise…your mouth on me is *never* going to feel bad. Spread me open and put your tongue on me. Right. Fucking. Now."

Fucking hell. "Yes, Coach." My hands shake, not from nervousness, but in eager anticipation of fucking tasting the woman I've wanted for so long, of making her feel good. I slide one arm under her thigh, carefully spreading her legs apart. My breath hitches as I stare at the wonderland before me. *Kennedy Kramer believes in me.* There's no more questioning. No more doubt. No more hesitation as I slide my tongue along her soaking wet slit. She tastes like my every hope and dream, and I nearly explode with how fucking good it is. She moans, the rumble vibrating through her body as she writhes against my face.

My hips buck, my length begging for attention. Begging for my hand. *But this isn't about me, this is about her.* I adjust slightly, paying attention to every cue she gives. She bows off the bed, and I take that as a hint to use more pressure. She relaxes, and I explore more of her, trying to find that spot. Her spot. The one that sends her over the edge when I find it with my fingers. *I wonder if my tongue gives enough pressure.*

"JJ," she pants, "just a little more to the left and a little more pressure—*oh my God*. There! Right there." She can barely breathe, her gasps hoarse with pleasure, and I file the moment away. Her response lifts something in my chest, a quiet pride that I'm doing this to her. That I *can* fucking do this.

"Holy shit. Just like that," she moans as I flick my tongue against her clit. "Nothing feels as good as your tongue. Not toys, not fingers, not…" she trails off with a groan, grinding her hips into my face again.

The woman of my dreams is lifting her hips into my tongue, and fuck *if this isn't the best feeling in the world.*

She gasps as I slide a finger inside, the sound bolting straight to my dick. I tease inside until I feel her react, pressing the spot harder as I suck her clit. A breathless moan escapes her, her thighs quivering on either side of my cheeks as she finds her release with no warning. But I'm not stopping. Not until I know she's done. Not until I feel her clit throb against my tongue.

My pulse races as she continues to shake, holding her breath for what seems like ages. She's still grinding into me—fucking my mouth as her voice echoes around us.

She finally exhales, collapsing back against the pillow, her arms relaxing against her sides. "That was…*fuck*, that was…"

"Good?"

She smiles as she slowly shakes her head. "Good would be the understatement of the century. You are fucking amazing, you know that?"

My cheeks flush. I've been told countless times I play great—praise is guaranteed with the job if you do well. But not with her. *This settles deeper.* I know deep in my chest that I couldn't have done this any other way. I couldn't have done it with anyone but her.

She motions for me to join her, and I crawl up beside her, leaning in for a kiss…hesitation stops me as I realize she may not want my lips on hers after what I just did. But, as usual, she throws my doubt out the window and pulls me in, a soft moan reverberating into my mouth. Our tongues dance, my body desperate for hers as I pull myself flush against her curves.

"Off," she demands as she pushes my T-shirt up. Tugging it over my head and tossing it aside, I lean back on my elbows with a groan as she rakes her hand across my chest, down my abdomen, right to the waistband of my joggers. Her eyes catch mine, her hand inching toward my raging hard on.

"Kenni..." My voice cracks. "You really don't have to do this. This is about helping me. Making sure my...*skills* are up to par. You don't need to—"

"Stop. This isn't how sex works—we *both* leave taken care of. This isn't a one-way street. You've finished before, twice, without even touching yourself. And it was the fucking hottest thing in my life. But," —her touch dances across my thighs— "I'm glad you didn't finish yet." She tiptoes her fingers around the base of my shaft, and goddammit, I'm fighting to stay in control. *Black licorice. Overtime loss. Low social media engagement.* "Now that you've had a taste of me," —her fingers still, light as a feather as she touches my cock through my sweats, my hips bucking at the contact— "I want a taste of you."

"Fucking hell," I groan. "I'm not going to last long."

She pops her smoldering eyes up to mine. "In case you haven't noticed, I don't care if you come in your fucking pants, last two seconds or two hours. You make me feel unbelievably good I want to return the favor." My dick twitches when she reaches the tip. I drop my head onto the pillows. "You okay, pretty-boy?"

"Yes," I whisper with a shuddered breath.

She kneels between my legs, leaning forward with her fucking gorgeous, full tits hanging down like the most perfect pears straight from the holy grail of Genovia for my pre-game snack. *I need to make this a new part of my routine.* She pulls my joggers and boxers down in one move. Her eyes widen as my dick bobs free.

"God*damn*." She licks her lips as a wicked grin spreads across her cheeks. "It is *really* unfair how fucking perfect you are."

"You're gonna give me a big head," I joke breathlessly, trying to maintain my composure for at least the two sections she mentioned.

"I think we're already there." She winks as she licks up the full length of my cock.

My entire body writhes as I white-knuckle the sheets. "Holy shit." She places her mouth around me, her lips fully surrounding my swollen head and licking the pre-cum from my slit. She flicks and swirls her tongue around me before taking me deeper into her mouth. My abs tighten as I place my hand on her head. Not to hold it down, just to give her quiet reassurance that she's perfect. *She's everything.* She's my every wish, and now she has her goddamn lips wrapped around my dick.

Maybe this is heaven.

She moves up and down my cock, her hands gripping my thighs. I suck in a sharp breath as her teeth graze my skin, the muscles in my abs clenching so goddamn tight I know I'm going to be sore in the morning. *Fucking hell; she knows what she's doing.* Going down farther, she takes in my entire length, and I can feel the back of her throat. Holy mother fucking balls, I can't hold it much longer.

"Fuck," I groan, "I'm so close."

I ease her back and instinctively grab my dick, barely stroking it before my body jerks, cum spilling onto my hands and dripping down my cock. I settle deeper into the mattress as I come down from my high. I've done this so many times before. Thinking about her, imagining it was her. This time, though...it was *with* her. Her hands, her body, her mouth on me.

"I think I might die right now," I barely whisper.

She kisses her way up my body, inch by inch, finally settling next to me, resting her head on my chest. "Don't die, pretty-boy. You have a lot of talents to share with the world."

"I'll keep that in mind," I say with a wry smile, kissing the top of her head as her fingers mindlessly run across my stomach.

We lie in silence, basking in the aftermath of our orgasms, as I feel her breathing slow, the most perfect woman finally asleep in my arms. My cheeks lift as my heart soars. *I can't believe this is my life.* I gingerly kiss the top of her head, careful not to disturb her. Fuck…I can't believe I just went down on Kennedy Kramer. I fully understand that quote from The Little Mermaid about it being better down where it's wetter. I've never done that, too scared to even try before. Too scared to trust someone enough to try. I bite my lip—*goddammit, why is my life so much like that movie?* Ursula tricked Ariel for her own gain, and that's exactly what Angelica did to me. *Fucking sea witches.*

But just like Ariel, I survived. My very own Prince Eric rescued me and is sleeping peacefully against my chest. If only Kennedy could ram a ship into the fucking sea witch that held my life hostage for so long. *God, the money I would pay for that to happen.*

I rub circles on her back, my body filled with a warmth I never thought possible. We've slept in the same bed before, but this feels different. Words on the tip of my tongue I've not dared to say give me hope that maybe, just maybe, she would stay. That maybe she feels this undeniable pull, too. Hope that maybe we could find our way to forever.

48
jordan

"Fuck you, Walton!" I shout at the Colorado Storm player who will *not* get off my goddamn back, shoving me into the boards *again*.

"I mean, if you're into that, I can make the arrangements," he chirps back, panting and out of breath. "But how about I fuck your jaw with my fist instead?"

I grit my teeth, dropping my shoulder into his pads. *God, I hate this guy.*

We're in game seven of the second round against the team with the player I hate more than the fiancé villain guy in The Notebook —*fucking Chase Walton*. Every time we play the Storm, one of us ends up in the box with bruised fists. He's a cocky, pompous, over-the-top son of a bitch, but shit...he's a damn good player. *Wait... why is this description sounding so familiar?* Rage sets in my jaw like a puck to the face. *Shit on a hockey stick...he's the 'me' of the Storm.* Well, now I hate him even more. I have no choice but to prove I'm the better Bougie of the two of us. And in a game seven, series-clinching, 'if we win, we go to the final round and play for the Cup' situation, that means only one thing. Full-on Bougification.

"You know what, Walnuts? I *would* like to make arrangements for that. You, me, a romantic rendezvous in the locker room? Sounds like heaven."

"Shut the fuck up, Doucher. Guess that new girlfriend of yours isn't fulfilling your needs. Clearly, you need a stud like Chase Walton to satisfy you."

"You sound sexually frustrated there, bud. Maybe you're the one who has the problem with your woman fulfilling your needs?"

His face turns redder than the goal light as he throws his stick and gloves. *Got him.* As much as I hate the guy, I do keep up on my celeb gossip, and he has it bad for his woman. *Relatable.* My chest surges with pride—I knew *exactly* how to get him to drop gloves first.

I drop mine as the crowd goes wild. A game seven on the road is never easy, but if I can get this motherfucker to throw the first punch because of my stellar chirping and sprinkle in some of my top-notch acting skills…our power play is killer.

"Talk about Zoe like that again, you won't have a mouth to speak with, Boucher!" he spits.

"You started this, Walton! And we all know the Zamboni gets more pussy sitting on it than your dick."

A sharp pain hits my jaw. I was waiting for it. I knew it was coming. But he doesn't know what I have up my sleeve. I dramatically collapse to the ice as if I just got knocked out by Mike Tyson. I lay on the ground for a moment, acting dead to the world. I've done this before. It's another Bougie special. I call it The Opossum. The arena goes silent, gasps and murmurs humming around me. I fight my smirk. *If nothing else, my acting skills are great.*

"Walton, in the box. Roughing," the ref announces.

"What the fuck? He's fine! He's fucking faking! You're not giving him an embellishment call?"

"He's out cold, Walton; now get in the goddamn box."

"Boucher started this!" he screams as the official skates him across the rink.

A whiff of smelling salts hits me before I crack my eyes open and find Zack Reeves and Hayes Larson standing over me, along with the Riders' medical personnel.

"You okay, Bougie?" Larsy asks.

"My jaw hurts like hell, but we could use a break and a power play." I wink. "I'm fine, but keep acting like you're really worried, and we'll be all good."

A wicked grin twists Larsy's face while Zack seems more than a little pissed.

"This could have gotten you, *us*, in even more trouble, you know that, right?" Zack admonishes.

"Z, the fact that you doubt my acting skills is really hurtful." I pout, shifting my jaw side to side. "What'd he get? Two? Four? Five?"

"Two, but we'll make it count," Larsy says.

"I have to walk you back to the bench, Bougie," Dr. Gregory says as he helps me sit up. I hear half of the crowd clapping, the other half booing me. I may have been known to embellish a time or two, but I *actually* got punched here, so that helps me sell it.

We head back to the bench, Walton still screaming from the box that he knows I was faking. He's a smart guy. I fight the smirk I'm dying to send his way. He really is the 'me' of the Storm, but today I was the wind that blew that storm in another direction. I'm restless on the bench as I get evaluated, but my team is up a player, so mission-fucking-accomplished.

I glance at the Jumbotron. We're tied. Getting another goal before the second period is over is crucial. We need the momentum to swing in our direction, and the fist that swung at my face was the exact directional change we needed. As I look down the ice to see my teammates set up a play, the red lamp lighting up behind the goal, I know it was worth it. Everyone on the bench jumps to their feet, cheering and screaming. We're up 2-1.

I'm proud of myself. My antics. The way I served them up on a silver platter to get our team an advantage.

Until I look at the crowd.

In the box where the WAGs are sitting, I see Maggie and Olivia on either side of Kennedy. They all flew out since we are either going to the next round or our season's done. But they aren't just standing beside her, they have her in their arms, almost like they are…consoling her? *Fuck*. Is Kennedy…is she crying? My breath catches in my throat, knowing she's right here but still out of reach. The game isn't over. I'm stuck. I'm stuck here. Unable to ask what's wrong. Unable to comfort her.

The horn sounds signaling the period's over, and the team heads back to the locker rooms. But I can't move. I can't breathe. My heart sinks. *What's wrong? What's going on?*

"Bougie, you okay, man?" Larsy asks as he bumps me on the bench, my frozen ass blocking his way. "I thought you said you were good after that hit."

I stand up, my eyes still fixed on her.

"Yeah…I just…" I jut my chin toward the suites. "Kennedy looks like she's crying up there, and I'm kinda freaking out."

He looks up, his brows narrowing as he sees what I'm seeing. Larsy sighs, putting his arm around my shoulders. "Come on; let's go back to the locker room. We'll text them real quick and figure out what's going on."

I nod, following his lead. "Yeah. Yeah, good idea. We'll text them." I glance back. "Do you think she's okay?"

"Jordan, listen. Olivia and Maggie have been at this for a while.

They're used to the violence of what we do. You took a nasty punch and literally played dead. If I had to take a wild stab in the dark at what's going on, she's worried about you."

Oh my God. The blood drains from my face. I never thought to walk her through this. She's not a super huge hockey fan like Olivia and Maggie. She doesn't know shit about what I've done in the past or the lengths I'll go with my antics. She doesn't come to many games. *She doesn't know.* I feel sick to my stomach, like Walton punched me there instead of my face. God, I never wanted to hurt her. I never wanted to make her cry.

But in the midst of all this chaos, something else hits my chest. Something I never had with a woman that wasn't my friend or family. Something that makes me feel like I'm flying through the clouds above the arena.

My smile feels almost manic. *She's worried about me.*

49

kennedy

He's on the ground. He's on the ground, and he's not moving. He's just lying there. A knot twists in my stomach, one far worse than any turbulence I've ever experienced. I've been in literal near-death situations from my Guard duties, but nothing has given me the sense of dread I feel right now. It's one thing when you're facing your own death. It's another entirely when you're fearing it may happen to someone else. Someone you actually care about. *Even if you're not ready to admit it yet.*

My hands are shaking, my legs are wobbly, and tears are welling up in my eyes. *What the hell happened to him?* I jump to my feet, my hands wrapped around my waist. *And what the hell is happening to me?!*

Olivia puts her arm around my shoulder, both of us watching in horror as Jordan lies motionless on the ice. "You, okay? God, I didn't think about the fact that you're so new to hockey life."

I can't answer, my voice refusing to work as I tremble in her arms.

"Kenni," Maggie reassures me, "he's probably fine. Your man

does this a lot. He was most likely trying to draw a penalty and get the Riders a man advantage. He's famous throughout the league for doing this. Stop me if you've heard this before," she says in a sarcastic tone, "but Jordan Boucher is quite known for his theatrics."

I huff out a little laugh that interrupts my tears for a moment. "I guess so. But...how do you know what's real and what's fake with someone like him?"

"You're the one *fake* dating him," Olivia says, making air quotes with her fingers, "you tell me. How does one know when something is fake or has turned real?"

I narrow my eyes as I sniffle, slowly turning my head to face her. "It's like you said. I'm not used to this. It's different when the person living in your apartment is the one lying on the ice. I am allowed to worry about my fake boyfriend."

"Sure you are," Maggie snorts, her tone dripping with snark. "I'd be worried about my *roommate* to the point of tears dripping off my chin, too, in this situation. So..." She sniffs. "So..." She sniffs again. "Worried. Platonically, of course. This is all fake. You would never have real feelings for that man."

I turn my glare to Maggie, the bitch having the audacity to flutter her eyelashes at me.

"Anything you'd like to share with the class, Kenni?"

"Look! He's sitting up!" Olivia shouts, tapping my arm. "See? He's going to be fine."

I see the trainers helping him stand before ushering him back to the bench. *At least that guy on the other team got a penalty.* God, I want to karate chop that guy in the face for hurting Jordan. Also, if his perfect little face is injured one little bit, I *am* going to retaliate.

I watch Jordan sit on the bench, the trainers tending to his face, the crowd going somewhat silent again, except for everyone in our suite starting to scream. We scored a goal. We're winning. I don't even care. I mean, I do, because I know it's important to the team, to the fans, to *him*, but all I feel is numbness until I know he's okay. *Does he have a concussion? Does he need stitches?* I don't see blood, but we're pretty far up here.

Oh shit. My heart stops. *I have to go to the airport now.* Fresh tears fill my eyes. God, I fucking hate this. This is why I don't come to many games, because now I have to leave to prepare myself to fly the team home and focus on my job.

That's when I lose it.

Full-on tears streaming down my face, ugly crying, hiccuping sobs rack through me. Dammit, there are probably cameras on me, too.

"Aw, Kenni, it's going to be okay! I promise he's fine. Hey, I'll text Hayes, and hopefully he'll see it and text back before the next period," Olivia says, rubbing her hand down my back as Maggie does the same. I collapse against Maggie's shoulder, no clue how I lucked out moving down the hall from her and gaining this group of girlfriends. I don't know how I'd survive without them, *despite their meddling in my love life.*

"I'm sorry, guys. It's just…there's a lot going on right now. I think this was just the final straw for me, from holding in all my emotions for the past couple of months. I'm just…" I groan, burying my head in my hands, "yes, I'm fucking worried about him. Apparently, through all this, I caught fucking feelings for him, and it's overwhelming as fuck. Being in this world is all so new. Hell, even being in the same apartment every night when we're home is new. He's nothing like I ever expected, but everything I needed. And he's so fucking sweet! Why does he have to be so nice?" I laugh, the sound watery. "He set up that damn espresso maker he got me and makes a vanilla almond milk latte every morning before he leaves. He even figured out how to make a heart in the foam!" Maggie smirks, Olivia's eyes shining with understanding. "You know how they say some people have old souls? Well, he's a twenty-three-year-old with the heart of a Millennial. He watches Saved by the Bell reruns as a part of his pre-game routine before every game, for God's sake. Every game! *And* he watches an endless amount of rom-coms with me. Did you know he can practically recite Sweet Home Alabama by heart?"

"I'm not surprised. Once, Zack and Kara brought one of their kids to meet us for dinner, and there were a lot of 'you have a baby in a bar' quotes that night." Olivia giggles.

I'm genuinely sad I wasn't there to see that.

"We were watching 13 Going on 30, and he made me get up and do the Thriller dance with him. He had to drag me off the couch, but dammit…it was kind of fun."

Olivia hums, dropping her head on my shoulder, and watches the Zambonis clean the ice.

"He was so nervous around me when this all started. I couldn't figure out why. Then he told me he was my secret admirer, and it all clicked. And as much as it pains me to say this out loud…you were right. Dammit, why are you always right? He was nervous because he liked me. I should be pissed. I should hate him because he couldn't just man up and say what he was thinking. But… goddammit, I kind of like that he didn't!" I collapse into my seat. "Why am I so drawn to the fact that he's the most caring, compassionate, selfless, kind-hearted person I've ever met? And why the *hell* would he want to be with a sarcastic, I hate the world, fuck the man, woman like me? I was such a bitch to him for so long. And he doesn't even seem to care! But he should care, right? I ignored him for months. God, I'm such a bitch. And now he could be hurt? Really hurt? I want to take back every time I ever snubbed him on that damn plane."

Another wave of ugly tears hits. I can't hold them back. I don't want to. They have been walled up behind a dam that's cracked wide open; there's no putting them back or stopping them.

"Kenni, look at me," Maggie says, her fingers finding mine. "You can't change the past. Let me tell you from experience, no matter how much you want to, that shit is set. Vladi and I have had our issues, specifically about how we treated one another when we should have listened, but somehow, it brought us closer together. And everything you're saying right now sounds a lot like you care about Jordan. Take your regrets and pour every ounce of them into loving him back for the rest of your life."

I swallow hard, my eyes staring widely at hers. "Maggie...I don't know that we're in love."

"Love comes in a lot of different ways," Olivia encourages me. "Hayes and I fell in love super fast. Maggie and Vladi? They took some time to see it. But everything you've just said? Your brain might be having a hard time catching up to your heart, but that's love."

I sniffle as I pull them in for a hug. "I mean this in the most *loving* way, but I hate you both so much right now. Thank you." I swipe the mascara from under my eyes. "Maybe you're right. Fuck, I don't know. But I have to pull myself together and get ready for work. I'll see you all back in Milwaukee."

"We love you, Kenni!" Maggie and Liv shout as I grab my bag and head out. I take a deep breath, trying to calm myself down a bit, as a burst of warmth floods my chest like a waterfall. Standing in the hall, still in uniform with his hair dripping sweat, skates off, in his socks and slides, and completely out of breath and ready to burst through the door is the man I've been worried as shit about.

"JJ! What...what are you doing here—"

He interrupts me, pulling me in and pressing his lips so tightly into mine I am not sure they'll ever come apart. I grip his shoulders awkwardly with all this gear, losing myself in this man. This feeling of warmth, of being in his arms? Nothing else matters. Not anyone who sees us. Not the fact that he is a hot, sweaty mess. Not the raw emotion I purged in the suite. It's just us, in this moment, and it's perfect.

We finally pull apart, and he immediately brings me in to hold me in his arms for another stolen moment.

"Kenni, I'm so, so, *so* sorry. I took that punch to draw a penalty. I didn't think to mention I do that sometimes, and I'm sure that scared the hell out of you. I saw you crying, and I got my skates off as fast as I could to catch you before you had to leave for the airport. I'm *so* sorry. I never meant to scare you."

The tears fall again—I couldn't hold them back if I tried.

"I'm just...dammit, I'm just so glad you're okay." I sob into his jersey as I squeeze him as tight as I'm able to. I can't let him go. My pulse quickens, as goosebumps scatter across my skin. *What if I don't ever want to let him go?* "I thought you were...I thought it was..."

"I'm right here, baby. I'm fine," he says as he holds my head against his chest, rubbing my back and soothing this ache in my heart. "You can't get rid of me that easily. You'll have to drown me in maple syrup to kill me and, even then, I'll drag you in with me."

I let out an exasperated laugh. "Don't you dare threaten to drown me in that horrible stuff. Let's at least drown in blueberry compote if we're destined to have a food-related Romeo and Juliet-style death. Deal?"

"Deal. Listen, I have to get back to, you know, the game."

"JJ...oh God! I'm so sorry I took your focus away from the game—"

"No." He cradles my head in his hands. "Nothing, *nothing* is more important than you."

My heart flutters in my chest, the words hitting me like a freight train.

"Thank you for checking on me." I can't help but kiss him again. "But get your ass back down to that locker room and win this damn game. Got it?"

"Have I told you I love it when you boss me around?" he whispers, a smirk on his face.

"No. But I'm not going to lie, I like this dynamic a lot more than I should." We both laugh as he kisses me one last time. "Now go. I'll see you on the plane."

50
kennedy

Sitting in the FBO at the airport, my pulse is still flying through my veins like it's gaining altitude, my heart soaring knowing he ran through an entire arena to get to me. Getting myself mentally prepared for a flight after all that is rough. Trying to focus on anything other than the score of the game is...also rough.

I have never been a huge sports fan. I enjoy going to a game once in a while, but have never really been the diehard fan that checks scores and keeps up with stats and standings. But now? There's a minute left in the game, the Riders are still up 2-1, and I'm waiting with bated breath for the damn clock to hit zero. If they win, it will be a while before the flight with post-game celebrations. And I'm going to hug the crap out of my damn pretty-boy when he gets here. I don't care if the team says shit, hoots and hollers, or whistles like we're in high school. Him coming to check on me means I threw all the rules out the window.

If they lose, they'll be packed up and headed out before I know it. I freeze, my blood going cold. *If they lose, our arrangement is over.* Date through the playoffs, and then we break up. If this was supposed to be a quick, easy, no strings attached arrangement, then why the fuck are my eyes burning? Surely, he wouldn't want to break up, not after what happened today. The way he found me, comforted me, and kissed me. Today, everything went way beyond fake dating.

Everything's changed for me. I pick at my nails. *Does he feel the same?*

Fuck. *I am a professional.* I set my phone down and focus on my flight plans on my iPad. *I can do this.* My training taught me to compartmentalize during tough situations—I can't show my emotions here. I've pushed them aside before, and I'll do it again now—flip a switch in my brain and focus on the task at hand.

As soon as I power up my iPad, my phone buzzes. It's face down. I stare at it, biting my lip as if that will somehow make the outcome what I want. We either won or it's going into OT. Also, apparently, I'm talking in hockey terms now? *Grilled Cheesus, what is happening to me?* I pick up my phone like it's a loaded weapon, flipping it over to see a notification of the final score flashing across the top of my screen.

> "Steel Riders 2, Storm 1. Milwaukee Advances to the third round."

I jump up from my seat, screaming and crying and wanting nothing more than to be back with my friends at the arena to hug them and celebrate together. I'm so damn proud of them. All of them. They've worked so hard this season.

Jordan talks about them all the time, a little hitch in his voice and an unconscious smile showing how much they mean to him. The fact that he's so close with his family and they can't always be here, but he does have his found family through the team, brings tears to my eyes. He talks about them every day like he'd do anything for any one of them. I smirk, knowing he absolutely would.

Another notification pops up.

> **HANNAH**
> I just saw the score—so exciting!! Wish I could have been there. Hopefully I can make a game in the next round and we can catch up some more! 🖤🏒

It's been nice having Hannah to chat with about some of what's going on.

> **KENNEDY**
> Hopefully you can make a game in Milwaukee, so I won't have to leave early! Stupid job stealing our girl time, but a girl boss never stops! See you soon!

A few of the flight crew peek in after hearing my screaming, immediately joining in on the celebration. We can't drink champagne, so we toast our coffees and Diet Cokes and freak out in this small space, unbelievably excited for our clients to make it to the next round. We work hard to make their travel as seamless as possible. Early mornings. Late nights. Insane turnarounds. But seeing it from the other side—seeing how exhausted Jordan is after a game, how many bumps and bruises he has—the team makes my job feel easy. *He* makes my job feel easy.

Funny enough, the one person not here is Chadd. He's usually here by now, annoying everyone in his wake. He doesn't *have* to be at the FBO right now, but now that the game is over, we need to get the plane ready for departure.

Not waiting around for him, I shrug and head to the jet. Stepping onboard, I hear a voice, the tension in my shoulders lessening. I should have given Chadd the benefit of the doubt that he was here preparing for the flight. Then I hear a second voice. And that second voice is not speaking. It's *moaning*. My eyes bulge out of my face as I turn to see Chadd sitting in the Captain's seat with Mara on his lap. Thank God they are both fully clothed, but there is a significant amount of grinding going on. And dirty talk I could've gone forever without hearing. I quickly take a step back, my hand balled into a fist at my side as I assess my options here. They are in a heavy makeout-dry hump session in *my* fucking flight deck. *Doesn't he know he could get fired for this?*

Okay, option one: I do nothing. I hide in the shadows and wait for someone else, like Theresa, to come in and start being loud while getting snacks ready for the team.

Option two: I confront them. I'll probably seem like the bitch, but then again, I don't care what Chadd McAsshat thinks of me at this point. He's being unprofessional, and I'm going to call him out on it. I grit my teeth, cracking my knuckles in a moment that would make Jordan proud. *You know what? It's on.*

I walk in confidently, hang my hat up on the hook behind my seat, and start building my nest.

"Oh! Hi Chadd. Nice to see you again, Mara. Let me know if you'd like to deploy the oxygen masks since you two are clearly out of breath."

They instantly pull away from one another, but only Chadd seems mildly shocked as he shoves her and adjusts himself. Mara stands up, leaning back slightly to give me a good once-over. "Hmm."

Oh, she did not just 'hmm' me. That's *my* line. *What the fuck is with these two?*

"Well, if you two are done, I'm going to need your friend to head out. As the captain, *you* should know we need to do our pre-departure briefing and get this jet ready for takeoff, not whatever you two were doing."

Mara gives me the 'you are a giant bitch' look as she straightens her shirt before leaning down to grotesquely kiss the fucking douchebag with full-on tongue. *Let me go find a barf bag.*

"I'll see you later," he says, smacking her ass as she makes her way out.

"Bye. Sooo nice seeing you, Kennedy!" she throws over her back on her way to her actual seat in the cabin of the plane.

I snap my head toward him. "What the hell, Chadd? I have to touch those buttons."

"Don't be jealous, sweetheart," he snorts, "you had your chance."

"Don't call me sweetheart. Can we just get on with flight prep, please?"

He smirks. "Sure thing, sweetheart."

Fucking fuckhead prick; I hope he impales himself on a stick and not in a fun way. My jaw clenches. He's calling me sweetheart now just to get on my nerves. He knows I can't do a damn thing about it either. *Fuck.*

With our pre-flight checklists done, I scroll through the Riders' social media accounts as I hear applause behind me. They're here. *He's here.* The team files onto the plane, and I hop up from my seat to greet them all as they enter. If Chadd can have his girlfriend mauling his face in the flightdeck, I can at least give my boyfriend a hug as he walks on the plane after winning a big game. As I step into the galley, I see fucking Mara sitting in the front row with her sunglasses on. *What the actual fuck is with the sunglasses?* I feel my brows touch my hairline. *Chadd sure knows how to pick 'em.*

I see player after player walking in as all the flight crew, including myself but excluding Chadd, come out to high-five them. Hayes and Zack both stop to give me a hug as they pass by. Vladi gives me a nod, which seems on brand.

It's agonizing waiting for him, but finally, that dark hair and million-dollar smile make their way through the forward cabin door. Biting my cheek, I can barely stand it as Colton Taylor takes his sweet ass time, walking at turtle speed past the crew. Jordan's eyes finally meet mine, and I don't give a shit if I'm the pilot on this plane or not. My eyes burn with tears *again*. He shakes Theresa's hand, his eyes continually flicking toward mine. The minute she lets go, I grab him, pulling him in for the biggest hug ever. Without even thinking about it, my lips are on his. I can't figure out what's possessing me to do this, but every cell in my body wants me to keep going. How did I go from finding this guy to be the most annoying person on the planet to not being able to keep my hands and my heart from him?

We finally pull back. "Hi," he says shyly.

"Hi."

"That was a hell of a greeting."

I slap him on the arm. "It was a congratulatory hug. Don't get too excited."

"Hug *and* kiss. What kind of congratulatory greeting do I get if we win the Cup?"

I lean into his ear. "It won't be a kiss, that's for sure."

He chokes, his knees nearly buckling under him. "And don't think we're not going to discuss how you scared the shit out of me earlier today. It's time for another lesson, pretty-boy."

I pull back, seeing his eyes wide as can be. My heart races, and I realize very quickly that, complicated or not, win or lose, I do *not* want this to be over. This may have started as fake, but these goddamn feelings coming over me are pretty fucking real. And it's time to stop fighting it.

51
jordan

"Vladster! We made it to the third round!!!" I say as I take my seat next to him, nudging him with my elbow. "Aren't you at least a little excited?!" We never sit apart. Ever. He acts like he hates it, but I know he secretly loves me. I'm sure of it. *I'm 91% sure of it...* The damn man is so hard to read. He never shows a hint of emotion, even after a big win like this. Me? I'm ready to skydive out of the plane with excitement, whereas Vladi looks his normal, calm, cool demeanor, not a hint of excitement showing on his face.

"We are not done yet," he says stoically. "I will celebrate when our names, specifically yours, are on the Cup. Mine is already on there from before I came to Milwaukee. But you and everyone else on this team deserve it. We play hard. We fight hard." A ghost of an emotion flickers across his expression. "There is something special about this group."

My smile widens knowing he does actually like us all. "Damn straight! You can at least smile about that, can't you?"

He huffs a quiet laugh as a half-smile creeps up his face. "Perhaps," he quips, putting his earbuds in before takeoff.

"Vladi, wait! Can I ask you a question?"

"Of course." He removes the earbuds and shifts in his seat to face me.

Whip me, beat me, take away my charge cards...Vladi is talking! I force my mouth closed. *I got an 'of course' out of him.* This is monu-freaking-mental! Between the adrenaline I have from that kiss and the fact that Vladi's willing to let me ask him a question, taking out his earbuds and everything, the plane doesn't need to fly. I'm pretty sure I just grew wings and can fly us home. *Calm down, Jordan.* It's only the man you've dreamed of being BFFs with being very nice to you. *Focus and ask your question.*

"How did you, um...how did you know you were in love with Maggie?"

I notice a flicker of compassion cross his face as he searches for the right answer. He is a man of few words normally, but I can tell he's really mulling this over.

"I knew she was special from the moment I met her." His eyes go out of focus, a darkness clinging to him. "But it took me a long time to realize it was love as I'd never experienced that before. You hear people talk about it. They write songs, stories, even poetry. *Classy* poetry, Jordan. But to feel it—it is something completely unexpected. It felt as though my heart was caving in and blowing up at the same time. It honestly took all my friends, Larsy, Zack, even you, for me to realize what it was I was feeling. When you feel it, you simply know."

Well shit. All the emotions of today have tears forming in my eyes. "I'm...I'm your friend, Vladi?"

He doesn't look at me, staring at the headrest in front of us. "You are my friend, Jordan. There are days I question your sanity, but...you were there for me when I needed you. You helped Maggie when she needed you. We are both grateful to have you in our lives. That is what friends are, yes?"

If I ignore the burning in my eyes, that means it isn't real, right? "Vladimir, You're gonna make me cry."

"Do *not* cry. Let us get back to what we were talking about, yes?" I nod, zipping my lips and sitting on my hands. "If you ask me, someone racing through the arena between periods to make sure the one they care about is okay sounds a lot like what someone in love would do."

I swallow down the knot clogging my throat. "Really?"

He slowly nods. "I told Larsy this once when he asked the same thing about Olivia. There's a Russian saying: when love is not madness, it is not love. Risking your recovery time in such an important game, risking getting benched or fined, facing *my wrath* if my defenseman was not back in time—you did whatever it took to make sure Kennedy was okay. That sounds like madness to me." He puts his headphones in and turns on his music, ending the conversation on his terms.

I flop back against my seat, my shoulders dropping as if every care in the world melted away. *If there is one thing I am crazy fucking mad about in this world, it's her.* I've been that way for months. And she's seen the real me, and she's still here. She was *worried* about me. A warm breath catches in my lungs—I've never had anyone outside of my family worry about me. When I saw her crying today, it felt like my chest was crushing in on itself. She was hurting and it made me hurt just as bad. I bite my cheek. *Vladi, as usual, is right.* I love her. I was already 99% sure, but hearing it from Russian Yoda's mouth means it must be true.

When we finally take off, my chest lifts with pride—we made it another round. *My team truly is something else.* But I have even more pride in the fact that the woman who was worried about me, the one I am crazy about, is the one flying this plane. Nothing can take my smile away. Without a shadow of a doubt, I am in love with Kennedy Kramer.

"Oh my God, I almost forgot to tell you," Kenni says casually as we ride the elevator up to her apartment. "I caught Chadd and his creepy girlfriend dry humping each other on the plane tonight!"

"What?!" I whip my head around to make sure I heard correctly. "Holy shit! They were doing cock stuff in the cockpit? I don't even feel like anyone can roll their eyes at me for making this joke; it wrote itself."

She snorts as she playfully glares at me. "*Technically*, it's called the flight deck now. They changed it because cockpit implied that you had to have a cock to fly it."

My eyes go wide. "Oh shit, sorry I didn't—"

"You're fine." She laughs, placing her hand on my arm. "It really doesn't bother me. Now we joke that when two women are flying it's called the clit pit and it's hijack proof since a man could never find it."

I gasp, placing my hand against my chest. "Kennedy Kramer, did you just make a *joke*? I couldn't be more proud. However, I would like to point out that *I* would have no trouble finding it. Given I have the world's best clit coach at my disposal. Oh my God, should that be on a mug? Like Michael Scott's World's Best Boss one? It should totally be on a mug."

She cackles, falling against me. "If you get me a World's Best Clit Coach mug I will drink out of it every morning."

"I'm getting you a travel one so you can take it on flights," I joke, her laugh warm against my neck. "Oh! Speaking of plane tea, did you see Mara with her damn sunglasses again?"

"Oh my God, *yes*. What the fuck is with the glasses?"

My heart soars. As if Kennedy wasn't already the most *fantastic* woman ever, it appears we both love to gossip. "Right? The fuck are those about? Who does she think she's Audry

Hepburn? *God.* Her and Chadd McPooPirate make quite the couple."

"I love your nicknames for him." She snorts. "Thank God they were fully clothed because I do *not* want to think about Chadd's," —her face scrunches like she's trying not to be sick— "sweaty bits and pieces all over that seat. I mean, it's kind of hot to think about doing it on a jet, but not those two."

"Smashing in the *flight deck*?" I wink finally using the correct terminology. "For sure hot. Between those two? Gross." I gag. "I bet he has old balls."

Kennedy snorts out the cutest laugh. "Let's see…how would you say this? One-hundo percent that dude has nasty, old man balls."

"Chadd McOldBalls," I say as we arrive at our floor and nearly fall out of the elevator in a fit of laughter, trying to be quiet since it's after two in the morning and I don't want to get her kicked out of her apartment. *God, I love laughing with her.* The fact that we can joke around like this is like the high after a big win. I love that she finally feels comfortable enough to joke around and laugh and let out her own feelings. I've seen her be like this around our friends, and my heart skips a beat knowing she's letting me see this side over her too.

As we approach the door to her apartment, she struggles with the key fob. *Again.*

"You've lived here how long and you still can't open this door?"

The side eye she gives me could cut through a steel beam. But I love it. "Well, *excuse me* Mr.Perfect. I know how to do a lot of cool stuff like, oh, I don't know, flying a fucking plane. Refueling fighter jets while in the air. Did you know I'm a fucking Major? This lock just sucks ass!"

I hold my hand out, and she immediately hands the fob over. I set it directly on the lock and the door immediately pops open.

"I hate you so much," she grumbles with a laugh.

I kiss her cheek. "No, you don't."

"I don't, huh?" she snarks as we step into the apartment and I drop our stuff on the floor. "What makes you say that?"

Maybe it's the fact that we won tonight. Maybe it's the pure exhaustion of trying to pretend I didn't like her for months. Maybe it's the fact that she was crying in my arms earlier today, but a jolt of something surges through me. It's steady, calm, certain. It pushes me forward like that first night at the bar. It's a feeling only she gives me. *Fuck it.* As soon as she shuts the door behind her, I cage her against the wood with my hands. I lean in closer, our lips a breath away. "You were worried about me today. Very concerned, actually. Most people don't hate people they show *concern* for."

Her face flushes, warmth radiating from her skin in the sliver of space separating us. "Maybe I just didn't want you to come home and be all whiny because your face hurt. You would be *insufferable*."

I hum, my eyes flashing with delight. "My jaw *is* killing me. But there is only one thing I'm suffering from right now." I breathe, pressing my thighs around her leg. "And it's not a broken jaw."

She sucks in a quick breath, her body shivering at my words. "What's gotten into you tonight, pretty-boy?"

"You. Kennedy, you're what's gotten into me."

52
kennedy

Our tongues collide, our hands roaming over every inch of one another with an intensity I've never felt before. Kissing him is…it's everything. Every time is a new experience.

The first one at that restaurant was me testing the water, dipping my toe into a pool I didn't realize I'd want to be diving into so deeply until right now. Some have been sweeter, while others have been more heated.

Today? Today, this man is on fire. He burns with a passion and determination that's going to set the world ablaze. *For me.* I want him to embrace every bit of confidence he's gained. Normally, I like to be the one in control—not tonight. The slickness between my legs is all I need to know that this change in dynamic in him, seeing him finally be so forward and being so sure of himself, is exactly what I need.

"You know," I say against his lips, "I did say it was time for another lesson earlier. How about tonight?" —I drag a finger down his chest— "you tell me what to do."

"Oh, my dear sweet Kenni, what do you think this is?" He

stands back, his gaze filled with a hunger I've never seen in him. He's no longer the shy man I first met. No. This is a crazed man starved for something only I can give him, and a warmth burns low in my core at the thought. He's starved for *me*.

Goddamn, this is a good look on him.

"Do what you tried to do that first night here." His tongue wets his lip. "Undo my belt."

Holy shit. Now *I'm* the one ready to come in my pants. I saunter toward him, reaching for his Gucci buckle, making quick work of the latch, unzipping his slacks, and letting them fall to the floor. Something flickers in his gaze. The softness remains, but there's an edge to it now—like the enforcer in him just stepped on the ice. *And he's here to play.* He pulls me in, pressing kisses along my neck, my pulse point, everywhere he can reach as I slowly unbutton his dress shirt. I push it off his shoulders, his kisses still raining over me as he shifts his arms free. I step back to get a good look at his ripped chest. Every time I see this man's body, I am reminded by the heat pooling in my core that he really is hotter than hell. *Christ on a cracker.*

I run my hands across his chiseled pecs, down his abs, and finally, I run my fingers inside the waistband of his boxer briefs. His fucking sexy-ass, tight-as-hell boxer briefs. I slowly move my hand down to grip the one thing I've been dying to feel all fucking day. Wanting it in my hand, my mouth, my pussy. I know we'll get to that last one, but *fuck,* it's hard to fight the urge to just climb on top of him and go to town. But right now, I'm only focused on giving him a reward for a hard-fought game and some newfound confidence.

"*Kenni.* Fuck. Get on your knees. Take it out. I want to feel your lips around me again tonight," he says with a quiet, tender voice. Even with his newfound boldness, he's still so gentle. So sweet. So purposeful.

As directed, I fall to my knees.

"Wait!" he says quickly, walking over to the couch to grab something. He returns and places a pillow before me. "I don't want your knees to get hurt on these hardwood floors."

Goddammit, can he be any more of a walking green flag?

"Thank you," I whisper, kneeling on the throw pillow. "I would have been fine, but…thank you."

"You are a fucking queen—nothing but the best for you."

"Okay, stop!" I tease, "You're giving me a complex and making me want to take over again."

We both quietly laugh, my pulse skipping a beat at how easy things are with him.

"Come here," I say, grabbing his ass and pulling him close, finally able to free the dick that's been trapped in his boxers for hours. His cock bobs in front of me, waiting for me to devour it. My tongue wets my lip. *Fuck, this man is incredible.* I tap his legs to have him step out of them, needing full, unhindered access to this man. My mouth waters as I curl my fingers against my knees, waiting for his instructions.

"Put me in your mouth. Show me how much you want it."

I do as he says, taking him in. My core clenches around nothing, aching to have him fully inside me. For now, my mouth will do just fine. *I can be patient with Jordan.* For the first time since we've been together, he's asking for what he wants, on his terms, in his own way. A spark flickers through me, driving my every move. It's fucking hot as hell to see him take back the control that was ripped away from him so unfairly. And the fact that I'm the one who gets to help him get it back?

It's everything.

53

jordan

The way her mouth feels around me is unbelievable. I didn't think anything could feel better than the first time she did this—in the Mile-High city, no less—but somehow it does. Never in my life have I felt so wanted, needed, and ready to do whatever she says. Except tonight, *I'm* the one in control. My skin buzzes in anticipation. Kenni has helped me overcome so many fears. And I'm conquering another one tonight—*I'm the one doing the talking*. I'm the one telling her what I like. Not to mention the fact that she's doing all this in her pilot uniform with that sexy as fuck scarf tied around her neck. The fact that I'm the one telling someone in uniform what to do is turning me on even more. It's taking me out of my comfort zone. It's scary, but there's no one else I'd rather walk this path with than her.

The way her tongue rolls around the ridges of my cock has my skin prickling with every stroke. The warmth of her breath makes my dick flinch in her mouth. She's got one hand wrapped around my shaft, twisting and turning as she slides me in and out over and over again.

"Fuck, that feels so good. You feel so good. You're incredible."

Her eyes smile up at me, her gaze meeting mine. With something as simple as a blink, she's encouraging me. Telling me to keep going. Reminding me I can do this. Knowing that she gave me the strength to do this. She reaches a hand down to cup my balls, squeezing them with just the right amount of pressure. The warm sensation deep in my abdomen is building so fast. Her every move, every glance, spreads fire outside the bounds of what I thought I could do.

"Kenni...*fuck*...I'm not going to last long. That feels... goddammit, you know what you're doing."

"Hey," she says hoarsely as she pulls back, rubbing her hands up and down the sides of my legs. "As long as it feels good, it doesn't matter how long it lasts. Now, tell me where you want to finish, pretty-boy."

Holy fucking fuckballs...*I was not anticipating this question.* My stomach twists as my cock twitches at the possibilities.

"Umm...could I—"

Her nails dig into my thighs. "No thinking. No asking. There is no right or wrong answer here. You tell me, with authority, where you want to come." Her eyes search mine. "Do you need to use your safe word—"

"I want to come on your face." The words fall from my mouth without even thinking. *Apparently, that's what I want.* I bite my cheek, my dick pulsing in agreement.

Her brows raise as she gives me a wicked smile. "Interesting choice," she says, and my panic hits my gut. But, as usual, she finds a way to calm me down. "That's what I would have picked, too. Tell me when you're close."

She places her mouth around my cock again, licking and sucking and twisting in ways I didn't know were possible. Every nerve in my body responds—*this is going to end before it begins.* I don't even care. She feels so good. And she's so beautiful. And she's so perfect. A fuse lights low in my body, every muscle tensing, building and building until I can't hold back anymore.

I don't want to hold back anymore.

"Fuck…Kenni…I'm…*oh fuck* I'm gonna come…"

I pull back as I explode, grabbing ahold of my dick, my hips thrusting forward as my release drips down her face. *Fuck.* Seeing her like this is sexy as hell. My knees go weak seeing her lips, beautifully swollen, her face glistening with my release.

"Jordan. That was…shit, that was hot," she says as she stands up. "Let me just go clean—"

"No! Stay there," I say, racing to grab a washcloth. As I return, I gently run the damp fabric over her delicate skin, her beauty somehow magnified in the soft glow of the dim apartment lights.

"I'm so proud of you, JJ," she says as I finish. "I'm proud of what you and your team did tonight. Proud of what you did here tonight for yourself. And most of all," —she leans up to press her lips against mine— "I'm so proud to be standing by your side through all of this."

I swallow the lump in my throat, my heart ready to explode. I want to blurt out how I feel. Those three words would change everything. *But she thinks we're friends.* And I love that. I've always wanted to be best friends with my wife.

I swear to all things hockey, I will make this woman my wife.

"There's no one else I'd rather have by my side, Kenni. You're everything to me." I pull her in for another kiss, suddenly realizing I'm completely naked while she's completely clothed. "Is it okay… no wait; I'm in charge still, right?"

"Yes," she snorts. "You like being in charge, pretty-boy?"

"I'd like it a lot better if your clothes were on the floor." I reach forward, unbuttoning her shirt inch by inch, each little piece of plastic a gateway to what's underneath. I slide my hands inside, pushing the fabric from her shoulders and letting it fall. Kennedy slowly reaches up to take her scarf off, her eyes dancing with an emotion I can hardly believe.

"No," I say, gently grasping her hand. "The scarf stays on."

She blinks. "I like this side of you."

"I've been dreaming of you in nothing but that scarf for months now, and now that I've been granted my wish, I'm not letting this opportunity pass me by."

She lays her palm over my racing heart. "What else have you been dreaming about?"

I reach around behind her, unclasping her bra, slowly dragging it down her shoulders, exposing her chest to me. "This. You. Us."

A blinding smile lights up her face. "Is it living up to your expectations?"

"Better than I ever imagined. This is fucking perfect, Kenni." I pull her close, kissing her with the same energy I have skating down the ice. Getting lost in everything that is Kennedy Kramer, I palm her cheek with one hand, running my other across her tits. *Goddammit, this woman.* Not breaking our kiss, I reach down and undo her belt, her pants, sliding them both down. *I need more.* More of her body against mine. More of her skin on mine. More of her.

I need to be naked beside her.

"I need to taste you again. I have been starving for your pussy all day, and I need it. *Now.* Let's go to bed."

54
kennedy

This fucking man no longer needs a coach. He has graduated from training wheels and is full-on riding the damn bike. With his tongue. On my clit. *Grilled Cheesus this man.* His fingers inside me curl, hitting that spot and nearly sending me over the edge. I thread my fingers through the thick strands of his hair, pulling his face toward my hips and writhing into his face. *I need more.* I want this man, fully, completely. I need him inside me. I need him to soothe the ache I feel both there and in my heart.

"JJ, that feels so damn good. Fuck. I need more. I need you inside me."

He jerks back, his gaze fixed on mine. His chest heaves, every breath a thought he's not saying out loud.

"Kenni...I want to—"

"Please, baby. *Please...*" My pleading turns into a full-on whimper, "I need you so bad. I really want this. I want you. I want—"

"Frites."

My body goes numb. Paralyzed. Struggling to find air as I register what he just said.

What *word* he just said.

His safe word.

"Oh." I swallow down the lump in my throat. "Okay. I hear you. We're stopping. I just...I got caught up in the moment and...Jordan, I'm sorry. I never went to pressure you—"

"No! No. Kennedy, this is my issue. I want to be inside you. More than you will ever know. It's like not fully breathing, knowing we haven't connected in that way yet. I just...I feel so fucking lame saying this." He throws his arm over his eyes, hiding from me. Hiding from what he's about to say. "When I'm with a woman again, I want it to be...I want it to be forever. I don't want to be what the media says I am. I want to make sure we're both on the same page. I want to know that she's dying to be with me as much as I'm dying to be with her. I don't want there to be a doubt in my mind that she loves me the way I love her."

My stomach twists into knots I'm not sure I can untangle. But I hold it in. He deserves this. He deserves to have a fairy tale redemption. I want him to have that.

Even if it's with someone else.

"Jordan, I completely understand. You don't have to explain yourself. We've known this all along. This was just..." I force a smile he can't see, "...we're just helping each other out, right? It's fine."

He peeks at me under his arm. "Kenni...I'm so sorry."

"Stop. Don't be sorry. Come here." I motion for him to come lie next to me. "You're fine. It's all fine. I promise. Okay?"

"Okay." He places a kiss on my cheek, and we lie in bed next to one another for a few moments until his exhaustion catches up to him and he falls asleep.

But I don't.

My breaths are short. My eyes fill with tears I'm desperate to hold onto. My body trembles as I try not to let it all out. He needs to know he's completely safe with me, regardless of the fact that I somehow caught goddamn feelings for him during all this. *Fuck my life.* I sneak out of bed and hop in the shower; *I cannot let him see me like this.* I can't let him see me completely broken.

The minute the water hits my skin, the tears my eyes have been desperately holding onto fall uncontrollably down my face. I'm ugly crying over my own stupidity for falling for this ridiculous, stupid guy. He's too young. And too funny. And so damn sweet and actually not stupid at all. He lights up my whole damn world. I slam my palms over my mouth, desperate to stifle my sobs. I want him to have the most special moment ever. *He fucking deserves it.* He cares for everyone. He has the kindest, most gentle heart, the most enthusiastic spirit. He makes me laugh like no one ever has before.

Why the hell am I crying about this? I wanted to help him. I have helped him. I thought he'd let me help him with this one last step, too. My throat goes dry, my body collapsing in on itself. *Does he not want me to be that person? His forever?*

"Goddammit. My fucking stupid friends were right," I whisper to myself. I've totally fallen in love with this guy, and now I'm not sure if he loves me back.

Fuck.

I lean back under the water as I take a deep, calming breath. Let's assess my options. Lists and plans never fail to calm me down.

Option 1: I let him go, get through this fake dating thing, and move on.

Option 2: Tell him my feelings and face possible rejection.

Option 3: Drink some gin.

Option 4: Stay in the shower and never leave.

Option 5: Google if it's weird to drink gin in the shower.

Option 6: Move to New Zealand and start a new life.

Option 7: Figure out if they have gin in New Zealand and how soon I could fly a plane there.

Option 8: I could—

Before I can fully form another thought, the shower door opens and arms band around me so fucking tight I can't breathe. Just like in the arena earlier today, but this is even more intimate, even tighter.

"Kenni, I'm so sorry. I never meant to hurt you. I fucking love you so much, and I never want you to cry because of me ever. Never ever. Please forgive me; we can go fuck like rabbits right now if it means you'll never cry over me again."

My breath hitches. *Did he just say what I think he said?* He loves me? *Holy shit.*

"What did you say?" I whisper, my voice raw.

"I said, please forgive me. Come on, let's go back to bed; we can do whatever you want. We can fuck like porn stars all night long. Just…please don't be upset…I can't take it."

I take a step back, my eyes finding his through the steam. He's so upset—I don't…I don't think he realizes he said it.

But I heard it.

"Have you been crying?"

"I mean, yeah. When I saw you were crying, I…" he chokes, wiping a tear from my face as we stand under the spray of the water.

I can hardly breathe. *He said he fucking loves me.* I want so badly to say it back, because I fucking love him too. But an idea pops into my brain, setting a plan in motion that I have to see through.

"Baby, let's go back to bed. I want you. I want to be inside you; I swear, Kenni, I trust you," he says, trying to tug me from the shower.

Despite my tears, I can't stop the smile creeping across my face at his willingness to give up everything for me. *This man.* I drag my feet, pulling him to a stop.

"No, no, no. That's not how this works. I know you trust me. I trust you, too. But we're not pity fucking because I'm crying. I'm not upset because you didn't want to go there tonight. I'm just... overwhelmed."

"You're trapped in a glass case of emotion like Ron Burgundy?" he teases through a sniffle.

I can't help but laugh. He has a pop culture reference for everything. "Yes. Exactly like Ron Burgundy." I cup his cheek, "Hey... you know what I just realized?"

"What?"

"You planned a nice, fancy date for me, but I never planned a date for you. Since you have an off day, let's have a date tonight. Okay?"

"You, Kennedy Kramer, are asking me, Jordan Boucher, out on a date?"

"I am. But only if you go back to bed and cuddle with me. I've heard that helps your tears dry faster."

He smiles through another sniffle. "I know you're just trying to make me feel better, but I'm not going to turn down cuddling with you. And I read a very scientific study confirming that about snuggles and quality sleep as well."

"Good." I grin. "Then it's a date."

The date where I'm going to tell him I love him too.

55
jordan

"Heard you got reamed by Coach again," EJ grunts as we do a quick conditioning skate. Even though we have an off day, most of us like to keep our muscles warm. "I thought this whole Kennedy thing would help you not have as many issues, but now he seems even more pissed off."

I shrug. "Meh. He'll get over it. I had to get to her. I had to let her know I was okay and make sure she was too. That's more important than hockey."

"Not in the fucking playoffs, it's not," Tay chimes in. "You couldn't have just sent her a text?"

I flash him a wicked side-eye. "Tay, she was *crying*. Jordan Boucher does not let his woman cry. He performs the grand gesture of running to her through an entire arena with Don't Wanna Miss a Thing by Aerosmith playing in his mind to show her what she means to him."

"You're comparing this incident to saving the world from a giant asteroid when your girlfriend was just upset you faked a hit to get us a power play?" Tay scoffs, shuffling a puck around with his stick. "Whipped."

"What? It's basically the same thing."

"Bro," EJ says. "You're lucky Vladi didn't murder you. You should have seen his face when you ran out. He. Was. Livid."

"He's my friend. We talked it out on the plane last night."

"Yeah, you and Kennedy also 'talked it out' on the plane last night," EJ says. "Man, I need to find someone to do that with after a game. What a way to release some energy. You think that Mara girl is available?"

I shiver. "She's *definitely* taken. Also, she gives off a weird vibe. Besides, what happened to Natalie?" I ask.

He shrugs. "It didn't work out. She was nice, I just wasn't into it."

"I didn't realize you two broke up," Tay says with a catch in his throat.

"Yeah. It, uh…just happened a couple of days ago. It was mutual." EJ shoots a puck down the ice. "But, Bougie, you and Kennedy seem to really be going well!"

I smile at the thought of other people seeing us as an item. "Yeah, really well actually."

"I still can't believe you settled down with one woman. I've been living through your adventures, bro!" EJ shouts. "Now I have to watch it on reality TV, and that's not nearly as fun."

"Yeah…that lifestyle isn't really all it's cracked up to be. Trust me. And Kenni is…she's everything."

"Sounds serious," Tay says, firing off a slap shot harder than normal. "You say the magic words yet? I figured wanting her after all this time, then finally having her, you'd have said I love you on the first date."

My heart drops. Last night. The shower. Everything slams into my brain like a bad cross-check. *Holy fucking shit.* I'm 99.68% sure I said it last night. I was so overwhelmed with her being upset and me dealing with my own emotions, I think I blacked out. *Fuck...did I say it?* Ohmygod, ohmygod, ohmygod.

My stomach twists. *Shit, what do I do?* Is she freaking out? Is she moving all of my stuff out of the apartment? Is she installing a lock she can actually work to keep me out? The only thing I know for sure is that I need to get to her. Right. Now.

"Guys, I gotta go."

"Where the hell are you running off to?" Tay shouts after me, clearly annoyed I'm leaving them a man short for drills.

"I gotta go check on my woman!"

I hear EJ mutter something about how often I need to check in on a grown woman, Tay mumbling something in agreement, but I don't care.

Make fun of me all you want. I need to make sure I didn't royally fuck this up.

I stand in the elevator pressing the button for the tenth floor over and over again like it's the delete key on my computer and I'm trying to erase what I just typed. There's no deleting this. I swallow hard. Once you spit out a word, especially *those* words, you can't take them back. *Did I say it? I think I did. Is this elevator smaller than usual?* My lungs are heaving, trying to find a steady rhythm to breathe. *Is there air flowing in here?* I watch the numbers, four, five, six, seven...*how fucking far is ten from seven?!*

I burst into the hall when the doors finally open, sprinting to her apartment like a breakaway on empty ice. I hold the key fob to the lock on the door.

Nothing.

I try again.

Red light.

My hands shake as I try again and again. My guts twist and turn like there's a goddamn tug of war going on in my stomach, my lungs still not figuring out how to fucking breathe like a normal human. *Did she change the locks so I can't get in? Fuck!*

I pound on the door with every ounce of strength. "Kenni…it's me. Please open up! Let's talk! Did you change the locks? Oh my God, please answer!"

No answer.

I bang on the door again. "Kenni, are you home? Please, let's talk!"

Nothing.

I drop my head against the door in defeat. *Look what you did now, Boucher.* The jiggle of the handle is the only warning before the door finally pops open, causing me to stumble inside until a pair of warm hands steady me.

"Jordan?!" Kennedy's voice is filled with concern and worry, and everything I've ever needed. "You weren't supposed to be back for another thirty minutes. What's…" She scans me over as if I'm an injured puppy. "Are you okay? What's wrong?" I wrap myself around her, cradling the back of her head so fucking tight against my chest, my mind can't convince me it's not real. She hugs me in return, rubbing circles on my back. "This is quite the greeting, but…what's the matter?"

"I thought…I thought…*Shit.*" I try, but fail, to keep my voice steady. "I realized what I said in the shower last night. I said it. Like…*it* it. I love you. Of course, I fucking love you, Kenni. But I was an idiot, and I said it too soon, and now I'm terrified that it freaked you out and you were going to run, and I had to get here as soon as I could, and then I got here and thought you changed the locks, and…oh my God, you smell good."

She laughs, the sound melting the tension in my body, rocking us back and forth. "No, I did not change the locks. I'm surprised someone with your skills struggled to open it. Not as easy as it looks, huh?"

I laugh through my sniffles. "It was *one time,* and I was panicking that you were going to shut me out forever. You've lived here for over a *year,* and you still can't open the damn thing!"

"Hey. Look at me." She pulls her head back, her gaze finding mine as she cups my cheek. "I'm here. I'm not going anywhere, pretty-boy," she says with a smile that tugs at my chest. She loops her arms around my neck and stretches up on her toes, her gaze steady as she presses her lips against mine. The heaviness lifts, my heart finally finding the steady rhythm I've only ever found in her arms. The way she calms me, commands me, chirps me…she's everything. *I honestly don't think my heart could beat for anyone but her.* I tighten my grip, worrying she'll slip out of my reach. And then it hits me—the reason why I feel like I could still lose her. The heavy pull in my gut tugs me back, breaking our kiss.

She hasn't said it back.

I swallow hard, my voice cracking when I talk. "So, you're not going anywhere? And you're not freaked out?"

"Do I look freaked out?" she asks, her gaze unwavering.

"No. But you…you didn't…" My gaze drops. "You didn't say it ba—"

"Jordan," she interrupts, gripping my chin and pulling my eyes back to hers. "Do you remember what I said last night?"

I sniffle. "That you were trapped in a glass case of emotion?"

"Yes. I also promised you a date tonight. Go get changed." She nods toward her bedroom. "We have somewhere to be."

I blink, confused as fuck as to what's happening. "You still want to go on a date with—"

"Jordan! *Go,*" she teases, shooing me down the hallway.

"Okay! Okay! Geeze!" I tease back, running off to change. I

pause in the doorway, glancing over my shoulder at Kennedy's casual jeans and T-shirt combo. Every muscle in my body is tense as fuck as I count my heartbeats and jump into the shower, needing to get practice off me so I can look my best. *She isn't running. I didn't scare her away.* She planned a date…a date for *me*.

Time to bust out the glass slippers and a tiara because I feel like a mother-fucking Disney princess.

My hand hasn't left hers, our palms glued together as she drives us to wherever the fuck we are going. I wanted to drive, but she insisted on keeping it a surprise. *As shaky as my hands are right now, it's probably safer if she's driving.* Her thumb, slowly grazing mine, keeps my heartbeat steady.

"Kenni…what are we doing at the airport? Please tell me we aren't going skydiving 'cause I'm kind of scared to death of… well…death."

She throws her head back and laughs as she pulls into a parking space at the County Airport. "We aren't going skydiving. Trust me, I have *zero* desire to jump out of a working plane. I was thinking more along the lines of landing the plane on the ground."

"You're…" I suck in a sharp breath, once again stunned at this woman's ability to surprise me. "You're taking me flying?"

"Don't they do this on those reality dating shows? I think I saw it on an episode of *You're The One*. They went on a romantic helicopter tour. I don't have a helicopter, so you'll have to forgive me, but I do have a small plane. I thought—"

"Did you say romantic?" I interrupt, my pulse thrumming in my ears.

She flashes me a wry smile before she hops out of the car and starts walking toward the hangar, knowing I'll follow.

She knows I will fucking follow her anywhere.

I race to join her, catching up just as she reaches the open bay door. Kennedy grabs my hand, pulling me along beside her as we walk to one of the small aircrafts. *Whoa...* "Is this your plane? Like...you own it?"

She smirks, one brow raised. "You're not the *only* one who can buy a plane," she says as she does her walk around. "Now, hurry up and get in—we're on a schedule."

We settle into our seats. There are so many fucking screens, gauges, buttons, and levers that I'm afraid if I breathe too hard, I'll break something. I feel like I'm in some sort of bizarre arcade playing a game left over from the 1900s.

"Am I supposed to put my feet on these pedals? Why does this feel like a recumbent bike?"

She shakes her head. "Keep your feet on the floor for now. Those are the rudder pedals." Kennedy points to the back of the plane. "That's how you taxi the plane to get to the runway. You really know nothing about flying, do you?"

"Not a damn thing other than my phone needs to be on Airplane Mode." I grimace, feeling ridiculous for not knowing more. "Do you steer with your feet? What's the Mario Kart controller for?"

She snorts. "This is not a car, or a video game, and this is not a steering wheel—it's the yoke."

I blink. "So basically everything is backward from a car. Got it."

"Sort of." She laughs. "You know how hockey has icing but involves zero cupcakes? Flying has a lot of terms like that—names that sound familiar but mean something totally different."

"True! And now I want a cupcake." I lick my lips, rolling my eyes as I picture the perfect yellow cupcake with chocolate frosting. "Wait. So, then how the hell does all this work?"

"Think of the rudder pedals like how you move around the ice with your feet. That's how you change directions. The yolk controls other things, like the pitch and roll. I'll show you some of the fun stuff once we're in the air."

I smile as I get strapped in, put my headset on, and watch her work her magic. The way she checks everything. *She is so damn smart.* There are a billion switches in here, and she knows exactly which ones to use when, not even hesitating before flipping them on and off. She commands every situation, even when it's just the two of us. My heart has been pounding all day, but seeing her like this, with my life completely in her hands, is making all that blood pump straight to my dick. I would adjust myself but I'm scared I'll elbow a button by accident.

Fuck it—she's seen my joystick before.

She taxis the plane onto the runway, talking to air traffic control and getting clearance for takeoff.

"Magneto, check," she says, her voice sexier than ever in my headset.

"Magneto? Like X-Men?"

"Yes. *Exactly* like X-Men." She peeks over at me as she continues her pre-flight routine. "The whole plane is run by magnets. You don't have anything metal on you, do you?"

Oh shit. I fumble for my wallet, my watch, the jewelry I never wear, trying to think of anything metal I have. *Will that make the plane not fly?*

She snorts, placing her hand on my thigh. "JJ, I'm joking. Take a deep breath. Remember, I fly you places multiple times a week. This is no different. I get to see you at work all the time, now you get to see what I do."

My shoulders relax as the fluttering feeling behind my ribs intensifies even as she gives me nothing but shit. *I fucking love it.*

I watch in awe as she talks to the control tower and they clear us for takeoff.

"You ready?" she asks, glancing my way.

My pulse is at full throttle, like it's trying to win some sort of competition. "Fuck yeah."

As we race down the runway and lift off into the air, my breath catches. This is more than a flight. *This is pulling us into uncharted airspace.* Something deep in my heart pulls loose. Like every bit of altitude we pick up frees me from things that have weighed me down for years. But it's not the air. It's not the plane. It's not the instruments or the engine. *It's her.* This woman I've been drawn to for months. I can feel it in my bones. She still hasn't said those three words yet, but for some reason, this flight feels like her way of saying them without speaking at all.

She feels it too.

"You doing okay over there, pretty-boy?" she asks in the calm pilot voice I hear her use on our flights.

"Kenni...this is...this is unreal."

She scoffs. "You fly all the time."

"Not like this. Not with you. You know I like it when you're in control."

"I might have picked up on that," she says with a laugh. "I wanted to bring you up here at this specific time because I knew the sunset would be stunning today. Look."

I'd been too focused on everything Kennedy was doing inside, I forgot to look out the window. The oranges and yellows radiating across the ground are breathtaking. *Goddammit, this needs to be part of a poem.*

"It's...it's...fuck..." I rub the end of my sleeve under my eye.

"It's beautiful, isn't it?" she says softly.

"It is, but..." I swallow the lump in my throat. "It's us."

"Us?"

"Yeah." My smile is bittersweet; my eyes locked on the hills beneath us. "You've been the light in the sky I've been searching for my whole damn life. I could see you in the clouds, but it all seemed so out of reach. You were so far out of my league. Not to mention, I was trapped in this cycle I thought I'd never get out of. But seeing the sun come down and kiss the ground like this? It's like you coming down to get me. And you know what happens every night when the sun disappears? In the morning, it comes back up. You grabbed me and pulled me back up with you. You got rid of the darkness and finally dragged me into the light."

She blinks quickly as she eases into a turn. She clears her throat. "I've spent my whole career trying to hide my emotions while sitting in this seat. To stay calm, stay focused, do my job. Yet here I am, choking back tears on a flight that's just for fun."

"Sorry, I didn't mean—"

"Don't you dare fucking apologize for the most beautiful words I've ever heard. I just wish I weren't flying a damn aircraft so I could wrap my arms around you. So I could look you in the eyes and tell you…" Her voice trails off.

She's holding something back—she's holding back from saying it.

My cheeks heat as I smile wider than the sunset we're flying over. "You were the one who wanted this to be romantic."

She huffs a laugh and shakes he head. "Point taken. How about we head back to the airport? I have more surprises, and I can't hold all this in any longer."

I wipe my face again, my sleeves soaked with more happiness and relief than I've felt in forever. I've been in love with Kennedy Kramer for a while. But now? My stomach dips, but it's not the plane. It's the inkling I have about her feeling the same.

"Ninety-eight, ninety-nine, one-hundred," Kennedy told me to stand in the hallway and count so she could get a couple of things ready. I have no clue what's happening, but I'm bouncing on my heels, I'm so fucking excited. I click the fob on the lock, my hands steadier now that I saw she was still in the apartment and still let me in.

As I push open the door, I hear *Kiss Me*, the most romantic song of all the '90s movies, playing in the background. Then I look around and see a trail of rose petals leading down the hallway toward the bedroom. *What in the rom-com is happening?!*

"Kenni? What…what is going on? How did you…you could not have done all this while I was in the hallway, so how…"

She flashes me the most brilliantly beautiful smile as she grabs my hand. "I recruited a little help from Maggie. Here," she hands me a gift bag overflowing with tissue paper. "Open it."

"You got me a present?" I gasp, flinging the papers all over the floor and tearing into the bag as fast as possible. I reach inside and pull out a box. My brows narrow, my eyes darting between the gift and Kenni. "You got me…a Bougie Bobblehead? Why would you give me my bobblehead? You know the team gave me one, right?"

She snorts. "That's not yours." She takes a step toward me. "It's mine."

"It's…" My eyes fly to hers, a knowing smile lifting my lips.

"Jordan Boucher, will you please autograph my Bougie Bobblehead?"

My cheeks ache from my smile. "Seriously? Now?"

"I have felt bad about this for a while, and I wanted to make it right."

I take my little mini-me out of the box, grabbing her Sharpie to sign it before handing it back. "You got me rose petals to ask me to sign my bobblehead?"

She nods. "That's part of it. I wanted to make it up to you. Not just the bobblehead. *All of it*. The fact that I ignored you for months before I really knew you. All the ideas I had about who I thought you were. And for last night."

"Kenni, no. Last night was—"

"Let me finish," she says, placing a finger on my lips. "You used your safe word last night. I respect that. I will *always* respect that. But after we stopped, I thought..." she runs her finger down my arm, grabbing my hand. "I thought maybe it was because you didn't want it to be with me. When I first met you, I would have been fine with that. I thought you were too self-absorbed, too rich, too young, too immature. But over these past couple of months, I realized none of that was true. You are the most kind-hearted, caring, thoughtful person I've ever met. And when you jumped into the shower, saying we could fuck like rabbits because you fucking loved me so much, I realized I was wrong to think you would ever want to be with someone else.

"You were willing to give up something you've been holding onto so deeply for so long, just to comfort me. I realized that's how much you loved me. You'd give everything up for me. But you shouldn't have to do that. Ever. For anyone. I...I wasn't about to let you give that up."

I squeeze her fingers. "After last night, I was just hoping I didn't scare you off. That I—"

"I'm right here." Her palm curves around my cheek, her eyes bouncing with warmth between mine. "And I'm not going anywhere. Not today. Not tomorrow. Not ever. Because I love you too, Jordan. Somehow between the fake dating, having a creepy stalker hellbent on keeping us apart, and being your clit coach, I fell in love with you."

My hands shake as my eyes go wide. *Did she just say what I think she said? Ohmygod, ohmygod, ohmygod...This is my moment.* "You... you love me?"

She nods, biting her lip. "I do. And I wanted to show you with a grand gesture that was, well, you."

"Kenni, I'm..." I look around the apartment, the petals blurring together. "This is the most thoughtful thing anyone has ever done for me. No one really...no one outside of my family ever..." My lungs are trying to take in air, but somehow the tears welling in my eyes are stopping my lungs from doing their job. "Thank you."

"I love you, Jordan. You do so much for everyone else, it was beyond time for you to get a grand gesture too."

"I love you so much. I've loved you from the day I saw you step out of that flight deck on the plane. I love how much we laugh together, how much shit we give Chadd together. I love everything about you. I always imagined what it would be like to be with you, but my dreams didn't even compare to how amazing you are in real life. I love you so much—"

I barely finish the words before she pulls me in, our lips colliding in a frenzy of passion. All of my hesitation disappears. Every ounce of worry finally evaporates out of my head. It's just us, here in this room, as the rest of the world fades away. I don't need the world anymore anyway.

Kennedy Kramer is in love with me.

56
jordan

Carrying Kennedy down the hallway, her legs wrap around my waist, our mouths completely entangled with one another as if we're permanently joined together like we'll never break apart—and fuck, I never want to.

"JJ, wait," she whispers, pulling back just enough to let the words escape, not wanting to come up for air either. "I want you to see."

My brows narrow. "See wh—"

I can't breathe. *Is there air in here?* I may need an oxygen mask deployed in this apartment because, as I glance around, a trail of rose petals lines the floor all the way to the bed, and the entire room is filled with the soft glow of candles, floral arrangements, and more petals lie on the bed in the shape of a heart. A rush of warmth rises in me, bringing to the surface everything I've been longing for. She did this. *For me.* I can't think. I can't move. I open my mouth trying to find words, but, for once in my life, I think I'm speechless. I, Jordan Joseph Boucher, am at a loss for words.

"Do you like it?" She bites her lip. *As if I would ever not like anything she did.*

The tiniest bit of air finally hits my lungs as I try to say something, anything. "Kenni. This…this is…holy shit, you went all out. You did all this for me?"

She slowly nods. "You deserve it. And hey…" She pauses, dropping her forehead to mine. "If you're still not comfortable, we don't have to do anything more than what we've already done. We will take this as slow as you want. I just wanted to show you that I—"

"Stop," I interrupt, not wanting to delay this moment any longer. "It's my turn to talk." She tilts her head as a smirk crawls across her lips, but she doesn't say a word. *Good.* I close the distance, my lips a breath away from hers, like she's the finish line I've been sprinting toward for my entire life, and it's finally in sight.

"I'm ready. So. Fucking. Ready. Last night, I wasn't sure if you felt the same way I did. It messed with my head, with my heart, and I spiraled. I froze and I panicked. But now? When I thought I'd scared you away I realized I didn't want to chance that ever again. I love you. So much. I'm all in. Last night had nothing to do with you —that was all me. And now that I know you feel the same way?" I spin us around in the kind of rom-com moment I've always dreamed of. Her head falls back in laughter, her hair flying as my heart nearly bursts out of my chest. Setting her down, she's still clinging to my neck, her cheeks flushed with a smile that will live in my memory forever. "Nothing is coming between us tonight. I finally have Kennedy Kramer and it's more than I ever could have dreamed of."

I press my lips into hers, more gentle and more delicate than before, soaking up every second as I drag her to the side of the bed. She moans into the kiss, sparking a frenzy in us both and igniting a full-blown fire I never want to burn out. We frantically undress each other, our kiss only breaking to shove clothing out of the way, tossing each piece and not giving a shit where it lands.

We fall onto the bed, her hair fanning out across the sheets, her smile meeting mine with a glimmer I can't tear myself away from. As I tuck a stray hair behind her ear, I am once again fully in awe of this woman's beauty. Every curve, every line, every single inch of her is perfection. I slowly place kisses down her neck, sucking hard as I reach her pulse point, her body bowing off the bed.

"JJ," she pants, "don't you *ever* doubt how good you are at this." She groans as I kiss down her body, my lips finding her nipple, her flesh pebbling beneath my tongue. My dick is rock hard, pulsing, and aching to be inside the only woman I've truly ever wanted. My chest pounds as I stand at the edge of the moment I've dreamed about for so long.

I drag my hand down her abdomen, sliding between her thighs and running a finger through the slickness she's worked up; every drop of it for me. I circle my fingers around her sensitive clit the way I know she likes it. Just the right amount of pressure, just the right spot. The first time we did this was a lesson. But now? I'm pleasuring her. Every gasp from her mouth, every move of her hips, is an affirmation tI'm doing things right. And with this woman and the confidence she's given me, I'm starting to feel like I can do no wrong.

"Fuck…you've got me so close," she moans through panted breaths, her chest rapidly rising and falling with every word. A whimper escapes her as I pull my fingers back. "No. I need more," she whines, her voice shaky with need.

A smile spreads across my face as the woman I've been dreaming about for months is whimpering. For me. *Goddammit, this is everything.* I lean down, whispering in her ear. "Patience. I've made you come with my fingers, with my mouth. But now? Now

I'm going to make you come with my cock buried deep inside you."

She gasps. "Do it, pretty-boy," she teases. Her hands cup my cheeks, pulling my face to hers, our lips meeting once more as my cock nudges her entrance. I start to slide forward, needing, *aching* to be inside her.

And that's when I realize I've forgotten a critical step. *Fuck. Shit fucking fuck.* Goddammit, I am an idiot. I pull back, her eyes wide. Clearly catching the worry on my face, her hands soothingly run along my arms.

"Jordan, we don't have to do this; we can seriously wait."

"Oh God, no! It's not that. It's…I don't have a fucking condom. I came straight from practice and, ya know, I don't typically need those there. You don't happen to magically have one here, do you? Is that weird to ask?"

A wave of relief washes over her face. "It's not weird. But," she says with a defeated smile, "sadly, I don't."

My head drops. *Fuck my life.* I finally get the woman of my dreams in bed, and I'm unprepared. As I mentally beat myself up, her gentle hand cups my cheek again.

"Listen. I don't know if you're okay with this, but I am on the pill, and I'm all good health-wise. And I'm guessing since it's been a while for you…you're okay too?"

I swallow hard. *Ohmygod. Is she implying what I think she is?* "Yeah, I'm good. But…are you sure? Like…*sure*, sure?" My eyes flicker between hers, searching for an ounce of hesitation or uncertainty. "Fuck, I want to feel you around my dick so bad, but I don't want to make you uncomfortable."

"Bet," she says with a wicked grin.

I can't hold back the laugh that escapes me. "Kennedy Kramer, look at you using Gen Z slang. I fucking love you so much."

The corners of her lips tip up. "I love you too."

I kiss her again; no one is able to ground me, calm me like she does. I place myself at her entrance once more, desperation pulsing in the air, and slowly push my hips forward, feeling how wet, how warm, how perfect she is surrounding me. My gaze never leaves hers as I slide inside, my muscles tight as I fight the desire to melt with ecstasy. She shudders with a shaky breath as I push a little further.

"You, okay? Tell me if it's too much."

"It's fucking unreal. You will *never* be too much," she groans, making me lose every ounce of my self-control. I thrust fully inside her. An electric current hums under my skin, every nerve coming to life at once. Fucking hell. *There is no way I'm going to last very long bare inside her.* And I don't fucking care. She loves me. I love her. And if I have my way, we'll have the rest of our lives to fuck all night.

Her hands tightly grip my back as she wraps her legs around my waist, pulling me closer. My heart beats out of my goddamn chest as I slide in and out of her. My hips feel like they are on autopilot, instinctively moving faster, deeper, harder. My pulse hammers, my thoughts spinning as I burn this moment into memory, clinging to every tiny detail and never letting them go.

"I'm so close. I'm gonna…"

"Let go. I want to feel you come undone around me."

She writhes, and I feel her fucking tight pussy clench around me, and *fuck,* I can't hold on any longer either.

"I'm right there too. Come with me. Let me feel you, Kenni."

She lets out a silent scream as I thrust over and over again, my hips bucking against her as I spill my release inside. I glide forward one last time as the euphoria washes over me. My entire body trembles, sweat beading like raindrops on our skin. I find my breath, leaning down to capture her lips once more.

"Kenni…that was…that was…"

"Everything."

I smile. "Yeah. Everything."

I pull myself back from the glorious wonder that is the woman I love and lie next to her, pulling her in so damn close I feel her heart thundering against mine. *I never want this moment to be over.*

"You doing okay, pretty-boy?"

"I'm more than okay. I'm here with you. I just made love to the only woman I've ever wanted. And she's not here to trick me or laugh at me or post about me online. I mean...I assume I did okay. Do we need to do a pulse check?" I tiptoe my fingers down her abdomen.

She lets out a loud laugh. "You had me pulsing, alright, but you're welcome to check anytime. I normally don't come like that with someone inside me. But apparently, your dick is as magical as your personality. Always making sure everyone leaves smiling and satisfied."

I squeeze her tighter, loving this side of her that shines through whenever we're together. "I knew there was a dirty joke inside your badass exterior."

"I have my moments," she says. "Now...let's go clean up and stuff our faces with blueberry pancakes."

part four
june

57

kennedy

"I, Kara Reeves, would like to officially initiate the newest member of the Riders WAGs, Ms. Kennedy Kramer! Cheers to Kennedy, and cheers to the Riders making it to the Stanley Cup Finals!" Kara announces at brunch as we all clink glasses and drink our mimosas at Walt's. This is the first time we've all been together since the playoff travel schedule is so intense and I've had to miss the last few due to being on the road during the third round. And now, after I confessed to them that we are actually dating, they are over the moon excited. My heart flutters in my chest, because—same.

"Thank you all. I never felt like I wasn't a part of this group, but now that we're officially dating, it does make it all seem a bit more real."

"Annnddd???" Maggie asks in a singsong voice.

"And what?"

"We want to hear you say it again!" Olivia chimes in.

I roll my eyes, shaking my head at them both. "This is the *last* time I'll say it." I point at my two friends. "You were right, okay? You were right about him."

They all cheer and laugh as Maggie throws her arm around me. "We are so happy for you, Kenni. Jordan has a heart of gold, and you two are the 'it couple' of the playoffs. A hockey player *and* a pilot? Two people in uniform who both happen to be hot as hell? This is a marketer's dream."

I try to scowl, but I can't shake the damn smile from my face. "Okay, okay, calm down. We're just dating, Maggie. We're not walking down the aisle and having a thousand babies."

"Not *yet*," Kara pipes in. "But that boy is so head over heels for you. I guarantee he bought a ring the day you two got into your fake dating predicament…just in case he needed it."

"Pssht. There's no way he has a ring yet," I spit out as my friends all look at me with raised brows. My heart skips a beat. "Wait…do you all know something I don't know?"

Olivia laughs. "No. We just know Jordan, and that seems pretty on brand for him."

I swallow the lump in my throat, suddenly wishing there was a little more air in here. *Does he want to marry me?* Oh God…he did say he didn't want to sleep with someone unless it was forever? *Fuck…do I want that?* And fuck…is it weird that I think I do?

It's been a month since we've been dating, *actually dating*, and every day is like one of the rom-coms we watch when we both have a night free. I never pictured myself wanting, or needing a lot of attention from someone. Whenever I pictured my future, we'd both have our separate lives, we'd be together when we could, screwing whenever we got the chance, but these past few weeks have proven one thing to me—that thought was just like the game they play in How to Lose a Guy in 10 Days…bullshit. I don't even know what's come over me.

A few months ago, I was irritated to occupy the same space as him, finding everything about him, except his hot body, extremely annoying. And now I find myself counting down the minutes when I know he's headed home from practice. I feel a pang of sadness when he leaves before me in the morning. An ache in my chest when I have to head to the airport early for a flight. Not to mention the way we've actually been fucking like unhinged, wild animals at night.

The moment he finally let go? *Damn, did he let go.* The man is insatiable. And I'm here for it. He comes in the door, and we barely make it to the bed. More often than not—*we don't.* I'm fairly certain every square foot of my apartment has been defiled. I have never felt so wanted or needed in my life because, as much as I ache for him, I know he's aching for me just as bad. *How the hell did an uptight, skeptical person like me get it so bad for a pompous ass professional athlete?* Probably because he's nothing like that at all—he's so much more.

Just thinking about him has my heart and my stomach twisting. Or...no, wait. My stomach is *actually* twisting. More like churning and not in a good way. *Fuck, why is the room spinning?* Am I this worked up over the thought of marrying him? Sweat beads on my forehead, panic rising in my throat. No wait...that's not panic rising, it's...*oh fuck.* What the hell is going on?!

"Kenni...you look a little pale. Are you okay?" Olivia says, concerned, placing a hand over mine.

"Yeah...I, I think I just need to go to the bathroom," I say, speed-walking to the restroom. As soon as I close the door, I lunge for a stall, barely making it in time for my breakfast to no longer be in my stomach. *Holy shit.* Did I accidentally grab Jordan's regular milk for my coffee instead of the almond milk? *Shit, I need to pay more attention.* Or maybe it's from the stress of the stalker being eerily quiet, like the calm before the storm.

"Kenni...are you alright?" Maggie worriedly asks through the stall door.

I flush the toilet and wipe my mouth with the back of my hand. "Yeah, just...that just hit me fast. I think I grabbed the wrong milk this morning."

Silence fills the bathroom. "You sure?"

I open the stall door, walking past her to the sink. "Yep. I'm better now." I wash my hands, the cool water soothing my clammy skin. "I think I'm going to head out, though. I'm super tired this morning."

"Kennedy," Maggie says, using my full name. *Fuck.* In Maggie speak, full names are never a good sign. "Are you sure it was the milk? I know you guys are banging all hours of the day. You know I'm right down the hall, right? No judgment here, of course, but when I came by to grab a few things to take to Vladi's the other day...I could hear you from the hallway."

I glare into the mirror, meeting her eyes. "Yes, *Maggie*, I'm having sex with my super hot, young, full-of-stamina boyfriend. What about it?"

"Is there any possibility you could be...you know?" She pauses, and my stomach sinks. *Don't say it...* "Pregnant?"

My gaze drops to my hands, rubbing them together as I shake off the thought, convincing myself she's lost her damn mind. "No. There's no way. I'm on the pill."

She gently nudges my shoulder with hers. "Is that all you're using? Cause that's not foolproof."

"I don't need a sex-ed lecture, thank you very much. I'm not pregnant. I can't be. I had my period..." My eyes widen, finding hers in the mirror again. "*Shit*...when did I have it last?"

Maggie winces, looking at me like it pains her to say more. But she does. "It wouldn't hurt to grab a test—just to rule it out. You're right, it was probably just the wrong milk this morning. But if you keep drinking the right milk and throwing up, it might be something else."

I nod. "Yeah. No big deal—I'll just grab a test. Just to rule it out."

"Exactly. We're just ruling things out here. Insert a pilot analogy; you have to rule things out. I'm sure you have one."

I huff out a laugh. "Yes, we rule out problems all the time."

"See? You do this all the time! Truly, no big deal. Now, come on; I'll give you a ride home."

I pull her into a hug. "Thank you. Thanks for being my friend and my neighbor and pushing me to love that man. I'm...I'm so happy," I say as a tear runs down my cheek.

"Love you too, Kenni. You know, now that I think about it, I bet it *is* the 2% milk that's making you so emotional."

I glare at her out of the corner of my eye as we leave the bathroom. "Ha ha. Very funny. I take back my thank you."

"Bitch, you know you love me. Now let's go get a stick for you to pee on."

58
jordan

Thirty seconds. Thirty seconds to figure out how to score on this team. Again. We're tied at one goal each in game six. This is do-or-die—we lose, we go home. Win, and we live to fight it out in game seven. At home. In front of *our* fans. Thirty more seconds to figure out how to get to that final game instead of busting out the golf clubs after a season-ending loss.

The worst part? We're playing fucking Montreal. *My hometown.* Growing up, this was *my* team. I had posters on my wall of all the players. Jerseys, tuques, key chains, T-shirts, you name it. All with Montreal stamped across it. And now I'm playing for the other team and trying my damnedest to be the reason my favorite team loses. My head and my heart are in a full-on battle as if they're in a boxing match on the ice. The blood racing through my veins fuels my adrenaline with the surreal situation of loving and hating this team all at once.

The one benefit? My family is here. My *home* is here. Having them in the stands warms my heart, sending a surge of pride through me. They've been flying back and forth to Milwaukee for all the home games in this round, too, but something about us all being here, back where my hockey career started, helps push my game even harder.

I'm dying for a chance to introduce Kennedy to my family and show her around my hometown, but between my game day routine, practice, rest, games, media, and her job, there just hasn't been a chance. I glance up to where the rest of the WAGs are sitting. I hate that Kennedy can't be here during the third period during away games. She skipped the game entirely tonight and is already on the way to prepare for the flight home. My teeth grit. Chadd has been a complete self-absorbed jackass lately. Kenni says he's been somewhat behaved during their flights, still insufferable as fuck, but she's trying to make sure he has no excuse to blame her for anything, and she didn't want him to think the game was a distraction. And while I'm sad she's not here, I'm so proud of her for being such a badass bitch pilot.

Especially with all the Chadd bullshit. Lately, outside of the flights, he and his girlfriend, the Edna Mode impersonator with her short black bob and constant sunglasses, have been everywhere. Every time I see them, they're fucking making out, or she's sitting on his lap, full-on groping one another in public. I mean... okay, *maybe* Kenni and I are doing the same thing, but Chadd's just...gross. And something about him just doesn't sit right with me. If I didn't know for sure he couldn't have taken some of the photos of us, I would swear he's the one behind all of this. I shove a player into the boards channeling all my anger for that dick pilot into my game—at least something good comes out of knowing that asshole.

But *fuck*...I can't dwell on any of that right now. I have to focus on winning this damn game. Montreal's goalie stopped the puck after a killer shot by EJ, so we have a face-off right by the goal. Momentum is in our favor, even if the crowd is against us, and

Coach calls a time-out to draw up a play, letting us catch our breath and forcing Montreal to stew and stress.

"Alright, boys, this is it. Let's get the goal here so we don't have to go into OT, and we can head back to Milwaukee to win this fucking thing at home. Bougie, Tay...that puck does not cross the blue line. We stay in their zone, got it?"

Tay and I tap gloves. "Got it, Coach."

The arena is electric as the puck drops and Zack takes the face-off, but he doesn't win. *Fuck*. Montreal has control, working to clear it from the zone. *I don't fucking think so*. The puck is almost to the blue line as I channel every ounce of energy into beating it there. And thank fuck I get there right on schedule, stopping puck with my stick to keep it in the o-zone. I pass across to Tay as our offense gets in place. *This is the play*. The one we've practiced so many times, I can do it in my sleep.

Tay passes to Larsy, who fires it right back at him to keep the defenders on the retreat. As Tay shuffles the puck, I know it's coming my way. And...fuck me...I see the shot. EJ has one of their defenders distracted, positioned exactly where Montreal's goalie can't see me. *The shot's mine*. I pull my stick back like a loaded weapon as the puck heads my way. Swinging forward, I fire off a one-timer. The puck sails through the air, high above his blocker. Larsy sees it and heads toward the net for a rebound.

But we don't need it.

My teammates scream and throw their arms in the air as the puck hits the back of the net right as the clock hits zero. My grin is instantaneous as they all dogpile on me with pats to my helmet. We fucking did it. *I fucking did it*. We forced a game seven back at home. *One more fucking do-or-die game to win the whole damn thing*.

"JJ!" The cheering from my family echoes in the hall outside the locker room after the game. As I approach, my mom nearly takes me out despite her five-foot frame, tackling me as she gives me a giant hug.

"We're so proud of you, JJ! All those days sitting at the rink while you practiced are finally paying off," my mom says as we all laugh.

"You're almost there, bud," my dad chimes in as he pulls me in next. "We're all coming to Milwaukee for the next game. Wouldn't miss this for the world."

Hannah grabs me the moment I'm free, squeezing the shit out of me. *Damn...I love having a family full of good huggers.* "It's unreal, JJ! You deserve this, and so does your team."

My eyes are burning, the emotions of everything that's been going on finally sinking in. "Thanks, everyone. I'm still in shock, I'm playing in a game seven for the Cup."

"Sooo," Hannah says in a singsong voice, completely derailing the celebration. "Now that we've got all the congrats out of the way...when can so I see Kennedy? I'm *dying* to see her again."

"She's at the airport. *Apparently,* she has to make sure the plane is working, review flight plans, checklists, safety protocols, blah, blah, blah," I tease. "Actually...it's pretty fucking badass."

"Language, Jordan," my mom scolds.

I cringe. "Sorry, Mom."

"Oh my God." Hannah quickly comes to my defense. "Aunt Maria, that's mild compared to half the stuff these players say."

"I don't care that everyone else is cursing," Mom snaps back. "If they all jumped off a bridge, would you follow after them?"

We all laugh and roll our eyes as I kiss Mom's cheek. My mom will never see me as anything but the five-year-old in skates begging for a snack at the concession stand after practice. And I kinda love it.

"Bougie!" EJ comes up behind me, putting his arm around my shoulder with a ridiculous smirk on his face, his cheeks flushed. "Are you going to introduce me to your family?"

I let out a loud sigh. "This is Erik Johanson, but the team calls him EJ. These are my parents, Joseph and Maria, and you've met my cousin Hannah before."

"Nice to meet you, Mr. and Mrs. Boucher," he says, stepping forward to shake their hands. Then he turns to Hannah and does the same, holding her hand for a few seconds longer than I'd like. "Hannah, a pleasure seeing you as always." His voice practically oozes flirtation. I grit my teeth. *I hate it.* "Are you coming to Milwaukee for the next game?"

"I'll be there," she says with a smirk.

"Nope! EJ, time for you to go." I shove him down the hall, breaking up their little love-fest. "Did I mention Hannah will be joining a convent next week? She's off limits. Got it?"

"I was just saying hello, not asking her to the prom. Calm down, Bougie!" he shouts over his shoulder, walking away, then has the fucking audacity to blow her a kiss. "Bye, Hannah. See you in Milwaukee!"

My parents share a look with one another, giggling to themselves. I suck my teeth, seeming to be the only one irritated at the thought of EJ hooking up with my cousin, who is my best friend and might as well be my sister. Just as I'm about to tell Hannah to stay the hell away from him, Tay walks up to see the commotion. We just won the game, but he looks like he's seen a ghost. *That's fucking weird.*

I shake my head, trying to focus on the fact that my family is here. "Tay, have you met my parents before?"

He forces a stiff nod. "Very nice to see you again, Mr. and Mrs. Boucher. Hannah..." He pauses, offering her a soft smile as she flashes him one back. "Good to see you again, too. I gotta go get my knee iced before the trip home. See you all in Milwaukee." He darts toward the training room, glancing over his shoulder one last time.

That was fucking weird too. *What the hell is going on with my teammates tonight?* I'll deal with these jokers after we win the Cup.

"Nice to see you again, Colton!" my mom yells back.

"I'd better get going too," I say, "See you all in a few days."

We all say our love yous and goodbyes, and I head toward the bus, my steps heavy. The weight of not being able to spend much time with my family always hangs on me. I love them all so much. My mind wanders to the blonde bombshell waiting for me at the airport. Maybe after the season, we can spend a week with them. I haven't seen Kennedy since early this morning, and I'm eager as hell to celebrate with her.

Finally stepping onto the plane, beyond exhausted from a grueling game, I peek down the aisle to see Kenni in the flight deck. I take a step toward her, only wanting a quick kiss since I see her looking over checklists, as a hand grips my arm.

"I wouldn't go in there if I were you," Theresa says, shaking her head. "Captain Ainsworth is in a shitty mood, for some reason, and I have a feeling you going in there will make it worse for Kenni."

My hand balls into a fist at my side, the excitement of seeing her quickly turning into rage. "If he's mean to her, even the slightest bit, you'll come get me?"

She nods, squeezing my bicep. "You know I will. Have I not passed along your coffee to her all season long? I've always been Team Jordan," she says with a wink. "I'm working the front tonight, so I'll keep an eye on her. You know he won't touch her with half this plane ready to beat the living hell out of him if he does, but that doesn't mean he won't be a complete asshole when he thinks no one is looking."

I roll my eyes as my teammates continue to file in behind me. "Isn't that his attitude most of the time?"

"No comment," she snorts, gesturing into the plane. "Take your seat, please, Mr. Boucher, so we can get you all home."

I head down the aisle to take my normal seat next to Vladi. He already has his earbuds in, which means he wants to focus. I sigh, already missing our deep conversations. I'll save my existential question about life for later and leave him be. I put on some music, take some deep breaths, and close my eyes.

Do I have nerves about the next game? Yes. But more than that, the fear sitting in the back of my mind at all times creeps to the front—this damn stalker and what he wants. I'm constantly worried about Kenni. We're together a lot, but I worry about her when she's alone. Is someone following her to the airport? Is someone hanging out in the building across the street from her apartment and watching, waiting to see when I leave? Did they somehow take that photo of us on the tenth fucking floor with a drone or something? *Fuck.* I pinch the bridge of my nose. I don't need this added stress during the playoffs.

Sinking into my seat, I chew on the inside of my cheek. I just want to spend time with her. I want to get to know every detail about every minute of her life before we met. I want to hear about her time in the Air National Guard. I want to hear about what she was like in high school. I want to hear about the old boyfriends I need to beat up because they didn't treat her right. *Then thank them for fumbling Kenni so hard she found me.* She's the air in my lungs and, if that was ever taken away from me, I wouldn't survive.

I send a quick text to Ray. I'm hoping he's got some sort of update on stalker-gate at this point because I need something, *anything*, that will calm my nerves.

> **JORDAN**
> Hey Ray…Any leads?

> **RAY**
> Nothing new. We talked to the guy that runs the coffee shop across the street from the apartment, but he hasn't seen anything unusual. And he's run the place for ten years, so I don't think he suddenly got a fixation on either of you. Looking into some new leads, but nothing concrete. I'll keep you posted.

Fuck. I run my hand down my face. I want this fucking guy caught.

> **JORDAN:**
> Thanks for the update. 🗝, 🎧, 🚫💀, 🚫🧸

I was hoping this would take away the worry over all this, but all it did was make me more worried that we have zero information. *Who the fuck is doing this?*

59
kennedy

A warm hand wraps around my body as I lie in bed, making me hum as I burrow deeper into the wall of muscle behind me. Waking up curled into him has become my new favorite thing. Being woken up with his hard dick pressed against me? Even better.

Normally, the sun creeps in at this time of day to wake me up, but the curtains might as well be super-glued shut after we got the photo of us dancing in here. A shiver runs up my spine thinking about what else might have been photographed without us knowing. I certainly do not need nude photos of me leaked on the internet. As a female in my profession, things are difficult enough. A chill runs through me that we still haven't figured out what the hell is going on, and Jordan's security people are coming up empty trying to find a lead.

I cannot for the life of me figure out who the hell would be doing this. After Chadd was extra bitchy to me on the last flight, I still feel like that weasel is somehow to blame. Jordan had Ray do a background check and some digging on him—came back clean. Not even a parking ticket. *Bastard.*

He had a bug up his butt while we were in Canada, but I don't know what that was all about. *And I don't care enough to ask.* We won. Our flight was smooth. What more could he want? *Maybe he is secretly betting against the Riders?* Whatever the reason, he doesn't need to be fucking rude during every minute of the flight. He even mouthed off to Theresa, telling her to stick to drinks when she popped in after the score posted online, asking if we'd heard the team won. I have never seen her so pissed, her face turning the same color as the in-cabin fire extinguisher. To be honest, I'm surprised Chadd is still alive after that. *Shame. I would've helped her take him out.*

I take in a deep breath and slowly let it out, sinking into the body behind me. I'm not going to worry about any of that right now. Today is game seven, and I'm so damn proud of this man hugging me so tight. I fight back the mist in my eyes. This team, this town, really deserves it. I'm so glad this game is at home. I can be there, fully present, and not have to worry about where the team is flying next. No flight plans, no bitchy Chadd, and I can drown my nerves with Ginny in the suite. Just me, the WAGs, and twenty thousand people screaming for our team. Whatever the outcome, though, I'm going to be there for him. If he's celebrating, I'll help him fill the Cup with blueberry pancakes from Millie's. If they lose, I'll hold him in my arms until he cries himself to sleep. Either way, we'll be together. And that's all that matters.

He stirs behind me as I absentmindedly rub my thumb on his arm.

"Morning," he says, his voice still groggy. "What time is it?"

"A little before seven. What time do you need to leave?"

He tucks his face into my back, placing a gentle kiss along my spine. "Eight."

"You ready for today? I was just about to get up and get out of your hair. I know you have your game day routine, and I don't want to get in your way."

"Kenni...no," he whines as he squeezes me so damn tight, I never want to leave. "You're never in my way. I want you here. Plus, you *know* my routine, and it doesn't start until *after* I head out for morning skate. I come home and take my nap. Then I make my Genovian pear and cheese snack and do the dance routine to Go for It from the greatest episode of Saved by the Bell of all time, where the girls make a music video, and Jessie gets addicted to the caffeine pills because she's under so much pressure and was so scared. And, for some reason, Zack comforts her by telling her she'll get through this. It helps me get in the right state of mind before a game. *And* it's a good reminder that drugs are not the answer."

I roll over in bed, facing him with a smile. "You're so damn cute, you know that? You have the craziest pre-game routine, but I love every bit of it. And that *is* the greatest episode of that show. You know, now that I think about it, you were a lot like Jessie around the satanic Care Bear. You were so...*scared*." I giggle as he pinches my arm, quickly kissing it better. "You're such a big baby."

"Oh...so you're calling me baby now?"

I shake my head. "I called you *a baby*...that's very different."

He tucks a piece of hair behind my ear. "Is it now?"

My heart races with an idea, something I've wanted to do to him for so long. "Very, very different," I whisper. "In fact, would you like to prove that you're not a big scaredy-cat baby?"

"Well, I'm *not*, so tell me what I have to do to prove it. Unless it involves a talking bear, then I'm one-hundo percent out."

"Same," I snort as my gaze locks in with his, neither of us daring to blink. "Do you trust me?"

"Always."

Warmth spreads through my chest knowing he trusts me enough to do literally anything to him. "What's your safe word?"

He shakes his head, his lips tight. "Kenni…I'm *never* using that again."

"JJ, listen, you didn't scare me away last time, and you won't scare me away if you use it again. You're always able to use your safe word anytime. I hope you know that."

"I know." He nods as the words sink in. "Wait a sec…do *you* have a safe word?"

I scoff. "I do—tonic water. You have something planned I'm not aware of? You're as green flag as they come, pretty-boy."

He lets out a loud sigh. "*Fine.* You're right. And you know what? That's a badge I will wear proudly." He pulls me in for a kiss, moving his hips into me, and holy lord, he's rock hard. Heat courses through me, my core slick with want. *The things I want to do with this man.*

"Okay, pretty-boy. Lie back."

He does as I ask while I reach into the nightstand to get something I've been dying to use.

"Kenni…holy fucking hockey stick. Is that your scarf? And…are those…ohmygod, ohmygod, ohmygod," he rumbles, his eyes wide and his interest piqued.

I smirk, loving the control I have over him. "Yes. This is my scarf. I'm going to cover your eyes with it. And yes, these are leather handcuffs I'm going to use to tie your hands to the bed."

"Fuuuck."

"You need to use your safe word?"

"Do you see the raging hard on I have right now? My safe word can go fuck itself."

"That's what I like to hear," I whisper in his ear as I tie the scarf over his eyes. Then one by one, wrap the cuffs around his wrists before securing them to the hidden hooks on the sides of my bed.

"Is this where you put a ball gag in my mouth?" he teases.

My brows practically hit the ceiling. "Would you be into that?"

He shrugs. "I mean...you never know 'till you try, right?"

God, I love this man.

"I love the enthusiasm for trying new things, but your mouth is the one thing I need from you right now. I'm going to straddle your face, and you're going to make me come. Understood?"

He groans low, his muscles flexing under his skin. "*Fuck* yes. But, you know I'll eat you out morning, noon, and night. You don't have to blindfold me."

"Oh, I know, but how am I supposed to use this giant flog if you can see me?"

"What?!" he shouts, nearly jumping off the bed.

My shoulders shake. "I'm just kidding. Although...I do have a soft, little flogger we may try later. But let's just take baby steps."

"You are a sneaky little thing, you know that? Now, sit on my face. I wanna taste you."

I straddle him, holding onto the headboard, letting my pussy touch his lips. His tongue slides across my wet core like he's done this a million times. I love being eaten out, but this angle, the power to move myself without the constraints of lying in bed, is fucking unbelievable. Being able to ride his tongue, my hips circling as if I were riding his cock is so empowering. I'm already on the edge. The angle makes my clit pulse in anticipation as my heart races in agreement. The thought that I'm the only thing he can breathe, the only thing he can taste? *Fuck*, just thinking about being his everything has me nearly coming undone despite him barely touching me.

And fuck if he isn't my everything too.

"You're doing so good, pretty-boy. Licking my cunt like that? Letting me ride this pretty face?" His moan rumbles through me like a vibrator right on my clit. Fuck, this is going to be over before I've even gotten started.

I reluctantly pull away, but just for a moment, while I reposition myself so I can give him some pleasure too.

"This is so goddamn hot. Why is this so hot?"

I steady myself, my heart nearly pounding out of my chest, realizing why this feels the way it does. "Remember when I said sex can be just a release, but when there's an emotional connection, it's so much more? *That's* why it's so hot, JJ. This connection we have, the trust we have with one another, it makes everything better."

"So you're wise *and* sexy? God, do I know how to pick 'em."

"Yes, you do, pretty-boy. Now, finish me off while I suck the cum out of your cock."

His hips buck. "Holy shit. You're not gonna have to suck that long."

And I don't. The feeling of having him in my mouth, while he has me in his, is beyond euphoric. My core and my heart are both on fire knowing that this is real. That it's special. And dare I even think that it could be forever?

It only takes a few moments before we both find our release. He thrusts into my mouth, each pulse a wave of pleasure as I swallow him down and shake uncontrollably above him. This connection we have—the physical attraction, the emotional resonance—my heart thrums, never having dreamed anything could be like this. And now I never want to let it go.

Once we've both recovered, I remove the scarf and cuffs and lie curled next to him, sharing a quiet moment as if the rest of the world doesn't exist.

"Baby, I love you so much. I thought I was in love with you the first day I saw you, but that was nothing compared to how I feel about you now. You're the queen of my fucking world, and I will worship the ground you walk on every day of my life." He pulls me in for a kiss, our lips colliding once more. "Also, I'm officially petitioning the league to change my number to sixty-nine, because that was fucking awesome."

"You'll always be sixty-nine to me, pretty-boy. Now, go shower. You have a game to win tonight."

After he heads off to practice, I stumble into the kitchen to grab something to eat. I'm starting to wonder if the smile on my face was drawn on with a permanent marker since I can't seem to wipe it off. I really hope our morning adventures don't mess up his routine...cause it *sure* as hell was a nice addition to mine. As I open the fridge, my stomach begins to churn. *Ugh*. Why does it smell awful in here? Is it the pizza from the other night? It's not that old; how can it be bad already?

I've never smelled something as awful as this, and my stomach curls in a way that lets me know it doesn't like it either.

"Shit!" I groan, racing to the sink and throwing up. *Dammit*. I turn on the faucet to wash away the reminder of what just happened and splash cold water on my face. *God, that hit fast*. Bile threatens to rise again, remembering I threw up on the plane mid-flight the other night. Thankfully, I was already in the bathroom, so Chadd didn't see. Or anyone else, for that matter.

My chest tightens. My breaths shortens. *Fuck*. I've been avoiding this. My knuckles go white at the edge of the sink. It has to be some sort of stomach bug. Right? I'm not...wait...am I? I quickly open my tracking app and see the message, *three days late*.

That's nothing. I've been a few days late before. This is just a bug. Also, there's no way in hell I can let Maggie be right about this. She'll *never* let me live it down. But I did promise her I'd buy a test just in case. And I did—just to rule it out—but I never said I'd *take* it.

Fuck. I guess it's time.

I dig in the bathroom cabinet for the box carefully hidden behind my tampons. Because who would ever look back there? *Although Jordan doesn't really seem scared of any of that stuff.* If I needed them, he'd probably be calling me over the speaker phone in the store, asking if he should buy regular or super flow.

Reluctantly, I pull the test from the box and empty my bladder on the tiny stick.

I set it on the counter, picking at my cuticles. *Five minutes.* Five fucking minutes. I walk around the apartment and back. Surely, it's done marinating.

"It's only been thirty seconds?! Shit." I groan watching the timer move slower than a sloth.

However, my heart races like my jet is headed down the runway for takeoff. *I can't take this.* I've got to get out of here for a few minutes.

"Coffee…I need coffee," I mumble.

I throw my shoes on and head to the shop across the street to get a nice, freshly brewed vanilla latte with almond milk. Since we fooled around this morning, Jordan was a little rushed, and I told him not to worry about making my latte. Coffee makes everything better and solves all of your problems, right? I mean, not that this is a *problem,* problem. I've always wanted kids. It's just…we haven't been together that long. *Does he even want kids?* A pit forms in my stomach. *Probably should have asked him that before I tied him up and sat on his face.*

Well…coffee is for sure going to solve this problem. I'm going to come back after five minutes, and it's going to be negative. One thousand percent negative.

60
jordan

Walking into the arena for morning skate, I pull open the door right as someone else flies out. "Oh gosh! Sorry," I say as they bump into me, both of us stumbling.

But as I turn to see who it is, my stomach churns. *Fucking Mara.* She whips her head around to look at me, her sunglasses on the ground at my feet. I pick them up for her, despite her audacity, and her eyes meet mine. A chill runs down my spine as she quickly looks away while snatching her glasses from my hand. She sneers like I just stole her diamond necklace. Then, just as quickly as she ran into me, she storms off with a childish grumble.

Okay...rude much? God, that was fucking weird. I've never been this close to her; if anything, she seems to keep her distance from me, but she's giving me the creeps more than usual. My pulse races, a worry that hasn't been there before, blanketing me. *Something's off.* I pull out my phone to shoot a quick text to Ray.

> **JORDAN:**
> Hey...can you dig into Mara? She works for the Riders. She's the broadcasting assistant for the team and also Chadd's little cartoon villain-looking girlfriend. Short gal with a black bob haircut. Always wearing sunglasses.

> **RAY**
> On it. Get back to you shortly.

I shiver as I walk into the arena. Not because of the cold—I'm used to that—but because of that weird encounter. My jaw tenses, something heavy in my gut I can't put a finger on. *Maybe it's just the nerves for tonight's game?* I've only waited to play in a Cup game my entire life, so nerves are not out of the question. I start counting my steps. Nerves help amp you up for a game, too, if you know how to channel them right. *That's all this is...right?* I shake it off as I head down the hall to the locker room.

"Hey, Bougie," Tay says as I walk in.

"Hey, man. You ready?"

"As ready as you can be for something like this. I can't believe we're here. And we have a home game. Can't get any better for us! Your family here?"

"Yeah, they have a suite for tonight. All my sisters are coming too."

"And Hannah?"

My teeth clench, and I reply a little more curt than usual, "Yeah. She's here. Can you help me keep EJ and his bloodsucking vampire mouth away from my cousin? The last thing she needs is to date a hockey player. They were like...making eyes at each other the other night."

He aggressively laces up his skates in the cubby next to mine.

"I'll do my best. But you and I both know EJ and his relationships are out of my control."

"Shit, Tay. I didn't mean to—"

He shrugs, fiddling with his paracord bracelet. "I'm used to it. I'll keep my eye on them for you, though."

"Thanks, man..." Quickly trying to change the subject, it dawns on me that Tay usually has the inside scoop on all things Riders. "Hey, what do you know about that Mara chick that works here. Is it just me, or is she weird as fuck?"

He shakes his head. "All I know is that she's the production assistant for the broadcast team. From what I understand, she keeps to herself, so I honestly don't hear much about her. Why do you ask?"

"I just bumped into her and got a weird vibe. And..." I groan, "remember me telling you about the weird texts I was getting?"

His eyes pop to mine. "Jordan, *please* tell me that's not still going on. Does Kennedy know?"

"Sadly, yes to both. Whoever it is has decided to start a group chat; apparently, not responding pissed them off. My security is on it, but we still haven't gotten any leads. They just keep saying to stay away from each other. But Tay...I can't let her go. She's my person. I fucking love her. She's my forever."

"Then don't let her go. When you find the person you want to love forever, you don't ever let go." He stands and places a hand on my shoulder. "I hope you catch whoever is behind this soon. And know you can ask for help if you need it. Despite what you like people to think, I see the real you. And you're a good friend, Bougie."

I choke back the lump in my throat. I cannot fucking cry today until this game is over. If I start now, I don't think I'll ever stop.

"Thanks, Tay. You're a good friend, too. One of the best. Now, let's go get ready to beat the shit out of Montreal tonight."

61

kennedy

"Miss Kennedy!" Hazel, the barista, greets me as I walk up to the counter. "Want the usual today?"

A knot twists deep in my stomach. *Why do I have a feeling 'the usual' is going to be the farthest thing from my reality soon? Also, is this my last chance to have caffeine? Alcohol? Lunch meat? Fuck.*

"Yes, please. Can you throw an extra shot in there today? I need the kick."

"You got it. That'll be—"

"Oh! Let me pay for that," a female voice, that sounds vaguely familiar, says from behind me. I turn to see the last person I ever expected to pay for my coffee standing there.

Mara.

"Oh. Mara. Hi. You don't have to do that."

"No, no, no. I insist! I think we got off on the wrong foot." *You mean you got off on Chadd's dick in the flight deck when you weren't supposed to be in there? Yeah...I'd say that's getting off on the* wrong foot. "Let me get your coffee. I'd like to apologize for earlier, and... catch up. Join me? I was just ordering another."

I think about the literally ticking time bomb sitting in my apartment, my stomach still rolling from what could be waiting when I get back. "I really should get going. It's a big day."

"Just one coffee. Please?" She places her hand on my arm. "I really want to make it up to you. I don't have a lot of female friends, and with you and Chadd working together, I'd like to at least be on good terms."

Shit. I really don't want to talk to her, but...*goddammit,* why did she choose today to be nice? *Ugh.* I suppose I should not be a total bitch and just hear her out.

"Sure. One coffee won't hurt."

"My table is right over there by the bathroom. Seriously...go have a seat. I'll grab our drinks."

I smile politely and walk over to where I see her laptop and her infamous sunglasses. *I cannot figure this girl out.* But, then again, I had very preconceived notions about my own man at one point, convinced he was the furthest thing from what he really is. I tap my fingers on the table. *Maybe I should give her a chance, too.*

She sets our drinks down and takes a seat across from me. I take a sip and Grilled Cheesus, this coffee is glorious, even if it's a little bitter today. They probably switched to a dark roast, but I don't even care. This extra shot is *exactly* what I need. I need coffee like I need oxygen.

"Thanks for sitting with me for a bit. I just wanted to apologize for what you walked in on with Chadd and me. We got caught up in the moment, and...you know how it is traveling with someone you're seeing. Sometimes you just can't resist."

A smile sneaks out before I can stop her from seeing, thinking back to how I've dreamed about mounting my own boyfriend in the flight deck on multiple occasions.

"I get it. And I appreciate the apology. Most people wouldn't do that. How are things going with you and, um...Chadd?" I ask, barely able to say his name without bile rising in my throat.

"Oh, fine. He's really helped me out a lot. As I said, I really don't have many friends here in town, so he's helped me kill time and have someone to hang out with. And he's helping with a little side project I have going on."

I let out a loud yawn, not realizing how tired I was when I walked over here. I take another huge gulp of my coffee, obviously needing a stronger dose of caffeine. *Maybe I should have gotten two extra shots in this.*

"Sorry, it's not you, I'm just tired from a lot of travel lately. He's helping you with a project? He doesn't seem like a DIY type of guy."

She grins, something hidden behind her eyes.

"We have a few similar interests, so it works out. How are things with Jordan Boucher? I have to admit, I'm a little jealous. You guys seem to be pretty serious."

I grip the coffee in my hand a little tighter than usual. But despite my irritation with her saying she's jealous, I still can't help the way my heart pounds thinking about him. "Yeah. It's pretty serious. He's amazing."

"Amazing, huh?" She taps her lip, her gaze sharp. "Interesting. That's not a word I would have ever thought to use with Jordan."

I let out another yawn. God, I am so fucking tired all of a sudden. I pick at the sleeve on the cup, fighting to stay awake. Not to mention it's a nice distraction from the near certainty that I'm not walking back to a negative result with this sudden exhaustion. "Yeah. He's not quite what—"

As soon as the words leave my mouth, my stomach churns, and the room starts to spin. *Oh God, this is a repeat of what happened at Walt's.*

"Kennedy...are you okay?" Mara asks in a concerned voice.

Fuck, I am *not* okay. "I'm...you know, I'm not feeling well. I think I should be going."

"You look really pale. Let's get you in the bathroom. It's right here. You look like you might be sick."

She's fucking right. "Yeah...I do feel like I might be sick."

"Here, let me help you up," she says, helping me from my chair as she walks me down the hallway toward the bathroom. I can't even keep my eyes open. *What is happening?* And just as quickly as we approach the door to the restroom, it passes by, and she leads me outside the back door of the coffee shop.

"Mara..." I fight to drag my heels, but my body is not cooperating. "Where...where are we going? The bathroom was right there. Whose car is this?" I can barely finish my sentence as she opens the car door.

"I think you need to go to the emergency room, *Kenni*. You don't look like you're feeling very well."

And that's the last thing I remember before passing out in the passenger seat of Mara's car.

62

kennedy

Why does my head feel like it weighs a thousand pounds? I try to crack open my eyes, but I'm still so fucking sleepy that even when I do wake up enough to look around, everything looks blurry. *Am I in the emergency room?* This does not feel like I'm in a wheelchair or on a gurney. My hands tremble as I squeeze my eyes closed, count to three, then try to open them again. I don't think this is a dream. My throat tightens, my breaths too close together to do any good. *What the hell is happening?*

"Wakey, wakey, Blondie," Mara's singsong words echo throughout the dark space. "I need you awake for the call I'm about to make."

I try to lift my hand to rub my eyes, but I can't. My arms won't move. And they are behind me. *What the...* My eyes struggle to focus on her. *Am I fucking tied up?!*

"Mara...what the hell is going on? What call? Where are we?" I struggle to get the words out, but things are slowly coming back into view. Bile rises in my throat as I realize this is not the hospital. This is very, very wrong.

"Oh, Kennedy. Sweet, naive Kennedy. You two really are *so* easy to manipulate. I can only assume you're trying to get his money too? He was so easy to trick the first time, and now I've gone and done it again! Only this time, I tricked you, too." She claps her hands together, holding them up to her face, an evil smile behind them. "You know, I'm really quite proud of myself! The way I slipped that pill into your coffee. The way you trusted me, just like he did. It was *too* easy. And bless your heart—you really thought I wanted to be your friend." Her eyes trace every inch of me, their scorn sharp. "I don't think we're really friend material." She makes air quotes as she steps toward me.

The fog lifts just enough for me to truly see the bitch in front of me. The drowsiness morphs into rage and panic, electricity screaming through every nerve, my spine snapping to attention. My blood is torn between freezing in my veins or igniting and burning through me right into her. "What are you talking about?! What do you mean, last time you tricked him?"

She lets out a villainous laugh. "Oh...Jordan and I go *way* back."

My mind spins. My blood settles on the raging inferno option as it floods through my veins as fast as it can, with some sort of drug still in my system. *Holy. Fucking. Shit.* "You...are you...Angelica?"

She tilts her head with an evil grin. "Awww...I see he told you about me! He was always *so* obsessed with the one and only Angelica Pierce."

My pulse thrums in my ears, unable to hear anything but my rapidly beating heart. "What the fuck are you doing? He gave you money to go away. What more do you want?"

"Oh, sweetheart. I want what everyone wants. More money. And *you* are my ticket to being rich forever. That boy is crazy about you, and his family will pay anything to get you back just to make sure their precious boy is protected. When I leaked that video of us,

I got a nice payout, thinking that would set me up for life. But it didn't. I got a nice car out of it, rented a fancy-as-fuck apartment, but quickly realized the million dollars wasn't going to last long if I kept up the luxurious lifestyle I was always meant to have."

She looks down at her manicured nails as if they are going to give her some magical answer.

"Hmmm, how do I explain this to you?" Her eyes pop up to meet mine as if a lightbulb went off in her brain. "Once you fly first class, you can't go back to flying coach. I decided I needed a better payday. I got a little plastic surgery done—a few things I wanted to fix and a few things to change my appearance enough that no one would recognize me from my past. The goal was always to catfish him and get pregnant. Can you imagine a Boucher family child support check? And with his reputation, catfishing him into a meetup was going to be easy. But that was a bust because of *you*. That naive as fuck little simp Jordan Boucher fell for you," she scoffs. "Did he tell you he lost his virginity to me?"

I swear to God I'm going to kill her once I get out of these restraints.

"It was so easy to hack into his email. Who makes their password 'hockeyplayer68'? And to see thousands of dollars in gifts being sent to some bitch Kennedy Kramer, made me see red. I tried telling him, telling you both, to stay away from one another. But you just couldn't listen. Then I saw your kiss plastered all over the media and realized there was a much easier way to get *my* money." Rage bubbles up, ready to burst out of my chest. "*You.* What a joke."

Shit. How the fuck do I get out of this? And where is Jordan? Fuck, I hope he's okay. I haven't even gotten a chance to tell him I took a test yet. *Fuck, I don't even know the results!*

Okay, Kennedy, focus.

You're in an active capture situation. Survive. Evade. Resist.

Escape. Okay, we're surviving. I do a quick scan of the space, assessing the situation. There's a knife on an old wooden table across the room, but she's not using it on me at the moment. *Shit.* I don't see any other weapons, but that doesn't mean she doesn't have any. I grit my teeth. I've already failed at evading and resisting. *Fuck me for thinking she was nice enough buy me a coffee as an olive branch.* But I can't worry about how I got here...only how the hell to get out of here. Wherever the hell we are. I need to keep her talking and distracted while I figure out if I can escape from this chair as a start. I feel with my fingers behind my back—hard plastic digs into my skin. Has to be zip ties. *I can get out of these.* I just need to wait for the right moment. The haze is still heavy, tugging my eyelids down. I take slow, deep breaths in through my nose, hoping the oxygen and that extra shot of espresso will help me wake up.

I need a plan.

"Speaking of a joke, let's call up your little boyfriend, shall we?" She shakes my phone in her hand.

I swallow hard. I can handle myself here. I don't want him getting in the middle of this. I wish I knew where the hell I was—that would help considerably if I can get out of this chair. *Think, Kennedy...think.*

"Hi, baby. Everything okay?" his deep, sexy voice pours out of the phone. God, even in an active capture situation, I am melting for this man.

"Well, hello there, Mr. Sunshine."

His voice hardens. "Who the fuck is this?"

"Oh, Jordan...you really don't remember this voice? It's your *former* girlfriend. The one you couldn't *wait* to be with. I'm here with your *current* girlfriend. You know, the one I told you to fucking stay away from. But..." She tsks, "you two just couldn't listen."

"Where the fuck are you?!" His voice is filled with an anger I've never heard before. "What did you do to her? I swear to God, Angelica, if you touched one hair on her head—"

"Oh, calm down. She's right here. We were just getting better acquainted. Say hi, Kennedy!"

"Jordan! I'm..." My voice cracks, "I'm okay."

"Baby, I'm coming to find you. Where are you?"

"Ah, ah, ah! Not so fast. Before I drop you a pin for where we are, I'm going to need proof of a nice little deposit."

"Don't give her money!" I shout before she can pull it away from me. "I can take care of myself."

"Kenni, no..." He says, voice laced with worry. "I can't...fuck, I can't lose you."

Tears threaten to spill down my cheeks, but I take a deep breath and force them back. This whole ordeal is worse than when I accidentally bought a fall-scented candle, and it made my house smell like maple syr—oh my God. My jaw falls open, my eyes finally opening wider. *That's it.* "Jordan, don't give in to her demands. I'll be fine. Just...go on with your day game routine; make your peanut butter and maple bacon sandwich and watch your game tapes. Watch them and study the time on the clock, just like you always do."

"What? Kennedy, I don't—"

"Pretty-boy, *listen to me*. Watch your game tapes. And, whatever you do, don't wire her the money."

"Shut the fuck up, Blondie," she snaps. "As for you, Jordan, contrary to what your latest fling of the week says over there, you cannot get out of this. Neither can she. You have one hour. Ten million in the account I'm about to text to you, then I'll send you a pin of where your precious little pilot is."

"Angelica, don't do th—" she ends the call before he can finish, a self-satisfied smirk on her face.

Shit. Please don't let him wire her the money. If he does, this will never end. I push every ounce of my energy into willing him to find me. He'll do anything to protect me. He *promised* he'd never let me go. I wiggle my wrists behind me, making sure I can get my hands free when the time is right. My gut screams at me like a siren —even if he gives into her demands, she won't keep her end of the bargain.

63
jordan

Go on with my game day routine?! Fuck. That. Kennedy's got to be fucking kidding me, telling me not to come and look for her. I don't care if she fell in a goddamn volcano—I'm jumping in after her.

I pace around the apartment, eerily reminded of when I was pacing outside her hotel door before our first date. That same panic flutters in my gut, but this time it's accompanied by pure dread. Where the fuck could she be? Is Angelica going to hurt her?

"FUCK!" I pound my fist against the kitchen counter.

Stay calm, Jordan. I call the one person who always helps me in these types of situations, as I nearly wear a hole in this floor walking back and forth. *Who cares...I'll replace it.* I can replace floors, windows, phones, and cars. A sharp pain nearly sends me to my knees—what I can't replace is *her*.

"Jordan? What's up, bud? You never call me before a game; it's bad luck."

"Dad. Fuck my routine. It's an emergency. I don't care if I never touch the Cup outside of a museum in Toronto. It's…it's Kennedy."

"What? What about her? What's going on, son?"

"Angelica," I say, nearly vomiting from speaking her name. "She has Kennedy. She's asking for ten million in the next hour or...or...*fuck*, I don't even know what she's going to do, but it doesn't sound good."

"Angelica?! What?! Why didn't you tell me sooner?"

"I didn't..." My voice cracks. "I didn't know, Dad. I don't know what's happening, but I can't lose her. I can't. I'm afraid that even when I find her...You know she's crazy. I don't know what she'll do."

"It's okay, JJ. Calm down. Have you called Ray yet?"

"Can you call him? I'm going to see if I can find any signs here of what happened. I left to go to morning skate, and as soon as I got back, I got a call from fucking Cruella demanding money," I mutter, making my way around the house, back to the bedroom where we woke up and enjoyed each other only a couple hours ago.

"Does anything look off?" he calmly asks. God bless him, he's trying to keep me calm. *I'm not sure it's helping.*

I scan the room, letting my dad know what I see. "The bed's made, which she usually does. Her sneakers are gone, so she must have gotten dressed to go somewhere. Let me check the bathroom. Maybe she didn't get..." I freeze. Paralyzed, I swallow the lump in my throat as my eyes catch on something on the counter. Something very out of place. My heart pounds, a spark of fear and excitement coursing through me.

"...dan? Jordan...are you still there?"

"Yeah...yeah, I-I'm here. Hey Dad? I'll call you back. I'm, um... I'm gonna see if I can ping her phone to see if it's here. You'll call Ray?"

"Will do. Jordan? Don't do anything to put yourself in danger."

"Thanks, Dad. Love you."

"Love you too, bud. Be careful."

I throw my phone toward the bed and practically sprint to the bathroom counter to pick up the smooth piece of plastic. I've never held one of these in my hands before. This little device, one I've seen on commercials since I was a kid, changes everything simply by the placement of a line. Two lines, actually. Two lines forming a symbol glaring back at me. My eyes go wide as if I'm in a staring contest. I don't think I could blink right now if I tried. My heart beats in a way that melts every part of me. *Nothing else matters now.* Not hockey. Not money. Not anything I've worked to achieve in my life.

This? This is all that matters now.

I'm even more determined to do *anything* to find her. I will scour every inch of this town, this earth. Even though this started as fake dating, it was *never* fake. Not for me. Not for one minute. She's always been my real-as-fuck girlfriend. The one person I somehow always knew I could trust. The one person who has seen the real me and accepted me regardless. The one who completes me. The love of my life.

And the woman carrying my child.

64
jordan

Where the fuck could Ursula have taken her? My heart stops. Oh my God, it's not just her...it's *them*. I have to find *two* humans now. *Wait, what if it's twins? Triplets?!* I mean, with my athletic talents, I would not be surprised at all if I had multiple strong swimmers. Holy shit, I'm gonna be a dad. The way I already have baby names ready to go. *Okay...calm yourself down.* She's pregnant. That's all you know. Let's just focus on finding the woman carrying one or more of your children before naming them all and crying tears of joy.

I open my laptop to track her phone. Surprisingly, her last location shows here, but it also says last tracked an hour ago. I hit the button to ping it, crossing my fingers, but...silence. *Fuck.* Angelica is smart, the bitch, I'm sure she has it turned off or destroyed. *Double bitch.*

Think, Jordan. How can we find her? She was being weird on the phone. *What did she say?* My mind whirls as my stomach churns, trying to replay every word. She said just to go through my pre-game routine. She knows there is no way in hell I'm leaving her kidnapped while I make my pre-game meals and take a nap. *Wait...she told me to make my peanut butter and maple sandwich.* She knows I hate maple anything, and that my pre-game snack is always the traditional Genovian dessert. *Is she talking in code?* Fuck, does maple mean something?!

She also said to watch the game tapes like I always do. *But...I don't watch game tapes.* She knows I only watch reruns before every game. Why would she tell me to watch game tapes? And study the time on the clock...the fuck? Why would I watch—

I feel my eyes bug out of my own skull. *Her watch.* She has her watch on! Holy shit. I pull the laptop up again and search for her watch location. When I see the map, rage surges in my veins once more. *You've got to be fucking kidding me.*

I grab my phone and keys and race out the door, hoping I'm not too late.

Parking my car, I send a text to my dad and Ray so they know where I am. They told me to wait. To be smart. They told me, under no circumstances am I to get out of the car and try to find her. *Fuck that shit.* She's somewhere in the *goddamn arena* I'm supposed to play in tonight, *of course,* I'm going to scour every inch of this place until I find her.

She's here, and there's no way in hell I'm sitting in my car waiting for backup.

I know this is the part of the movie where someone says this, then something bad happens. But even when that happens, it always works out in the end, right?

Stepping out of the car and shutting the door behind me, I think about texting Jonesy. He used to work security here; maybe he knows some places I wouldn't think to look. But before I can pull out my phone, I see someone approaching my car in my peripheral vision. My hands shake. Blood pumps through my veins with rage.

"What the fuck are you doing here?"

"Hello Jordan. Always so nice to see you," Chadd says, his fist hitting my face.

65
kennedy

I'm annoyingly groggy as hell, but it's a little more manageable. The haze is still there, but I can keep my eyes open for longer. *Baby steps.* My goal is not only to survive, but to escape. Dammit, I haven't seen the results on that little stick in my bathroom yet. But the idea that it could be positive? My heart melts at the thought. And my adrenaline kicks in with full force—I'm here to fight. For me, for Jordan, and for the potential of what may be growing inside me.

While Angelica is busy on her phone, I glance around again, trying to get a sense of where the hell we are. It's like some sort of abandoned warehouse or storage facility. There are paint cans, a broken ladder, and random bricks strewn about on a hard concrete floor, all covered in dust and spider webs. Tall cinderblock walls close us in with no windows—we're underground.

I look to see if there is anything I could use as a weapon if I get free. This chair is metal, so picking it up and swinging it at her is an option. But first, I need to get out of this zip tie. If it were in front of me, this would be much easier, but right now, my only option is to create friction against the chair and try to snap it. I just have to keep her talking and distracted while I do it. I'd rather be force-fed black licorice than have a conversation with her, but this calls for an act of desperation.

With her distracted and seemingly doom-scrolling, I'm afforded a few precious moments to start my plan. I rub the back of my wrist against the metal on the chair—feeling a slight bit of heat as I do, which is exactly what I need. I'm jolted from my actions as a muffled noise fills the space. *Is that a boat horn?* Angelica seems unbothered—as if she was expecting it—but she glances my way, giving me a smarmy smirk. My gut churns, and not in the potential morning sickness way. *If I don't get out of here before she gets what she wants, I won't be getting out of here at all.* I shove the panic threatening to rise down as hard as I can. I've been in near-death situations before. I've come out stronger, wiser, and harder to break. *Focus on the plan, Kennedy.*

"So, you moved to Milwaukee just to extort money? I came for the beer, cheese, and insane abundance of festivals in the summer."

Her glare turns angry. "Don't even try it. You think I didn't Google 'tactics to get out of a kidnapping situation' before I did all this?" She swaps her phone for the knife on the table, running her finger along the side of the blade as she turns it over in her hand. "You're not going to be able to talk your way out. I'm not an idiot."

Well, that's debatable.

"I'm simply making conversation while we're just sitting here in this dark, musty space. I would never try to talk my way out of this."

Angelica stands from her chair, stalking her way around the space. I'm sure she knows this is all bullshit, but I just smile and keep talking. "Have you found a good financial management firm yet? With all this money, you'll certainly need help. I know a guy. I can hook you up if you want."

She scoffs. "What makes you think I'm not capable of managing my own money?"

"Well, the Bouchers gave you a million dollars, and you already blew through it. Seems like you might not want to make that mistake again."

Angelica steps over to me, knife aimed at my throat. I press into the back of the chair. *Maybe I pushed her a bit too far.*

"What do you know about money? You have a good job. You don't know what it's like living like a fucking peasant in a one-bedroom apartment that doesn't even have a water line to hook up to my nugget ice maker—I have to fill that damn thing up every day!! And now you're dating a rich boy to get his money too? That's the real crime here, Blondie. *You're* taking *my* meal ticket."

I push my shoulders back. "That's where you're wrong, Angelica. I am not dating him for his money. In fact, that's the thing that turned me off the most about him."

Her eyes fill with confusion as if she can't comprehend why I would hate someone for their money. "You're a fucking liar. *Everyone* wants money," she huffs as she pulls the knife back, looking at her reflection in the blade.

"I *hated* the thought of being the girlfriend of some rich playboy who dropped money on ridiculous things just because he could. That's not me. I'm not flashy. I've worked too damn hard for what I have. I thought he was cocky and conceited and rude and..." my voice trails off as my eyes well up. I'm not a chronic crier, but this guy has somehow unlocked the sappy part of my brain and, the worst part is, I'm not even mad about it. Not even a little bit. Not even at all.

She darts her eyes between me and the weapon she's still fiddling with, her scowl lethal enough to kill a wandering rodent with a single look.

"I was quick to judge him. I thought I knew his type; I see them all the time at work. It turns out I was wrong. He's kind and sweet and cares about everything and everyone. He has the biggest heart." My smile is genuine despite the fear humming through me. "I didn't even know someone could have a heart that big. He watches all my favorite rom-coms. He does ridiculous dance routines in my living room just to make me laugh. He even got me a Taylor Swift autographed guitar that Olivia *still* gives me a dirty look about every time I mention it. Funny," I say with a slight laugh under my breath, "that was the only gift he got me before we were together that I actually liked. Honestly, he's made me feel like the richest woman in the world, but not with his money. With his heart. He makes me feel like I'm the most important person. That's why I fell in love with him, Angelica. He could lose every cent to his name, and I would still love him. I don't care if he only has a dollar in his bank account or a million; it's who he is that stole my heart."

"Nice try, sweetie," she spits, "but I'm not buying that crap. Those are all the things that make him *weak*. Nothing but a fool." I grit my teeth, wishing I could make Jordan's dream of poking her eyes out with skewers a reality. *I see the appeal.* "Just wait…you'll be just as annoyed with his sweetness one day, and all of this will come back to haunt you in the end. Well…" She smiles as she rotates the knife in her hand. "That's if I decide to let you go."

This fucking bitch.

A loud knock on the door startles me, but I use the distraction to continue rubbing the zip tie against the back of the chair, desperate to create enough friction to finally break it.

"Let's see who our mystery guest is, shall we?" She walks over to unlock the door. As it clicks open, I see none other than the man I just declared my love for being shoved in, a bag over his head, blood on his shirt. A chill runs up my spine. A gun. Pointed at him. And the person forcing him in holding the gun?

I fucking knew it.

"Well, well, well. Nice little reunion we have going on here," Chadd sneers with a stupid smirk on his face, as he yanks the bag away. "You were right, Angelica…he came running to try and save her."

"Jordan!" I yell as Chadd shoves him into a chair next to me and zip ties his wrists. "Are you okay? Oh my God…You're bleeding."

"I've gotten hit worse on the ice. He caught me off guard when he punched me, put a bag over my head, and told me to walk. But I'm fine." His smile is painted red. "Are you okay?"

I lean toward him, nearly toppling my chair. "I'm fine. She didn't hurt me. Just fucking drugged my drink to get me here."

"She drugged you?! Fuck, we have to get you to the doctor right away…this can't be good for…" He squints. "What the fuck is Mara doing here?" he asks, his voice shaking.

"Awww, Jordan, you haven't changed a bit," Angelica interrupts, her voice mocking. "I'm *so* disappointed you don't remember your *favorite* girlfriend. Still a fool for any woman who gives you attention. Truly, it was so easy to manipulate both of you. It's pathetic."

His eyes go wide as his jaw drops. His hands shake, his face white as a ghost's. I fight the urge to bust out of these zip ties. I hate being tied up right now, not being able to comfort him, hold him as he slowly realizes the same thing I did when I first woke up here.

We've been fucking duped.

66
jordan

I think I'm gonna be sick. *She's been here this whole time.* Spying. Threatening. Texting. Taking pictures. *It was all her.* The woman who fucking ruined my life. And even worse—I got Kennedy dragged into this, too. Fuck. I can't hold it back. Everything crashes in. I jolt forward, retching onto the filthy concrete floor as the last few months of fear and panic tear their way out of me. I blink away the tears from being sick, and this entire fucked up situation. The love of my life and the mother of the unknown number of children is tied up in a chair beside me. *Get your shit together, Boucher.* I wipe my mouth off as best I can on my shirt as my mind races through the past few months—everything I should have seen and didn't.

"Angelica? It's been you this whole time? Fuck, now I realize why I was so creeped out this morning when you bumped into me. What the hell happened to your face?"

She lets out a loud sigh, her eyes rolling back. "I don't have time to keep repeating myself. Blondie," —she waves a knife at Kennedy — "fill him in."

I look to Kennedy. Wishing I could hold her. Wishing she could hold me through all this.

Kenni explains that, apparently, my former girlfriend, stalker, and now kidnapper altered her appearance to try to get more money from me. *What the* actual *fuck?* I need a Zack Morris time-out right about now because my brain is about to freaking explode.

"Mara has been Angelica this whole time. Holy fucking fuck." I turn to face the woman who has made the last few years of my life absolutely miserable. "What more do you want from me? My family already paid you. You ruined my life, Angelica! Can you just leave me the fuck alone for once?"

She shakes her head. "Unfortunately for you, that money just wasn't enough."

Her words echo through the space as my jaw tightens—how could someone do this to me, to *us*, just for money? "You two were the ones behind all of this? The texts, the creepy photos, reporting Kenni for the bad landing when it was Chadd McFuckFace flying. God…I knew you had something to do with all this, asshole! Fuck both of you."

Chadd saunters closer to us. "Well, *I* certainly couldn't be blamed for the shaky landing. I figured we could at least divert their attention to Kennedy until all of this got sorted out. So, how about us getting our money?" he says as he walks over to put his arms around Angelica.

"Not now," she grumbles, pushing Chadd away from her. He winces, almost like he did that night when I told him Kenni was my girlfriend. *Yikes bikes.*

"Fine. What's the plan here, sweetheart?" he asks, stepping back from her, completely defeated. *He is totally pussy whipped. And honestly…same. Just for the good woman in this room.*

A pit forms in my stomach. All along, I thought Chadd was the bad guy and Mar- *Angelica* was just his little minion. But…shit…it was the other way around. The gears in my brain start turning like a cheap-ass blender trying to crush frozen fruit for my smoothie. *He gave up his weakness, just like an opponent on the ice.* He's more fucking whipped than a horse on a racetrack.

I have an idea.

Angelica continues to ignore Chadd, stalking toward me and waving a knife in my face. "That depends. Is my money in the account?"

"My dad's working on it. This isn't like the movies. You can't just move ten million dollars at the drop of a hat. There are forms that need signing, and co-signing—this shit takes time."

"Well, he'd better hurry up. You have a game to get to tonight, don't you? Time's ticking. And now that I have you both, I think I should maybe ask your family for more. Maybe…ten million each?"

"Angelica, don't do this! I have nothing to hide. You have no leverage on me."

"I don't? So, you don't care about the woman sitting next to you? What if she suddenly, I don't know, weren't here anymore?"

I grit my teeth, shifting and twisting and using every bit of my strength to get out of this chair, but fucking Chadd McStalker tied these super tight. "I swear to God if you touch another hair on her head, I will *end* you."

She smirks. "Funny, you're making threats, but I'm the one with the weapons here. I have the power. I'm the one with all the control. Just like always. Admit it, handsome, you *lose*."

The sick feeling from earlier still lingers in my stomach, churning and clenching and making me want to sit and cry. *Of course,* this is all happening hours before the biggest game of my life. I bite the inside of my cheek. I want to just crawl into a hole and die.

"Angelica," Kennedy speaks up. "Just let him go. This is the biggest game of his career. Can't you just let him have this *one* thing? Look...I'll stay here; you can keep me until all the money gets sorted out. Including the extra ten million."

I whip my head toward her. "Kennedy Kramer...hell *fucking* no. I'm not leaving you here by yourself. We're going to get out of this, okay? Surely someone from the arena staff will need to come down here for," —I look around the empty space, noticing nothing but some broken shit no one would ever need— "something..."

"We're in the fucking arena?!" Kennedy whisper-yells.

"Oh, Blondie. I've been plotting this for months. Why do you think god Bridget fired for selling her tickets, and there was suddenly an opening with the Riders? Oopsies! Did I forget to mention that? It just so happened that this all came together like a perfect storm right before game seven, making my plan even more diabolical, and guaranteeing that I'll get my money so he can play in his precious little game."

I would give anything to see a giant piece of the ceiling crush her right now. As much as I want to channel all my hate toward that, I can't focus on her. This is my time to fight. For Kennedy, for our child, and for once, I'm gonna fucking fight for myself. So, I set my sights on the one person I know I can goad into a blowup.

Chadd.

He's still standing back from us, his arms crossed, face red, gun still in his shaky hand. He's not looking at Kenni and me, thank the hockey gods, his focus is on *her*. *He's still pissed*. Still miffed at her dismissal moments ago. I may not be able to physically reach him, but if there's one thing I'm good at, it's my acting. A slight lead over my poetry skills, but still. He's just another opponent *under* my ice. And that happens to be where I thrive.

"Wow. Impressive Angelica. Bravo. I would clap if I didn't have my hands tied behind my back, but kudos to you. Really. You managed to get Bridget fired *and* convince Chadd to date you so you could get insider information on Kennedy to take her down as well." I cock my head to the side, raising a brow. "And all you two could come up with was reporting her for a bad landing? I thought you were smarter than that. We all know that if we pull the tapes, it will be clear as day Chadd was the one flying that night."

"Congratulations, Einstein, you figured it out," Angelica scoffs with a smirk. "Any other earth-shattering discoveries you'd like to unveil? What happened to Amelia Earhart, perhaps?"

Chadd moves to stand beside her. "She didn't *convince* me to date her. We met at a bar; she was all over me, not surprising since I'm a catch, and we hit it off."

"Oh really?" I snap back, looking at the scum of the earth woman standing next to him. "Is that true, Angelica? You were all over him because he's so hot, and you wanted to date him? Not because you wanted to use him to get insider information on us? Specifically, to have access to a pilot to help you take Kennedy down?"

Angelica narrows her eyes. She knows exactly what I'm doing, but she doesn't seem to give a shit. She turns to Chadd, giving him a fake smile.

"Mar—I mean, Angelica, you said this was all for both of us. I could get rid of Kennedy, and you were going to get the money so we could be rich. Together. That was all true, right?"

I fight the smirk dying to creep across my face. *I've got him right where I want him.*

"Oh, Chadd, about that—"

"I'm telling you, Chadd," I interrupt, knowing I have to choose my words carefully to direct this anger toward her and not me, especially *while he's still holding a gun.* "Been there, done that. She's playing you like she's been playing us."

"No! No, you're wrong, Boucher. You're *dead* wrong," he says, walking over to me, gun raised. My pulse races. My breaths are short. Sweat beading on my forehead, but not for me. I need to protect *her*. Shit...I need to protect *them*. She's carrying my child, and we haven't even had a chance to talk about it. *Dear hockey gods, please let this plan fucking work.*

"She just admitted it! She tricked *you* this time—not me. Sucks, doesn't it? She played you like a little fiddle, and she's just standing over there smiling, waiting for her payday so she can drop you faster than you finish. Not to mention, she told everyone about your tiny wang."

"I do not have a tiny..." —he turns to face Angelica— "you told? You know I'm embarrassed about that; you said it was okay and that size didn't matter because I used it just fine."

Angelica shrugs. "I mean...it *is* a little on the small side. But I swear, I didn't tell anyone."

Chadd's face becomes beet red, full of rage and fully pissed off.

Perfect.

Her eyes widen as he stalks toward her. The loaded gun now aimed away from me—but directly at the backstabbing bitch.

"You...you tricked me? You said you *loved* me. Was it all a lie?!"

Angelica steps back, her hands raised in surrender. "Chadd... don't fall for this. He's trying to get you all worked up. This was just an arrangement. I...I do love you. I *love you* for getting me the intel I needed. For getting me even more access to the Riders. But... I'm not really *in* love with you. You knew that, right? Listen, let's just put the gun down so we can talk."

"No!" he shouts, the gun shaking in his hand. "You *humiliated* me! I'm...I'm going to fucking kill you."

"Chadd, don't do this. Please!" she pleads, taking another step back. But it's no use. Chadd's finger is on the trigger, and I'm stunned as a loud bang rips through the air, piercing my ears. Angelica screams and falls to the ground. But Chadd falls as well.

What the fuck just happened?

67
kennedy

My sweet, wonderful, and fucking smart as hell boyfriend goaded Chadd into getting upset at Angelica and bought me more time to get free. *That man is brilliant.* After painstakingly rubbing the zip tie along the chair, I finally feel it snap. *Thank. God.* And they are still arguing, too distracted to see I've gotten my hands loose. I glance toward a brick within reach—the best weapon in my vicinity. He's fucking aiming a gun at her, his finger on the trigger. *He's going to shoot her. And then we'll be next.* This is my chance. I bolt from the chair, throwing the brick at his head as hard as possible in my somewhat foggy state.

BANG!

By some act of God, I nail him right in the head. Angelica is bleeding on the ground, and Chadd is knocked the fuck out. *Thank you, Reserve beer league softball.* My heart races, my vision swimming as I see Jordan unscathed, outside of a cut on his face, staring at it all in complete shock.

I exhale the breath I've been holding in, my pulse easing as the tension lightens. *We're okay.*

"Kennedy! What…how?! Are you okay?" he shouts from his chair, straining to get to me. Nodding, I grab the gun and Angelica's knife and quickly cut him loose.

I wrap him in my arms. "I'm okay. Are you okay?" Warmth radiates through me as we hold each other so fucking tight I'm afraid we'll both suffocate. But I don't want to let go. Tears I've been holding back let loose, and I'm now a crying hot mess, sniffling into his chest. "You stupid, stupid, *smart* man. I can't believe you came here for me. But I'm so glad you did. You worked your magic and gave me a chance to work mine."

He cups the back of my head, clutching me to his chest. His tears spill out, falling onto my face and making me cry harder. God help me, I kind of love that he's a crier.

"Baby, I wasn't going to leave you here with her. I wasn't going to stop until I found you. Not for one second. Especially when I saw she had you here somewhere in my arena. I basically live here! I was going to tear the place down brick-by-brick," he says as I smile up at him.

"I know you would have. I would have done the same for you."

"Yeah, 'cause you're a total badass and I fucking love that about you. Speaking of your badassery, how the *hell* did you take down Chadd?!"

I snort. "Well…Angelica, Mara, whoever the fuck she is…made a few mistakes. One of them was not realizing I'm smart enough to get out of zip ties. Once I got my hands free, I waited for my moment." I lean back, cupping his cheek, my thumb brushing against his skin in awe at his part in all this. "JJ, I couldn't have done it without you. You s*neaky* son of a bitch got Chadd all worked up over her. Fucking brilliant."

"Yeah. Well, my acting skills are *quite* amazing." He smirks.

I tilt my head, unable to stop myself from giving him shit, even in this situation. "And you're *so* humble."

"I know, right?" he says as we both laugh, relieving just a bit of the tension. "How did she even get you down here?"

I sigh, upset I fell for her fake nicety. "She fucking drugged my coffee. I don't remember anything after that."

His eyes widen as a streak of panic races across them. "We have to get you to the hospital right away. That can't be good for the baby."

Frozen, I suck in a sharp breath. My heartbeat pounds in my ears as I stare at him, trying to figure out what he's thinking. *How does he know when I don't even know myself?* "What? How? How do you..." my voice trails off, seeming to not know what words are anymore.

He tucks a piece of hair behind my ear. "You left the test in the bathroom. It had a plus sign. That's positive, right? We're going to have a baby?" he asks with a shaky voice as tears well in his eyes once more.

"I left before the five minutes were up, so I didn't get to see the result. I was too nervous. It was...it was positive? Holy shit." I swallow the lump in my throat. "I'm pregnant?"

He nods ridiculously fast, making this all seem even more real. "Yeah, baby. You are. *We* are."

Holy *fucking* shit. I swallow hard, preparing for my next question and hoping the answer is the one I'm longing for. "And you... you're okay with this? I know I'm older and ready to settle down, but you still have so much life to experience and I—"

"Kennedy Kramer, would you look at my face?" he says with the biggest damn smile I've ever seen. "I could not be more fucking excited. I have always wanted a family. *Always*. Honestly, after everything that's happened these past few years, I was beginning to think that would never happen. But with you? I will have a thousand babies with you. I have so many names picked out, we're going to have a hard time narrowing down the list. I also may have asked Siri for some stroller recommendations while I was driving like a madman to find you."

I shake my head and grin. "I was so worried you wouldn't be ready for this. But I should have known. You get excited about everything. I couldn't be happier! I love you, Jordan; I want to have babies with you, too. Maybe not a thousand, but at least this one." I settle back against his chest. "You're going to be the most fun dad ever. And don't worry, I know full well I'm going to have to be the disciplinary in the relationship."

"Well...we have already established you like to be the one in charge," he says with a smirk.

"I'm not even going to argue that." I snort. "You like it though."

"Never said I didn't," he says, pulling me in for a kiss. I nearly lose myself in him before I quickly realize two things. First, he just puked, like, five minutes ago—*may not be the best time for a makeout session*—and two, Angelica's waking up, letting out an agonizing moan.

"Shit," I grumble, dropping my head back to look at the ceiling. "I kind of forgot about those two. Also...how the fuck do we get out of here? Where the hell are we?"

His gaze bounced around the space. "I have no fucking clue. Chadd had a bag over my head the whole time he dragged my ass down here. I thought I knew every inch of this building, but not this place. Did you see where they have our phones?"

"Mine's over there. I'll call the police; you tie them up. Then let's get the fuck out of here. You have a Cup to win."

68
jordan

The police arrive quickly and work with the Riders personnel to figure out where we are. Apparently, there is a storage room no one uses anymore. *No shit.* It had some water damage, which forced them to move almost everything to another part of the arena, letting this one just stay empty. Angelica, somehow, stumbled upon it and thought this would be a fitting place to hold Kennedy hostage.

We watch as our kidnappers are hauled away on gurneys in handcuffs. I should be thankful neither of their injuries were life threatening, but I can't say I'm not a tad disappointed they will still exist on this earth. Hopefully, they will be spending the rest of their lives behind bars. The EMTs and the Riders' medical personnel check us out as well. Outside of the cut on my face, which is not out of the ordinary for me, especially during a game, I'm good to go. Kennedy checked out fine as well. *Thank you, hockey gods.* All her vitals are great, but they want her to get some bloodwork done and see a high-risk pregnancy doctor as soon as possible. I lean back against the wall outside the medical room, the cool brick settling me. *Our family is okay.*

The calm evaporates quickly as I realize I have to turn my attention to the other part of my life. The fucking Cup final. Game fucking seven to be exact. It's ninety minutes till game time, and fans are already filing in. I haven't done my pre-game routines, meal prep, or had a nap. I run my shaky hand through my hair, tapping my foot at warp speed. *I don't play well without my routine.*

"Hey." Kennedy grabs my hand. "What's wrong?"

My shoulders slump. "I didn't get to do any of my pre-game stuff with all the…ya know…kidnapping and attempted murder. I don't typically play well unless I finish my routine. Vladi's superstition is easy—sit next to me on the plane. Although I heard a rumor he has some good luck charm he keeps with him too, but no one knows what it is. But for me? It's my whole fucking game day routine."

She squeezes my fingers. "Oh shit…Jordan, this is all my fault. This is like the biggest game of your life, and today has ruined it."

"No, Kenni, absolutely not. This is all Chadd McKidnapper and She-Who-Must-Not-Be-Named's fault. I'll push through. We can't change what happened, and I'm beyond thankful to have you back and safe and *here*. I just have to rely on my skills and pray they're enough for tonight. I'll just channel the adrenaline from almost dying into the game. I just have to get out there and go for it."

Kennedy freezes, a spark in her eyes. "I have an idea. Wait here!" she yells over her shoulder as she races to the vending machine down the hall. She frantically taps her phone on the card reader, racing back to me with two items in her hands.

I narrow my brows. *What the hell?* "Cheese-it's and jellybeans?"

She nods with a reluctant smile. "I know it's not the *traditional* Genovian cheese and pear dessert, but it is cheese crackers, and these jellybeans are pear flavored, so…close enough? And…" —she swallows hard, nervousness creeping across her face— "I have another idea."

She steps back, looking around the tunnels as if she's double-checking no one is around. Something tugs behind my rib cage—I can feel it in my gut this is another rom-com dream come true. "Grilled Cheesus, I can't believe I'm about to do this, but...here goes," she mumbles under her breath.

I try not to react, to stay calm so she doesn't lose her nerve—but it's no use. A smile creeps across my face as wide as the entire rink as I watch the love of my life singing about putting her mind to it, going for it, and breaking a sweat along with every hand motion of the Go For It song from Saved by the Bell. She doesn't quite have the pizzazz I do, but damn, it's the cutest fucking thing I've ever seen. I race to join in, doing all the moves with her and goddammit this is the best moment of my life.

The moment she's done, I pick her up, swinging her around in the hallway, and kiss her harder than I've ever kissed her before. *This is it. The woman of my dreams.* Well, she *was* the woman of my dreams. Now she's the woman of my present and my future. No more dreaming needed. She's here, in my arms, and I'm going to go fucking win the goddamn Cup for her.

As if I wasn't exhausted enough from the day's activities, the game goes into overtime. Montreal decided that me being fucking kidnapped was not a reason to go easy on me or my team. This game has been brutal. We each scored one goal in the first period and not another since. Three minutes left on the clock for the first OT and fuck, we need to score. I'm resting on the bench between shifts, willing my muscles to keep working, convincing my lungs they have a little more space left to keep breathing.

"You alright, Bougie?" Tay asks, sliding down the bench next to me. "I know it's been a day and if you need someone else to swap out, we all understand."

I take a sip from my water bottle as I debate his question. My body is tough, but even I'll admit this game has been rough on me after not having my full pre-game routine. *Maybe I should*—Out of the corner of my eye, I see something sparkle from one of the suites above.

Kennedy.

The WAGs all have jackets for the playoffs, but she went and got hers bedazzled for me. She *hates* bling like that, but she said it was an homage to my sparkly personality and 'the damn leopard' in her apartment. *She still refuses to call him Neil.* But seeing her up there cheering for me is the *only* motivation I need to keep going.

"Yeah, I'm good. Just got my second wind. Let's fucking do this." We pound our gloves together as we wait for our teammates to skate to the bench for a line change. *Go time.* Hopping over the boards, I race toward the back of our goal where Vladi has the puck waiting. I pass to Zack, following him up the ice into the offensive zone. He sends it over to Larsy, who gets a good shot off but it's blocked before a full-on scuffle for the rebound breaks out. Out of the corner of my eye, I see Tay creeping up to the other side of the goal where no one is looking. *Fucking genius.* I can tell Larsy sees it too, gaining control of the puck and shuffling it over to Tay, who pulls back his stick and aims for the goal. Montreal's goalie tries to shift across to stop it.

But he doesn't.

The puck hits the back of the net, and the entire arena explodes. We clobber Tay as the entire team flies off the bench. Gloves, helmets, sticks, everything goes flying as we scream. *We fucking did it!* We fucking won the whole enchilada. We hug, scream, and slam each other against the boards in excitement, the weight of the moment truly sinking in.

"Fuck yeah! Colton Taylor with the game-winning goal!" I shout, pulling him in for a hug.

"TAY!!!!" EJ screeches as he comes running over to him. "You fucking won us the Cup! My best friend won us the Cup!" he whoops as he cups Tay's face and kisses him right on the lips with a huge *mwah*, then disappears to continue celebrating with the rest of the team. Tay stands stunned, his hand shaking against his lips. *Yikes bikes.*

"Boucher!" Coach Cal walks over in his suit and dress shoes on the ice. "I told you no more pre-game antics, and you just couldn't resist getting yourself kidnapped on the day of the fucking Stanley Cup final game?" I narrow my brows. *Is he really upset about this?* "I'm fucking kidding. Pull all the antics you want after this damn game…you're a Stanley Cup champion!"

"Jordan!" Vladi wraps his arms around me, pulling me in for the world's biggest hug. From the world's biggest hug hater? *Nobody pinch me.* "Now we celebrate. We celebrate as teammates and friends, yes?"

"Fuck yeah, Vladster. Fuck yeah."

69
kennedy

"Drinks on the house for the Stanley Cup Champion Riders!" Walt yells as the boys file in with the Cup. They've been up all night partying, going to various bars in Milwaukee, and being treated like the royalty they are. I was lucky enough to go home and get some rest after an extremely long day. Jordan refused to let me stay by myself, so Maggie invited Olivia and me to her place for a sleepover. Before we left the arena, though, I finally got the chance to meet all of Jordan's family after the game. They are the loveliest people in the world, and I can't wait to get to know them more. Even more than that, I'm excited to tell them, along with my own family, that we are starting one of our own.

But right now, my focus is all about celebrating this team. More specifically, Jordan. My boyfriend. My partner. My love.

They parade the Cup through the bar and set it on a giant table in the middle of all of us. Everyone tells me this is the most difficult trophy to win in all of sports, and yet—it seems to be at home here. The wood paneling on the bar and the year-round multi-colored Christmas lights found in nearly every Milwaukee bar give a feeling of history. The things this bar has seen, the things this trophy has seen, all seem to mesh together like it was meant to be here all along.

I can relate.

My heart flutters as my boyfriend drops into the seat next to me. Despite the fact that he's barely able to stand upright, I still want to hold onto him and never let him go.

But, if I'm being honest, he could maybe use a shower.

"It's 11 in the morning, pretty-boy, how many drinks have you had?"

"Kenni, baby...I'm...I forgotten...forgetting..." He lets out a deflated sigh. "I lost count. All I know is I almost lost you yesterday, and now I'm losing count of drinkies."

I can't help but laugh at his ridiculous, drunk speech. This is the first time I've seen him hammered. I would normally be irritated, but as all the other WAGs clued me in, this is what they do when they win the Cup. Party hard all night, then crash *hard*. There will be a parade in a few days, and the whole town will celebrate, but right now, these guys are a bunch of drunken fools. Walt's was the first and last stop on this tour of debauchery, and we WAGs get the distinct privilege of driving all their drunk asses home.

I couldn't be any happier.

"Kenni...I'm gonna just lay my head on your shhhoulder for a minute. I'm sooo tired," Jordan mumbles as he collapses into me.

"Okay, you do that." I snort as soft snores rumble in my ear. "I think maybe it's time we head home."

He jolts up. "Not yet! I gotta ask Maggie something," he says, reaching across the table toward her. "Did Kenni tell you we got kidnapped?"

Neither Maggie nor I can hold back our cackles, our grins identical as our eyes lock.

"Yes, Jordan, she told me what happened. I'm glad you're both alive."

"Me too," he slurs, leaning back against my shoulder. "Baby, I love you so much. You have my baby, okay?"

I gasp. I try to play it cool, patting him on the arm and hoping no one heard. "Yes, JJ, we'll have babies someday."

"Nooo, Kenni. You have my baby *now*. Like…nine months. You already have my baby. It's right here," he says as he pats my belly.

Oh shit.

It's loud in here, and everyone else is involved in other conversations, which means no one noticed Jordan's confession. Except for one person. *Maggie.* Of course, she heard it and is looking right at me, her eyes wider than I've ever seen. I return her look with a pleading stare, silently begging her not to say anything. She nods with a wicked smile and a silent, *I told you so.*

I roll my eyes. She was right. *Why are my friends always right about this shit?*

Honestly, I'm glad they were right and even more glad to have them in my life. Maggie, being my neighbor, led me to this amazing group of friends. My being the Riders' pilot led me to the incredible, but very drunk, man on my shoulder. And fake dating him is what led to us embarking on a lifelong journey together. I cheers Maggie, knowing my friends were probably right about another thing—Jordan already has a ring. Not the Championship one, he'll get this fall, but one for me. I can feel it in my gut. And when he asks, my answer will be yes. This ridiculously handsome, kind-hearted man, stole a piece of my heart he gets to keep forever. Resting my cheek against his sweaty hair, I can't believe how my life has changed. *Jordan can have the whole damn thing because he's given me his in return.* The only person we'll ever be sharing with is the little one that'll be making their appearance next year.

As we head to the car, I can't help but think about what's in store for us. Car seats, strollers, diapers, late-night feedings. And with two really crazy jobs, we'll have to figure some things out. It's too overwhelming to think about now, but we'll make it work. I'm not worried at all, honestly. The way we were so in sync yesterday, teaming up to defeat evil, I know our kids are going to have the best parents ever. If we can survive Angelica and Chadd, I know we can survive angsty teenagers. I cringe, glancing at the man by my side. I may regret that statement in about 15 years.

"Come on, pretty-boy, let's get you home."

"I love you, baby. I love you so much."

"I love you too, JJ."

I squeeze his fingers, my body exhausted, but my heart full. This has been my dream for as long as I can remember. Having a husband, a family, and a place to always hang my scarf. I can fly solo, but since meeting him? I never want to do life alone again. It's funny—I always pictured Jordan with his head in the clouds. A dreamer. A performer. A complete goofball. And me? I'm the pilot. Serious. Focused. Always in the air and in control. Yet, somehow, he's the one who keeps me grounded. It's more than I ever imagined.

It's everything.

epilogue: part 1

jordan

Six Months Later

*Psst! Hey you. Yes, **you**. The one reading this book. Yeah, I can see you. Did you think I didn't know you've been sitting there reading this smutty little romance book? God, I love it so much. I don't know about you, but this one is one-hundo percent my favorite. Listen, Ellie says I'm not supposed to talk to you, but I figured you'd want a little recap of what's happened in the last few months.*

So...we're pregnant! Holy shit, right? But you knew that already, didn't you? I'm actually in the middle of the baby shower right now. My entire team is here, and all their wives, girlfriends, and both of our families. I know showers are supposed to be for the mom-to-be, but I was not about to miss the gifting event of the century. This shower is just as much for me as it is for her. Similar to the gender reveal that I meticulously planned, I wanted everything to be perfect.

We had the party at the arena. I recreated my Ice Ice Baby routine,

Epilogue: Part 1

except this time, I had my pyrotechnics guy hook me up with colored flames that would shoot out of my hands for the sex of the baby. Kenni and I had no idea until the flames went off.

One pink. One blue.

Twins. I knew I had strong swimmers, and I was fucking right! And now, we get to introduce a little Kenni and a little Jordan into the world. I was honestly hoping for twin girls, just because I grew up with all women, and I am somewhat terrified to raise a boy. I was a terror of a child, so I can only imagine my own spawn combined with Kenni's being a handful. But, regardless of their personalities, they are both going to play hockey, and both are going to learn to fly. If they want to, of course. But…I have a feeling they will. Kenni has promised me we can go flying together after the babies are born. But I won't let her until there are not four of us sitting in the flight deck.

She's going to take a little break from work for a while to focus on the babies. I did end up *Crazy Rich Asians* buying the Riders' private airline company, so she can now do whatever the hell she wants. She won't be flying for the Riders for a bit—we can't both be on the road with babies. But she can take on private clients whenever she gets an itch or wants to keep up her flying requirements until she's ready to come back.

And if she wants to go back to flying full-time? I'll give all this up to be a stay-at-home dad.

We've moved into my house. She really hated how big it was, claiming it was too much house, but with twins and a full-time nanny, plus having space for our families to stay when they visit, her apartment wasn't going to cut it. Yeah, I know. Full-time nanny sounds like Richy Rich 101. But, with my job, I can't always be here to help her, so it's the only option. I've heard how excessive it is from her a billion times; she's convinced she can handle this on her own, but I'm not taking any chances. She's the queen of my world, about to give birth to the prince and princess of my world, and she's not going to be struggling when I'm away.

Epilogue: Part 1

Shit...it's time to open gifts, and I'm being summoned....I'll be right back.

"Awww." Everyone collectively ooos and ahhs at the gift Kenni opens, tears filling her eyes again. Walt and Johnny got us onesies that say 'I'll have a bottle of the house white' and 'brewed locally with love.'

"Johnny got one of those insect machines to do crafts, and he can't stop making things," Walt says.

Johnny shakes his head. "For the millionth time, it's called a Cricut. And I'm making new merch for the bar's annivers—" he's interrupted by his phone buzzing in his hand. "Hang on, I gotta take this." He swipes across the screen and whispers as he walks out of the room. "Johnny's Travel Agency, this is Johnny. How may I assist you?"

"Did he *say travel agency*?" Maggie asks. "Why do I have a feeling he's been behind some of the rooming mishaps this group has had?"

Kennedy and I share a knowing smirk, realizing he was probably the reason we were in adjoining rooms. *I can't even be mad at that meddling son of a bitch.*

After all the gifts are open, Larsy stands, clearing his throat to address the group.

"Kennedy, Jordan. I want to say congratulations to you both," he says, making my heart soar. This group has become such a family to us, and Larsy saying a few words is getting me all in the feels.

Larsy smirks, shaking out his speech. "And Jordan, since you wrote me such a *lovely* poem for my bachelor party, I thought I would return the favor here at your shower." *Ohhhh shit. My heart is*

Epilogue: Part 1

no longer soaring. My heart is nosediving through the air and crashing on a tropical island in the middle of the ocean. "I'm not a poet, but I do happen to be married to a songwriter, so she helped me with the rhyming."

Kennedy is literally going to murder me in my sleep if this is anything like the poem I wrote for Larsy's bachelor party.

"H-hey Hayes," I say, patting him on the back, "that's sweet of you, man, but you really don't have to do this."

He looks at me with a wicked smile. "Oh yes, Jordan. I do."

"Larsy...my *parents* are here," I whisper to him, the blood draining from my face.

"Guess you'll have to wait and see how inappropriate this is then, huh?"

I glance at Kennedy, who has heard rumors of the poem I read at their destination wedding and is looking at me like she will, in fact, murder me. I bite the inside of my cheek, preparing myself for what's about to come. *There's no taking things back.* I made this bed, and now I have to lie in it.

"I've titled this...Bougie's Baby Shower Poem."
Oh God. Here we go.
"Today we celebrate Bougie and Kenni,
I'm sure this shower cost you a pretty penny.
You found a woman, and finally settled down
She was in the air, while you were on the ground."

Aww, this is kinda sweet actually.

"But you two came together, surprising us all
And you impregnated her with the sperm from your balls."

Epilogue: Part 1

Kennedy rolls her eyes at me. *Yeah. Okay. I'm definitely getting smothered to death in my sleep.*

"But that's as graphic as this poem gets
  Because we're here with all our parents.
  Here's to your babies being happy and healthy
  As if they even need that cause they'll be really wealthy
  And whenever you feel you're drowning in diapers
  Remember you're part of this family of Riders."

My eyes burn while the world goes fuzzy. *Dammit Larsy.* I give my teammate the biggest hug. "Thank you for only referencing sperm and balls in the poem."

"That is your gift. Not making that poem dirtier. Trust me… Olivia and I had some other ideas." We both laugh. "Now…go sit with your wife so we can get a group photo."

Oops! Did I forget to mention we got married? I bought a ring the day after we decided to fake date. Had my family jeweler on that shit in a flash. You never know when you're going to need to propose to your fake girlfriend, who you want to be more than your fake girlfriend. It was the perfect day, one of many we've already had. We were taking the Cup around Montreal on my day, with the glorious trophy my name is now engraved on forever. Name a better day to propose to your girlfriend and the mother of your future children. I'll wait.

Kenni never wanted a big wedding. But I did. And she indulged me. We got married before the season started. It was pulled together quickly, but when you have access to a lot of money, you can make things happen quickly. She had a few things she wanted, but the rest was all me. I'll have

Epilogue: Part 1

to let Ellie tell you the whole story sometime, because it was epic. But I'll save that for another time.

Right now, there's only one word to describe my life. Happy. We're about to have two little ones to care for, and I'm over the moon ecstatic, and terrified, in the best way. I have a beautiful wife, an amazing job, a great group of friends, and so many exciting things planned for our future that it would take years for me to list them all.

But for now, stay bougie, bitches!

Your forever friend and entertainer,

Jordan "Bougie" Boucher

epilogue: part 2

colton

I've always wondered what it's like being in prison. Being served three square meals a day with dedicated exercise time always sounds appealing. But staring at white walls and longing for freedom is what always made me question if I could really survive.

Turns out...I can.

Not in an actual jail cell, I'm a little too *by the book* for crime, but I am stuck staring through the bars at the freedom I've longed for for *months, years,* without a key to unlock the metal standing in my way.

It's fucking torture.

Not physical torture as I've seen in prison movies. *I wonder if that would be easier.* A shiver runs down my spine. *Nope.* This is much, *much* worse.

Sitting at a baby shower for Bougie and Kennedy, seeing the glow on their faces, the excitement of everyone here celebrating

Epilogue: Part 2

them tugs at something I didn't realize was there. I'm extremely happy for my friends. Bougie finally got his happily ever after. If anyone has the slightest inkling of what I am going through, longing for someone for so long but not being able to have them, it's him. *But he doesn't completely get it.* He found his love without risking everything. I can't do that. Confessing my feelings would ruin our careers. Our reputations. *Everything.*

Personally, I couldn't give a shit. My reputation is not much more than being a decent player in the NHL. I enjoy the game. I'm good at it. Fuck, my name is on the Stanley Cup! But losing all that would be nothing compared to this.

Because, of course, my fucking dumbass self-had to fall in love with the one person I can't have. My teammate, my roommate.

And my goddamn best friend.

We moved in together during the rookie season, both new to the city, and became instant friends. I'm the serious, responsible, level-headed planner. He's the carefree spirit that doesn't give a shit about bills or setting aside money for a hockey player's inevitable retirement. We balance each other, helping one another find a neutral zone within our lives. And when we both started making enough money to buy our own places, we just…didn't.

I think he secretly wanted me to keep paying the utilities and pay me back so he didn't have to worry about it. For him, it was continuing our friendship and living arrangements. But for me? It was about making sure he stayed. The masochist in me wanted to see him every day despite knowing he would never be mine. If torturing myself is what I wanted, that's exactly what I got.

Every time he clapped his hand on my shoulder.

Every time he brushed against me, reaching for a mug in the cabinet above the sink when I was rinsing out a dish.

Every time his foot brushed against mine when we sat on the couch.

Epilogue: Part 2

Fucking. Torture.

Then he decided we should go on a spur-of-the-moment trip to Cabo for the weekend. I fiddle with the paracord bracelet on my wrist, remembering what *almost* happened on that trip. We had a room with two queen beds. Easy peasy, right? Nothing could go wrong there.

We live together; this was no different. But after a few too many drinks, I stumbled into bed and only remember waking up with his arm across my chest, EJ having passed out in the wrong bed. *My bed.* I'll never forget the way my heart raced, the way my cock twitched, and the way my stomach twisted. Cherishing every detail, knowing it would be gone the minute he woke up.

Then he did.

I clenched every muscle in my body, waiting for him to panic. Ready to say it was no big deal. Ready to explain the morning wood as an everyday thing.

But he didn't panic. His eyes caught mine, his hand still glued to my chest. Nothing but silence in our gaze. I swear we lay there for an hour, but it was merely seconds.

He finally cleared his throat, saying the words I was expecting, "Sorry, Tay. I was wasted." I, of course, replied with what I had planned. Then we both went about the rest of our trip like it never happened. Like we were a couple of frat bros who bunked up after a party. And somehow, on a trip with my best friend, I never felt more alone.

But that morning, that one glorious morning in paradise, gave me more than a hard on. It gave me hope. Because I fucking saw it. It was deep and buried in his stormy eyes, but it was there.

He thought about it. He thought about *me*.

And yet, despite the time that's passed by, here I sit at a baby shower. I stare blankly out the window, still tortured by what

Epilogue: Part 2

could've been my freedom had I been bold enough to pull him in for a kiss that day.

But I didn't. I couldn't. So now I live my life every day wanting a man I can't have. The man is currently hiding in the kitchen with Hannah. They thought they were sneaky, wandering off separately, but I saw. *I always see.* I see his hand on her waist, hers on his cheek. I see the longing smiles and looks they give each other when they think no one's watching. I see the way they feel about each other.

And, like the fucking good friend I am, I agreed to keep their little secret all while trying not to lose my goddamn mind.

Bougie *specifically* told EJ to stay away from Hannah after her move to Milwaukee—he actually declared it to the entire team that she was off limits to all of us—yet somehow I get to be the secret keeper. *Everything is a goddamn secret around here.* I feel like I'm in a vault with someone on the other side trying to blow it wide open, knowing there's nothing I can do to keep it shut anymore.

This is why prison seems appealing.

Fuck even I have secrets. EJ doesn't know one critical piece of information. Well, *two* actually...

He doesn't know I am in love with him.

He doesn't know Hannah and I kissed.

Yep. That happened too. She visited Bougie earlier this year, and we all went out. I had a little too much to drink, mainly because EJ was dating someone else at the time, and Hannah and I just seemed to, I don't know, click? I was having a really hard time seeing Erik dating *another* girl who was completely wrong for him. *Probably because I'm in love with him.* The twisting in my chest aches knowing I will never have him—but I do want him to be happy. And seeing him with girls that are clearly only into him because he's a professional athlete is a knife to the heart. How does he not see they are glorified puck bunnies hoping to get a lifelong cash contract?

Epilogue: Part 2

How does he not see that he's worthy of so much more?

I sneak another glance into the kitchen at them. At *her*. I'm not quite sure if Hannah knew exactly why I was moping that night, but the way she set her hand on my forearm when I caught EJ making out with his girlfriend made me feel like she got it. Like she knew I needed a distraction. She sat with me the entire evening while everything around us disappeared. And, for a moment, I forgot. I forgot about the pain. The longing. The unrequited love. All because of her. There was something about the way her eyes sparkled when she talked to me. I felt like she could see into my every thought, conquer every inner demon. For the first time, I felt like someone *saw me*. In the midst of our laughter, she keeled over in hysterics, nearly falling off the couch we were sitting on.

But I caught her. I held her in my arms as our eyes locked, heat thrumming. Then she smiled, and that was it. The space between us all I could see. That was all it took for my entire existence to be upended. I had to have her. I leaned forward and kissed her. In the middle of a club full of people, but in my mind, it was only the two of us.

And she kissed me back. And in the most surprising moment of my life—I fucking loved it. I've always been more attracted to a person versus the parts and pieces they have. As the patron saint of sexuality, David Rose said, I like the wine and not the label. More often than not, it's been men that have had my attention, only because I'd never really found a woman I wanted in that way before.

Until her.

It felt like something finally clicked into place. Like when the equipment manager snaps my blade in place, and I'm finally able to glide back out onto the ice with no resistance. Just as I was about to take her out of the club and find some place more private, to do

Epilogue: Part 2

something I never thought I'd have a desire to do, a voice came over the mic introducing a guest DJ for the rest of the evening. We pulled back from our kiss, her face flush and her lips plump from being pressed against mine. I apologized, and she waved me off as she said the same. We both chalked it up to the alcohol, assuming that was probably for the best. That's what I keep telling myself anyway.

For so long, my chest has been aching, longing for something I thought I could never have. And there I sat with a beautiful woman, one who I wanted to be more than a friend, while she comforted me because I was desperately in love with someone else.

Then she met EJ.

Talk about fucking conundrum.

And now, here I am, keeping their secret relationship under lock and key. My prison cell gets smaller every day. Every hour. Every minute. Every breath. Every time I fucking see either one of them. Where he is goofy and carefree, she is professional and poised. Where she is small and fits perfectly in my arms, he is someone I want to be completely enveloped by, not being able to escape his hold. *I wonder if—*

"You want a piece of cake?" I nearly fall out of my chair as Kara stands in front of me with a plate of dessert.

"Sure," I say, taking it from her as she hands me a fork and napkin to go with it—along with a look that tells me she's here for more than playing host.

"You okay, Colton?" she asks. "You've been quiet today."

If only she knew. "Yeah. Baby showers just aren't my thing."

"Keep telling yourself that," she says with a knowing look and walks away. *What does she know?* Kara loves some piping hot tea as much as I do. *Does she know about mine?*

Fuck.

I stare at the piece of cake, the sugary pink and blue frosting

Epilogue: Part 2

staring back at me as if it's trying to force a thought in my mind. I can't even blink, my gaze glued to the confectionery fortune teller in my hand.

I think the fucking cake is right.

I don't want EJ. I don't want Hannah.

I fucking want them both.

afterword

Jordan and Kennedy's trip to visit Kellsie in the hospital was inspired by my real life cousin Kellsie. When she was battling Osteosarcoma, an aggressive form of bone cancer, I would often spend the night with her in the hospital to give her parents a break. She was so funny, so brave, and always wanting to help others. While she didn't have a hockey player best friend, many professional athletes would come and visit patients to brighten their day, and writing this book I knew Bougie and his heart of gold would be one of those athletes.

The Kellsie in this book is very much based off her personality. She was quite feisty and would absolutely have tried to vet someone's significant other. Sadly she passed away in 2011 just shy of her 21st birthday. I miss her every day, and I am so grateful I was able to honor her in this story.

acknowledgments

Thank you for reading Ice Deke! I am so grateful for all of the love the Milwaukee Steel Riders series has received. People reading my stories is one of the greatest privileges and I appreciate any of you that have picked up this book and I truly hope you enjoyed this one!

As always, a huge thanks to my husband, Mr. Ellie K. Drake. A little piece of him lives in all of my MMC's, this book was the way he has a heart of gold and always buys me the most thoughtful gifts. Okay so maybe Bougie's gifts were not always thoughtful. However, I'm still waiting on my diamond encrusted leopard, and there is one at the furniture store here in town so…wink wink Mr. Drake.

Thank you to my family who promote my books even though most of them don't read them.

To Casey, my editor. How we got this book finished with everything we've had going on, I will never know, but we did it! Thank you as always for immersing yourself in my stories. This was the most complicated plot I've written so far and I could not have done it without you! Also…did you know Zack Reeves is the Captain of the Riders?

Thank you to my alpha readers Amy and Christian for reading my first drafts and telling me not to throw it in the trash.

Thank you to the Diamond Dolls for keeping me sane, being a sounding board, celebrating each others wins, commiserating over the inevitable disappointments, and overall navigating the emotional roller coaster of being an indie author with me.

To Megan, for collecting me as one of your authors, being an awesome event assistant, and helping run the street team.

To Sandra at Maldo Designs for once again knocking it out of the park with the cover!

To Vampira Art for your amazing work on bringing life to my characters through your sketches!

To Lindi, my amazing friend and badass female pilot. Thank you for helping me learn all kinds of cool things about aviation, being a pilot, and shouting from the rooftops about my books. Thanks for reading this book in a very unpolished state to help me with all of the aviation terms. I hope I made all the female pilots proud.

To P, even thought you cheated when we played MarioKart, thank you for being the inspiration for a guy in his twenties with an extensive knowledge of chick flick movies. *Marla Hooch…what a hitter.*

To Jillian for proofing all my hockey scenes for accuracy and getting out a hockey coaching whiteboard to help me block out a scene. No gear bags were harmed during the writing of this book 😂

To Sarah for making my beautiful social graphics…so glad to have you as a part of my team!

To Mekhala for the amazing proofread and for reading the entire Steel Riders series ahead of time!

To my beta readers, Megan, Rachae, Ashley, and Sunny, thank you for helping polish up this book with your feedback!

And last, but certainly not least, to my street-team the Ellie-verse! You are the reason people find my books! I get emotional seeing the way you promote my books and help one another out in the group chat. Forever grateful to you!

also by ellie k. drake

Want to read more about the Milwaukee Steel Riders?

Book 1: Ice Contact

Book 2: Ice Block

Sign up here to receive a free bonus content about Zack and Kara Reeves called STAYCATION!

And stay-tuned for Book 4 to read Tay, EJ, and Hannah's story! Available for pre-order now!

Follow me on Instagram @elliekdrake for updates.

Subscribe to my newsletter at www.elliekdrake.com for bonus content, sneak peaks, and all the latest news in the Ellie-verse!

about the author

Ellie K. Drake is an author, wife, and dog mom. When she's not busy writing her latest novel, she enjoys reading her favorite genres, including romance, fantasy, and thrillers. Ellie has been making up stories her whole life, and finally decided to put them down on paper. Her stories are funny, swoon worthy, spicy, and always have a happy ending. Aside from her love for storytelling, she is also a musician, an avid baker, loves to volunteer for her favorite non-profits, and balances her creative pursuits with a full-time career in marketing.